"You don't frighten me," Thalassa said curtly.

"Ah, but I do, my tawny lioness. I frighten you dreadfully. But because you are a warrior, you hide it. And because you have decided you must submit yourself to my desires, you will lie sullenly beneath me like a clump of dead seaweed. Is that not so?"

"Just-get-on-with-it," she bit out through clenched teeth.

"It does not have to be that way, you know." His voice became a low, husky murmur, and she fidgeted as his warm tones seemed to enfold her. "And nor will it be," Dorian continued seductively, "if you can bring yourself to trust me in the smallest measure."

His long fingers slipped under her heavy hair and gently kneaded the tight muscles of her neck and shoulders. But even while her body was responding to his skill, her nerves were quivering with panic. This was not what she had expected—this unhurried and subtly arousing campaign to lull her fears. For a moment, part of her spirit sought to rebel. Then Dorian lifted her chin and bent his head to hers. . . .

ACROSS A
WINE-DARK SEA

≈ ≈ ≈ ≈ ≈ ≈ ≈ ≈ ≈ ≈ ≈ ≈ ≈

JESSICA BRYAN

BANTAM BOOKS
NEW YORK • TORONTO • LONDON • SYDNEY • AUCKLAND

ACROSS A WINE-DARK SEA

A Bantam Fanfare Book / April 1991

FANFARE *and the portrayal of a boxed "ff" are trademarks of Bantam Books, a division of Bantam Doubleday Dell Publishing Group, Inc.*

ISBN 0-553-28981-0

Published simultaneously in the United States and Canada

Bantam Books are published by Bantam Books, a division of Bantam Doubleday Dell Publishing Group, Inc. Its trademark, consisting of the words "Bantam Books" and the portrayal of a rooster, is Registered in U.S. Patent and Trademark Office and in other countries. Marca Registrada. Bantam Books, 666 Fifth Avenue, New York, New York 10103.

PRINTED IN THE UNITED STATES OF AMERICA

RAD   0 9 8 7 6 5 4 3 2 1

To Stephen, husband, lover, and friend. The Terran man who taught Dorian everything he knows, and who continues to be a never-ending source of inspiration. Thank you for never doubting that this book would one day happen, Steve.

And to Marion and Joseph Chudnow, Shirley and Sheldon Miller, and all the rest of my family and friends, for their encouragement and patience in dealing with someone who almost *never* answers the phone because she's writing.

Finally, a special thanks to Nita Taublib and Elizabeth Barrett, for seeing the potential.

AUTHOR'S NOTE

When I first decided to write this book, I was surprised and frustrated at the dearth of information regarding the Amazons. Books dealing with various cultures of the time abound, but most of them approach the Amazons as figments of man's imagination—creatures as fanciful as Bellerophon's winged horse—existing only to be vanquished, in order to show the superiority of patriarchal society. I found few research materials acknowledging that a viable culture composed solely of warrior-women may have existed in the distant time of which I have written.

An interesting irony is that the one book breathing life into the Amazons—therefore proving invaluable to me— was written by a man: *The Amazons of Greek Mythology* by Donald Sobol. I relied heavily upon Mr. Sobol's fascinating and thorough research of not only the history surrounding the Amazons, but of what their day-to-day life might have been. His insightful interpretations of the ancient myths made these colorful and tragic women live for me, and I am deeply grateful. I owe Mr. Sobol a great debt.

. . . Early summer in the year 1260 B.C.,
along the southern coast of the Black Sea . . .

≈   ≈   ≈

CHAPTER 1

≈ The long, wooden galley lay ominously on the sheltered cove, its one square sail furled against the warm, ocean-scented breeze. A group of men, hard-faced and bare-chested, lined the railing, their dark eyes narrowed in the dazzling reflection off sun, water, and sand.

Silence rippled over their motionless, sweating figures as waves lazily explored the hot beach, then drew back to the cool of the sea, lightly rocking the anchored ship. After a time, one of the men shifted restlessly and turned to the leader, a squat man with thick muscles bulging in his shoulders and arms.

"I don't like this, Kriphoros," the restless one said. "These unnatural creatures we're hunting fight like Alastor, the demon of vengeance. No slave-taking voyage is worth getting my gut cut open."

"Or your manhood sliced off," another muttered.

"Are you dog tongues or men?" Kriphoros's gruff voice seethed with scorn. "By the Great Bull, these are only women. And, unclothed and unarmed, they'll be as helpless against us as any other women."

The first man remained unconvinced. "I don't know," he said stubbornly. "These Amazons are man-killers. Everyone knows that. They hate all sons of Zeus."

Several men laughed at this, and the sound spread a stain over the clear, bright day.

"That's only because they don't know what it is to have real men between their legs," one said with a grin. "On the way back to Amnisos, we'll ride them hard, and by the time we put into port, those 'man-killers' will be as tame and docile as well-broken mares."

Kriphoros turned and scowled at the speaker, until the man's leering grin became a nervous, placating smile. "No one mounts those women without my permission unless he wants to be carved in pieces and offered to Scylla, that barking monster, on the trip home." Each man shuddered at Kriphoros's tone of dire threat. "Beautiful, unmarked slaves fetch better prices than bruised, ill-used ones, and I'll not allow your lusty spears to jeopardize my profits." Kriphoros's glowering stare roved along the row of silent, bearded men. "We'll take our pleasure of the cargo on the return voyage, never fear, but only when *I* say so."

One man suddenly stiffened. "I hear hoofbeats," he whispered urgently. "A group of them must be coming."

"Ready yourselves," the pirate leader ordered sharply, "and remember: capture them alive and unharmed. Nothing is more useless than a half-dead female slave."

Now the others heard it as well: the rhythmic thud of hooves on sand, the jingle of weapons, and the call of women's voices. A small band of Amazons had been out hunting and were now returning to their capital city of Themiscrya by way of the flat, curving beach.

Like ants pouring out of a hill, the pirates swarmed from the galley. A jumble of rocks at one end of the beach shielded their boat from their prey's eyes, and they crouched behind them. Hours earlier, they had stretched a thickly meshed hunting net on the beach above the waterline, and covered it with layer after layer of sand, sweating and cursing as they labored in the white-hot sun. Kriphoros's great fear had been that the ever-present wind would expose the trap. But it seemed the gods favored him, for all traces of the net and the ropes his men would pull to jerk it up around the Amazons' mounts remained hidden by the thick coating of sand.

The sound of horses grew louder, and the pirates leaned forward, eyes fixed eagerly on the peaceful beach, hands sweating on the hafts of their short swords. The leather thongs with which they planned to bind their victims twisted nervously in their tense fingers.

Abruptly, the first of the Amazons appeared, a tanned, black-haired woman mounted bareback on a snow-white mare. She was followed by five others, riding horses equally as fine as the white mare. All of the women were young, their flowing hair held back by silver or gold fillets, and their strong, lithe bodies clad in short leather tunics that exposed one breast and left their long, sleekly muscled thighs fully bare. At the sight of those round breasts and sun-bronzed thighs, the hidden men swallowed and licked their lips greedily, like hounds about to feast on the quarry they had just pulled down.

Talking and laughing, the women rode down the beach at a gentle canter. Their hunt had been successful. A fat doe was lashed across the back of one of the horses, and the party's thoughts were of returning to Themiscrya, bathing the sweat and blood of the hunt from their bodies, and roasting a venison haunch for dinner. Here in their own lands, they suspected no danger. This was Amazonia, the country of the Amazons, and only the most foolhardy of men would dare to cross its boundaries to do them harm.

In a sudden display of high spirits, a tall, night-black mare broke away from the group and raced ahead, following the hardened sand at the water's edge. At first, it seemed the mare was bolting, but the woman astride her rode as if she and the animal were one being.

The line of crouching slavers watched her hungrily, for this Amazon was truly magnificent. No older than eighteen, her body was slender, yet as finely muscled as a young man's. Her exposed right breast rose high and proud, and like the rest of her was gilded from the sun. Loose chestnut-colored hair, glittering with red-gold streaks, flowed back from her face, and her features were as flawless as those of a goddess. The pitch-black coat of the horse contrasted sharply with the rider's golden beauty, so that the two of them resembled one of the great gold and black striped cats that inhabited the far-off mysterious lands along the Great Silk Road.

On she came, and as she neared the rocks hiding the pirates, the mare swerved to higher ground. The rest of the Amazons were galloping now, having caught their companion's exuberance, and were rapidly catching up to her. The black mare's change of course put her directly in line with the concealed net. Within moments her pounding hooves were touching the net. . . .

Seeing this immensely desirable female so close within his grasp, one man could no longer maintain his discipline. With a hoarse cry he yanked the rope in his hands. Instantly, the other men did the same, despite Kriphoros's enraged, "Not yet!"

The hunting net rose out of the sand like some deadly underground creature, wrapping itself tightly around the startled horse and rider. With a scream of fear, the mare went down. The woman screamed, too, but with rage rather than fear. In an extraordinary display of athletic power and reflex, she vaulted off the animal's back, escaping the net's folds, and landed on her feet, furious and ready to fight.

Kriphoros bellowed with fury and struck the nearest rope holder a savage blow to the head. "Disobedient fools!" he roared. "You've ruined everything! Now take her and the rest of them, and be quick about it, or I'll kill you myself!"

Even as he spoke, the chilling sound of the Amazon war cry rose on the hot wind, drowning out the steady song of the ocean. The ululating ring of it froze the men's blood, but at the moment, they feared their leader's anger more than these women, who *were* after all, only women, and outnumbered women at that. In a dirty brown wave, they surged over the rocks with yells of their own, determined to take the unhorsed Amazon as their first captive. But unhorsed though she was, she was far from helpless. One of the pirates made a strangled noise and fell, clutching frantically at the arrow protruding from his throat. A moment later another, and then another toppled, showering their fellows with blood from pierced jugular veins as they died. Coolly, in one continuous motion, the woman pulled a fourth arrow from the quiver on her shoulder, notched it to her bow, and let it fly, to find a home in yet another man's throat.

The onrushing pirates faltered in confusion, then the rest of the Amazons, their shrill war cries terrifyingly loud, came thundering within arrow range. What followed was a massacre. Because this had been a hunting expedition, the women were not armed for war. They carried neither their crescent-shaped shields nor the *bipennis,* the famed Amazonian double-bladed ax. But they had all their other weapons—their spears, short swords, and bows—and these were more than enough to take care of the would-be slavers.

Even at full gallop, the Amazons shot their arrows with the same steadiness and accuracy as if they were on foot. A hail of lethally aimed projectiles struck the pirates before the horses even reached them. With hideous cries men fell, pinioned to the ground by pierced hands and feet, or impaled through the torso, neck, or limbs. A red-haired woman on a fleet bay surged toward her unhorsed sister, and as she swept by, the young warrior used her spear to vault effortlessly onto the mare's back. Seated so that she faced the animal's tail, she continued to fire arrows, each one as deadly as the last.

Complete pandemonium broke out among the pirates. Kriphoros's battle orders went unheeded as his companions either fled or fought, depending on the degree of terror each felt. Actually, it mattered little which choice was made. Death was the only result for all. Kriphoros's exhortations were choked off as a well-aimed spear pierced his chest and thrust its bloody point through his back. Several men tried desperately to loosen the net from the black mare, hoping to throw it over their charging foes. They died in the attempt as with fierce whoops, two women raced past and swiped heads from shoulders with their short swords.

Their leader dead, their numbers vastly reduced, the remaining pirates abandoned all thoughts of battle. As if one brain were animating all their legs, they bolted for the dubious safety of their ship. The Amazons cut them down as they fled, and only three lived to reach the deck. Such a small group could not possibly have hoped to man a twenty-oared galley, but they were fated neither to try nor fail at it. Two of them collapsed on the wooden rowing benches, punctured with arrows; the third died in the act of hacking through the anchor rope with his sword. As his body crumpled over the ship's vermilion prow, the rope strands parted, and with majestic slowness, the galley drifted into the outgoing tide.

Not all of the pirates were dead, however. Those who had been pinned to the beach had managed to pull the arrows out of their limbs and the sandy ground. Crippled and bleeding, they sought to crawl away from certain death. Men who had chuckled lustfully over how they planned to use their captive "cargo" on the return voyage found themselves babbling for mercy from the very women they had intended to abuse, then sell into slavery.

Their pleas fell on unhearing ears. Mercy to enemies was an undreamed-of thing, whether among the Amazons or any kingdom ruled by men. Indeed, in the lands dominated by men—of which there were far too many in the Amazons' view—the practice was always to kill male warriors and take only women and children into slavery. The wounded pirates knew this. Often enough they had ignored similar cries for pity, and sent the pleading ones to the dark world of the dead. And they had done it far more cruelly than these women, who now started them on their own shadowy journey out of the bright halls of the living.

Finally, only one still lived. Ironically it was the man who, a lifetime ago, had expressed his doubts about the entire undertaking. Silently, the six Amazons gathered around his prostrate form, and one of them knelt, gripping his beard so that she could sever his throat. Before her hunting knife could end the man's agony, Aella, the black-haired woman who had ridden the white mare and who was the oldest of the group, intervened.

"Why have you come here, O fool of a man, you, and your fellow fools?" she asked in the pirate's own tongue. She had recognized it from his companions' pleadings, and like most Amazons, she was fluent in more than one language. "Why did you dare trespass onto the lands of the Amazons, thinking to do us harm when we had done none to you?"

The pirate groaned. "We came seeking women to sell as slaves in the markets of Amnisos on the island of Crete, land of our birth. And the beauty of Amazons is well known."

"And the ability of Amazons to fight? Is that not known equally as well?" Scorn colored the voice of the young chestnut-haired woman known as Thalassa. Filled with contempt, she glared at the wounded man. This creature, she thought, this piece of dung, believed Amazon warriors could be bought and sold like cows in the filthy marketplace of his man-ruled land.

Gasping painfully, the man answered her. "We had heard that Amazons knew the skills of war. And yet only I believed the tales could be true. The others laughed at the thought of women defeating men in battle, and fighting from the backs of horses rather than riding in proper chariots—" His voice wheezed to a halt as the pain from his wounds welled up. Coughing hoarsely, he whispered, "Spare me . . ."

Aella gazed down at him coldly. "And why should we spare you? You, who came here to enslave us. Neither you nor your fellows would have spared us the living death of bondage to men."

"We would have trained you to be proper women," the pirate insisted, his voice weak and thready. "Not unnatural creatures who refuse their place. Demons, who would shrivel a man's staff between his legs and turn his seed to dust, rather than receiving it obediently as the gods have ordained—"

"As your *man*-gods have ordained, you mean," one called Eriobea said dryly. "But *we* worship the Goddess, Who is older and far more powerful than any god who believes a piece of flesh hanging between his legs makes him master over women."

But the pirate was no longer capable of listening. His voice became a bubbling, then a gurgling, as blood rose into his lungs and spilled out of his mouth. He shuddered once and was still. Asteria, who had originally knelt to cut his throat, rose and sheathed her knife. "So much for his request to spare him," she remarked.

Aella turned to the chestnut-haired woman and clasped her shoulder warmly. "Sisters, there will be a feast in Themiscrya tonight, for Thalassa has killed her first enemy!"

Among the Amazons, a girl was not considered an adult until she had killed a man in battle. Since only adults were allowed to mate, and thus reproduce their kind, this was an important requirement to fulfill. The practice ensured that only the strongest in the tribe bore offspring, and to the Amazons—alone in a sea of man-ruled kingdoms—nothing was more important than strength.

As pleased as she was by her companion's approval, Thalassa was more concerned about her mare, Alcippe. She disentangled the animal from the folds of the net, and while the others discussed how to dispose of the pirates' bodies, she absorbed herself in comforting Alcippe and checking her for injuries.

Tecmessa, the red-haired woman who had rescued Thalassa from the ground, suggested that their foes be heaped on a funeral pyre and burned honorably. "For we do not want their shades haunting this sunny beach and wailing that we gave them no resting place," she said.

But Hippothoe, whose name meant "impetuous mare," snorted like the creature after whom she was called. "Give an honorable burial to curs such as these? They are not warriors, but pirates, who came here to take us unawares and capture us like animals, and when that failed, they fought badly."

"And they pleaded cravenly for their lives," Eriobea added, "rather than accepting death bravely."

"All of that is true," Aella said. "But Tecmessa has a point. We can't just leave their bodies here to rot. Not only will their spirits remain, but their corpses will make this part of the beach unclean until the birds have finished picking the flesh from their bones."

Thalassa had been listening to the conversation with half an ear, and now she turned with one hand on Alcippe's lathered black neck. "Why don't we give them back to the sea?" she suggested. "They came here from the sea. Let her take them on the outgoing tide and do with them what she pleases."

It was the perfect solution. Everyone set to work dragging the still-warm bodies down to the waves. The task took some time, for there were more bodies than there were women to move them, but at last it was done. The sea accepted the dead men with the same vast indifference as she accepted live men attempting to navigate her immense, unfathomed depths. Casually jostling the bodies against one another, she floated them out toward the brightly painted galley that drifted, aimless and eerie, off in the distance. The six Amazons stood on the shoreline and watched.

"That was a good idea you had, Thalassa," Asteria

finally said. "The Greeks and Cretans worship a man-god called Poseidon, whom they say rules the sea. They believe that he lives in a great palace underneath the water. Perhaps he'll know what to do with those pirates."

"Well, at least we don't have to worry about them anymore," Hippothoe declared. "And now, Aella, can we go home? I'd like to cleanse myself in the river before the feast for Thalassa."

Aella smiled. "We could all use a good bath, especially Thalassa, since she's the guest of honor. It's not often a new warrior kills more than one enemy in her first battle."

Eagerly, the women cleaned their weapons and mounted their horses to continue the interrupted journey back to Themiscrya. All except for the guest of honor. Alcippe had strained a tendon in her foreleg. It was not a serious injury, but it would preclude riding her for several days. She would have to be led the rest of the way home, a distance of about three miles. Generously, the group offered to keep pace with the lamed mare, but Thalassa would not hear of it.

"Go on ahead. That way, Alcippe and I can take our time, and when we get home everything will be ready for my honor-feast. Anyway, I would like to think about this day, and walking with Alcippe will be good for me."

The others smiled at Thalassa understandingly. In their small, close-knit community, her independent and somewhat solitary nature was well known and accepted by all, for along with it went a heart as warm and open as the plain surrounding Themiscrya itself. So, calling their good-byes, the hunting party urged their mounts into a brisk trot and set off for home.

Thalassa watched them head down the beach, the carcass of the doe they had killed earlier that day bouncing on the back of Eriobea's chestnut mare. Alcippe blew into her comrade's own chestnut hair, and smiling, Thalassa caressed the velvety black nose.

"I know you'd like to go with them, but we have to walk slowly and carefully. I don't want you to hurt yourself more."

Thoughtfully, she looked around her. Except for scattered bloodstains on the white sand, the beach seemed to have resumed its air of peacefulness, but an aura of violent death still clung to the place. Vibrations from the screams of men dying in terror and pain shivered on the early evening breeze, and in the first shadows of dusk, Thalassa thought she could see their shades, hovering with reluctance as the sea pulled them out to follow the bodies they had inhabited in life.

The tide was fully out now, and the wooden ship was only a ghostly outline on the purpling horizon. Here and there Thalassa could make out the irregular shapes of men floating in the same direction as the boat. The waters around them were splashed crimson from the lowering sun, and to Thalassa it seemed that their blood, and not the sun, had dyed the restless waves such a brilliant red. She felt the strong presence of a consciousness other than her own emanating from the sea, almost as if a pair of eyes, piercing and intense, had fastened on her. With a little laugh, she shook off the feeling. Marpe, her grandmother, would chide her for being too fanciful. "That's what comes of wandering off by yourself so much," she would point out in her sharp, old voice. And likely, she was right.

Thalassa bent to pick up Alcippe's reins. Straightening, she glanced once more out to sea, driven by a strange desire to reassure herself that no mysterious presence lingered there. Alcippe gave a sudden explosive snort and pricked her ears toward the water. Thalassa followed the mare's gaze with curiosity, then her whole body tensed.

The head and shoulders of a man rode above the waves; a man who was directly facing the shore. And her. Thalassa blinked, straining to make out details in the uncertain light, but the apparition had vanished. The sea washed the horizon as it had before, and the only men riding the waves lay prone, all life gone from their outstretched limbs.

Gooseflesh rose on Thalassa's arms and the hairs at the back of her neck lifted. It must have been a trick of the light, she told herself. No one was out there who still lived. Such a thing simply could not be! Yet some unnamed instinct made her grip Alcippe's reins and back away from the softly whispering sea.

"Come on, Alcippe," she said to the mare. "Let's go home."

Those Cretan pirates had been more successful. Three Amazons had been out swimming, and the raiders had come upon them when they were too far from the shore and safety. Greatly outnumbered, the three women were quickly captured and bound. Rejoicing at their success, the pirates nevertheless lost no time in making for open sea before their captives could be missed.

Once they were safely away, the men decided to draw lots for the women. Each woman would service five different men every night. That way, the pirate leader reasoned, they would not only have the use of their beautiful captives' bodies, but the women would get a thorough breaking-in and be completely tamed by the time they went on the block. They might even have their bellies ripened, and women brought a better price if there was a good possibility they were with child.

The first two nights went exactly as planned. But on the third morning, in the grayish black of the false dawn, the captives managed to gnaw loose each other's bonds. They killed eight men before it became obvious they would be retaken. So, screaming their war cry in utter defiance, they leaped into the black, glittering sea. . . .

Of course, neither Thalassa nor her people could know all this. But the Moon-Goddess in Her kindness had brought the bodies of Her drowned daughters home, and even though the water had swollen their once lithe forms, and fish had nibbled their flesh, the bruises and bitten-through thongs were still there. It was not hard to know what had happened.

One of the dead had been Hippothoe's older birth-sister. From that day forth, Hippothoe had held an undying hatred for the black-bearded men of Crete, who all suspected were the ones responsible. That day, for the first time since her sister's body had washed up on shore, Thalassa had seen Hippothoe's face free of the smoldering frustration that had characterized it for three summers. The blood-price had finally been paid; the deaths were avenged and honor restored. Although, Thalassa mused, there had been little challenge in battling those craven pirates.

She had forfeited her right to take the head of one of her foes, a custom not only of the Amazons but of the Hittites, their powerful neighbors to the north. The skulls were lined with gold and served as drinking cups to commemorate a warrior's first victory. But Thalassa had demurred.

"A drinking cup should be from the head of an opponent I respect," she had said, "not a pirate slaver who lived by preying on the weak and helpless."

Thalassa stroked Alcippe's neck as they approached the beautiful headland at the mouth of the Thermodon. The greatest of all Amazon Mothers—Lysippe—had chosen to build the capital of Themiscrya along that lovely river after the long march over the treacherous Caucasus mountains and the swift conquering of unsuspecting Cappadocia. Clear and sweet, the Thermodon lived as a multitude of rushing streams high in the craggy, remote mountains surrounding Themiscrya. As they found their way down through the heights, these numerous small streams formed themselves into a broad, short river that gradually emptied into the sea the Greeks called the Pontus.

Verdant plains surrounded the city of whitewashed plaster buildings and neat wooden huts. The generous Thermodon had created rich pasturelands for the vast herds of shambling cattle and swift horses that roamed in unfettered freedom throughout the Amazons' lands. At the southernmost foot of the mountains, apples, pears, grapes, and nuts grew so plentifully, they could not all be gathered.

Inveterate warriors who trained extensively, even during their intervals of peace, the Amazons were nevertheless skilled farmers and horse trainers, vocations that were practiced as much for love as for necessity. They grew many varieties of grain, both for themselves and their much-valued horses, and to supplement their diet there was always hunting. The heavily forested woods teemed with game, and it was a rare night indeed when fresh meat was not roasted for the evening meal.

It was a good life. A life of health, exercise, companionship, and above all, freedom. Reflecting on this, Thalassa thought that to be an Amazon was the best thing in the world. They were their own masters, and no man could force them to live shut up in dark, smoke-filled houses, laboring for him like slaves, as those whom men called "wives" did. She was sure she'd rather die than be some man's "wife." Truly, as their great foremother Lysippe had said, "Marriage and slavery are one and the same, and there is no honor in either."

Themiscrya's fertile meadows came into view, waving green and golden in the dying sunlight. Here and there, the dappled hides of cattle and the glowing reds, blacks, browns, and whites of horses brightened the wide, living carpet. Off in the distance, the broad ribbon of the Thermodon shone silvery-blue beside the sun-washed city.

Alcippe's ears pricked forward eagerly as they neared home, and Thalassa realized how hungry, tired, and in need of a bath she was. A splash of color resolved itself into a group of riders. Her hunting companions, refreshed and dressed in their best finery, were coming to act as an honor guard for the newest warrior of the tribe. Thalassa grinned and tugged affectionately at Alcippe's mane. "Don't worry, my love," she assured the mare. "I'll see to your leg, and make you a nice mash before the celebration begins. And then I hope I have time to swim in the river so that I don't have to go dirty to my own honor-feast!"

The horse snorted and nuzzled her comrade's shoulder as if in agreement, and the two of them went on to meet the five women, who were already shouting boisterous greetings as they galloped over the grassy plain.

That night the resinous smoke of torches stung the eyes until late. Thalassa ate and ate as did everyone else, and still there seemed to be no end to the bounty.

Tender haunches of roast venison and beef reposed on platters of gold, accompanied by dozens of plump quail and waterfowl cooked to a brown and crispy turn. Round loaves of fresh-baked bread sat in fragrant piles next to silver bowls heaped with grapes, pears, and apples. Black puddings, made of blood and fat and roasted in the paunch of a calf, were devoured greedily, washed down with wine imported from the Hittites. There was also strong mead made from fermented mares' milk, and a thirst-quenching drink of barley meal mixed with water and flavored with mint. For dessert there was more fruit and heaps of lightly baked golden cakes sweetened with wild honey. It was truly a feast to remember.

In the great stone banqueting hall, Thalassa had been given the place of honor among the queens of Amazonia. The Amazons were governed by a tribal system of three leaders, the current ones being Hippolyte, Oreithyia, and Antiope.

The system of laws by which the Amazons lived was entirely uncomplicated. The only recognized crimes were theft and lying. Queens were treated with the loving but informal respect due older sisters, rather than the slavish deference given to the royal monarchs of Minoan Crete or the mighty Hittites. Therefore, Thalassa felt comfortable sitting with the rulers of her people, and they in turn treated her as a peer. Oreithyia, in particular, had many questions about the afternoon's events. She was the war queen, and the responsibility of defending Amazonia's borders against attack fell to her.

Oreithyia, Hippolyte, and Antiope were sisters, and as they sat together in the firelit hall, the resemblance between them was clear. Like all Amazons, they were tall and small breasted. Each of them had long hair the color of midnight, handsome, finely etched features, and the same level, dark eyes. Hippolyte, the oldest of the three, looked especially striking to Thalassa that night. Belted around the waist of her gold-stitched leather tunic was a magnificent sword belt worked in the finest silver, crystal, and gold. Normally made from leather, this particular sword belt was worn for ceremony rather than function.

The Amazons' sword belts—or girdles, as some called them—symbolized their way of life. In a world where women were defined by which man they belonged to, the girdles of the Amazons proclaimed that they belonged to themselves alone. And the belt of Hippolyte, glittering with its own fires in the light of the torches, was the most beautiful of them all.

Now Hippolyte entered the conversation between her sister and Thalassa. "We had better be mindful of watching our lands more closely," Oreithyia was saying. "For there is not a man born who is worthy of a woman's trust. They are all of them enemies to our kind, and those from the islands of Greece are the worst.

"They have torn the Goddess from Her holy place and set man-gods there instead. Nothing would give them

greater joy than to destroy those who follow the Mother, enslaving us as they enslave the women of their own lands."
Oreithyia's strong fingers tightened with rage on the stem of her goblet.

Hippolyte smiled. "And still, men have their uses, sister. For how could we get our daughters without them? And trading allows us to have many things we would not otherwise enjoy. Even more important, it keeps us aware of happenings in the world of men, and is it not better to know of the treaties and wars they hold between themselves, than to be caught off guard by a surprise alliance?"

But Oreithyia would not be reassured. Her dark gaze wandered over the faces of her sisters, troubled flames burning in the depths of her eyes. "Our tribe is like a single lioness, ringed by packs of hungry jackals. And of late, I've had dreams—dreams of a black-bearded man from the land of the Greeks, a man who will bring us great harm. I have prayed to the Goddess for guidance, but she has not answered . . ."

Her voice trailed away, and Oreithyia gazed abstractedly into her wine. Hippolyte stroked the war queen's long hair and murmured, "Worry not, my sister. It is true that there is only one tribe of Amazon, but a strong lioness can kill many jackals, and strength is something we have in abundance. When it suits our purposes, we will deal with men, taking from them those things we value, and guarding ourselves against them the rest of the time."

Antiope, the youngest queen, teasingly nudged Thalassa. "Well, next spring Thalassa and I will have a chance to get something of value from a man when we go up into the mountains. Won't we, Thalassa?"

Thalassa grinned back, relieved that the conversation was taking a lighter turn. She and Antiope were age-mates, and they had grown up hunting, riding, and practicing warfare together. Two months earlier, Antiope had slain her first enemy in a campaign against the Colchians, a subjugated tribe in the eastern territories, who had mounted a brief and unsuccessful rebellion. Now both of them were adults, and when the spring mating season arrived, they would go into the northern mountains that separated them from their neighbors, the Gargarians.

Every year for two months, the same ritual took place. Though the Gargarians were a patriarchal tribe, the Amazons respected their warriors for their strength and bravery. Centuries before, when the Amazons had first migrated to this region, the wise Lysippe had taken steps to ensure the continuance of the young tribe. She made a treaty with the Gargarians, promising them freedom from attack in exchange for a yearly mating. Fierce fighters themselves, the Gargarians had by that time experienced enough of the Amazons' savagery in battle to prefer them as partners for rutting.

The arrangement worked. Each year, warriors removed their girdles and went to the mountains. There, they joined the Gargarian men in offering sacrifices, then the two groups lay together, coupling at random and in the dark. Daughters born of these secret unions were kept and sons were returned to the Gargarians. A man gladly accepted any boy brought to him, for sons were always welcome, and who knew but that he was not the child's true father?

Thalassa's gaze wandered over the torch-bright hall. The huge wooden doors had been flung open to the warm night, and now that the feasting was done, people were wandering about, visiting with one another and nibbling on the remains of the meal. In the center of the vast room a dance had begun. Amazons of all ages were swaying in an exuberant circle, waving their arms and stamping in rhythm to the whistling accompaniment of pipes. Such a dance was always performed before battle, only then it was armed warriors who danced, shaking shields and quivers and shrieking until they had lashed themselves into a killing frenzy.

Tonight, though, the dancing was for pleasure, and grandmothers, children, and women in the prime of their strength laughed and circled as their shadows leaped crazily on the firelit walls. Outside, several warriors had begun to spar playfully with their short swords, and the watchers' encouraging shouts came through the door to mingle with the wild strains of the pipes.

Thalassa's gaze lingered on the young girls. She wondered what it would be like to feel her belly swell with the weight of an unborn daughter, and afterward watch that daughter grow before her eyes. But the music of the pipes was creeping into her blood. Antiope was pulling on her to join the dance—Hippolyte and Oreithyia already swayed among the circle—and with a laugh Thalassa put thoughts of childbearing out of her mind. For she was young and strong, life ran hot through her veins, and this—this was her celebration night!

Two days later, Thalassa awoke before the sun with a restlessness upon her. That was unusual, for she generally slept with the easy peace of the young and healthy. Perhaps, she mused, it was because for the first time in her life she had the privacy of her own hut.

Girls shared common living quarters with age-mates or stayed with mothers, aunts, or grandmothers until they had attained adulthood. Then they were given the option of living alone. Most of them tried it for the sheer novelty, yet opted later to share larger houses with one or two close friends.

Thalassa rolled onto her back and stared up at the thatched ceiling. It was strange not to hear the steady breathing of her youth companions or the sleepy muttering of old Marpe. Throwing the woven coverlet from her naked body, she rose from her pallet of furs and stretched luxuriously. The small hut was dark, but against the log walls the shapes of her weapons stood out among the shadows. After a moment, Thalassa pulled a tunic over her head and buckled on her bronze sword. Picking up her crescent-shaped shield, she pushed the door-skins aside and stepped out into the dawn.

The sun had just begun to paint the jagged peaks of the mountains with red fingers, but the plain and the sleeping city were still in the grip of night. Mist lay along the river, heavy and white and low under the looming mounds of rock and timber. Nearby, a bird awoke and chirped halfheartedly, and in the distance the ocean rolled up onto the shore and washed back into itself with a rushing murmur.

Thalassa took several apples from one of the storehouses, tucking them into her tunic, then wandered off toward the indistinct shapes of the animal herds. A low nicker floated out on the still air and she spoke softly, recognizing the greeting of her mare. Alcippe trotted up, her limp almost gone, and Thalassa stroked her sleek neck while the horse crunched an apple. One of the stallions the

Amazons kept for breeding—a big, powerful bay—pricked his ears and stalked over to them, nickering deep in his chest. Thalassa fed him an apple as she rubbed his broad forehead, and the animal nudged her affectionately in return.

"The elders say," she told the stallion, "that you can't be our comrades the way mares can because your tempers are too uncertain. And Oreithyia says stallions are like men and can't be trusted, but I don't know. It seems to me that animals are as different as people, and that you would make a very good companion, indeed."

The big stallion snorted as if he agreed and lowered his head for another apple. Alcippe jealously shoved Thalassa's other side. Laughing, she divided the last two apples between them.

"That's all," she said, spreading her empty hands so they could see for themselves. "Go and eat grass now, before all your friends come to see why I don't have apples for them."

Obediently the stallion ambled away, but Alcippe showed no inclination to rejoin the herd. She watched as Thalassa retrieved her shield from the dew-laden ground, then made as if to follow her.

"No, no, love," Thalassa admonished gently, tugging on the silky black mane. "You have to stay here. I'm going down to the beach to practice with my sword. I'll be back to see you later."

She headed off across the grassy plain, and this time Alcippe did not try to follow. But as Thalassa walked away, the mare gave a long, ringing whinny, an almost human sound that she had never made before. Later, Thalassa would remember Alcippe's neigh and grieve she had not listened to the warning it carried. Yet at the time she thought only that the mare wanted to go for a gallop on the beach, the poor thing not realizing her leg hadn't fully healed.

Thalassa strode far down the beach in the uncertain light of the early dawn. She felt no sense of unease at going to the sea alone, for she had pushed the unnerving apparition of the other day out of her mind. And true to her word, the ever-cautious Oreithyia had doubled the number of mounted sentries who patrolled Amazonia's borders. The chance of pirates being able even at night to slip past the sharp eyes of those experienced women riding the wooded slopes that overlooked the ocean was virtually nil.

The sun was clearing the craggy peaks when Thalassa finally found an exercise spot that suited her. Despite the earliness, the pale, cloudless sky and warm air foretold a hot day, and Thalassa was glad she had decided to practice before the heat rose.

Her supple body eased into the rhythm of feints and parries from long practice. Her arms and legs moved in a slow, elegant dance that needed neither music nor formal steps. The flashing sword seemed disconnected from the arm of the woman as the blade wove its own clean, rapid pattern through the salt-scented air. The weight of the shield balanced Thalassa, lending a stability and power to the deceptively artless flow of the weapon, as it sliced and slashed with bronze deadliness.

From the time they could walk, girls trained in the use of arms, singly and in groups. Thalassa enjoyed the blood-pounding challenge of competition, but something in her had always responded to the call of lonely places by the sea where she could push her strength and skill to the limit with only the waves to observe.

When finally she stopped, the oxhide shield hung heavy on her left arm, and her sword arm throbbed with the healthy ache of exertion. Carefully, she laid her weapons high up on the beach and flexed her tingling muscles. Her soft leather tunic was drenched with sweat, and distastefully she stripped it off and walked down to the water.

At other spots along the coastline, the breakers boomed and frothed in white fury, but here they foamed up onto the sand and receded with hypnotic gentleness. Later, as the morning advanced and the wind came up, these waves would pound the beach too. Now, though, they were calm, their murmurous voices inviting Thalassa to enter the cool, sparkling depths.

She did. Her golden body shone against the deep blue of the sea as she waded in up to her waist. The little waves washed around her, and through the cool, flat sand beneath her feet she could feel the ancient pulse of the rumbling surf. Gulls wheeled and cried overhead, and Thalassa let herself sway with the sea's rhythm as she gazed out over the far, rippling horizon. Finally, she took a breath and dove. Her wet chestnut head broke the surface a little way out, and with strong strokes she began to swim.

For all their nearness to the sea, the Amazons had never sailed, never sought to navigate its breadth. Their province was ever that of the horse. But they were good swimmers, and Thalassa was better than most. She loved the sea, loved its vast, lonely solitude and the mysterious songs it sang only to her. Most of all, she loved to swim away from shore, then float on the ocean's rolling breast, her face turned up to the sun, at one with the sea, the sky, and herself.

On this day, as on other summer days, she swam until the beach was nothing more than a faint, white line set between the glittering blue of the water and the rich green of the thickly wooded slopes. Spreading her arms, she lay on the wide sea as comfortably as though it were her bed of furs.

Time merged with the sweep of water and the steadily brightening sunlight. Thalassa lost track of how long she rocked on the placid surface of the water, relaxed and half-dreaming. Eventually, though, her meandering thoughts turned to breakfast, for she had given all the apples to Alcippe and the stallion and kept none for herself. Easily dropping her legs, she treaded water as she looked out to sea.

A thin border of morning haze clothed the horizon, and the sky above it was a pristine blue. Thalassa paused to let the beauty of it fill her soul. The instant before she turned to swim back to shore, a man rose in front of her.

She recoiled, shock and terror surging through her. There were no ships about. No enemy could have gotten past Oreithyia's sentries. Where in the name of the Mother could he have come from? And she hadn't so much as a knife with her. The man's features blurred, leaving only a fragmented impression of startlingly blue eyes, as she whirled and flung herself wildly toward land.

Powerful arms closed around her, and a broad, wet chest pressed against her back. In all her life, Thalassa had never felt the touch of a man's body. The feel of that firm, smooth flesh was no less frightening than his appalling appearance, rising from the very depths of the sea. But she was a warrior and would not give in to fear.

Twisting savagely in the man's unyielding grasp, she fought to get her arms free and keep her head above the water. She was strong, and she battled with agility and determination, but there was something inhuman about the power of this man's embrace. He held her easily, without apparent effort, and the heaving ocean did not seem to impede him as it did her. Thalassa's superstitious dread returned full-force, and she frantically redoubled her struggles.

One of the man's arms loosened, and for a wild moment she thought she had gotten free. She lunged forward even as she felt strong fingers probe hard into the side of her neck, just below the ear. Pain exploded with such unexpected intensity, she cried out before she could stop herself. Salty seawater washed into her mouth, and through a haze of throbbing dizziness, she felt the man's hand grip the other side of her neck.

This time, the pain was blurred beneath a warm cloak of numbness that spread with incredible speed throughout every part of Thalassa's body. In horror, she realized she was slipping, either into unconsciousness or death, and was completely unable to help herself. She no longer felt any pain, but her eyes had closed and, regardless of her mind's desperate commands to open them, she found she could not. The man held her gently now, as gently as the sea had rocked her, and as the dark tide finally took her, Thalassa felt his lips brush her temple.

Although the struggle had been furious, it had lasted only seconds. The man cradled Thalassa's limp form as his penetrating gaze swept the distant beach to make sure they had not been observed. Satisfied, he looked down at her still face.

"I'm sorry," he murmured in a tongue she would not have understood had she been awake to hear it. As the gulls wheeled overhead, strangely silent, he gathered her more closely in his arms and disappeared beneath the waves with scarcely a ripple.

CHAPTER 3

≈ The mysterious man dove deep under the sea. He was taking his captive home. Indeed, she was the sole reason he had journeyed into these waters.

All through the day and well into the night, the man swam, following ancient routes known only to those of his kind. He left behind him the cool depths of the Pontus and headed west, toward the warmer climes of that great salt expanse the Greeks called the Inland Sea. He swam swiftly and with power, for he had a long way to go and no time to waste in the going of it.

Into the straits of Bosphorus and through the raceways of the Dardanelles with their whistling winds and treacherous currents, the swimmer ran, cradling his precious burden. He entered the dark waters of the Aegean, blood-red under the dying sun, and made for the isle of Crete, although he had no intention of passing so near the heavily populated island that his presence might be noticed.

Late in the night he angled toward a tiny, unnamed island sitting like a piece of fallen moon in the star-bright ocean. Only the white-bellied monk seals visited this island or the underwater cave beneath it, and even they were not about when the man entered the domelike cavern and laid Thalassa on a patch of damp sand. As the waves echoed through the dark chamber, he knelt beside his insensible companion and examined her carefully. Opening a pouch attached to a soft belt around his waist, he withdrew a small, needlelike spine and pricked Thalassa's arm with it. After re-tying the pouch, he lay down, drawing the unconscious woman's head onto his chest. He was asleep instantly, and for the next several hours did not stir, even when a curious seal swam into the cave and flopped down on the sand next to him.

Dawn was just beginning to turn the sea a dull gray when the man awoke. The seal had gone, leaving only a flat patch in the sand to show it had been there. Thalassa still lay as if dead. The man checked her again, piercing her arm once more with the sharp spine before lifting her limp body into his muscular arms. Within moments, he had resumed the journey, his powerful legs propelling him and his burden through the water with effortless speed and power.

Men who sailed on the surface of the sea would have found their sleek wooden galleys left far behind by the lone swimmer for he belonged to a race different from the folk of the land. His was a far older and stronger race that walked on the land and enjoyed the sun, but called the sea their home. And Thalassa—this woman he had come so far to find—was to join his ancient and powerful people, however unwilling she might be.

The swimmer brooded on this as he traveled. Twenty years ago—a mere instant in the long-lived eyes of his people—the Elders had foretold this young woman's birth. The kingship had still been in the capable hands of his father when the Ceremony of Choosing had been held for him, as it was for all the males of his royal house. To mingle their ancient blood with the hardy life-force of landwomen was a vital necessity. It assured the seafolk's continued health, and for the king it was a sacred duty.

The selecting of such a woman was no easy task, though. Only a rare few were born with the physical and emotional capabilities that made adjustment to the seafolk's world possible. And these precious ones were like the most prized of jewels—occurring within the Terran population at infrequent, and often difficult to predict, intervals. They were always female. Even the Elders, with their ability to read the future, to look into a mother's womb and examine the unborn life therein with their vast telepathic powers, did not know why this was so. But it was.

The fact that his designated mate had been born to a tribe of women whose way of life was based on separation from men mattered little to the Elders. All that mattered was that Thalassa's blood would mingle compatibly with his, creating strong, healthy offspring. And her mind contained the necessary qualities to take on the telepathic abilities of the merfolk—those abilities that were the key to their survival in the universe of the sea.

After he had succeeded to the throne several years earlier, it had been only a matter of finding Thalassa, and then waiting for her to mature. But the young king had not anticipated the guilt he would feel when he took this woman whose lifepath was destined to weave with his. It was a cruel way to introduce his chosen one to her new people, he reflected sadly. But the Elders had selected her, and there was no gainsaying that sacred pronouncement.

Another day and part of another night the man swam. The Aegean had been left behind long before and he was well within the blue and sparkling Mediterranean, those familiar waters of his birth. As he neared his destination—a remote spot near the coast of North Africa—the swimmer descended deeper and deeper into the depths. The sun had set, leaving the moon to sail through a starry sky and light the ocean's restless face with silver. Eventually, even this fitful light was left behind as the man dove hundreds upon hundreds of feet down.

Directly ahead, a huge, many-tiered shape loomed out of the darkness, and the swimmer made for it eagerly, his journey finally at an end. The first part of his undertaking had been successful, but that had been the easy part. The hard part would begin when Thalassa awakened to find herself torn from the world and life she had always known.

The man smiled ruefully as these thoughts passed through his mind. His task would be made no easier by the fact that Thalassa had been raised to distrust all men, and forcibly abducting her was far from the best way to overcome such teachings! Still, he'd had no choice, and with time and patience, he hoped she would one day understand that.

It was the softness of the bed that at last woke Thalassa. All her life she had slept on furs, straw-stuffed pallets, or the hard ground and been perfectly comfortable. The Amazons certainly could afford the luxuries of thick cushions and silk coverlets but they were a nation of soldiers. They were trained to live simply, without frills. Therefore, the feel of the wide, soft couch was an alien and disturbing sensation, and Thalassa jerked her eyes open in confusion. Disoriented memories had swirled behind her closed eyelids, but the sight that met her was even less reassuring.

Gone were the whitewashed huts and buildings of her people, or the friendly familiarity of the vast gathering-hall. She had never seen this gorgeously appointed chamber and could not remember being brought there. Her stomach clenching in fear, she sat up, desperately seeking to orient herself to the strange surroundings.

The chamber was not large, but what it lacked in size, it made up for in sumptuousness. The walls and floor were a pale, translucent green, reminding Thalassa of a precious stone a Hittite trader had once shown her. "Jade" he had called it, and had told her that it was very costly and came from the lands along the Great Silk Road. Interspersed with the milky green were intricate designs set in mother-of-pearl and gold. A thick white rug lay on the floor, and a brilliant fresco painted in blues and greens adorned the ceiling. There were no niches in the walls for torches or oil lamps, but the chamber glowed with light. As Thalassa pondered this mystery among all the other mysteries, the unmistakable ring of male voices came to her ears from beyond the chamber.

Her reaction was instantaneous. She sprang out of the bed, reeling as a wave of dizziness smote her from head to toe. Weakness assailed her in all her limbs. Her neck and head throbbed fiercely, and ominous thoughts ran hazy and unfocused through her brain. Never in all her strong and healthy life had she felt like this, and it unsettled her even more than the male voices or the opulently luxurious chamber.

She shook her head, trying desperately to gain control of her mind and body before whoever was outside decided to come in. Something smooth and cool rustled around her, and she looked down to see that someone had dressed her in a loose, soft gown of bright violet.

The color of royalty, she thought, bemused. Only the Phoenicians knew the secret of the rich purple dye, rumored to be made from rare sea snails and so costly that only the nobility could afford it. Hesitantly, she touched the silky cloth, almost expecting it to dissolve in her hands like the dream this must surely be.

In another moment, her age-mates would start shouting for her to wake up and come hunting with them. The familiar morning sounds of Themiscrya would greet her ears—the nicker of horses, cattle lowing in the distance, the opening of a door.

Thalassa froze. Intensity filled her now, the intensity of a cornered animal awaiting its chance to fight or flee. A young man entered the room, alone, and as far as she could tell, unarmed. Dark-haired and with glittering blue eyes, he was dressed in a thigh-length scarlet tunic that left his arms bare and exposed a massive chest that gleamed smooth and brown against the red material. He was barefoot, and magnificently worked gold glittered from the arm-rings around his muscular biceps and the necklace encircling his strong, tanned throat.

Thalassa stared at him. He was the biggest man she had ever seen. In a world of short, dark men such as the Scythians and Hittites who surrounded Amazonia, this frightening stranger stood out like a giant from one of the stories the grandmothers told the very young. Among her own people, Thalassa was considered tall, but this alien creature dwarfed her. She speculated that the top of her head would barely reach his bronzed shoulder, and this realization in itself was profoundly disturbing. Worse, it frightened her, and fear was something she knew she should never show an enemy.

Throwing her head back, she fixed the man with hard

eyes and demanded fiercely, "What is this place and how have I come here?"

The stranger studied her. "The answer to that is rather complicated," he said gently.

His voice was deep and musical. It made Thalassa think of the sound the waves made in the underwater sea cave she sometimes swam to when she wished to be truly alone. He spoke her language perfectly, but with an odd, lilting accent she could not identify. She had heard Greeks, Cretans, Scythians, and Hittites all twist their jaws around the difficult tongue of the Amazons, and this stranger sounded like none of them. Nor had any man she encountered spoken her language so fluidly.

"How is it you speak my tongue?" she asked warily.

"I speak many tongues."

Such a reply was scarcely reassuring. If anything, it only increased her already considerable uneasiness. She itched to investigate the elegant chamber to see if there was a second way out, but dared not take her gaze off this ridiculously tall man. A chilling thought suddenly flew into her mind, and her eyes blazed.

"If you have brought me here to make me a slave, you will regret it. Amazons do not submit to slavery. We recognize no man as master, and we die well!"

The stranger gave her an attractive smile, his even, white teeth flashing. "There is no need for you to die, I assure you. My people do not keep slaves. It is not our custom nor will it ever be."

Confusion momentarily overwhelmed her fear and anger. Slavery was as commonplace as the rising of the sun. *Everyone* kept slaves, including the Amazons. Enslavement was a fate that could befall anyone at any time, and strength in battle was the only protection against loss of freedom. That a person as wealthy and powerful as this man obviously was saw no need for slaves was a concept that completely bewildered Thalassa.

"But who serves yo—" she started to blurt out, then caught herself. This was no time to worry about other people's customs. She was in desperate straits, and had to find a way to escape the man's silken prison without further delay. If this strange man-creature had no slaves, what then did he want with her?

Cautiously, keeping the broad bed between them, she took a few steps toward its foot. The thin gown whispered against her skin, reminding her that she was weaponless, and the man stood between her and the door.

Thalassa was trained in unarmed combat, as all Amazons were. Yet she was uncomfortably aware that it would not be easy to overcome a man of such size and obvious strength, and the long robe would impede her movements. Unused to restriction of any kind, she longed to tear off the unfamiliar garment, but there was no way to pull the gown over her head without becoming totally vulnerable to attack in the process.

Sensing her roiling unease, the man said softly, "Lady, I know there is much you do not understand, and much that I must explain to you. But believe me, I mean you no harm."

"And do you always carry off by force those to whom you mean no harm?" Her tone was scathing, for despite the foggy confusion of her memories, she was increasingly certain this disquieting stranger was responsible for her being there.

The man's answering laugh rumbled through the room, then he sobered and gazed at her seriously. "How much do you remember of what happened before you woke up in this chamber?"

She glared back. "It is *I* who should be asking questions, and you who should be providing answers. You, who have dared to arouse the anger of an Amazon warrior! How have I come here and why? What is this place? Cease dancing with words and speak plainly to me!"

The man's piercing sapphire gaze rested on her face, as if he were debating how to respond. Finally he said, "You are in my palace . . ." He paused for a heartbeat, then finished quietly, "Under the sea."

Silence then. A silence as deep and overwhelming as the sea that supposedly surrounded them. She did not really believe him, Thalassa told herself, but there was something in the way he was looking at her that stilled the denials springing to her tongue. A thought occurred to her, and unconsciously she took a step backward. "Are you a god, then? The man-god of the sea the Greeks worship— Poseidon?"

The man shook his head, smiling. "No, Lady, neither I nor any of my people are gods, although you will find our ways very different from any you are familiar with. And in the beginning at least, rather difficult to comprehend."

She stared at him. "I do not understand. One cannot be under the sea. One can be in or on top of it but *under* it . . . That is impossible . . . you are creating tales."

"Indeed, warrior-woman, it is no tale but the truth, and sooner or later, you will have to accept it."

"I accept nothing, and you have told me nothing! I am not a child to be fooled with silly stories—"

"Would you like me to show you, then?" the stranger interrupted with quiet courtesy.

Thalassa considered, biting her lip and thinking hard. She did not want to fight this huge man unarmed, not when her body felt so weak and ill. But it was either that or look at what he wanted to show her, and perhaps she might be able to find a weapon along the way and escape. In any case, she must not let those keen eyes of his see that she was unwell.

She threw her shoulders back. "Show me what it is you wish to show me, but I warn you, if you mean some trickery, you will regret it."

"Agreed," he said immediately, and turned to the carved red coral door. His hand on the mother-of-pearl knob, he glanced back at her and asked politely, "What are you called, woman of the Amazons?"

She impaled him with a stony gaze. "My name is only for those of my race, they who are my sisters and my mothers. An Amazon does not freely offer her name to a man, in friendship or otherwise."

Rather than being offended, the tall man only gazed at her with a disconcerting tenderness. When he spoke again, his voice made her feel as if she were being stroked by a great, warm hand. "Perhaps one day soon you will count me as a friend, and honor me with the gift of your name. I am called Dorian, and I would be pleased if you addressed me so. Saying my name will place no bonds upon you."

She watched him without answering, and after a moment, he pulled the door open and stepped outside. The instant he turned his back, Thalassa yanked the gown over her head and left it lying in a bright heap on the jade floor. Unencumbered by its clinging folds, she immediately felt better able to deal with whatever dangers lay beyond the beautiful, alien room. She whispered a quick prayer to Artemis for protection and then, filled with caution, every aching muscle taut with the readiness to defend herself, she strode to the doorway.

The stranger stood in a wide, arching corridor, glimmering with subtle shades of coral that varied from a deep rosy hue to the palest pink. In brilliant contrast, the smooth, cool floor appeared to be black coral, flashing with rich, polished highlights.

The beautiful passage was empty of people—suspiciously so—and Thalassa stared warily into it. With a cordial gesture, the man indicated that she should accompany him. She did so hesitantly, stepping as though the smooth black floor were studded with spikes, and taking great care to keep a safe distance from the man.

Unceasingly her gaze darted about, analyzing and observing with the alert instincts of a trained warrior. Thalassa possessed an excellent memory for detail. It had been drilled into her since childhood that one's life often depended upon the ability to take note of escape routes and quickly memorize landmarks. Now, her keen senses heightened by fear, she took careful heed of the corridor's many twists and turns, studying them with an intensity that bordered on desperation.

At length, they entered a huge, brilliantly lit chamber that echoed with the sound of voices and the singing gush of water. She saw the water spurting out of elaborate fountains set within the glistening black floor, and she saw the people.

They crowded the vast hall, entering and leaving by corridors identical to the one she and the stranger had just passed through. Many carried bags of an odd-looking shiny material over their shoulders; others sat or stood by intricately carved tables on which all manner of objects were arranged. The rise and fall of the alien language they spoke rushed against Thalassa's ears. It was almost as if she were listening to waves washing against a beach, rather than the sound of human voices.

Why, it seemed like a giant marketplace, she thought in astonishment. But of all the wares displayed for sale, only the brightly colored fish were familiar, and Thalassa was far less interested in them than in the men and women milling about.

The folk who inhabited the palace of this man-creature called Dorian were everywhere she looked, strolling singly or in twos and threes. Some were clothed, either in robes similar to the one she had found herself wearing, or in the scanty tuniclike garment her enigmatic companion wore. Others were as naked as she, and seemed totally comfortable with their nudity, as if this were their natural state. They certainly saw nothing out of the ordinary in Thalassa's lack of clothing, and nodded at her in the most friendly of fashions as they passed.

Without exception, they were tall and beautifully formed, men and women alike, and the latter exhibited none of the submissiveness Thalassa associated with women of man-ruled tribes.

Repeatedly these foreigners smiled at her, studied her, pointed her out to their companions, and whispered to each other as if she were the most fascinating of creatures. In the whole of her life, Thalassa had never been the object of such intense scrutiny. Nor had she ever seen so many foreigners in one place at one time—and all of them seemingly spellbound by her!

It was unnerving. A powerful desire to run back to the green chamber gripped her, though the safety it promised was dubious. Do not shame the Mother by such cowardice, she berated herself. Squaring her shoulders, she glanced at the stranger, and was taken aback to see that *he* was watching her as well, smiling.

"Why do they stare at me so?" she asked sharply.

His smile widened. "They have been expecting you and your arrival pleases them."

"Why?"

He hesitated, and a shiver raced down her spine. Determinedly she ignored it. If all these people were in this palace of his, then there had to be a way to get in and out, and surely she would find it.

Even as she reassured herself with this thought, one of the strange folk approached her. A youth of about sixteen, he was dressed in a pale yellow tunic that matched the startling blondness of his unruly hair. She met the boy's gaze for a cold instant, then with a lift of her head started to pass by him. But stepping forward, the youth intercepted her.

"So you are our lord's chosen one. It is said that you come from the land of the Amazons. Is it truly so?"

He spoke the language of her people, but unlike the flawless pronunciation of the one called Dorian, this foreigner mangled so many of the words, Thalassa had difficulty understanding him. Dorian, however, did not.

"She does indeed," he said, also in Thalassa's tongue. "And will you let her become a bit more used to us before you begin plaguing her with your questions?"

The youth cast his lord a look of respect tinged with resentment. "I will," he said sullenly, then added a burst of something in his mysterious language that seemed filled with the rushing murmur of the ocean. Thalassa's companion answered in the same tongue. The sound of it bemused her, so that when the youth once again fractured the familiar tongue of her people, she looked at him blankly.

"I have never been on land, but I am told that yours is rich and fertile. How sad that you will not—"

"Boy," Dorian warned.

The youth subsided, opened his mouth as if to protest, then apparently thought better of it. Glancing up at Dorian, Thalassa saw why.

The courteous, gentle stranger she had met in the green chamber was gone. In his place stood a man whose face was as dark and lowering as the thunderclouds that swept over Amazonia's mountains in summer. The menace stamped on his features made him seem taller and even more formidable than she had first thought. In silence she watched as the boy ducked his head to them, then quickly made his way off through the crowded hall.

"What did he mean, he has never been on land?" she

demanded, praying that only her ears and not Dorian's could detect the trepidation in her voice.

He looked down at her, still brooding. "Come," was all he said, and began once again to walk.

Caught between her perusal of his curious people and the possibility Dorian would lead her to an exit, Thalassa hurried to match her strides to his. But she could not let the matter rest; some unnamed force drove her to persist. "Why will you not answer me? What meaning had his words?"

"I have said that we live under the sea," he told her evenly. "Does it not make sense that the younger ones among us may never have set their feet upon the land?"

He led the way out of the crowded hall. Stunned and at a loss for words, Thalassa followed him.

As they proceeded down another great curving hallway, Dorian watched his unwilling guest from the corner of his eye. Her efforts to memorize the twisting pathways of his abode were obvious, and he admired her courage in the midst of this bewildering situation. Ah, but she was so hostile, he thought, sighing. He was not sure it was wise to inflict the shock of the vast windows on her, yet the Amazons were a pragmatic people known for their mental as well as physical strength. And Dorian intuitively sensed that despite the upheaval it would bring, nothing less than actually viewing where they were would convince his intended mate that he was being truthful.

So they continued in their cautious way, with Dorian taking care to respect the distance Thalassa set between them. Her nudity was as natural to him as his own, for among the seafolk, going unclothed was the rule rather than the exception. Still, he took pleasure in covertly admiring the long, clean lines of her body.

She was as beautiful as a finely tempered sword blade, he thought, with her skin the burnished shade of the bronze her people made their weapons from. He had not been able to tell the color of her eyes when she was on land, and later in the ocean, there had been no time. Now he saw they were a clear hazel, ornamented with flecks of gold that made them glow like the eyes of a cat. Combined with her chestnut hair and golden coloring, they gave her the look of a tawny lioness—exciting and unpredictable.

At length, the corridor divided into two branches veering in opposite directions, and at the point of divergence stood a huge window. Thalassa stopped, her eyes widening, her body freezing in mid step.

"It can't be," she whispered. "By the Sacred Mother, it can't be." She whirled around to confront Dorian. "You *are* a god!" she accused. "Poseidon lives in a palace beneath the sea—a palace that must look like this!"

"Perhaps he does," Dorian agreed patiently. "But not in this one. And as I have told you, my name is Dorian, and I am not a god . . ."

But she was no longer listening.

CHAPTER 4

≈ A violent trembling seized Thalassa, then she spun about and ran as if possessed by demons. Footsteps, swift and inexorable, sounded behind her, and warm hands fell on her shoulders.

"I know it's a surprise," Dorian's deep voice said quickly and soothingly. "But truly, Lady, there is nothing to fear. Let us talk."

With a strangled exclamation, she twisted out of his grasp and struck at him—a skilled and deadly blow that he avoided with terrifying ease. In a movement too fast for her panic-stricken eyes to follow, he encircled her waist with one long arm, drew something from a fold of his tunic, and jabbed her arm with it.

The effect on Thalassa was almost immediate. Her legs buckled, and suddenly the stranger was supporting rather than restraining her. Frantic with fear, she struggled to force back this latest threat—an obviously magical sleep he had just induced in her—but it was no use. A languorous fog surrounded her, and through it she heard him speak with an oddly compelling reassurance.

"Gently now. It's too soon for you to be flinging yourself about so madly. You need rest and quiet. Be calm, Lady. Nothing terrible is going to happen. You will only sleep for a little while, and no harm will come to you."

Dazed and nearly asleep, Thalassa felt her feet leave the ground as the man swung her easily into his arms and began walking along the corridor. Horror at being so vulnerable rippled along the last remaining strands of her consciousness, but by the time Dorian reached the green chamber, even those strands had parted under the power of the enchantment he had put upon her.

The mind-shattering vision she had glimpsed drifted into the stuff of dreams as Dorian tucked the bed covers around her. Even in the deep sleep that followed, what she had seen wove itself relentlessly into her slumber.

The images continually repeated themselves. The window, made from a thick, foreign substance and lit in some unexplainable way to reveal what lay beyond; a gigantic realm of rugged mountains, each one higher than the most towering peak of Amazonia's familiar range; jagged cliffs and crags plunging into sloping valleys and vast, level plains; all of it looming out of the eternal night of the ocean bottom. Life inhabited this inconceivable world, generating its own eerie illumination. Fantastic creatures roamed the depths in front of her, glowing with unearthly, colored lights in the shifting darkness, seeming to fly rather than swim through the ghostly shadows.

Thalassa had flung herself away after only a moment, but the underwater kingdom and its luminescent denizens remained in her mind, merging into one frightening impression of nightmares beyond reason. They haunted her sleep, mingling with the face of a black-haired man, whose probing blue eyes seemed to see into her very soul. Finally, waking up became a relief—until she opened her eyes and saw him sitting in a chair next to the bed.

Dreams and reality warred within her as Thalassa willed the Goddess to undo the spell of this being who looked like a man and return her to the safety of her own people. Minutes passed, and the one who called himself Dorian did not move. Neither did Thalassa. It seemed, she thought in despair, that the ancient Mother had no power there, and that she was truly in the hands of a demon or a god, after all.

"What do you want with me?" she whispered, forcing herself to meet his steady gaze.

Dorian looked into the hazel eyes filled with apprehension and barely disguised fear. "I want nothing that might hurt you," he said gently. Guilt stabbed him as he spoke, for he had already hurt her merely by bringing her there. And he could see she did not believe him.

"If 'nothing' is what you want, then why am I here?" she asked, nervous anger coloring her tone.

"I did not say I wanted nothing from you," he corrected. "I said I don't want to hurt you."

He paused to let the significance of his words sink in, then went on. "I know you are afraid because you believe me to be something other than a man, but this is simply not so. I belong to a race that is far older and stronger than the people who live on the land and sail on the sea without knowing her secrets. Yet we are much the same as the men and women of your world. Being unaccustomed to our ways, you must think we have powers and abilities only gods could have, but that is because what is different and new is often frightening until you become used to it."

The sleep-drugged mists had been clearing from Thalassa's mind while he talked, leaving her coldly aware of the precariousness of her position in the exotic bed. Pushing herself up, she rolled away from him to the edge of the couch and gained her feet.

The physical discomfort she had felt on awakening the first time had lessened, although it was far from gone. The purple robe had been put on her again; she touched it, her suspicious gaze fastened on the man. He continued to sit, totally relaxed, in the chair by the bed.

"I do not want to become used to your ways," she said in a voice made rough by fear. "I care nothing for men or the customs of men, be they gods or mortal. I want only to rejoin my people. And I still do not understand what sorcery brought me to this place or what it is you want from me. But I do know that whatever it is, man of the sea, I will not give it until you release me!"

Despite the bravery of her words, she suddenly looked young and lost, and Dorian had to remind himself that even though she was a skilled warrior who had killed men in battle, she could not be more than eighteen years old. In the view of his ancient people, she was an infant, and he would have to go slowly and carefully with her. But it would be a mistake to let her think there was any possibility of returning to the Amazons.

"I cannot release you," he said quietly. "And it was no sorcery, but my arms that brought you here. I wish I could say this more gently, Lady, yet there are no soft words to tell it. You will never rejoin your kin. Your life is with my people now."

Thalassa's eyes widened until they seemed to fill her whole face. Consternation, rage, and disbelief swept through her in a mighty storm. Never again to see the beaches, plains, and mountains of her home? The faces of her friends and loved ones? Never to ride on Alcippe's back and feel the sun and wind on her face? To dance and feast in a firelit hall surrounded by the warm security of being with her tribe?

"No," she declared, hardly aware that she had spoken. "I will not stay here. I am a woman of the Amazons, and *they* are my people."

"Once," Dorian agreed. "But no longer. I have great respect for your tribe, Lady. They are indeed a noble people to be descended from, and in you I see everything that is best about them. Yet it would be cruel to leave you with the false hope that you might one day resume your old life. My world has much to offer. In time, you will discover it is so."

"Never!" Thalassa cried on a rising note of hysteria. "You can't keep me here. I'll escape. My sisters will search for me, you foul son of a diseased cur, and when they find me, they'll take pleasure in cutting the manhood from your body, if I haven't done so already!"

Dorian waited for the outburst to end, then asked softly, "My fierce warrior, how do you think they will find you?"

She stared at him, wild-eyed, as the full import of his question struck her.

"We are far beneath the waves, Lady," he went on, "as you have already seen. In fact, we are not even in the sea that borders Amazonia, but in another, much larger ocean far to the west. And both of us know the strength of the

Amazons lies in their skill on horseback. They do not sail upon the sea. Even if they did, it would not matter, for no person born on land is capable of diving this deep."

Still unable to speak, Thalassa stood on shaking legs as his musical voice removed each clinging hope of rescue with the implacability of a finely honed knife. Had Hippothoe's sister and her companions felt this utter hopelessness when they were bound on the ship of the Cretan pirates, their only future one of endless rape and servitude?

"I know these are bitter words for you to hear," her captor was saying. "But it will be better if you realize quickly there is no way for you to escape."

There was, though! Her eyes hardened as she remembered the story of how her captive sisters had escaped the slavers. She'd never felt such empathy before. "Escape is always possible if one does not fear death," she said, and was astonished at the controlled coldness of her voice. "No Amazon may live without freedom, and I would rather die than live in dishonor as your slave."

The man frowned. "I have already told you that we do not keep slaves," he said with a touch of impatience. "You are as far from being a slave as it is possible to be."

"And yet I am not free!"

He regarded her thoughtfully. "No, you are not. But that is only a temporary state of affairs. One day, you will be free—freer than you can possibly imagine."

Tendrils of fury raced along her strained nerves at his imperturbable calm. Her voice lost its coldness, becoming thick with frustration and outrage as she snarled, "All I can imagine now is that you hold me captive in this evil place, and by Artemis's holy quiver, I do not know why! Freedom is an absolute. One is either free or is not. Who are you to dare withhold or dispense what is mine by right?"

The man looked at her gravely. "I am the ruler of the sea-people," he said at last. "And long have I searched among the women of the landfolk before finding you—you, whom I have chosen as my mate." There, he thought. He'd said it, and now that he had, what would she do?

For the moment, it appeared she would do nothing. She stood as if carved from stone, looking almost as though she had not heard him. But she had. Thalassa's mouth felt drier than sun-cured leather, and her tongue was a huge, awkward thing that had forgotten how to press against lips and palate to form words. This incredible man-creature was waiting for a response, and she struggled to find her voice.

"It is against our laws to take a man as mate," she eventually got out. "The only purpose a man serves is to help us get daughters. Beyond that, he is either an enemy or a nuisance."

To her astonishment, he laughed. "My beautiful adversary," he said, his broad shoulders still shaking with mirth, "in my travels, I have come across many men who would fit into one or both of those categories. But believe me, there are many other purposes a man might serve—purposes far more pleasant than you might think." Smiling at her, he let his voice become beguiling and intimate. "It would be my great joy to show you that a man can be much more than an enemy or a nuisance."

Thalassa frowned, bewildered at his caressing tone. Again, rage gusted through her as she recognized that she was this man's prisoner and that the fundamental tenet of Amazonian belief amused him. If she could have killed him at that moment, she would have. Only the memory of the magical sleep he had forced on her kept her from rushing at him as he sat there, his white teeth flashing in a teasing grin.

She drew a deep breath, then shouted, "May the raven-beaked woman of vengeance pluck out your eyes and strew your liver upon your accursed ocean! May maggots feast on your living brains, and loathsome creatures burrow and crawl deep within your man-parts until your screams of agony can be heard from one end of the world to the other! May the most poisonous of scorpions replace the food you eat so that their venom spreads throughout your hideous, repulsive man's body—"

"Peace, ferocious lioness," Dorian interrupted with a pained expression. "I can see it will take some time for us to become friends." The corners of his mouth twitched, and with a glint of mischief lighting his eyes, he could not resist adding, "But 'hideous' and 'repulsive'? Do you truly find me so unattractive?"

Thalassa's hands clenched into fists until the tendons in her arms stood out in ridges. When she finally spoke, her

CHAPTER 5

≈ Far from Amazonia, and even farther east of Dorian's deeply hidden abode, through miles and miles of the Great Mother Sea's heaving breast, lay the kingdom of Greece. And in that man-ruled country, the great hero Heracles was unleashing terror throughout the land.

First, he assisted the men of Thebes in defeating their powerful overlords, the Minyans, and in destroying the Minyan capital of Orchomenus, where all male inhabitants were put to the sword and all women taken into slavery.

This victory gave Thebes possession of the rich cornfields in the Copaic Plain where the river Cephissus emptied into the sea, and for this prize, Heracles was heaped with honors. Among them was marriage to King Creon's eldest daughter and the prestigious appointment of city protector. But Heracles was not content.

Next he vanquished Pyraechmus, king of the Euboeans—an ally of the Minyans when they had marched against the Thebans. Heracles ordered the living body of Pyraechmus to be torn in two by unbroken colts and left unburied beside the river Heracleius.

This final excess vexed the gods so much that they drove the mighty hero mad. In a fit of insane rage, he mistook six of his own children for enemies, killed them, and flung them into a fire, together with two of his beloved nephews.

Recovering his sanity too late, Heracles felt all the agonies of an arrogant man brought low by forces beyond his control. His great size and bulging muscles were useless against the mightier foe of death. He, who had brought the final darkness to so many, found himself in a black misery worse than that which he had meted out. His most precious possessions—his children—were dead by his own hand. And he owed a blood-price that could never be paid for the sons of his brother, as dear to him as his own sons had been.

He shut himself up in a darkened chamber for days, avoiding all contact with anyone, male or female, royal or slave. Finally, he emerged and endured more days of seemingly endless purification rites. He traveled to the Oracle at Delphi. The *Pythoness*—this most sacred of priestesses through whom the gods spoke—instructed him to reside in the walled city of Tiryns, and there serve its king—his cousin, Eurystheus—performing twelve labors that Eurystheus set for him. And thus, the stage was set.

Eurystheus had a daughter, Admete, an easily bored and spoiled girl who was ever searching for new amusements. Had she become an Amazon, she would have been kept too busy to become bored.

Admete, of the privileged class, had servants to perform onerous work. Therefore, she had the time to think about tales she had heard. She dwelled on one: Hippolyte, queen of the Amazons, possessed a magnificent golden girdle given to her by Artemis herself. Admete decided she wanted the girdle, and the Amazons were simply an obstacle to getting the bauble she coveted for its novelty.

Months went by, and each day she begged her father to dispatch Heracles in pursuit of this latest toy. Finally, wearying of her tantrums, Eurystheus ordered the hero to undertake the mission—the ninth of his labors.

Heracles had heard of the Amazons, and was not about to take them lightly. He also had his own reasons for traveling to Amazonia.

One of his ancestresses was of the Danaids, Hyper-mnestra, one of the fifty daughters of Danaus, king of Lerna. In the kingdom of Lerna on the Peloponnese, the ancient matriarchy had still held sway, for this was in the days before patriarchal custom had vanquished the rule of women throughout the Greek mainland. Besieged by his powerful and greedy twin brother Aegyptus, Danaus agreed to marry his fifty daughters to Aegyptus's fifty sons, with or without their consent, in order to avert war.

In matriarchal culture, freedom over one's person was the most original of rights. Added to that was the fact that inheritance always went with the daughters. So the Danaids were not only being deprived of their free will, but through the politically compelled marriage, they would lose their birthright as well.

Outraged by their father's betrayal, the sisters plotted to kill not only Danaus, but their unwanted bridegrooms on the wedding night of the mass-marriage ceremony. And this they did.

But on the following morning when the Danaids emerged rejoicing from the bloody bedchambers, they discovered that softhearted Hypermnestra, seduced by the beauty of her bridegroom, Lynceus, had allowed him to escape. In breaking faith with her family, Hypermnestra had broken matriarchal law. For that, she was punished severely.

Generations later, her descendant, Heracles, still remembered the incident, and he vowed never to rest until the last matriarchy was wiped from the earth. In his eyes, rule by women was an abomination—an offense against the natural order. The Amazons, with their complete contempt for all things male, were the personification of everything Heracles had sworn to destroy. Spoiled Admete's desire for Hippolyte's girdle was to him an opportunity to depose and ravish those creatures who dared to place themselves on an equal footing with men.

Preparations went forward carefully. Heracles gathered the highest-born youths in Greece and divided them under twenty-nine officers, who were themselves mighty heroes. Included were Theseus, king of Athens; Peleus, later the father of Achilles; and his brother Telamon, who would one day sire the great Ajax.

From Corinth, the center of shipbuilding in Greece, nine galleys were commissioned. They were built of seasoned alder, poplar, and fir—woods chosen for their buoyancy. Each galley was forty-oared, with one square canvas sail, and tall masts of the finest pine. Boars' heads and serpents decorated the prows, and as the final step, the boats were painted in the brightest vermilion.

In late spring—the best season for sailing—the war fleet set forth. Through the Gulf of Corinth and out into the Ionian Sea they sailed, and then into the wine-dark Aegean.

In the manner of Greek navigation, Heracles and his fleet followed the coastline. With their one square sail, they were at the mercy of the wind, for they could sail only with it. If the wind became an unfavorable gale, the hapless men could merely toil at their oars, and when human strength failed, they were blown off course.

Like all Greek fleets this one traveled by day and anchored by night. Heracles's navigators maneuvered among the islands and headlands that dotted the Aegean Sea, always seeking to keep some familiar landmark in sight. The fleet stopped at Paros, an island renowned for its marble, then sailed on through the Hellespont and Bosphorus, to the land of Paphlagonia. Finally, they reached the Pontus, which Heracles renamed Euxine—"hospitable to strangers."

Into that sea of dark lapis-blue water, the fleet slipped and headed eastward. Now the watch was doubled, and Heracles ordered shields to be lashed together on the landward side of each ship, thus forming a bulwark against Amazonian arrows.

The land bordering the sea was low at first, then it rose in towering mountains, cleft with deep gorges and clothed in thick forests or sun-dappled woods. Beyond reared still higher peaks, crowned with snow and spearing the very heavens themselves.

On the second day, a shout went up from the pilot's watch. Since dawn the man's fearful gaze had been fixed upon the craggy slopes of this unfamiliar country, and at last he had spied a mounted Amazon, gliding like a shadow through sunlight and shade. His cry brought the men crowding onto the decks. Imaginations on fire, filled with curiosity and awe, they pointed and muttered. But the lone horsewoman appeared unconcerned. Silently, as though she were a cat stalking a flock of chattering water birds, she paced the fleet, an eerie figure to these men who had never seen a woman bestride a horse, much less carrying weapons.

Throughout the morning, she appeared and disappeared. In the afternoon she was joined by a second rider, then a third. The forested slopes had flattened into scrubland that gave only the sparsest of cover, yet those on board the nine galleys had the persistent sense that the dry riverbeds and stunted trees concealed far more than they revealed. Stabbed by unseen eyes, the Greeks, fascinated by the three women, watched while wondering how many more of their sisters lay hidden.

Presently, a dip in the shoreline was sighted, and a river mouth. As the fleet hove toward land, broad green plains came into view, and beside the shining river stood a city of wood and stone houses thatched with brush.

The air was suddenly filled with the sound of hooves thrashing into shallows, as the Amazons discarded their almost supernatural use of cover and rode boldly to the water's edge. Quivers bounced against hundreds of bare, tanned shoulders, and sunlight flashed off the blades of battle-axes and the bronze points of spears. But despite their ominous show of arms, the women did not seem hostile— merely watchful.

Heracles stood with his mighty legs planted like tree trunks in the prow of the lead galley and shouted his orders. In response, the scarlet-painted fleet sailed with stately speed across the harbor of Themiscrya, and events that would be chronicled as history and legend came to pass on the cloudless summer day. . . .

CHAPTER 6

~~ Hippolyte stood in the queen's house, looking out of the wide, square window cut into the white-washed stone wall. The wooden shutters that protected against cold and rain were thrown open in the heat of summer, affording her a clear view of the harbor and the approaching flotilla.

A frown creased her forehead as she noted the shields lashed to the sides of the galleys and the number of men straining at each vessel's oars—men who were obviously well armed. Light footsteps sounded behind her, and without turning the queen knew her younger sister had entered the room.

"It is a great force," Antiope said breathlessly, joining her at the window. "Do you think they mean to fight with us?"

Hippolyte shook her head in negation. "Not unless the sun has addled their wits. Only fools or madmen would come upon us so openly if they intended ill. Still, I would feel easier if Oreithyia had not taken such a large force of our warriors to attack the Cappadocians. Whoever these strangers may be, they are not simple traders."

"We could kill a few of them," Antiope suggested hopefully. "And then their fellows would be very cautious about remaining in our favor."

"Or they could kill a few of us in return, and then there would be a battle and many would die. You must learn to think, sister, not be directed by the hotness of your warrior's blood. We are prepared to fight, if need be. At the least we should see what they want before we slice them to pieces."

Antiope sighed in frustration, but the wisdom of Hippolyte's words was inescapable. "It would be far more interesting to slice some of them in pieces," she grumbled. "After all, they may be the ones who carried off Thalassa."

A look of great pain filled Hippolyte's eyes as she thought of their chestnut-haired kinswoman who had vanished so mysteriously two mornings after her honor-feast. Searches had turned up only her weapons on the beach, a puzzling discovery that had led to much speculation. Oreithyia's sentries had seen no sign of ships in the waters of Amazonia's coastline, and no enemy could have possibly infiltrated their territory by land. So what had become of her?

It was a mystery unsolved. And the loss of Thalassa's proud, generous, giving self was keenly felt by all. Antiope, in particular, missed her age-mate. They had been close friends, and Thalassa's disappearance haunted the youthful queen. She would have liked nothing better than to avenge herself on the ones responsible, and as far as she was concerned any man would do, including these strangers in their scarlet galleys. But Hippolyte was not so intemperate.

"I doubt it was these men who took Thalassa," she said gently. "Such a large force would not have gone unnoticed by our lookouts. They could not have been here on the day she vanished."

The fleet had continued to advance, and Hippolyte turned from the window. "I have given orders for the leader of these men to be brought to a private audience with me. Go down to the beach, Antiope, and greet him as befits your station. Then conduct him and his officers back to the palace."

Antiope nodded obediently, but when she spoke her

voice was curt. "If that is your wish, sister, then of course I will do it. But I will also hope that one of these strangers acts disrespectfully, thus giving me a reason to cut off his head."

Hippolyte laughed and gave her a slight push toward the door. "Remember the laws of hospitality, little sister. Let them see how noble a tribe we are."

Antiope strode down to where the boar's head prows of the crimson ships nudged eagerly toward shore, like tired horses seeking their stable after a long journey. The mounted Amazons made way for their queen as she passed, and the silent men took note of this strikingly beautiful woman, so young, yet so regal.

The eyes of young Theseus—the exceedingly handsome red-haired king of Athens—gleamed with special admiration, but not for Antiope's queenly bearing. He studied her shapely thighs and pert, thrusting breasts. He could take such a one as her back home, he thought, and breed sons upon her. And what sons they would be!

Unmindful of these disrespectful thoughts, Antiope planted herself at the water's edge with the same arrogance displayed by Heracles, who still stood in his place on the lead galley. "I am Antiope," she called, "youngest of the three sister queens who rule the noble tribe of Amazon. Who are you, and what is your business?"

She spoke in Greek, for it was evident from the appearance of the strangers and the design of their ships that they were neither Hittite nor Egyptian, and Greeks were the only other people she knew who were adept at traveling by sea.

It was a logical conclusion, and had a man arrived at it, Heracles would not have given it a second thought. But he believed in the inferiority of the female intellect, and such an intelligent deduction from a woman startled him unpleasantly. His bearded jaw dropped. He bit back a sharp rejoinder and forced himself to answer courteously.

"Greetings, O most noble Queen. I am Heracles, son of Zeus and beloved of the gods. These men who follow me are among the most noble issue of Greece's highborn, and have traveled with me on this great, perilous journey from our land to yours at the command of Eurystheus, king of Tiryns, the mighty and most powerful city of walls."

To his barely concealed annoyance, the young raven-haired queen appeared unimpressed. "It is a long way to travel merely because one man tells you to," she remarked dryly, and mocking smiles flashed across the faces of the mounted women nearest her. Heracles frowned, but before he could respond, Antiope continued. "Hippolyte, our eldest queen, has requested that you meet with her in private audience. You and your most senior officers will accompany me. As for the remainder of your men, they must stay on your ships, until"—she finished ominously—"we have discovered your king's purpose in sending you here."

Heracles struggled to keep both dignity and temper intact. His province had ever been that of the physical. Courtly speech did not come easily to him, and being forced to treat a woman as his diplomatic equal was enough to make the words bind in his throat.

"You honor us, noble Lady," he finally managed to say. "Allow me a few moments to gather my officers." Antiope nodded her assent, and Heracles turned to Theseus. "Unwomanly, ill-mannered creature," he muttered. "She needs a man to teach her decent behavior."

"She does indeed, Lord," Theseus agreed with a delighted grin. "But she is young enough to learn the folly of this unnatural life. And a king needs spirited sons, which he can only get on a spirited woman."

Heracles grunted as he beckoned to the men he wished to accompany him. "It is the man and the potency of his seed that makes strong sons. Any woman's belly will swell with a spirited son if the seed that fills her comes from a strong, spirited man. She is nothing more than the vessel in which a man plants his heirs."

Theseus's grin widened as he followed Heracles along the deck. "Well, if a man is going to plant sons, he may as well sow his seed in a beautiful container," he said, thinking of how pleasurable it would be to have that lissome young queen serving as his container.

Heracles and the seven officers appointed to go ashore with him gathered on the small foredeck. Theseus was among them, as was his good friend, Peirthoos, king of the

Lapiths, the brothers Peleus and Telamon, and a slender, young man called Soloon, whose attractive face carried a perpetual sneer. Soloon turned to Heracles and said, "That uppity wench mentioned Hippolyte, my lord. Is she not the one possessing the golden girdle we have come here for?"

"She is," Heracles said gruffly. "And since she is the eldest sister—a wrinkled frog of a woman she must be."

"Don't despair, Lord," a muscular officer named Tiamides said cheerfully. "Despite their attempts to act like men, these creatures are still women, and all women have two weaknesses: honeyed words and shiny baubles. Both of which we possess in abundance."

Heracles gave his characteristic grunt. "Well, let us go visit this hag queen and see if we can barter. With all of them positioned on the beach, armed and mounted as they are, to engage in battle now would be the act of a fool."

Swinging his powerful body about, he made for the stern where the ladder used for getting on and off the galley was kept. One by one, each man followed him down the wooden rungs into waist-high, sun-warmed water. Because of the narrow drafts of the keels of the ships, they could be brought into shallow water without fear of foundering, and therefore the fleet of Heracles had been able to anchor quite close to shore. The men remaining on the galleys clustered at the rails, watching nervously as their lord and his party waded in toward the Amazons.

Despite the heat of summer, Heracles had donned his famous lionskin cloak, girding it high on his loins to keep it dry. The pelt—flayed from the lion with its own razor-sharp claws—represented the first of his labors for Eurystheus. He had freed the city of Nemea from the monstrous, man-eating beast, losing only one finger in the process. During the struggle, he had discovered that the sharpest weapons had no effect on the huge animal, and had strangled the lion to death. Now the skin served as armor, and the gaping, white-fanged head as a helmet that protected him from all weapons of bronze, iron, and stone.

His officers, although not garbed so dramatically, presented a fine appearance. All of them comely and well built, they were clothed in full-skirted summer linen tunics; white as befitted their rank, and short to show off their strong limbs. In further keeping with their status as Greek aristocrats, each man wore a gold torque around his tanned neck, and bore both a long and a short bronze sword, held carefully away from the damaging bite of the salt water.

The Amazons who awaited them appeared no less splendid. Antiope stood proudly in a red-dyed tunic that glowed brightly against her bronzed skin. Gold adorned her sinewy arms and slender neck, and held back her long hair. A short sword was belted around her small waist. In one hand she clasped a crescent-shaped shield, and in the other, its companion—the beautiful and deadly efficient *bipennis*.

This terrible ax had come to symbolize the Amazons' ferocity in war and was uniquely theirs. Nearly the height of a man, its double blades—honed from the finest bronze and embellished with symbols of the Mother Goddess—could destroy an enemy either from horseback or on foot. As soon as she was big enough to heft one, a girl was trained in the battle-ax's usage, until by the time she reached adulthood she wielded it as if it were an extension of her body.

Flanking Antiope was her honor guard: tall, noble warriors dressed in brightly colored tunics with the characteristically bared right breast, and armed in the same manner as their queen. Had Thalassa's destiny been different, she would have been part of this elite company, for it was composed of many of her age-mates, including Aella, Hippothoe, Asteria, and red-haired Tecmessa.

In thoughtful silence, their lovely faces impassive, the women observed the strangers as they sloshed onto the beach. To the Greeks—accustomed to blushing, eye-lowered deference—these women who stared directly into their eyes were an uncomfortable surprise. Amazon eyes were made to be looked *at* rather than looked *into*, and so Heracles and his entourage found themselves pierced by hundreds of spearlike gazes that measured their progress as coolly as any man's. The wary hush around them was broken only by the occasional stamp of a horse's hoof, or the jingling of bridle rings as restive mounts tossed their heads.

When he reached her, Heracles looked down at Antiope. He was immensely pleased that he towered over her. At six feet two inches, however, he towered over all the men of his world as well as these women. "Very well, Lady," he said. "Conduct us to your noble queen."

If Antiope was daunted by the mighty hero's size, she gave no sign. Wordlessly she turned and led the way up the beach. The men fell in behind, flanked by her guard and a dozen or so riders whose nimble horses pranced and curvetted in the hot sand.

As they walked, the visitors looked about eagerly, torn between the desire to study the beauty of their escorts and the urge to view this fertile land, rich with the smells of ripening grain fields, lush pastures, and abundant fruit trees. The sun lay hot upon their bare heads; it glittered off whitewashed houses, burnished the placid river, and lit up the plain of Themiscrya with all the verdant luster of high summer. Bands of glossy horses wheeled and dipped about the group, nickering equine greetings, then pausing in flight to stand with heads raised and ears pricked as the humans went past.

Theseus, who had contrived to walk near Antiope, glanced at Heracles. Reading permission in his leader's eyes, he respectfully addressed their royal guide. "Your horses are magnificent, Lady. I breed fine horses myself, and never have I seen any to match these. My sire, the great Poseidon, gave horses to the Greeks as a gift, but surely he must have given some to your people as well, for such animals can only come from the gods."

Antiope's dark gaze brushed past his. "Such animals come from careful breeding and good care, which you should know if you breed horses yourself," she pointed out. "And Poseidon is a man-god. We worship only the Mother, who gives us all the gifts we need."

It was an inauspicious beginning, but, unabashed, Theseus tried again. "Do you always let them roam free like that? Are you not afraid they will wander off if left unconfined?"

"And why would they do that? We raise our horses to be our friends and comrades, not our servants. They stay by us out of love, and no force is necessary to keep them here."

"But what if someone tried to steal them? They are extremely valuable animals, Lady."

Antiope laughed—a sound which was pure music to the

enamored Theseus's ears—and said something to her companions in the Amazon tongue. The other women laughed in turn.

"No one would ever be so foolish as to attempt that," she explained, switching back to Greek. "For he would first have to get past the patrols that constantly watch our borders. And even if by some intervention of the Goddess he succeeded, we are all of us very light sleepers. If we did not kill him, the hooves of our horses, who are not fond of men, surely would."

This disclosure rendered the youthful king temporarily speechless, and as he was thinking of something else to say, they arrived at Hippolyte's palace.

The palace could not match the ornate splendor of the dwellings the highborn Greeks, influenced by their wealthy overlords of Minoan Crete, were used to. Even Theseus, who ruled Athens—still only a minor power—inhabited a far greater home than this. But despite its lack of grandeur, the queen's house was an airy and comfortable refuge from the growing heat of the day.

The men were ushered into a spacious vestibule, furnished with simple elegance and cooled by wide openings cut into the white stone walls. The rich furs that covered the plaster floor in winter had been rolled up to reveal colorful depictions of horses and other animals sacred to the Amazons. Hittite traders had supplied the large tasseled cushions and ebony carved benches that composed the room's furniture, and at Antiope's gesture, the visitors seated themselves.

Male slaves entered, bearing nine-footed stone tables inlaid with crystal, which they placed about the room. They left, and presently one returned, bringing water in an ample pitcher made from beaten gold, along with an equally large basin of pure silver. Beginning with Heracles, the slave knelt before each man so he could make his ablutions. When this was done, the other servants reentered, laden with drinking cups and jugs of finely glazed black ware decorated in bright reds and yellows.

The visitors appreciatively sipped the beverage served them; a river-cooled mead mixed with pale honey and flavored with barley. The laws of hospitality regarding their

reception were being followed with impeccable courtesy—
something they had never expected from this infamous tribe
of manhaters, these savage freaks of nature who were
supposed to fall upon any male with bloodthirsty delight the
first moment they saw him.

Heracles and the other men were actually a little
disappointed to find these unnatural women so civilized.
How could they return home as all-conquering heroes if
their female opponents refused to give them the opportunity
to triumph in the name of manhood?

It was indeed a ticklish problem, especially for Heracles, who more than any of them was obsessed with the idea
of vanquishing this aberrant female society. True, he had
not wished to engage in immediate battle, and was relieved
it had been avoided. But he had given a great deal of
thought as to how the story of this exploit would be
recorded by the tale-singers, and these blasted women were
not cooperating!

He and his men were supposed to come in peace, asking
for a boon from the vicious Amazons with the nobility of
true heroes. The treacherous creatures would refuse and
attack like a pack of rabid she-wolves. The valiant men
would be forced to defend their lives and would, of course,
acquit themselves bravely. The entire Amazon nation would
subsequently be crushed into ignominious submission by
the superior men, and Heracles would return home victorious.

What he had not expected was to be received in such a
gracious and . . . well, *manly* fashion by those he intended to destroy.

Moodily he drained a second goblet of the delicious
mead, then looked up as Antiope addressed him. "If you are
sufficiently refreshed, Queen Hippolyte awaits you in her
statechamber. A slave will conduct you there."

Heracles promptly rose to his great height. Several of
his men made as if to rise with him, but Antiope and her
warriors intervened with polite but unmistakable decisiveness. "Your men will remain here," Antiope said in an
emphatic voice. "They will not be harmed. We do not kill
guests, unless," she added deliberately, "they give us
reason to."

Heracles ground his teeth together. The protocol of her actions was undeniably appropriate. It was customary for rulers to meet leaders of an expedition such as his in private. But the presumption of this female still angered him. How dare she issue orders and threats to men as if she were an equal, rather than a lowly woman whom the gods ordained should obey commands, not give them? By his father, great Zeus, these females needed to be taught manners!

"Very well," he said, meeting Antiope's level gaze. "I look forward to meeting your queen."

Throwing his huge shoulders back, he placed a hand on the hilt of his long sword and strode forcefully after the slave. They passed down a short corridor and stopped before an oaken door sheathed in that most precious of metals, copper. The servant opened it and bowed his august companion inside, then silently closed the door after him.

"Good day to you, stranger," a low, musical voice said, and, stunned, Heracles beheld the most magnificent woman he had ever seen.

A tunic, white as snow and embroidered in silver, clung to Hippolyte's tall, stately form, and matching silver fillets glittered from the midnight-dark hair that flowed down her straight back like stars in a moonless sky. Gold, copper, and yet more silver caressed her arms and adorned her long, elegant neck, leading up to a face that was an older, more regal, but no less beautiful version of her sister's. Around the queen's slender waist rested the coveted girdle, its priceless jewels ablaze with fires so brilliant, they dazzled the eye.

Heracles knew he should return her salutation, but dumbfounded by the unforeseen beauty of this Amazon ruler, all he could do was stare.

"Why do you not speak?" Hippolyte asked with a touch of impatience. "Is it that you have no tongue?"

"Indeed, I have a tongue," the hero blurted out before he could stop himself. "But you are as far from a wrinkled old frog as it is possible to be."

Horrified at himself, he gulped, then said bravely, "I am sorry, Lady. I am a simple man, a warrior, who is unused to mouthing perfumed courtesies in the manner of court diplomats. My skill lies in weapons, not words, and in my stumbling fashion, I was trying to say that I find you beautiful. If I offended, please forgive me."

For the first time in his life, Heracles had spoken to a woman with self-effacing honesty, and he was astounded at how the words had come unbidden to his lips—but then he had never seen a woman who looked like this one.

Far from being insulted, the queen smiled, a smile that made her seem even more glorious.

"You do not offend, stranger. We Amazons are also a simple people, who value skill with arms above courtly speech, particularly when that speech is used to cloak a person's true intentions."

Heracles could not help but be impressed by her perceptiveness. If she were a man, he found himself thinking, he would consider her worthy of his friendship. It confused him to have such thoughts—as everything about this woman and her kind seemed to be confusing him, betraying and distracting him from the cause of his mission. Clearing his throat, he drew up his mighty frame and launched into a ponderous explanation of his royal task.

Hippolyte listened with evident patience, but an observer more astute in such matters than Heracles would have noticed that her attention was not in her ears. Instead, it was in her gaze, which roved over his hard, bronzed torso, his massive arms and legs, the silky black beard curling about his cleft chin, and those piercing black eyes.

What a magnificent daughter would result from coupling with him, she mused. Tall and strong and beautiful, just like the two of them. Twice now she had gone to the annual spring meeting with the Gargarians, but had not conceived. She was little concerned by this, for it was not at all unusual and she was still young with numerous years of daughterbearing ahead. But as queen, it was essential she produce heirs. Seeing this splendid man before her, Hippolyte decided that the Goddess had a hand in why her belly had not yet ripened. Obviously, this man's presence was a gift from the Goddess.

The thought made Hippolyte's mouth curve with another smile. Seeing it, Heracles inquired somewhat anxiously, "So you approve of our mission then, Lady?"

Hurriedly, Hippolyte brought her mind back to the

matter at hand, and mentally reviewed what Heracles had told her. "It is a most extraordinary request," she said gravely.

"Yes, Lady, it is. But we have not come empty-handed like beggars. Indeed not. We are prepared to bargain."

"Is that so? And what do you intend to offer for this sacred girdle which is the symbol of my queenship?"

"Many things," Heracles said expansively, encouraged by her tone. "Tall pots with wondrously colored patterns, made in the fashion taught us mainlanders by the Cretans, the most skilled of all potters. Fragrant unguents created from the costliest of spices: sage, cyperus, saffron, red and white safflower, ginger-grass, fennel, rose, and mint, as the master unguent-maker told me. Combs made from the finest ivory, mirrors of polished copper with ivory handles. And then there is the jewelry, Lady. Earrings of heavy gold, and long ropes of beads, crafted from amethyst, carnelian, amber, and gold. And from the island of Lipari, we have brought that rich strange substance known as obsidian, which," he added with awkward daring, "shines as black as your hair, noble Queen."

He did not mention that the idea of bringing trade goods had originally angered him. He and his highborn crew were not common traders, he had vehemently protested to Eurystheus. Better, he had declared, to stock an extra store of arms to fight off the blood-mad females than useless fripperies. But Eurystheus had insisted, reminding Heracles of his vow to the Oracle that he would render total obedience to the king of Tiryns. Now the hero was glad his lordly cousin had prevailed.

Hippolyte, however, was shaking her head. "And what do we need with perfumes, combs, and jewelry? You forget, Heracles, that we are not soft, pampered Greek women, but Amazons. We live a warrior's life, just as you do, and therefore we value the same things. Warriors have no use for perfumes or fancy combs and mirrors. Bathing in the river keeps our bodies clean and sweet smelling, and our hair can be braided or tied back by other simple means when we hunt or fight. And as for heavy earrings and long ropes of beads—of what possible worth are those? They would only get in our way, and we would feel as silly in them as you would."

She paused, then said reflectively, "The only thing you mentioned that has any value for us are the pots and the obsidian. At least from the black stone we can make knife blades and arrowheads. But some pots and a few measures of obsidian are hardly fair exchange for my girdle. Have you nothing else?"

Heracles stared at her, crestfallen. It had never occurred to either him or Eurystheus to bring along trade goods that would appeal to warriors. Despite their ferocious reputation, the Amazons were, after all, women. And did not women have the same weakness—vanity?

"My lord Eurystheus thought these things would please you," he said stiffly, and was surprised when the Amazon queen smiled at him.

"No doubt there are many women of the man-ruled tribes who would be greatly pleased by your ornaments. So I suggest you take these riches home with you and distribute them to women who desire such baubles. There is only one treasure I would consider worthy of being offered in trade for my sacred belt."

Heracles's strong brow furrowed with the effort of his thoughts. "And what is that?" he finally asked, totally perplexed.

"A daughter," Hippolyte said serenely.

He stared at her uncomprehendingly for a moment, then his jaw dropped as the meaning of her words became clear. "You mean you desire one of us to lie with you?" he exclaimed incredulously.

Hippolyte threw her head back with a laugh that rang out as easy and free as any youth's. "I desire *you* to lie with me," she said, her voice bubbling with humor. "It is certainly nothing to be ashamed of. How else do you think we Amazons continue our race?"

Briefly, she explained the mating arrangement with the Gargarians. "So you see," she finished, "the Goddess has brought you here for the holy purpose of giving me a daughter. For you are a comely man, Heracles, and fit to mate with a queen such as myself. Between us, we will make a truly noble daughter, and that is a treasure beyond price. It is worth far more than any jeweled girdle, another one of which our skilled smiths can easily make."

Heracles shook his head in wonder. "Lady, you and your people are not at all what I expected."

And he meant it. He could not decide which aspect of these astonishing creatures confused him more, their beauty, their civilized behavior, or their practicality—especially with regard to lying with men. Women in his world did not offer themselves to men. They waited to be taken. The question of choice was the sole prerogative of man.

Yet, here was this woman—and even though she *was* a queen, she was nevertheless only a woman—choosing her bed partners as if she were a man! It was a new and not entirely welcome change, and the mighty hero found himself feeling both flattered and uncomfortable.

"You make it sound as if a man is nothing more than a stallion, to be used for stud," he grumbled in an effort to hide his unease.

Hippolyte's black eyes flashed. "And do not you men view women in the same light—as mares to be mounted and bred?"

Without waiting for an answer, she went on more calmly. "Surely you must realize our ways are very different from yours, man of the Greeks. We Amazons belong only to ourselves. We obey the will of the Mother, and not that of any man. There is no marriage custom here, as there is among your man-ruled tribes. Indeed, it is against our laws for an Amazon to live with a man or form any type of permanent alliance with one. And yet, women and men need each other to create children. To not discuss such things plainly is complete foolishness. We will sleep together, and you will enjoy my body, as I will probably enjoy yours. Then you may depart in peace with the girdle, and with the blessing of the Goddess I will bear a daughter. What could be simpler?"

"Nothing," Heracles said thoughtfully, his gaze resting on her lovely face, matched only by her wonderful body. "Nothing," he said again, and suddenly spread his massive arms wide, a great roar of laughter booming from him.

"Lady," he cried, "a man would be twelve kinds of fool

to refuse an offer such as yours, for you are the most beautiful and desirable woman I have ever seen. Your customs are outlandish, but I can think of nothing I would like better than to sleep with you!"

Hippolyte grinned back at him, a grin that was more like one from a comrade than a future lover. "Good," she said happily, and turned to pour them both some wine.

Still, her astute brain was ever mindful of her responsibilities as queen, the chief one being the safety of her people. She had not forgotten for an instant that nine galleys lay in her harbor, each of them filled with heavily armed men.

"Let us drink a goblet of wine together," she said, all business again, "so that we may speak of your many men and the weapons they carry. For it is a large force you brought here, Heracles. And one that gives cause to doubt your peaceful intentions."

CHAPTER 7

≈ Dorian strode naked through the narrow passage-
way, frowning with thought. The area through
which he walked was the most ancient part of his abode,
dating back to the end of the Time Before, when his ancestors first conceived the idea of building places such as
this. Unlike the warmth and light of the rest of the abode,
this part was damp and dark, cut from the living rock of the
monolithic mountain that had housed his clan for uncounted
centuries.

Dorian, gifted with superb vision and a body inured to
extremes of heat and cold as were all his kind, scarcely
noticed the gloomy cold. Absently he followed the corridor
into a small unlit cavern, the central feature of which was a
large pool.

Wraiths of steam rose pale and ghostly out of the black
water, drifting and coiling lazily up to the cavern's craggy,
arched ceiling. An eerie phosphorescence danced off the
pool's surface—*spirit laughter,* his people called it—and it
provided the dank chamber's only illumination.

Dorian found his way unerringly over the mist-slick

floor, to the several stone steps cut into the edge of the pool. Eight figures reclined there, an equal number of men and women, all of them unclothed and all of them extremely old. The eerie light gleamed off their wet limbs and long, tangled hair, casting fitful patterns over the heavy armbands and necklaces adorning sun-browned necks and arms. Their faces, as they watched him approach, were pensive.

Dorian lowered himself into the water. "The peace of the deep places be upon you, Revered Ones," he said, and sighed as the pool's fierce, caressing heat enfolded his body.

"And upon you, my child," one of the women responded. Ripples of dark water spun away in long, uneven circles as she sat up. "So, it is done?"

"It is. Three moon-tides she has been here, and not a whit less prickly than the moment she awoke."

"And the Ceremony of Matebonding. Have you told her of it yet?"

Dorian's sigh, this time, had nothing to do with the volcanically heated pool. "No. She wants little enough to do with me as it is. I've asked Aricia to tell her."

"She'll get over it." The man at the farthest end of the pool spoke with utter confidence, his voice sounding hollow in the cavernous chamber. "What's important is that you took her when you did. Her people are about to bathe themselves in the fire and blood that seems the inevitable fate for civilizations of landfolk. A shame, really. It was quite hopeful to see a tribe of women acquire the power these Amazons attained. Yet they have proved as death-mad and violent as any man-ruled race."

Dorian trailed a hand through the steaming water. "Can you blame them? How else are they to survive, given the way men view women on the land?"

The old man shrugged. "That may be. But their desire to slaughter men, or of men to slaughter them, is of little concern to us, as long as the one woman is kept safe."

"Indeed," said another of the Elder women. "No harm must be allowed to come to her. From what we have seen in the Shell, another such woman may not be born into the world for thousands of years. To leave this one amongst her birth kin as blackness approaches would be the height of foolhardiness."

Dorian nodded. The contempt his elders felt for the ways of landfolk coiled about the dark chamber as pervasively as the steam rising from the pool. None shared more heartily in that contempt than he. Yet the young Amazon's stricken expression when he told her she would never see home again haunted him. It was one thing to make love to a pretty Terran woman on a deserted beach at midnight; it was quite another to tear a woman—even a landwoman—from hearth and kindred for all time.

"Perhaps the Shell misspoke its visions," he said, "and the blackness you saw may not come after all."

The woman Elder's voice was cool. "Such a possibility exists, of course. Destinies can be rewritten according to the actions of those who write them, and nothing is infallible, not even the Shell, or"—faint amusement colored her voice—"us, for that matter. But you know as well as we risks should not be taken in a matter such as this."

"Yes." The resignation he felt surprised Dorian. "I do know."

"Guilt is piercing you, my son."

The man who spoke sat in the pool's darkest corner where the steam was thickest, the heat most intense. Dorian could barely see him, but he did not have to see him to recognize the speaker. Nomar, the most ancient of these ancient ones, a man whose eyes, it was said, saw further back into the merfolk's hazy past than anyone.

No one knew how old he was. Despite his advanced age, though, the venerable Elder stood half a head taller than Dorian himself, with a sturdy bronzed body and a glorious mane of silver-white hair that fell well below his boyishly narrow waist. Brushing strands of that silvery hair from his lined face, Nomar continued.

"To feel so is natural. I have never known a son of the royal house not to wonder if what he does in this matter is right."

"I don't wonder about the rightness of it," Dorian said abruptly. "It's the causing of pain to she who is to share my life that bothers me."

Nomar's smile was serene. "It is all one and the same,

is it not? In any case, when you have put the Sea Spell upon her, things will be easier. For her, and for you."

Dorian made no response, and Nomar's smile became a shade less serene. "You must do this soon, Dorian. Before the Ceremony of Matebonding or after—it does not matter—though it will make her more tractable if you do it before. But it must be done."

Angry thoughts roiled through Dorian's mind. He held them back with an effort. It would do no good to voice his sentiments here. He knew only too well how the Elders would react.

The views of Jabari, even the speaking of that notorious philosopher's name, still elicited scorn, not only in the Elders, but in most merfolk. At one time, Jabari and the ideas she espoused had been on the lips of all who swam the seas. But that had been long ago, and Dorian had not been born until centuries after the final tragedy.

Dorian did reject the principles of Jabari as roundly as the Elders did—except for one. The ancient philosopher had had much to say about the Sea Spell, and her reasoning had struck a reluctant chord in Dorian. It was incongruous that her teachings on the subject should affect him so, for he disagreed with everything else she had ever said. Yet there was a wisdom in Jabari's observation about the Sea Spell, a wisdom he found difficult to ignore.

"Well, I see no need to hurry about it," he said gruffly. "The woman is safely held here, and until her physical change is complete, she obviously cannot leave the abode."

The woman Elder who had first spoken shook her head. "You are being cruel, Dorian. It would be kinder to lay the spell upon her now. Then she would cease pining for what she has lost and settle down more happily to her new life."

"I, cruel?" Dorian could no longer contain himself. "It is the custom that is cruel! Why should I have to beguile and enchant my mate, binding her to me with invisible chains that enslave her to my will? Have we not progressed enough as a people to forego such things? The sea-people dance within the rhythm of life. We are one with the Great Mother Sea and know all of Her secrets, yet we hold to a practice that would be more suited to the landfolk, had they the knowledge to do such things. Which, thank the tides, they do not!"

A long silence answered him, broken only by the gurgle and splash of water against stone. Dorian struggled with an irrational desire to laugh. For just a moment, he was a boy again—his eyes having looked on the world for less than one hundred years—an untried and mischievous boy who delighted in shocking his elders. Then Nomar cleared his throat, and the moment was gone.

"I see there are still some who give credence to the philosophies of Jabari," he said.

"I do not—" Dorian began, but the old man slapped his hand against the rocky side of the pool.

"She was as wrong then as she is now. A brilliant woman, but with a head as thick and hard to penetrate as this rock. Three centuries did I argue with her, to no avail. Now she and her followers are dead, and we—we live and grow strong. And do you know why?" Nomar's voice rose. "Because we keep to the old ways, the ways that have always ensured the survival and well-being of our people. You are charged with protecting that trust, Dorian, as your father and all your fathers before you have done through the ages."

"Venerable Elder," Dorian said, his tone clipped and harsh, "I am well aware of my duties as king. I need not be reminded of them."

"Then speak no more Jabari-inspired nonsense about the Sea Spell! The ritual was devised for a purpose, and it does the chosen one not the slightest harm. If your own mother still lived she would tell you that herself—she who was taken by your father in precisely the same manner in which you took this woman!"

Dorian sighed. That was entirely true, he thought glumly, but it made the task ahead of him no less pleasant. And his mother's life upon the land had been harsh. Born to the Accadians—a landfolk who had later developed into the powerful Babylonians—she had been given in slavery to a loutish man who had raped and abused her. But, despite that harsh treatment, she might have been drawn to the mermen because the Accadians had worshiped the sea in the form of Oannes, a god they depicted as a merman.

But, Dorian thought, his Amazon mate was very different, and convincing the Elders of that seemed well-nigh impossible. The heated water splashed and ran from his tall form as he rose from the pool. "I will fulfill my responsibilities," he told the assembled Elders in a curt voice.

"We know you will, my son," Nomar said gently, "and the compassion you feel toward this woman is only to your credit. Yet, just as we preserve this part of the abode to remember our beginnings and our past, so must we preserve the traditions that keep us strong. As Elders, we would be remiss in our own duties if we did not remind you of these things."

"I understand." He didn't, but there was no point in arguing further. "I've already chased that young seal-pup, Valya, away from her," he added, climbing out of the pool. "He is fascinated with her—the first Terran he has ever seen."

"And he is not alone." The woman Elder's tone was somber. "It is natural for ones of that seeding to be fascinated with the land, since they are still too young to have been allowed to visit it for themselves. But Valya is of Jabari's original clan, and he and his friends have recently developed an interest in her that worries us."

Dorian looked down at her in concern. "Have you looked into the Shell?"

"Yes, although it showed us nothing. It rarely does in matters that concern only the merfolk. But it is all the more reason for you to place the Sea Spell upon your chosen one quickly, to prevent her from inflaming them with tales of the land."

"And," Nomar added, "I suggest you not speak to her of the ill winds that fly toward her birth-people. There is naught she can do about it, and it will only make her transition more difficult."

Thalassa glowered at the blond-haired youth who had entered the jade chamber. With great deference, he held an enameled tray laden with dishes. As if, she thought savagely, she were the most honored of guests, rather than a powerless captive.

"Here, Lady," the youth said haltingly in her tongue. "We believed you might be hungry."

Thalassa ignored the steaming bowl he proffered. "And who believed so?" she asked harshly.

"Our lord Dorian. He ordered that you be given—"

"He is not *my* lord. Neither he nor any other man!"

Silent and uncertain, the boy stood motionless, still holding out the bowl, a foolish look stamped on his sun-darkened face. Perhaps it was the very foolishness of his expression that sent a tiny stab of guilt through Thalassa, for this hesitantly friendly young man threatened her less than anything else in this incredible place.

Still, she knew little about how to converse with a man, much less one who lived under the sea! In truth, she had never even held a conversation alone with a male, until her disastrous meeting with Dorian. Her fists clenched. She would have gladly foregone *that* experience to be back safely in her hut, her accursed decision to go down to the sea alone never made.

The youth shifted nervously from one foot to the other. "I am called Valya," he said suddenly. "It was not I who was supposed to bring you food. The lord Dorian would be angry if he knew."

"Why?" Thalassa asked the question dully, not really caring. The animosity between her captor and his subjects was of no concern to her

"Because I would ask you things—things about the land."

She regarded him with a bit more interest. "Is it true you have never been on land?"

Valya nodded eagerly, pleased that she was speaking to him. "Yes, Lady, it is true. And not only for me. Most of my"—he used a word in his own tongue—"have never placed their feet upon land. Small islands, yes, places that only we know about. But as for the great lands of your kind, we have never walked there."

"But how do you live?" Thalassa shook her head incredulously. "Surely, the Mother did not mean for Her children to bide in this way."

"The sea is our mother. Whatever we need she provides for us. Food, shelter, anything we may wish."

"Yet your faces look as if you visit the sun." The horrible thought was being borne upon Thalassa that if what this boy said was true, then the same fate awaited her. Desperate to convince herself otherwise, she insisted, "Such cannot be. For if you stay in these deep places, your skins would not be so brown!"

"Yes, but we do not stay beneath the sea all the time, only to gather with our kin for visits, resting from a long journey, and"—he paused—"and for ceremonies."

This last word brought Thalassa's gaze sharply to his face, but unheeding, Valya rushed on.

"We swim upon the sea's breast, we play with the other seafolk, the dolphins and the—I do not know their names in your tongue. But I cannot yet go to visit the land, not until I am older and have gained more wisdom, the Elders say. But I am wise enough now, and I wish to see for myself the things I have heard of. Lady, are there mountains on land like those beneath the sea, and are they covered with something called 'trees,' as numerous as the sea urchins?"

"Yes, that is so," Thalassa said slowly, even as her mind raced. It was a marvel that this odd boy-creature had never seen a tree before. And it was terrifying. But could his desire to see land possibly be of any help to her?

"And the folk of the land?" Valya asked eagerly. "What are they like? Do they kill all four-legged creatures, or else enslave them to toil and do their bidding until they die?"

Alcippe, her beloved comrade whom she had raised from a foal, enslaved? "No—" she started, but a new voice overrode her.

"Yes, that is precisely what they do. And they are equally fond of killing and enslaving each other. Such is the way of the landfolk."

Neither of them had noticed Dorian's entrance, so silent had he been. They jumped in guilty surprise. Thalassa, in particular, was mortified by her dull-wittedness. She glared at the towering man who called himself ruler of this place. Dorian paid her no heed. His unnaturally blue eyes were fixed on Valya.

"Did I not tell you to let her become more used to us before rushing at her with your questions?" he asked, the stiff set of his jaw belying his calm tone.

Valya looked embarrassed, the way, Thalassa mused, she must have looked when old Marpe caught her filching apples from the winter stores. Pain stabbed her. By now her disappearance must have been noted at home. Was Marpe wailing for her vanished granddaughter, thinking her dead or, even worse, taken into slavery?

Uncomprehendingly she listened to the two men, now speaking in their own language. Valya sounded defiant, Dorian coldly angry. The discussion escalated until, with a black look, Dorian thundered something in a tone that made Thalassa glad his ire was not directed at her.

Apparently Valya had been ordered to leave, for he stomped toward the door. Turning in the doorway, he thrust out his chin, said, "I will speak to you again, Lady," and marched out.

The elaborately carved door closed behind him with a resounding bang, and Dorian muttered angrily under his breath. Thalassa was hot with shame. How could she have quailed before this man—even though it had only been for an instant?

"Are you truly a king?" she demanded truculently.

His piercing gaze left the door and fastened on hers. "I have said so."

"Well, then." She forced herself to meet his eyes and speak as scathingly as she could. "You must be a weak king indeed, for your people behave disrespectfully toward you, as though they bear you no honor."

He stared hard at her, and she saw the muscles in his jaw clench. Abruptly, his face cleared. "I suppose it must seem that way to one who comes from the land," he said in a silken tone, "where people have no understanding of either honor or respect."

"My people understand both, man of the sea!" she spat.

Ignoring her, Dorian walked over to the marble table on which Valya had placed the tray of food. "I see you have not touched this."

Thalassa said nothing. Lifting a bowl, he strode back to her. "You must eat, Lady. Three of your days have passed, and you have taken nothing." He held out the bowl, filled with a soup redolent of unfamiliar spices and peculiar but savory smells.

She glanced at the fragrant broth, steaming in a dish of beaten gold so fine, it resembled a delicately crafted leaf. She looked away, muttering, "I do not want your food."

"Nevertheless, it is what you need. And sooner or later, you will have to eat."

"Then it will be later—much later! For I would rather starve than eat your otherworldly fare, which is most likely poisoned!"

A smile played on Dorian's lips, but since Thalassa was not looking at him, she did not see it, though she did hear the implacable note in his voice. "The soup is not poisoned, Lady. Indeed, it would be the act of a fool to bring you all this way only to poison you, and trust me, Lady, I am no fool. I also have no intention of letting you starve, so I suggest you eat this before it cools. I think you will be pleased at how good it tastes."

Thalassa set her mouth in a tight, mutinous line, refusing to acknowledge either him or the steaming broth. She could feel him watching her. He was standing so close, the heat of his body flowed out to enfold her. She could smell the aroma of his skin—an aroma compounded of salt air and sun. A strange scent, but not an unpleasant one.

His nearness unnerved her. She had never been this close to a man before. Oh, there were the traders of course, but they did not really count. In any case, they had certainly never unsettled her the way this huge man did. She tensed even more when he spoke again.

"Warrior-woman, if you do not eat willingly, I will have to lay force upon you, and that will be very unpleasant, for you as well as for me. You have not seen the full extent of my powers, and it would distress me to have to use them, making you act against your will in something so basic as the taking of food. Now, please, eat."

She swung around at last to scowl at his dark, impassive face. She was tempted to take his broth and fling it at him, but the threat beneath his courteously phrased words gave her pause. She was in over her depth. Despite her biting comments about his weakness, he still seemed to her either a god or a mighty sorcerer. Who knew what skills he possessed to make her do as he wished?

She snatched at the bowl, spilling some of its contents in her haste to minimize any contact with him, and took a reluctant sip. To her astonishment the soup was delicious, awakening a ravenous hunger she had not known she had. What it contained was as much a mystery as everything else about this place, but if poison was indeed one of the ingredients, it was well disguised. Under Dorian's approving gaze, she finished the broth, then at his gentle urging, a second bowlful as well.

The rich broth eased more than just her hunger pangs. It banished much of her dizziness and sent new strength rushing through her limbs. Feeling more herself for the first time since she had awakened in this incomprehensible world, Thalassa paced across the chamber, then turned to stare grimly at Dorian. Hatred and resentment smoldered throughout her being. The catlike eyes she fixed on him burned with malevolence for this man-creature who had deprived her of her freedom.

She yearned for the comfort of a weapon in her hands—even the dullest of eating knives would have been welcome—but whether by design or accident, Valya had brought food that required no utensils. She clenched her fists, wondering if it would not be best to forsake caution after all, and throw herself at him. Perhaps if she caught him by surprise?

The Mothers taught that force was generally the best way to deal with men. "They are heavy-footed and slow," Marpe had always said. "Dependent on muscle rather than skill, they are no match for opponents who understand the use of both. It is a rare man indeed who can stand against a fully trained Amazon warrior and live."

Thus had she and Thalassa's other elders instructed, and Thalassa had never seen any reason to doubt them. But could the realm of experience of the Mothers encompass this place? If Marpe and the other old ones knew of these "merfolk," they had certainly never said so.

Dorian smiled. "I can see by the expression on your face that our soup, flavorful as it is, has not improved your mood."

She said nothing, and his smile deepened. "Perhaps you would like something cool to drink," he suggested. He rose from the alabaster bench on which he had been sitting and strode to a small enameled table holding a silver jug and two goblets. Unstopping the jug, he turned to fill the cups. The instant his broad back was to Thalassa, she moved.

Hurling herself across the room, she locked both hands into a club and swung viciously at Dorian's kidneys, or at least where the kidneys on a normal man would be. It was a trained blow, aimed at one of the many vulnerable points on a man's body. It should have landed. Even without weapons an Amazon was a formidable opponent, and Thalassa was as proficient in hand-to-hand combat as she was in armed battle. In another setting, she likely could have killed a foe with no arms other than those given her by nature. But as Thalassa rapidly found out, Dorian was not like other men.

His huge body, which she had hoped would be unwieldy and slow, slipped away from her attack. Her fists struck harmlessly at empty air, and furiously she went for him again. But with an ease and gentle forbearance that was utterly maddening, Dorian evaded her again.

"Lady, you will tire yourself to no purpose if you persist in this," he said. "The strength of my people far exceeds that of those born to the land. And while I don't wish to sound boastful, I am considered among the strongest of my folk."

At the calm assurance in his deep voice, rage blazed white-hot through Thalassa's entire body. How dare he speak to her as if she was not a worthy opponent! If he was not a god as he so adamantly insisted, then he could be hurt. And by the Mother, she would be the one to do it!

Lightning quick she leaped for his throat, slashing with bladed hands. He stepped aside with almost lazy grace, and she found herself striking at air yet again.

Gazing at her, Dorian shook his head in mild reproof. Then—heaping indignity upon indignity—he smiled as if he sympathized with her! That drove Thalassa to heights of belligerence she had not known she possessed.

Screaming the war cry of her people, she launched herself at him in a storm of skilled kicks and punches, consumed by only one desire: to inflict *some* hurt, no matter how small, on this perplexing, frustrating foe.

But even this new series of attacks proved as unsuccessful as the others. Again and again, Dorian deflected her whirlwind onslaughts, moving with the cadence and force of the ocean itself. Within his muscular frame lay the might of that ocean, coiled and unleashed only enough to neutralize Thalassa's assaults.

When finally she stood on unsteady legs, panting and dripping from her mighty efforts, he shook his head again. "I hope your labors have shown you the futility of seeking to fight me," he said. "We of the sea are essentially peaceful, but we are fully capable of defending ourselves when circumstances require it."

Speechless, Thalassa glowered at him, waiting only for her breath to return so she could attack once more. Admitting defeat never occurred to her. She was an Amazon and would continue fighting until the heart in her breast exploded from the strain.

As if he had divined her determination, Dorian frowned and said sternly, "Lady, I have no intention of allowing you the opportunity of killing or injuring yourself through useless battle. I indulged your anger so that you would learn the fruitlessness of trying to hurt me, and also because I know how difficult this is for you. But do not presume on my good nature too far; I would not like having to use my strength to convince you of the uselessness in fighting me."

She could not mistake the warning in that suddenly inflexible tone, and despite herself, Thalassa shivered with apprehension. She had tried force and it had not worked, but there *had* to be another way. Somewhere in that massive, towering body, this creature in the shape of a man must have a weakness. It was vital that she find it. Otherwise . . . Thalassa's mind froze, and she could not bring herself to complete the thought.

CHAPTER 8

〰 The afternoon was well advanced when Heracles followed a slave back to the vestibule, where his companions anxiously awaited him. It took but one look at his face for them to see that the audience had gone well, and they crowded around him eagerly. Antiope and her escort had stationed themselves outside, but mindful of the women's listening ears, Heracles took care to keep his voice low as he described what had occurred.

"So we are to be welcomed and treated as honored guests?" Soloon asked in a tone that clearly indicated he preferred it to be otherwise.

Heracles shot him a lowering glance from beneath his black brows. "We are indeed," he said coldly. "And in return, I have pledged that we will act according to the laws of courtesy. My honor rests upon this pledge, Soloon, and woe to you or any other man who stains it."

Temporarily quelled, Soloon gulped and said nothing. But Tiamides spoke up. "Lord," he said, respectful, but clearly bewildered, "I do not understand. Do not all Amazons hate men and wish them dead? And did we not come here either to trick them into giving us the girdle, or slay all of them and take it by force?"

"We did," Heracles agreed. "But they are not foolish like most women, and therefore, not easy to trick. There are also more of them than I had planned on. It would be difficult if not impossible to slay them all. No, this is a far better way, and still we may return home covered in glory. Not only will we possess the girdle, but also the bards will sing of how we conquered these fierce Amazons with the strength and comeliness of our man's bodies without even needing to use our weapons."

"Ah, but we are in truth using a weapon," Peirthoos said with a lewd grin. "The most powerful weapon of all—that which hangs between our legs."

Theseus chuckled and cast a quick glance toward the door. "I can scarcely credit our good fortune, Lord. They actually want nothing more than to rut with us? And all the rich goods we carried here do not interest them?"

Heracles shrugged. "Hippolyte says they are warriors, and have no more use for such things than men would. Daughters are what interest them, and they mate only with strong warriors who will father strong offspring."

He was not aware of the approval in his voice as he said this. His deep animosity toward matriarchal societies had not changed, but in his way Heracles was as pragmatic as Hippolyte. There was little advantage in engaging a foe that outnumbered him if his objective could be reached another way. And what healthy man could not help but be pleased by a beautiful woman desiring him to father children on her? It was a compliment, both to his prowess as a warrior and as a man. And Heracles had ever been pleased by compliments.

Peleus poked an elbow into his brother's ribs and said happily, "Well, Lord, if it be your will that we battle these women with our bodies rather than our weapons, Telamon and I shall strive to oblige you—"

"And them!" Theseus put in quickly. "And the queen's younger sister—that toothsome Antiope—is one I shall strive, in particular, to oblige."

"Then let us return to the others," Heracles commanded. "For there will be a feast tonight, and we have much to do before then."

Heracles and his officers were conducted back to their ships by an escort that was noticeably more friendly than it had been. Only Soloon did not share the mood of the others. He walked slightly behind, a sullen, resentful expression on his handsome face as he watched his fellow officers flirting with the mannish she-wolves.

Heracles's decision angered and disappointed him, for Soloon was a man who was happiest when those around him were not. He had greatly looked forward to bringing these so-called warriors to heel, and he simply saw no reason to treat them as if they were men.

It was one thing for a slave girl to be offered to various men by her master. But females taking an active part in the process of selecting bedpartners broke all the laws of nature! Women who freely offered to sleep with strangers were whores, and in any case, Soloon had never been overly fond of the opposite sex—virtuous or not. He was fond of his life though, and he knew that should he anger Heracles, the hero could, and most likely would, kill him with one blow of his mighty fist. So he watched and brooded as if a personal wrong had been done him.

Soloon's gloomy countenance failed in any way to dampen the enthusiasm of his comrades. Those left on the galleys were soon eagerly rushing to do Heracles's bidding, so that they might ready themselves for the feast.

As he and Hippolyte had agreed, the men heaped their weapons into a great pile on the beach. An equal number of Greeks and Amazons were set to guard them in shifts that would change every few hours. Only Heracles and those officers chosen to accompany him to the queen's house were allowed to retain their long and short swords. The rest of the men could keep the knives they used to cut meat with, but that was all.

It was an effective arrangement for both sides. The Greeks' willingness to put up their arms was proof of their peaceful intent; that Amazons and Greeks would guard the weapons together ensured against treachery from either side; and that Heracles and his highest ranking nobles would keep their swords served the men's sense of honor.

Once swords, javelins, and spears lay in a large, glittering pile, the Greeks divided themselves into groups and took turns traipsing down to the river, eager to bathe away the sweat and dirt of their long sea journey. They discovered that a number of their hosts had the same idea, and the men found themselves made unaccountably shy by the bold, appraising scrutiny of the Amazons. To hide their embarrassment, from the women as well as from each other, the men shouted and laughed, making boisterous jokes and bawdy observations about the women, who watched in amusement, undeceived by their antics.

In the large space before the Great Hall, a magnificent feast was being prepared. Freshly slaughtered cattle already turned on huge spits beside tender haunches of venison and wild boar, the mouth-watering aroma of roasting meat floating up on the warm air. Ducks, geese, and partridges had fallen victim to Amazon arrows, and were being plucked for the cooking fires. Great quantities of bread— that basic food of all people—were baking. Peas, beans, lentils, and purple-flowered vetches, all cultivated by the Amazons themselves, were cooking. Baskets full of figs, pears, walnuts, almonds, hazelnuts, and plums stood just inside the Great Hall. Dried apples were brought out to be baked into flat, golden honey cakes.

The sun was dipping low, trailing long streamers of orange flame after it, when Hippolyte called for the repast to begin. As was customary, she invited Heracles and his second-in-command, the lucky Theseus, to share the royal board with herself and Antiope inside the Great Hall. The rest of the company was free to serve themselves from the wooden trestle tables and find seats wherever they could, which for a good number of them was outside in the soft, warm evening.

Soon the merry noise of feasting rang out. Wine and mead flowed generously. The men piled their plates with bread, fruit, vegetables, and slabs of meat. Cattle were not numerous in the Greek islands, so the juicy beef was a great treat, and after months of olives, dried fish, leeks, stale bread, and hard cheese, the array of succulent food was a delight to the Greeks. They stuffed themselves—all the while gazing at their hosts with adoring, appreciative eyes.

At last these strange Amazons were acting like proper women. Cooking was, after all, women's work, so it was tremendously reassuring to see them behaving as they should . . . in the one way, at least. It did not occur to the men that the banquet made in their honor had nothing to do with gender. The Amazons would have feasted any welcomed guests in exactly the same manner. Likewise, the hungry men did not stop to think that the savory pork and venison disappearing into their mouths had been hunted by women. Instead, they devoted themselves to enjoying this, the most delicious meal each man was sure he had ever eaten.

When their bellies were full to bursting, the Greeks leaned back and contemplated the night ahead. In the flickering orange light of the torches, the long-limbed Amazons in their short tunics, their hair unbound, appeared even more beautiful. They outnumbered the men, but since possessiveness was a trait unknown to the Amazons, the lesser number of men was not a problem in their eyes.

The Amazons saw nothing wrong in enjoying the physical pleasures. There were those who did not, and this was acceptable, even sympathetically understood. But pleasure was secondary to the getting of a child. Men were only the means to that end, and the arrogant Greeks would have been utterly horrified if they knew the true light in which their lovely hosts viewed them.

Normally the only opportunity for increasing their number came from the spring meeting with the Gargarians. Traders visited frequently—drawn by Amazonian leather, copper, and gold—but most of them were puny specimens, not considered worthy to mate with warriors. Then there were the war captives. But unless a large campaign was mounted, there were not many of those, and such captives always ended up being sacrificed to the Mother anyway. So that left the Gargarians, and now these Greeks—healthy, stalwart fighting men—capable of fathering many strong daughters.

Yes, it was a wise bargain Hippolyte had concluded with their leader, one which would result in the birth of new

Amazons. Many a young warrior of childbearing age picked at the remains of her meal and reflected that it was far easier to make another queen's sword belt than it was to make a daughter. And one of those warriors was Antiope.

Since she had killed a man, and since the Moon-Bull had begun his monthly visits, she was an adult now and ready to bear children. But spring was nearly a year away, and thus Antiope was still a virgin. Her gaze rested thoughtfully on the handsome, young Theseus, but she was not really seeing him.

Instead, she was remembering the honor-feast held for Thalassa; of how her friend had sat in the same place now occupied by this male stranger, smiling as Antiope teased her about mating with the Gargarians. Where was Thalassa now? Antiope brooded on that question, and sighed heavily.

Ah, Theseus thought smugly, glancing surreptitiously at Antiope when she sighed. She was as taken with him as he was with her. See how she gazed upon him! Leaning forward, smiling his most winning smile, he said, "A pensive look is upon your beautiful face, Lady. Could it be that thoughts of love have put it there?"

"Wha—?" Brought back to herself, Antiope murmured apologetically, "My thoughts were far away, stranger. What was it you just said?"

"I said that perhaps your thoughts were of love, Lady."

She nodded. "They are," she said honestly, "for I am remembering one of my kindred, a beloved age-mate, cruelly and recently taken from us by mysterious means."

Theseus's smile faded, and he sat back, his consequence stung by the blunt sincerity of her answer. Had Antiope been Greek, she would have responded differently—with demure blushes and words designed to flatter him. But Antiope was an Amazon. Flirtatious games were as alien to her as warfare was to the women of Theseus's world. Being so badly brought up, she has no notion of civilized manners, Theseus told himself reassuringly. But he could teach her.

"A maiden as fair as yourself should never think of unpleasant things," he declared gallantly. "And if you had a man to protect and care for you, your life would ever be cloudless and free of any unhappiness."

Antiope stared at him. "And what power does a man

have to prevent unhappiness?" she asked, more amused than irritated. "We Amazons are taught to protect and care for ourselves. We need look to no man to do it for us."

"But, Lady, why expose yourselves to hardship and danger if there are men willing to shoulder those risks and be responsible for you?"

"It is always better to be responsible for oneself," she said brusquely. "What happens to the women of your man-ruled tribes when their men are defeated in battle? They are taken into slavery, and because they have never been allowed to bear arms and learn to protect themselves, they are as helpless as newborns. That is not a good way to be."

"It is the way ordained by the gods," Theseus said stiffly, his manly honor smarting from both her tone and the uncomfortable logic of her words.

"It is *not* the way ordained by Artemis, our sacred Goddess," Antiope pointed out coldly. "And for myself, I am glad of it, Theseus of the Greeks. I would not like to be a woman of your people, always caged in a dark, smelly house and forced to obey the will of men. Freedom is worth any hardship, risk, or danger."

The youthful king gulped the contents of his goblet and reached for the silver flagon of wine next to him. He was unused to a young and beautiful woman refusing to be dazzled by his highborn rank and handsome appearance. Yet, in a curious way, this exotic girl-queen was immensely exciting. He felt challenged by her, and there was nothing Theseus's hot blood liked better than a challenge.

His good humor restored, he said, "Well, despite your low opinion of us, Lady, you must concede that without men there can be no children. So, even you Amazons cannot do without us and our seed."

Antiope simply nodded. "That is quite true. And it is also true that men cannot do without women, since it is we who bring children into the world. There is no shame in it. Such is the way of the Mother."

In the smoky glow of the torches, Antiope's hair shone with black-gold highlights, and the formal tunic she had donned before the feast gleamed white against her tanned skin. Theseus filled his eyes with her, and still could not stop looking.

"Lady," he said, and hoped she could not hear the slight tremor in his voice, "will you lie with me?"

"Of course I will," she answered in some surprise. "That is why we allowed you to stay here, so that we could get daughters. I hope you will not be disappointed by my lack of experience though, for I have never lain with a man before."

Theseus's shock at her casual attitude faded at the young queen's startling disclosure. She was a virgin! He made up his mind then and there that Antiope would never know any man but him—unless he gave her to another.

"Your lack of experience pleases me greatly," he assured her with a delighted, wolfish grin. "Indeed, I prefer it, noble, beautiful Antiope. It will be my great pleasure to instruct you in the arts of love." And, he thought confidently, once she'd had a taste of how things could be between a man and a woman, she would quickly realize the senselessness of her present life and be only too willing to leave it!

Unaware of his thoughts, Antiope frowned, puzzled by his pleasure at her inexperience. It certainly seemed more practical to seek out a bed partner who was knowledgeable. Also, his reference to love bothered her. Love was for sisters, age-mates, horses. Men did not enter into it at all, and she could not see why the physical act of making a child should involve this most powerful of emotions. She shrugged away her doubts, deciding she'd ask her more experienced sister later.

"I have my own small house," she said, "and if your hunger and thirst have been satisfied, we can go there."

Theseus's grin widened. "My only hunger and thirst are for you now, Lady. Let us go quickly."

As they left the hall, Antiope glanced back and exchanged a quick smile with her older sister. Hippolyte was sharing a cup of wine with Heracles, and the two of them looked as if it would not be long before they rose to seek the queen's bedchamber.

Outside, the moon had risen. All around men and women were pairing off, the couplings arranged with matter-of-fact efficiency by the women themselves. Bemused and willing, the men went along, most of them slightly drunk on Amazon wine, which unlike Greek wine was not watered. Their hosts, however, had remained clearheaded. Unaffected by either wine or mead, they laughed to one another about the Greeks' weak heads for strong drink. In twos and sometimes in threes, men and women wandered off toward the pale, shining sand, or into the sweet, soft grasses to lie down under the moon's great watching eye.

"I hope their ability to beget is better than their ability to hold their wine," one Amazon whispered to her friend as they walked to the beach with two somewhat unsteady males in tow.

They need not have worried. The Greeks were all healthy, young men who had long been without women. In the summer-scented night with the wine stirring blood already heated by the Amazons' beauty, they were only too eager to perform.

In Antiope's cozy house, Theseus's head was clear, for he had drunk only enough wine to free his desire fully, not impair it. Antiope had brought a jug with her from the hall. She filled a cup and handed it to him as he gazed curiously about him.

"Thank you, La—" he started to say, then caught himself when he saw what held the wine she was offering. A skull, bleached white and lined in gold, the red of the wine taking on an even deeper hue in its dry, bony depths.

Seeing his hesitation, Antiope laughed. "It is the head of the first man I ever killed in battle—that which made me a blooded warrior. Among us it is the custom to drink from the skulls of our foes. Is it not that way with you?"

"No," Theseus said lamely, feeling a little dizzy as he stared down at the scarlet-filled cup that had once been the head of a living man. How barbaric to teach this beautiful young woman such practices! he thought angrily. But she must not find him weak-stomached. Determinedly he lifted the skull in both hands and took a hearty swig before giving it back to her.

The strong wine sent a rush of heat through him, reawakening his desire and tightening his loins with anticipation. Silently they passed the skull back and forth until it was empty and then—still silent—Theseus reached for her.

She was taller than the women he'd known, as in fact all her people were. Of the Greeks, only he and Heracles overreached the Amazons, the rest of the men being of the same height or slightly shorter. Yet Antiope's tallness pleased Theseus. She fit into his arms as if she had been fashioned for that purpose alone, he thought as he bent his head to kiss her.

Never having been kissed before, Antiope had nothing to compare it to. Nevertheless, she found the strange contact unexpectedly pleasurable. Theseus's muscled body was warm and hard next to hers, and she could feel his manhood butting eagerly at her lower belly. Like a colt seeking its mother's teat, she decided, and giggled into his mouth.

Surprised, Theseus lifted his head. "Why do you laugh?" he demanded.

By the Goddess, she thought, men were touchy creatures! "I meant no offense," she said placatingly, "but I did warn you of my inexperience. I have never touched lips with a man before."

Ashamed of himself for forgetting she was a virgin, Theseus quickly apologized. "No, Lady, it is I who should ask forgiveness. I am a stupid lout; but let us lie down, and I will endeavor to make amends."

And so they stretched out on Antiope's bed of furs. Their mouths tasted again, and slowly Theseus drew the tunic away from Antiope's body. He caught his breath at the sheer beauty revealed to his hungry gaze.

"In the holy name of Athena," he whispered huskily, "your loveliness rivals that of any goddess on Olympus."

Sitting up, he yanked off his own tunic, proud to show his smooth, suntanned body and his lordly man's organ, thrusting arrogantly upward against his flat belly. Antiope gazed at him, more curious than aroused.

Without a doubt, she mused, women's forms were lovelier and far more practical. Men were so vulnerable, with their genitals bobbing about like fruit hanging from a branch, exposed to all sorts of dangers from a well-aimed sword, arrow, or knee. Yet there *was* a certain compelling attraction about this unfamiliar masculine body, an attraction she did not understand.

Theseus broke into her reverie. Grasping her in his arms, he kissed her deeply, and pressed his whole eager body tightly against hers. It was then that Antiope truly began to learn of the differences between men and women, and of how those differences made possible the most startling of pleasures.

Theseus's hands were gentle but sure upon her flesh. He touched and stroked and explored as if it were his intention to mark every inch of her. Antiope was astonished—first, at the delicious feelings emanating from his hands, then at the realization that she wanted him to keep on touching her. She had heard that the act of coupling could be pleasant, but she had never expected this! It was akin to riding a fleet horse on a clear, windy day—only better. Incredibly better.

His fingers slipped between her thighs, and very gently he parted her, delighted to find that she was already moist. Skillfully he searched out the tiny knob of flesh that led to a woman's pleasure, and teased at it until Antiope's entire body shuddered violently, and she cried out in the most uninhibited ecstasy he had ever heard from a woman. The intensity of her response excited him beyond belief, and unable to wait any longer, he spread her thighs wide with his knee and mounted her.

Expecting to butt up against the obstruction of her maidenhead, he was startled when the throbbing length of his member slid easily into her wet warmth. The shock of it—that and Antiope winding her satiny, muscled legs about his waist—almost unmanned him. *She was not a virgin after all!*

Moaning with pleasure, Antiope thrust her hips against him. All thoughts promptly fled from Theseus's mind, leaving nothing but the driving and plunging and rocking until, with a shout of triumphant elation, he shot forth long streams of his seed deep into Antiope's womb.

Legs and arms intertwined, they lay afterward in panting silence. Intermittent spasms of pleasure flickered through Antiope's woman parts, causing her to tighten reflexively on Theseus's embedded organ. The exquisite feel of it made him groan and pull her even closer to his sweat-damp body.

Antiope sighed, still lost in her own blissful sense of satisfaction. What a shame that men and women could not live together without the one seeking to enslave the other, she thought. It would truly be pleasant to enjoy this act of coupling more than once a year. If only males could be trusted! But of course, they could not be.

Stretching luxuriously, she murmured, "This business of daughtermaking is far more enjoyable than I realized it would be, Theseus of Athens."

He lifted his head and frowned down at her. "Why did you lie about being a virgin?" he asked in an accusing tone. "I would still have desired you had you been truthful with me, Lady."

Now it was Antiope's turn to frown. "Amazons do not lie. Ever!" she snapped. "I said I had never lain with a man before, and that is the truth!"

"Then why have you no maidenhead?"

"Maidenhead?" she repeated blankly.

"Yes, maidenhead," he said impatiently. "The barrier of an untouched girl, which only can be pierced and broken by a man, thus opening her body and enabling her to receive his lifegiving seed."

"Oh, that. I have heard the women of man-ruled tribes possess this maidenhead thing, but we do not. The grandmothers say it is because we live on horseback even before we can walk, so any virgin barrier is long gone by the time we are ready to mate. Perhaps the women of your land should learn to ride horses and labor with their bodies, rather than sitting in houses spinning and weaving all day. Then they, too, could rid themselves of these troublesome maidenheads, which are surely nothing more than an inconvenience."

Horrified at her attitude, Theseus stared at her, momentarily speechless. "Only lowborn women and slaves are expected to perform strenuous labor," he finally managed to say. "And it is simply not proper for a modest woman to spread her legs and bestride a horse the way a man would."

"Why? It is certainly a far less painful means of removing her maidenhead than being left torn and bloody the first time she mates. But then, since it is not you men who must bear the discomfort, that probably does not concern you."

"A woman's maidenhead is her most precious possession!" he sputtered, outraged. "It is the proof she brings to her husband that she has been kept virtuous and pure for him alone. The blood she sheds is confirmation that the sons he will breed upon her are his without question. If women were allowed to discard their virginity so lightly, how could a man ever be sure that his sons were truly the issue of his own loins, and not another's?"

Antiope shrugged. "Such things have no importance here. In fact, it seems rather silly to be so concerned about whether or not a girl has her maidenhead. Women of your land should be free to choose whom they wish to sleep with, just as we Amazons are. What difference does it make who the father is, as long as the child is strong and healthy and without blemish?"

Theseus shook his head. She would never understand. It was the nonsense these so-called grandmothers had filled her young head with since she was a babe. But he believed now that she had indeed been a virgin. And by the golden trident of his father Poseidon, she was beautiful! Despite his frustration at her wrongheaded ideas, he was already growing hard again.

Feeling his manpart stirring within her, Antiope smiled. "Let us not quarrel, Theseus. I would much rather try this business of daughtermaking again. My sister made a good bargain with your lord, Heracles. You and your companions will soon return home with the queen's belt, and we will be left with many fine daughters ripening in our bellies."

I hope my seed plants a son in your belly, fair Antiope, Theseus almost said out loud. But with an effort, he held his tongue. He was no longer in the mood to quarrel either. Anyway, there would be ample opportunity to civilize this comely young savage on the voyage back. For Theseus had made up his mind that even though woman stealing was an appalling breach of hospitality, he would somehow find a way to carry Antiope off when the time came to leave.

"Your royal sister did indeed make a good bargain, my lovely queen," he murmured, lowering his mouth to hers.

"I am pleased that you journeyed here," Antiope confided, when at last they had paused for breath. "I wasn't at first. Actually, I hoped one of you would do something that would give us cause to kill you, but now I'm glad there was no fighting between your people and mine."

"I am glad, too." Yes, he would take her with him, Theseus vowed as he began to move inside her. Only a fool would leave behind such a splendid creature as she!

Twice more that night Theseus and Antiope made energetic love. And while they were busily learning the sensual pathways of each other's bodies, Hippolyte and Heracles had finally gone to the queen's moon-washed bedchamber.

Despite the revealing Amazonian tunic, Heracles had still been unprepared for the absolute magnificence of Hippolyte when she stood before him in proud, glowing nudity. "By my sacred honor," he breathed reverently, "your comeliness would tempt the manhood of my noble father, great Zeus himself!"

"Let your god keep his manhood," she said with a low, rippling laugh. "I am only interested in his son's." The hero's claim of divine ancestry neither surprised nor impressed her. She had heard that many kings liked to declare themselves descended from celestial lineage. "Are you going to stand there all night like a moonstruck calf?" she asked humorously. "Or do you plan to uphold your part of our bargain?"

A slow grin spread across Heracles's bearded face. "I am a man of my word, Lady."

Roughly he tore off his own tunic and swept the laughing Hippolyte up in his mighty arms. But when he laid her on the bed and flung himself down beside her, his big hands were unaccustomedly gentle—almost hesitant—as if he still could not believe the beauty of her. He traced the sweet contours of breast and thigh, half afraid she would dissolve like a vision, leaving him alone and filled with need.

Not since the god-inspired madness that had caused him to murder his own children had he permitted himself the pleasures of sexual intercourse. Hippolyte's beauty made him feel awkward, as though he were a green youth taking his first woman. For long minutes, he was content merely to caress her and do nothing else.

But Hippolyte stroked him in return, twining her strong limbs about his body and running warm hands over the bulging muscles of his chest and back. Gradually Heracles's nervousness left him—to be replaced by a joyous, raging need that made his prodigious organ swell and grow. Many a woman would have been dismayed or even frightened by his size. Hippolyte, however, was pleased, and in the direct manner of her people, she said so.

"Your man's part is as strong and fine as the rest of you," she murmured approvingly. "Now, I have no doubt that we will make a glorious daughter to carry on my line." And she placed a slender, callused hand upon his pulsating member.

It was too much. With a groan Heracles threw himself upon her. "Lady, you could fire the blood of a dead man," he cried hoarsely, and buried his massive shaft to the hilt within her silky welcoming folds.

CHAPTER 9

 "The Mother's welcome to you. I am called Aricia."

Thalassa stared at the tall and stately woman who had entered the jade chamber. Her hair was as raven-black, her eyes as brilliantly blue, as Dorian's. She said nothing, hoping this unwelcome visitor would go away. When the woman did not, she said rudely, "It is blasphemy to use the name of the Holy Goddess in this place."

"I do not speak of She whom the Amazons worship," Aricia said with quiet dignity, "but of the Great Mother Sea, She who gave birth to all life, whether beneath the waves or above."

Thalassa sent her a flamingly hostile look, but undeterred, Aricia went on. "You must have many questions and fears about our life here. I would like to help you in any way I can. Perhaps you might find it easier to speak with me than with my brother."

"I have no wish to speak with any of you!" Thalassa burst out raggedly. Spinning around, she stalked to the other end of the room.

It seemed to her that she had been a captive forever. Alone, bereft of her home and kindred, imprisoned in an unimaginable world among strangers—far too many of whom were male—and more defenseless than she cared to admit, she had lost the fire of overt rebellion. But the need for freedom lived below the surface, scorching her with its heat, until she could think of nothing but its loss and of the one who had taken it from her.

In her entire life, Thalassa had never known a day of restraint. Discipline, yes, but the glorious discipline of training with beloved comrades under a clear sky; of feeling the blood pound through her veins, hot with strength and confidence; of galloping in unfettered liberty throughout the Amazons' lands, proudly secure in her tribe's and her own invincibility. Now that arrogance—so innocent and yet so proud—had been shattered, and Thalassa's independent spirit chafed at being controlled, the way a half-wild mare fights against a heavy bit.

Patiently, Aricia tried again. "It may not seem so to you, Lady, but my brother feels things very deeply. It grieved him to take you so cruelly from your home, but please try to understand. He had no choice."

"No choice? If he is a king then he can do whatever he likes."

"Not among us. The ruler of the merfolk must take his mate from the land. After the Ceremony of Matebonding you will understand these things a little better."

Thalassa turned and regarded her blankly. Valya had said that the sea-people came together for ceremonies. Was this what he had meant? "I will take no part in your ceremonies," she declared, "and your brother acts like no king I have ever seen."

"Ah. And how many kings have you seen?"

Thalassa did not answer, and Aricia smiled. "Lady, you must participate in the Ceremony of Matebonding. It is there that you will be acknowledged as Dorian's queen, in accordance with our most ancient customs. And as for his abilities as a ruler—would you like to see them for yourself? He is judging a dispute even now, and if you like, we can go and watch."

Thalassa wanted to refuse. In fact, she was certain that

she should. But the luxurious confinement of the jade chamber was driving her mad, and though she would have cheerfully died before admitting it to this elegant stranger, she was curious.

"My brother is a good ruler," Aricia said as they walked down the now familiar corridor. "Strong and compassionate, but wise enough not to interfere in our affairs without cause. Among us that is very important, for we merfolk are an independent people who do not need or desire a great deal of control from our king, as the folk of the land do."

They sound like Amazons. It was a traitorous thought, and Thalassa hastily pushed it from her mind. Aricia was explaining that kingship was passed on to the eldest of the royal line, regardless of gender. Upon the tragic deaths of both their aged parents in a recent undersea earthquake, Dorian, being firstborn, had ascended to the throne.

"It was a great sadness to lose our beloved mother and father," Aricia said softly. "Yet, in the way of our people they knew their time to leave this world was coming, and I do not believe they were sorry to go. Age affects even those of the sea if we live long enough, and both my parents were very old. Still, Dorian suffered."

An unexpected and confusing sympathy for her captor flowed through Thalassa. Clearly, this sister of his was trying to befriend her. Perhaps if she had been able to respond in kind, Aricia could have eased some of her feelings toward men, and toward Dorian in particular. But Thalassa was not yet ready to take such a drastic step.

One did not befriend enemies, and even though the women of these people behaved more like Amazon warriors than docile servants, they were still part of her abductor's kindred. What was far worse, they entered gladly into the one unforgivable sin—cheerful cohabitation with males.

So Thalassa kept silent. After conducting Thalassa through one winding corridor after another, Aricia brought her to the room where Dorian was holding court. Unlike the other chambers in the palace, this one had no door. Thalassa heard the sound of voices rumbling out into the hall as they approached, but by the time they reached the doorway, the voices had died away into a profound silence. She gave Aricia a curious look.

"Why do they not speak?"

The other woman gestured for silence. "You will see," she whispered. "But you must also be quiet and I will explain."

They entered the chamber. Thalassa was surprised at how small it was, and how empty. Then her gaze fell upon the irregularly shaped pool in the center of the room and upon those who stood about it, and her thoughts stopped.

In the center of the pool, bobbing back and forth in the gentle wash of the water, were two bluish gray creatures. She could only make out what seemed to be their heads— round bulbous shapes with long, sharp noses, toothy grinning mouths, and dark, shining eyes. Never had Thalassa seen anything like them, and she tore her gaze away to the figures grouped around the unknown beings. At least *they* appeared human!

Towering over all of them was Dorian, clothed in a floor-length cape of some silvery gold material, so bright it seemed to cast out its own light. Upon his dark head sat a wide gold band set with black stones, and though he must have seen them enter, his gaze was fixed not on Thalassa or Aricia, but upon the creatures in the pool.

Thalassa swallowed. No matter what disparaging remarks she had made about him, there was no denying now that this man was indeed a king, and a powerful one. The other men had their backs to her. One of them, a squat, powerfully built male, turned to glance at her. Thalassa saw his eyes—dark round eyes with no white in them. Not the eyes of a human being at all.

Her lungs constricted in her chest, and for a moment, she forgot how to breathe. The *thing's* equally stocky companions also glanced at her. Their eyes were the same. Liquid, long-lashed orbs that belonged in the face of a horse or a dog, not mortal men.

The Amazons possessed no sign to protect against the evil eye, but in that instant Thalassa wished desperately they did. This Dorian was indeed a sorcerer, she thought in terror, and these were his creatures. In the name of the Goddess, what was to become of her?

Vaguely, through the wild fears milling in her brain, she heard Aricia whispering to her. ". . . in the pool are two of the dolphin folk who have come as witnesses in this dispute. They look like fish, but they are creatures as warm-blooded and intelligent as ourselves. The others are Selkie folk, and they are known as the shape changers of the sea, able to take the form of a human or a seal at will."

The soft voice went on, and Thalassa forced herself to focus on it. "These Selkies say that merfolk have been encroaching upon one of their ancestral fishing grounds. It is nearly time for the migration of the tunny, a rich-tasting fish enjoyed by both our peoples, and to prevent conflict the quarrel must be resolved quickly, since the tunny will pass soon through the disputed area."

Thalassa turned huge eyes upon her. "But why do they simply stand there?" she asked hoarsely. "When will they speak?"

"They are speaking now—directly into one another's thoughts. It is the way the folk of the sea communicate, though when they are not in seal form, the Selkies can speak the tongue of the merfolk if they wish to."

Struck as speechless as those in and around the pool, Thalassa stared again at Dorian. In the glittering cape and golden diadem, he looked stern and forbidding. He had still not acknowledged her presence, though his sapphire gaze was trained on the squat Selkies now, rather than the dolphins.

Abruptly the latter emitted a series of shrill, squeaking whistles and clicks. The sound of it in the silent room was deafening. Thalassa jumped, her breath suspended as the strange *dolphin* creatures upended themselves in the pool. She caught a glimpse of long, sleek fish bodies tapering to broad, flat tails, then they were gone.

Aricia made an approving noise in her throat. "Good," she whispered. "My brother's suggestion that the clan of the guilty merfolk bear recompense in the form of food and allow the Selkies to harvest tunny in its own ancestral territories has been accepted. The difficulties are at an end."

Walking over to Dorian, the stockiest of the seal-people clasped his shoulder with a broad hand. Between each finger stretched a thin membrane. In what Thalassa had learned to recognize as the murmurous tongue of her captors, the creature said something. Dorian smiled and replied in kind. Then suddenly, to Thalassa's horror, the unworldly gaze of *all* these creatures was upon her.

Transfixed, she returned the scrutiny of the dark, blunt-featured Selkies. Except for their eyes they looked astonishingly like men—squat, heavily muscled, and hairy, but men. If she could have summoned up the will, she would have fled, but her bare feet felt rooted to the cool, damp floor. All she could do was stand there, utterly motionless. Aricia's musical voice rippled through the chamber. Despite Thalassa's consternation—or perhaps, because of it—she quivered with resentment. How tired she was of being spoken about in this language she could not understand!

But the Selkies were no longer interested in her. After another brief exchange with Dorian and Aricia, the creatures turned to the pool. One by one they dove fluidly into it, leaving Thalassa to stare abstractedly at the lapping water, wondering if they had really been there at all.

Dorian rubbed a hand over his eyes, then gave her and his sister a tired smile. "Well, it is over," he said. "And how glad I am. The seal-people were not pleased when they first came here. Convincing them of my good intentions was almost as difficult a task as the one I face in convincing you, my love." He spoke in her own tongue, but Thalassa only looked at him, still too stunned by what she had seen to banter with him.

"Do not tease her," Aricia said severely. "She is in no mood for your humor, such as it is." Lightly she touched Thalassa on the arm. "I am sorry, Lady. I did not stop to think of how the Selkies and the dolphin folk would affect you. They are so familiar to us . . . as familiar as the Hittites and Scythians must be to you."

"Don't coddle her, Aricia."

Dorian's voice was curt, and under the glittering headband his eyes were shadowed, as though he had not slept. "I'm pleased that you brought her here," he went on. "The sooner she gets used to our ways the happier she'll be." His words were directed at Aricia, but his gaze was on Thalassa. She flushed angrily at his forceful, deliberate words.

Aricia shook her head. "Brother—" she began, and

stopped with a sigh. "I will see you again, child," she said, turning to Thalassa. "Please remember what I said about wanting to help you." Dorian received a piercing look from the blue eyes so like his own, then Aricia departed.

Thalassa took a step after her, only to feel Dorian's long fingers close on her arm. "Stay awhile. Or is my sister's company so preferable to mine?"

Any company was preferable to that of a sorcerer! Thalassa thought fervently. Instead of speaking she concentrated on avoiding the steady gaze she sensed was bent upon her. A silence ensued, broken finally by Dorian's deep voice.

"How long do you think you have been here?"

The unexpected question took her off guard. Time—as she knew it—had no meaning this far below the ocean, and the accompanying disorientation had been overwhelming, almost unbearable. "How can I possibly know the answer to that," she muttered, "here in this place of disease and misfortune, where the life-giving sun of the Mother never comes?"

"Four weeks," Dorian said, as if she had not spoken. "Our people have an inner sense that enables us to mark the passage of time without depending on the sun."

Shock rippled through her. To have been there for so long a time! But Dorian was still speaking, and his low voice pulled at her with the persistence of an outgoing tide.

"I am king here, Lady, and among my people, the king's mate must come from the women of the land. It is one of our most ancient customs, and it has kept the merfolk strong and vital. But in order to dwell with us beneath the sea, the chosen one must be transformed. That is what I have done to you. When I took you from the waters of your old home, I began a process within your body—a process that will eventually turn you into a woman of the sea, with all the powers and abilities of our kind."

She stared at him. A man had no business speaking the Amazon tongue so fluently, she thought irrelevantly. He was lying of course, probably seeking to frighten her into obedient submission with these absurd tales. With the vision of dolphins and Selkies so vivid in her mind, she had difficulty denying anything he said. Yet she tried.

"The curse of Lysippe be upon you!" she hissed. "For there cannot be one word of truth in all the drivel that has just poured from your mouth. Whatever evil gods you worship will lose their powers and die of old age before I cease to think of you as an unnatural creature. You, and all those who dwell here with you!"

Be patient, Dorian reminded himself as a wave of exasperation rolled through him. After the long session with the Selkies, he was tired and hungry and less than tolerant of his unwilling guest's sharp tongue. Striving to keep irritation out of his tone, he said, "We travel through the sea in much the same manner as our distant brethren—the seals, dolphins, and porpoises. My people love the sea just as you yourself do. There is one difference, though. Each of us possesses gills, as thin lines on our necks. They make it possible for us to breathe water as easily as you breathe air. Therefore, unlike the seals or dolphins, we may stay underwater indefinitely, not needing to seek the surface to breathe air. It is a wondrous ability to have, and it has opened all the world's oceans to our people. Now you, too, have gills lining your neck."

"No! It cannot be." Her voice sounded weak, even to her own ears, but she plunged ahead anyway, her words gathering an angry momentum of their own as they spilled out. "Do you really think I can be tricked so easily? I am what I have always been and will always be—a daughter of the race of Amazons. And nothing you say can change that!"

"You've seen the great windows that look out on our underwater world. And I think that in your heart, you know I have spoken truly. How else could we live this far below the sea without the abilities I have just described?"

His mention of windows caused Thalassa's insides to knot and twist. Since that first dreadful encounter, she had adamantly refused to lift her gaze to the giant portals along the arching corridors of the coral abode. It changed nothing, yet denying what lay outside gave her some small measure of comfort, enabling her to maintain what little rationality she had left.

Now this diabolical man-creature wanted to destroy even those last few shreds of reason. He surely would not be content until he had reduced her to a witless imbecile, she thought. The very idea stiffened her spine.

"I have no liking for the things you have shown me thus far, man-demon, either in words or actions." Her brain was fast becoming a discordant mass of thoughts that clashed wildly against one another, and she took relief in concentrating them all into one sharp-pointed spear of hatred directed straight at this enigmatic, terrifying being. "I will never accept such madness, so you may as well leave me in peace!"

He shook his head. "You are stubborn, Lady. It is one of the qualities about you I admire. Still, too much of anything can be detrimental, and I think your common sense is now being ruled by obstinacy. That is not desirable, and it will certainly give you no peace."

Enraged by his self-possessed, level tone, Thalassa lifted a menacing fist. It was instantly caught in a grip of iron, and Dorian's magnetic gaze seized hers.

"Feigning blindness will not alter the truth," he said bluntly. "You are in my palace beneath the sea, and whether you will it or no, here you must stay. Continue to rail at me if you like, but do not continue to pretend the world outside this abode does not exist. It is unworthy of you, Lady."

"What you consider unworthy means less than nothing to me. Nothing!" she stormed, trying to yank her arm away. Overcoming him physically was not possible—she had learned that by now. His words rang true—yet she was determined not to acknowledge it for hand in hand with such acknowledgment went acceptance that all she held dear was gone forever.

She brought up her other hand to strike him, and he smoothly caught that one as well.

"Touch your neck, Lady," he suggested quietly.

His glittering gaze bore relentlessly into hers, and with an effort she made herself glare back. "I am no fainthearted woman of the man-ruled tribes, creature of the sea. I recognize foolish stories when I hear them, and they do not frighten me."

"Good. There is no reason for you not to touch your

neck then, is there? Since I have said only foolish things and nothing to be frightened of."

Outmaneuvered, Thalassa seethed for an instant, then jerkily raised her hand to explore the side of her neck. A sharp vibration of pain struck just as her searching fingers encountered a small, raised line directly below her ear. Immediately Dorian was forgotten as she hurriedly examined the other side. An identical pain flared up, and she felt herself go cold all over.

Dorian watched the change in expression on her fierce, lovely face with sympathy. This was a difficult time for her, and it would get worse before it got better. Much needed to occur prior to his chosen one's acceptance—both of him and of this life he had forced upon her—and none of it would be easy.

She stood rigidly in front of him, as though he had placed a holding spell upon her, and he sighed inwardly.

"The pain in your neck is only temporary," he said. "It will pass, just as the weakness and aching and dizziness you felt on first awakening here has passed. There are other changes that will take place as well. Your body will no longer react to cold, enabling you to swim in the most frigid of waters with perfect comfort. You will gain enormous strength and speed, both in the water and on land. You will age very slowly, so slowly in fact, that to those of the land you would appear not to age at all."

He decided to say nothing of the spell that would enable the sea, and him, to claim her as their own. This information was a heavy enough burden for her to bear at the moment.

Waiting for yet more explosions and denials, he let his gaze rove over her set face, but her response when it finally came surprised him.

"How did you know I loved the sea?" she asked in a voice that was barely above a whisper.

"Part of your soul speaks to the waves, and the sweep of water and sky, Lady. All I had to do was listen."

She stared fixedly at her hands, and he added reassuringly, "Once you've been with us for a time, the things I've told you will seem more natural. Now come, there is something I would show you."

≈ ≈ ≈

Thalassa looked blankly at the burnished coral wall in front of her. On it were four small black panels mounted in silver. She could feel Dorian's thoughtful gaze upon her and to cover her anxiety, she snapped, "Why have you brought me here to stare at a wall?"

"You will see."

He pressed one of the panels and stepped back. A grinding thunder reverberated throughout the hallway as the walls next to the panels suddenly revealed themselves to be giant doors, opening with ponderous majesty. Beyond was a bare, cavernous chamber, dimly lit by peculiar, tiny lamps that glowed fitfully in the darkness.

Thalassa jumped in terror, her body automatically tensing in defense against whatever frightful thing might come roaring out of the ghostly shadows. But moments passed, and no monster or any hideous being sprang forth to attack her.

Dorian waited for her to realize that. When he judged she had, he said quietly, "It's called an interlocking chamber. This is how we enter and leave the sea."

Fighting to regain her composure, Thalassa swallowed painfully. "All I see is a great, empty room."

"It is far more, Lady."

He pressed the panel once more. Thalassa was prepared for the rolling thunder this time, and she watched him distrustfully as the massive doors ground shut.

"Come a little closer," he invited, beckoning to her. "There is nothing to be afraid of."

She hesitated, and he smiled. "After all," he murmured tauntingly, "you yourself pointed out that it is only an empty room—a room which is now closed."

Lifting her chin defiantly, she stomped over to join him. Still smiling, he pressed another panel. "Watch."

A narrow window slid open, allowing them to see the shadowy cavern. Thalassa gazed into the eerie semidarkness. Even from the outside, the chamber had a feel of great antiquity and awesome power to it. Uneasy thoughts ran through her mind. Perhaps these creatures dedicated human offerings to whatever gods they worshiped there in that room, and as their ruler, Dorian had selected her as the latest sacrifice!

Riveted by such terrible speculations, she barely noticed when he touched a third black square. But her eyes grew huge in disbelief as openings appeared in the top and bottom of the far wall and water poured into the vast, open space.

"It's really quite simple," he said, apparently unaware of her shock. "The chamber can be operated either from these panels or by two levers inside. When the room is completely filled with water, two doors at the far end will open so that we can swim out into the sea. On returning, we close the outer doors and let the water drain back to the ocean. These inner doors I already showed you will open only after the chamber is totally emptied."

Thalassa stood as if she had not heard a word. The sea marched on in its relentless campaign to flood the enormous grotto, and through the rising tower of water, the oddly shaped lamps continued to shine, creating fantasy shapes that danced and glimmered in the watery gloom. Even after the ocean had submerged them, the lamps kept burning. It seemed to Thalassa as if the moon and stars had found their way through the openings of the walls.

If she could forget the man at her side and the cage that surrounded her, she could almost imagine she stood in her secret underwater cave looking out over the night-glittering ocean of Amazonia. But it was an illusion, and one that ended abruptly, with a muffled roar that vibrated the cool, polished floor beneath her feet.

The chamber had filled, and the inner doors Dorian had described were opening. Colossal slabs of volcanic rock, they resembled sides of mountains more than doors, and she stared transfixed at what they revealed: The very mouth of the ocean—black and gaping—its darkness made even more ominous because it lay outside the murky light generated by the lamps.

"You won't be able to go out for some time yet," Dorian said softly. "Your body must complete the adjustments, and the gills on your neck need to mature. When that happens, you will be ready to enter the sea as the rest of our people do."

His voice broke her trance, making her start as if he had

poked her with the sharp point of a dagger. "Why are you doing this to me?" she cried desperately. "Can you not see that I do not want you or any man? I will never bide willingly here, and I most certainly will not make you happy!"

"Ah, but you make me happy already, dear one. It is you, my lioness—with your fierce warrior ways, infuriating stubbornness, and proud spirit that blazes from your golden eyes—that I want. You, and only you."

His words rang strangely in Thalassa's ears. She stared at Dorian with little more comprehension of what he had said than the lioness to which he compared her.

"You cannot possibly want me," she said at last. "I know nothing of pleasing a man, and have even less interest in learning. I've already told you it is against our laws to take a mate, and I will not break the laws of my people. To do so means banishment from my tribe. I would be cast out, no longer an Amazon, and never would I give up my birthright and desert my sisters to be a *wife*." She spat out the word as if it were a curse. "A wife to you or any other man!"

"My ferocious Lady," he said, and his gaze was level although his melodious voice was soft, "you still do not realize, do you? Regardless of whether or not I want you, your life as an Amazon is over. Not because they have banished or would banish you for taking a man as mate, but because you yourself are changing. I am familiar with Amazon law, Lady, but sooner or later you will have to understand and accept the truth. You no longer belong to the people of your birth, but to those of the sea—my people."

Like that of a hunted animal, Thalassa's gaze swept the corridor crowded with passing merfolk, as if some path of escape that she had not previously noticed would open and show her the way home. But the delicately tinted rose walls glimmered at her in mocking solidity, and inexorably, her awareness was drawn back to the narrow portal that opened onto the chamber.

If Dorian was speaking truthfully, then there was only one exit from this place, and it lay through that awesome, black maw—that terrifying gateway into an alien sea full of horrors that only the Goddess knew. Horrors that she must face.

She shuddered inwardly at what awaited her beyond this interlocking chamber, and yet, it could be no worse than what awaited her here. The world she had always known was collapsing as surely as marble columns crumbled under the force of an earthquake, and she was floundering, frantically trying to keep her balance in a shifting, unfamiliar reality.

And this enigmatic creature—this *being* in the form of a man—was responsible. For everything.

CHAPTER 10

≈   "Lady?"
    Thalassa spun around to see Valya smiling
nervously at her. Two men and three women flanked him,
all of them young, well-favored, and bearing the same
tentatively eager smiles.

"What is it?" Thalassa heard the testiness in her voice
and felt the slightest stab of guilt. Valya was, after all, the
only one in this place of captivity who seemed somewhat
sympathetic to her plight. "Won't your lord be displeased if
he sees you talking to me?" she asked more politely. "He
seemed so when you did it before."

"Yes, but he's not here." Valya exchanged conspirato-
rial looks with his five companions. "He left a short time
ago, to visit the abode of the merfolk who have been
poaching on Selkie fishing grounds and tell them what
occurred in the council." Valya paused, then added reflectively, "He was in a most unpleasant frame of mind when he
departed."

Thalassa did not wonder at this. After the grievous
episode with the interlocking chamber, she had railed at

Dorian, summoning up every foul name at her command to fling at him, until finally, he had lost his temper. His eyes blazing blue fire, he had roared, "Lady, I have spent a very long while listening to the tirades of the Selkie folk and I am in no mood to listen to yours. The gods of sea and sky bear me witness, but you possess the most evil tongue of any woman I have ever encountered in all my years. If it were not for the Elders I would take you back to Amazonia and gladly bid you farewell. But you are burdened with me, as I am burdened with you, so let us both make the best of it!"

Holding Thalassa's arm in a tight grip, he had virtually hauled her back to the jade chamber. Now it gave her some small sense of satisfaction, hearing Valya, to know that she had upset Dorian so greatly. "May he sicken and die with the most painful of wasting diseases," she said, her words a virtual growl.

Her listeners traded shocked glances. "You must not speak of him so, my lady," one of the young women said. She appeared to be about the same age as Valya—a girl really—and her mastery of the Amazon tongue was far better than his. "He is our people's king."

Thalassa did not dignify the girl's words with an answer. Instead, she studied the six merfolk. How young they seemed! She could scarcely credit that Dorian had spoken the truth about the longevity of his people, for at the age of these youths, she had been already proficient in the skills that would one day make her a blooded warrior.

"If you are so fearful of angering your king," she asked, "then why do you risk his wrath by coming here?"

Suddenly all six of them had trouble meeting her gaze.

"Well?" she demanded.

Valya cleared his throat. "We wanted to talk with you before . . ."

Awkwardly he stopped. Apprehension shivering through her veins, Thalassa prodded, "Before what?"

Valya cast a helpless look at the others, and an auburn-haired youth finished for him. "Before our lord Dorian puts the Sea Spell upon you."

A treacherous weakness flooded Thalassa's limbs, and for a horrible instant she thought she might have to sit down. "You had better explain to me," she said slowly, "what this Sea Spell is."

A girl with hair as blond as Valya's gasped in surprise. "You mean he has not told you of it?"

"No."

"It is . . . it is a way to make you stay among us willingly. I do not know much about it. None of us do, because"—her mouth turned down—"we are too young. But we do know it is something only the king puts upon his chosen one." She gave Thalassa a small apologetic smile. "You see, only the chosen one is in need of it—being from the land and all—"

"I understand," Thalassa said grimly. She was at the breaking point. This, together with everything else that had happened, was simply too much to bear. That her situation could worsen did not seem possible, yet it had. What else lay in store for her?

It did not occur to Thalassa to dispute what these young ones said. If Dorian could call forth creatures such as she had already seen, his placing an enchantment upon her was all too possible. "Do you know when he plans to do this?" she asked faintly.

"Soon, I think," said another of the women. "Actually, we thought he would have done it by now." She grinned shyly at Thalassa. "But everyone in the abode is chuckling about the quarrel you and our lord had beside the interlocking chamber. Our lord is known for his cool head. Seldom does he lose his temper. In fact, I cannot ever remember a time when he has. Although," she added in a burst of candor, "I am not very old."

"But what is it that all of *you* want from me?"

They gazed at her solemnly, and Valya took over.

"Lady, there is a reason those of our years have never seen the great lands of your kin—or so the Elders say. Once, long ago, some of our people left the sea and went to live upon the land. The Elders of that time, and many of the sea-people, were very much against their leaving. But these merfolk were devoted to the teachings of a woman named Jabari, and when she left the sea they followed her, despite the strife it caused."

His words startled Thalassa from brooding over the latest threat to her. "Do they live upon the land now?"

"No. The Elders say that Mother Sea rose up against them in anger at their leaving and all of them died. From that time to this no one born of the sea has made his home upon the land. We are not even allowed to go there until a certain age, and even then, only after the king and then the Elders have searched our hearts, to make certain that we have attained sufficient wisdom to visit the great lands without being tempted to stay there."

"Why should it matter to them one way or the other?"

"Why?" Valya gazed at Thalassa as if he could not believe she had asked such a question. "Because the wise ones want no more tragedies to befall our people, and because our world must be protected from the prying eyes of landfolk, which might not happen if great numbers of us go to live in their world." He said this automatically, clearly reciting lessons carefully learned.

"But *we* would not endanger our kin." The words burst from a boy with flaming red hair who had not spoken before. "First of all, there are so few of us, only we six, and we would need little room—"

In a flash of insight Thalassa understood. "You want to leave the sea and live upon the land, don't you?"

Relief washed over the faces of all six. The blond girl said hurriedly, "Yes, Lady, we do, and we have heard that the lands your tribe inhabits are vast and rich. All we ask is some small corner of it to build our dwellings in. If you only could instruct us—explain the best ways to approach your people in peace—we would like even better to dwell among them. In return we would gift them with the sea's bounty whenever they desired. But there is little time."

"What do you mean?" Thalassa did not bother to explain that while the Amazons might accept the three young women, the men would surely be killed, or at the very least, driven away. She had more pressing concerns.

"All of us are at the age when it is customary to appear before Dorian and the Elders. Yet if we do so, they will surely see the desires and plans in our hearts and deny us permission to visit the land until we are very much older. We are not skilled enough to hide our thoughts from the power of the Elders, so with your help, we must begin our journey before any of us are called to the Pool of Understanding . . . and before our lord puts the Sea Spell upon you. For once that is done, you will be . . . changed."

Thalassa swallowed hard at the ominous words. "You ask help from me when *I* am the captive?" Her voice suddenly rose in desperation. "It is you who must help me," she cried hoarsely, "to escape from this place! If you do, then we will see what I may do for you."

The merfolk were silent, and she looked wildly from face to face. "Well? Why do you not answer?"

"Lady . . ." Valya stared at his bare feet.

"*Well?*"

The youth cast a pleading glance at his friends, who avoided his gaze.

"We cannot help you," Valya stammered at last. "You are the king's chosen one—selected by the Elders themselves—and you *must* stay here. It is ordained. You see, what we wish to do violates custom. In time, however, we hope the Elders will forgive us and see that we can dwell upon the land without bringing harm to the rest of our people. If the land displeases us . . . Well, we can return to the sea, accept whatever punishment is decreed, and be accepted once more.

"But to aid you in leaving the lord Dorian is . . . Lady, there is no worse thing we could do. We would be exiled—beyond the pale of our own kind for all time—we and our children's children all down through the ages. Lady, please do not ask this of us. Please do not."

"Get out."

"Lady—"

"*Get out!* If you are not willing to help me then cease flapping your useless mouths and leave me. *Leave me!*"

Shaking violently, her fists clenching and unclenching in impotent rage, Thalassa stalked to the far end of the chamber and stood with her back to the young merfolk. She listened as they whispered to one another for a moment, then their feet padded softly over the smooth floor. The door opened and closed, and Thalassa was alone.

Fury poured through her like heated spiced wine, and

she gladly let it take control. Its intensity was as cleansing as fire; its ferocity swept aside the unnerving terror of the mysterious Sea Spell. So Dorian thought to beguile her, did he? Well, she would show him what it meant to underestimate an Amazon! Him, as well as these spineless youngsters who feared to help her.

There was only one gateway from this diabolical place, and by Artemis's sacred girdle, she would take it. If what waited for her outside that terrible interlocking chamber was death . . . then so be it. At least she would have her honor—and escape the ignominious fate of being reduced to becoming a man's chattel. And might she not be able to escape successfully and return home? Dorian might be lying about them being in another ocean, simply to intimidate her. There was only one way to find out.

Determinedly Thalassa set off. Her head for directions stood her in good stead. Memorizing the routes on which her captors led her had become so natural, she had paid attention without realizing it to the corridors Dorian had taken to reach the interlocking chamber. Yes, the grandmothers had taught her well, not like the young of these merfolk, whose childhood seemed to encompass the learning of nothing useful, she thought contemptuously.

Well aware that creeping furtively along would clearly announce her intention to try to escape, she walked boldly, arms swinging, eyes looking straight ahead.

While bypassers glanced curiously at her, no one interfered with her progress, and presently she found herself standing before the wall containing the four panels. The Mother was obviously in favor of this undertaking, she thought, for the long corridor was deserted now and the awesome chamber stood empty. She stared at the shining black and silver squares and chewed her lip, feeling her resolve weaken.

Her entire being quailed at the thought of entering that vast, eerily lit space and waiting for it to fill with cold salt water, which would sweep her away . . . to where? She could still turn back. It was not too late, and no one would ever know of her cowardice. Except her.

Pressing her lips firmly together, Thalassa pushed the first of the panels, as she had seen Dorian do. She was prepared for the grinding roar of the opening doors, but the sound still made her jump. The chamber gaped ominously, beckoning to her with shadowy menace. She almost hoped Dorian would come pounding up and with a harsh, "What do you think you're doing?" drag her away before she could go any farther. But the moments crawled by, and neither Dorian nor anyone else came along the silent corridor to stop her.

Hesitantly she stepped inside. The chamber's stone walls and ceiling loomed about her, and she shivered, for the air seemed much colder than in the hallway. The tiny lamps flickered and danced in the gloom, and in the uncertain light, she could just make out the two levers Dorian had spoken of mounted on the far wall.

Her heart battering against her chest, she stripped off her short tunic and crossed the dim cavern. Gooseflesh rose on her bared skin. She wondered whether it came from the cold or fear. The levers were long, heavy objects. One was carved from red coral, the other from black, and both were set in mountings that appeared to be pure gold.

Thalassa studied them, remembering that Dorian had told her the red one controlled flooding the chamber, and the black emptied it. He had also said she was not ready to enter the sea yet, but she forced the thought aside. If she was going to do this thing, it would have to be now. If she hesitated any longer, she would lose her courage completely, or someone would come along to restrain her.

Drawing a deep breath, she placed a trembling hand on the red lever and pulled it with all her strength.

The doors behind her crashed shut with the echoing finality of a tomb. She had to fight with all her will not to yank frantically on the black lever and reverse what she had begun. Water misted saltily onto her lips, and she flinched as the sea came sweeping and curling around her ankles. Once started, the process was terrifyingly swift. Watching from outside, it had not seemed to be so quick. In a matter of moments the water had surged up her thighs, invaded her woman's parts, and was rising to cover her breasts. Thalassa clenched her jaw until it ached, reminding herself over and over that she had always loved the sea, that swimming came as naturally to her as breathing. The opportunity to use her skill would soon be upon her, for the water was about to engulf her face. In another few instants, she would be completely submerged. The flood would reach the vaulted ceiling, and the gigantic outer doors would open. . . .

Thalassa gulped the last remaining air into her lungs, and held it as salt water flowed over her face. The outlandish things Dorian had told her about—gills that enabled his people to breathe underwater—could not possibly be true. Stronger than any bizarre tales about such inhuman abilities was the instinct to hold her breath underwater. How long she would be able to hold it, she did not know. She could only hope they were not as far undersea as Dorian would have her believe.

With deceptive gentleness, the water floated her feet out from under her, and automatically she started to swim. Ahead of her the massive doors began moving. Vibrations rippled through the flooded grotto, jarring Thalassa's body back and forth, then drawing her with inexorable authority into the newly revealed ocean mouth.

Filled with a sense of utter fatality, of determination and of dread, Thalassa let herself be pulled forward. . . .

CHAPTER 11

~~ The sea closed around her, black and cold and filled with nightmares. It was deep. Oh, Mother, help her—how deep it was!

The stifling miasma of death spread malevolent, clutching fingers into Thalassa's lungs, and all hope evaporated. With bitter certainty, she acknowledged she would die there in the bowels of that foreign sea. Having no idea what the sensation of drowning felt like, she could only hope it to be over quickly.

The rush of salt water through the suddenly opened slits on her neck caught her totally unprepared. *Her captor had been telling the truth, after all!* But only in part. He had also said there would be no pain, but there was. Sharp, stabbing pain trembled throughout her body, following the rhythm of her breathing with precise spasms. It swiftly worsened, and with it came a sense of agonizing pressure, as if the weight of the mountains looming eerily around her was planted on her chest, rather than the floor of the sea.

The cold was numbing. It wrapped her body in layers of ice, froze the blood in her veins, and seemed to freeze the very thoughts in her brain. Desperately Thalassa sought to fix her mind on reality, but logical perception no longer had any meaning. In a torpid, heavy way she began to feel inordinately pleased with herself. An almost hysterical sense of joy invaded her whole being, and awkwardly, barely aware of what she was doing, she began swimming again.

Her movements were sluggish and uncoordinated. Trying to swim through this black sea was like swimming in a dream. The water felt as thick as mud, and it snatched at her limbs, slowing her still more. Her tongue, lips, hands, and feet all swelled grotesquely, and a bitter, metallic taste washed into her mouth. But still she tried to swim, driven by instinct to seek the surface of this ghastly ocean, which seemed to be doing its very best to smother her.

She felt she had been there for eons, a tiny insect caught in a vast pool of pitch, feebly seeking to lift its fragile wings out of the clinging tar. In reality, it was only moments before the sharp eyes of Dorian and his three companions picked her out of the gloom. Like arrows, they shot forward, surrounding her and sweeping her back toward the abode with the speed of hunting dolphins.

Lethargically Thalassa realized she should struggle. But strong arms and powerful, naked bodies pressed her close on every side, moving her so swiftly through the water that she could do nothing except be borne along. The sensation of speed was dizzying. It made her giddy with confusion and pain, and drove away her last coherent thoughts.

The unearthly structure she had just escaped from emerged abruptly, among a kaleidoscope of swirling impressions—the roaring sound of water rushing past her; the deep, unfamiliar male voices gabbling in a language that made no sense; and agony—agony such as she had never felt in her entire life.

Air burned its way into her constricted lungs, and she doubled over with a choked scream. Hands were all over her body, and she was powerless to shake them off. The pain left no room for any other feeling, and when a blackness as heavy as the ocean crushed down on her, Thalassa fell forward into it gratefully.

Later, Dorian sat beside the still figure lying in his bed,

frowning and lost in thought. The Elders had left some time ago. Their rigid disapproval rankled him like the salt blood of Mother Sea upon an open wound. Never had he seen the venerable Nomar so angry.

"Look on the result of your misplaced compassion!" the old man had raged. "What in all the universes of the sea possessed you to ignore our counsel and delay in placing the spell? Had you done so she would not have engaged in this folly that has almost taken her life!

"You are a mature merman and a king, Dorian, not some headstrong youth chafing under the customs that exist solely for the good of his people. Yet here you are, putting some foolish notion of pity above the welfare of your own people and your responsibilities as king. That empty-headed boy, Valya, may as well rule in your stead!"

Remembering the old man's tirade, Dorian winced. Strictly speaking, he was not bound by the dictates of the Elders. Their role was completely advisory, and a king could disregard—even defy—their counsel if he chose. Yet to the long-lived merfolk, among whom reverence for age was an almost inbred trait, such open defiance, especially on the part of the king, was virtually nonexistent. The very young with their natural rebelliousness often tested the old ones' patience, but even they did so with respect.

With their highly developed powers and vast wisdom born from innumerable centuries of living, the Elders were unique and greatly revered. No more than a dozen of them had ever lived at a given time, for in every generation only a few were born possessing what the Elders themselves termed "the gifts," those intangible abilities that determined a man or woman's rise to the exalted position.

Dorian would never be an Elder, neither he nor any other king. Rulers governed until they died, or until they voluntarily stepped down to make way for their successor. Which at the rate he was going, Nomar had pointed out acidly, was a highly unlikely event.

Pacing the tiled floor as his colleagues looked on silently, Nomar had demanded, "If she died what would have happened to the succession? These are sacred matters, Dorian. Only a child of her body can be your heir—"

"I know that all too well, Old One," Dorian had

interrupted. "But grant me the right to do these things in my own time."

"Why? What do you wait for? The life she will have with us is infinitely superior to the brutish existence she would have had on land. What awaits her in Amazonia? A few short years of health, then the decay and illness of old age—if she isn't killed in battle first, with her eyes gouged out and her body raped until she is in pieces."

Despite himself, Dorian had flinched. His life, though not nearly as long as those of the Elders, had provided him ample opportunity to see what Nomar described—and much worse. But picturing Thalassa's golden eyes and lovely body so horribly was . . .

"You don't need to convince me of the landfolk's brutality, Nomar—"

"Good, because then you will be able to convince her of how fortunate she is to have been taken from it. Put the Sea Spell upon her, Dorian, link your body and mind with hers so you can perform the Ceremony of Matebonding, and then—get busy making an heir!"

"She is a woman, not a seal cow in breeding season," Dorian said, and he did not mean the Selkies, who—despite their wondrous ability to take seal form, were essentially human—but the true seals breeding throughout these waters.

For this remark he received a cold, furious glare from eight pairs of eyes. "She is," Nomar said icily, "a queen. Or at least she will be when *you* begin acting like a king once more."

With those words he led the way out of the chamber. In the doorway, the last of the Elders, a woman called Dourika, turned around. "Let her rest undisturbed a while longer," she murmured in a sympathetic voice, "and then lay the spell while she sleeps. It will be easier for her so. She'll awaken and remember nothing."

But looking at the unconscious woman in his bed, Dorian wondered. This unwilling Amazon of his was a frustrating, prickly creature, who aroused feelings more akin to fury than amorousness in his breast. And yet the thought of seeing all that angry defiance fade into acceptance made him strangely sad.

In a deep way that he did not understand, she pleased him, this fierce sword-woman with her mane of red-gold hair and tawny, flashing eyes. Pleased him as no other woman ever had. Not the lovers he had taken from among his own kind, and not the many landwomen he had seduced over the centuries. Those women he had made love to on deserted beaches or visited in their beds, leaving them to awake alone the next morning and wonder if his presence had only been a magnificent dream.

So he sat by the bed, watching her sleep . . . and waiting.

Groggily Thalassa floated into wakefulness. Fever and chills washed over her in alternating waves, and pain beat through her entire body like an alien, throbbing heartbeat.

Never ill before, Thalassa had no experience to help her endure these frightening sensations. Death was not supposed to hurt once one died, and why was she lying on something so soft? She fought to gather her thoughts, but they skittered and leaped like yearling fillies, and she could not hold onto any single idea long enough to make sense of it.

A large, warm hand cradled the back of her head, and the unfamiliarity of it caused her to start violently. Pain twisted like a sword blade in her vitals, and for a horrible moment, she could not draw breath. A deep voice spoke comfortingly, and her horror increased. Sick as she was, she recognized the voice.

She had failed, either to die or to escape. It was the one clear thought that stayed in her fever-ridden brain, and it sat on her with all the evil weight of one of the giant seamounts outside this accursed place. She cried out in despair, and Dorian hushed her.

"No, no, my sweet. Be still. Nothing is going to harm you. Swallow a little of this now. That's it, just a little."

Something pleasantly hot was being tipped down her throat, and she could not summon up the strength to push her captor's hands away. She drank, then felt her head laid back down. Gentle hands massaged her aching temples and stroked the tangled hair off her forehead. She wondered hazily at the strange feel of it before slipping into a restless, fever-laden sleep.

Time passed, and Thalassa hovered in the cloudy realm between dreams and reality. At times she believed herself safely in the arms of her own kind; yet other times ominous images made her delirious with the fear that perhaps she was not at home after all. Finally, there came a day when she awoke with a mind that was lucid and unblurred by fever. She lay quietly in the huge bed, exploring an appallingly weak body, and dully realizing she was neither dead nor safe in her own land.

"I see you're feeling better this morning," the hated, melodious voice said.

She did not bother turning her head to look at the speaker. For one thing, she knew it was *he*, and for another, she did not have the strength.

Unfazed by her refusal to acknowledge him, Dorian studied her, then said dryly, "Well, if it was your desire to die, Lady, you certainly came far too close to getting your wish. Had I not returned early from my journey and sought you out to apologize for my temper, things would have gone badly for you." He sighed. "You are very brave and very determined and very, very foolish."

"I will try again." It was an effort even to talk, but she would not give in, Thalassa told herself fiercely. The next instant, a long-fingered hand turned her head on the pillow. Dorian leaned forward so that their faces almost touched, and his eyes burned down into hers.

"You will *not* try again," he said in a voice that reverberated with power and authority. "For the simple reason that I will not allow it. I have been patient with you, Lady, and I will continue to be patient, for I realize how difficult this is for you. But I did not bring you here to die, and if I must shackle you to my wrist to prevent another such ill-advised escape attempt, then so be it!"

Her eyes blazed with what fury she could summon. "So now you speak of chaining? You, who were so quick to tell me I am not a slave? You are as dishonorable and untrustworthy as all other men!"

Dorian's gaze still held hers, but seeing the desperate fear behind her anger, he gentled his voice. "You recite your elders' teachings because you are too young to have any experiences of your own. You are afraid and distrustful, and I can hardly blame you. The men of your world are not particularly trustworthy where women are concerned. But you know nothing of me—a situation I intend to remedy as soon as possible."

His words carried an implication that terrified her, and she shored up her rage. "I know more than you think, spawn of a sea-demon! How are you any different from the Cretan pigs who sought to trap me like a wild animal, or the pirates who kidnapped three of my sisters to sell as slaves? You carried me off and hold me an unwilling prisoner, and even though you cloak your intentions in honeyed words, the slave chains still rattle behind your back!"

Exhausted by the effort of such a long speech, she lapsed into panting silence. Dorian gazed down at her sadly. "I know that is how it must seem to you," he said. "But Lady, consider this: If we are linked together, am I not bound to you as much as you are to me?"

For a moment Thalassa's whole view of the world and men's place in that world tottered. Then logic intervened once more. "Not if you are the only one able to unlock the chains!" she snarled.

Their faces were very close, and to Thalassa's tremendous shock, she felt the quick contact of his lips on hers. Then he laughed and gave her a genuinely admiring look. "An excellent point, my love. Perhaps we should dispense with chains, after all."

Outrage struggled with fatigue, and outrage temporarily won. She jerked her head away from his suddenly caressing fingers and struck savagely at him. "Of course, what need have you of chains, when you can make me your slave by simply laying a spell upon me!"

He drew in a sharp breath, and his eyes suddenly pierced hers like daggers. She defiantly refused to look away, and both of them remained frozen in place for several seconds. Then Dorian said softly, "Someone has been talking to you, I see. Is that why you tried to flee?"

"Yes!"

He shook his head. "The Sea Spell will not make you a

slave. Whoever told you that is very ignorant, Thalassa."
His use of her name was deliberate, and he watched her
closely to see if his suspicions were correct.

Thalassa's eyes widened in horror at hearing her name
roll off his tongue. The man *was* a sorcerer, or even worse,
a demon! Her voice was hoarse with strain and her head
ached, but she forced the words out.

"By what magic did you learn my name?"

"None at all. You talked a great deal in your fever, and
I merely guessed. I realize we are not yet friends, but since
you did not share the knowledge willingly, no Amazon laws
were broken, were they?"

She did not answer, and he went on. "Your name is
beautiful, and it speaks of the sea. An unusual choice for a
people who live by the horse. I wonder if your mother knew
how well it would suit you when she named you."

Thalassa remained silent. It was true her name was not
typical of the ones Amazons gave their daughters, but she
had never had the opportunity to question her birth-mother
about it. She had met a brave and honorable death in battle
when her infant daughter was still nursing on mare's milk.
All Thalassa knew was what old Marpe had told her—when
she had been born, the Goddess had come to her mother in
a dream and bestowed Thalassa's name upon her, saying
that there was a destiny on this child.

A destiny . . . *Could the Goddess have actually pre-
ordained this fate?*

Thalassa's heart stopped, and she cried out at the cruelty
of it. Surely the Ancient Mother would never approve of the
abduction of an Amazon daughter! But what if the Goddess
was indeed involved? Then she was truly doomed, for there
could be no escape.

In the enormity of these revelations, she had forgotten
both Dorian's presence and the looming horror of the Sea
Spell. His voice jarred her from her thoughts. "If it
distresses you to have me use your name, Lady, I will not
do so until you give me permission."

"You lied," she muttered, not looking at him. "You said
there would be no pain, and there was." It was the nearest
she could come to admitting the beginnings of acceptance,
and the subtlety of it might have been lost on another man.

But not on Dorian. He touched her arm, marked by thin whitened scars left by the sword blades of sparring partners over the years of her training.

"I spoke truthfully, Thalassa, and if you had listened to me, there would have been no pain. It was too soon for you to go out. We are very deep below the sea, and no person born of the land could live for even the space of a heartbeat in these waters. You lived because you no longer belong totally to the land, although you do not belong totally to my people either. The transition is not yet complete, but enough change has occurred so that you were protected for at least a little while.

"Had we been any longer in reaching you, it would have been too late. As it was the midnight sea—which is what we call these deep waters—took a heavy toll on your body, for she does not welcome those who are not of her blood."

"You should have let her kill me then, for I do not want to be of her blood." Thalassa's voice was filled with pain. Even if the Goddess had ordained this to be her fate, she thought bitterly, she simply could not bear it.

Dorian's hand still lay on her arm, and abruptly she rolled away from the alien touch that sought to comfort her. He reached out and took her hand, callused and hard from her life as a warrior. He was not sure why she had suddenly stopped screaming at him and become more acquiescent, but he was prepared to take full advantage of this new mood for as long as it lasted.

"I am sorry, Lady, but it is too late for that. Your body will recover quickly, for you are very strong, and your next experience in the sea will be far more pleasant, believe me."

He was watching her face, and he saw panic flow across the fine features, even though she tried to hide it. "It was not a good introduction to the world of my people, I know," he said reassuringly. "But I promise you that nothing like that will ever happen to you again."

Thalassa scarcely heard him. Her mind was instantly full of a black ocean of icy mud that slowly crushed the life from her; the taste of dirty metal that tainted her mouth; and the demented joy that the heavy darkness was killing her.

Without being aware of it, she trembled violently and clutched Dorian's hand in a grip borne of utter terror.

He used his free hand to turn her face so that he could look into her eyes, silently persuading her to accept his reassurance.

"The things you felt," he said softly, "were only because your body was not ready for the sea. The blackness, the cold, the terrible feeling of pressure, the bitter taste in your mouth, and the sense of rapture were all because you are still partly connected to the land. The seafolk feel none of those things, and neither will you, once your body has made the full change."

His words brought Thalassa back to herself, and she stared at him in open-mouthed amazement. How could he know what she had been feeling within her body?

He smiled at the expression on her face. "Do not be surprised, Lady. My people have made their home in the sea since the beginning of time, and all of her secrets are known to us—as one day they will be known to you."

She yanked her hand from his grasp. "I do not want to learn the sea's secrets," she said waspishly. "I am a woman of the land, and *that* is where I belong. With the earth underneath my feet, and the wind and sun on my face, not here in this place of cold and darkness. I know the secrets of handling weapons, of warfare and hunting, and the language of horses. That is all I need."

"You are very young to decide that the world has no more knowledge to offer. Have you no wish to learn of anything more?"

"I wish to know when you plan to put this spell upon me!"

For the first time since she had met this enigmatic man, he had trouble looking directly at her. "I don't know," he said gruffly. "I should have done it before. If I had you would not now be lying here."

"Why—why haven't you then?"

"I said I don't know!" The impatience in his voice shocked him as much as it did her. He forced himself to go on more calmly. "Thalassa, this business of taking a mate is as new to me as it is to you. Custom requires me to do certain things, but I had hoped we could become . . .

more used to each other first. I did not expect you to be so unhappy here. The life I offer you is truly better than the one you would have had on land, yet I sometimes wish I could undo what has been done."

"And if you could?" Her voice seemed different to her, as if someone else were asking the question. "Would you overturn this deed and unbind me so I could return home?"

He did not answer, and the hope that she had thought dead surged up again. Shakily, fighting her fatigue and weakness, she pushed herself upright on the pillows. "Would you?"

The breath whooshed out of him in a deep sigh. "No," he said heavily, and even Thalassa, distraught as she was, could hear the regret in his voice. "It might not be safe for you to return to the land of your former kin, Lady. The Elders—who are the wisest of us all—think some sort of doom may be about to fall upon your people. That was why I took you when I did, to prevent you from being caught up in it."

All thoughts of her own fate promptly fled from her mind. Icy tentacles curled about her insides, and her gaze froze upon his dark face. "What manner of doom?" she whispered.

"I'm not sure. The Elders have foreseen men coming to the shores of your birthland, men who might do the Amazons harm."

"Any man who comes to our shores means us harm." Futile rage boiled up in her throat like bitter bile. "Including you. Do these Elders possess the gift of seeing?"

"As much as it is possible for one to possess such a gift, yes. No foreseeing into the future is ever infallible."

"But if there is even a chance of this coming to pass, they must be warned!" For the first time in her life, Thalassa reached out to a man. Desperately gripping Dorian's bare, muscled forearm, she pleaded, "You must let me go now. Don't you see?"

"No, and do not ask it of me again, Lady. The Elders have already accused me of being too softhearted with you. And perhaps I have been. Encouraging you to accept this existence is the kindest thing I can do for you. If an evil fate is truly in store for your people, there is naught you or I can do to prevent it."

She dug her strong, weapon-hardened fingers into his arm until a weaker man would have flinched. "Are you so lacking in pity then? What manner of person can be so heartless?"

Dorian stared at her. "A very old one by your standards. A man who has seen violence come to the folk of the land so many times, he lost count centuries ago."

"By the Goddess!" She released his arm and lifted trembling hands to her face. "You seek to confuse me with your sorcerer's talk! Well, I don't believe you, for you look scarcely older than I!"

"Look at me."

The rich voice contained an oddly compelling note that brought her unwilling gaze to his dark face. Despite the seemingly endless time of her captivity, she had never truly *looked* at the man responsible for her being there. She had seen him in the way one sees an enemy—as only a body with vulnerable spots and weak points that could be exploited in an attack. But now she gazed at Dorian, and it was as if she were seeing him for the first time.

The strongly featured face above her was intelligent and kind, with high cheekbones and a well-defined mouth that was sensitive and yet firm. Humor lurked around the full lips, but it was blended with an unmistakable stamp of decisiveness and strength that commanded respect. At last, her guarded eyes met his, and a frightening insight jolted through her, as if somewhere in a life beyond memory or consciousness, she had gazed into their depths and discovered a part of her very soul.

They were speculative eyes, full of an open-minded, unbiased perception, deep with self-knowledge and with mysteries she could not begin to guess at. Bewildering sensations washed over her. With difficulty she tore her gaze from those eyes, glittering with an ancient wisdom that sat strangely in his young face.

"You see?" he murmured softly. "I am far older than I appear, but there is no reason to fear or distrust me."

"There is every reason," she said, yet anxiety coiled around her even as she spoke.

The burden of the destiny placed on her by the Goddess almost buried her with its weight, and Thalassa's heart broke as she finally acknowledged it. She would never see Amazonia again.

CHAPTER 12

≈ The days had passed pleasantly with a gentle peace between Amazon and Greek. Like the males and females of certain animal species who come together only in the mating season, the women and men played and made love in temporary harmony, the clash of their disparate natures momentarily stilled under a serene summer sky.

Antiope and Theseus went riding and hunting together, and the latter was astonished at his companion's skill. Never had he seen such fluid grace on a horse, and he came of a people who were themselves good horsemen, treating their mounts with an unusual sensitivity. And as for her mastery of the bow and spear—Few, if any, men of his acquaintance could match it.

If it were not for the smooth, brown thighs gripping the horse's sides and the one exposed breast rising softly with the animal's motion, Theseus could have imagined that he rode side by side with a male comrade. But the stirring in his eager loins ever reminded him of the truth, and more often than not, their rides ended with the two of them locked in straining, laughter-filled combat in the cool seclusion of deep, wooded glades.

The Athenian king had not changed his mind about finding a way to steal Antiope, but lost in the delights of her splendid body, he found it easy not to think about the disagreeable and possibly dangerous aspects of such an action. It was far more pleasant just to enjoy himself with her. When the time came to depart, he would talk to Heracles, and they would devise a scheme. Theseus told himself this confidently as he played and rode about the country of his new lover.

But Heracles—caught up in blissful dalliance with the wondrous Hippolyte—seemed no more eager to leave than any of his men. The golden girdle had already been packed carefully away in a locked sea chest on the lead galley. A love gift well worth his manly attentions, Hippolyte had claimed with a roguish smile after their first night together.

As for Heracles, he could not get enough of the Amazon queen whom he had once ignorantly compared to a frog. Hippolyte was like no one he had ever known. That she ruled over a society representing everything he stood against was a profound contradiction, and Heracles was not good at resolving contradictions.

He was far from stupid, but neither did the great hero possess Hippolyte's complexity of character. He preferred to see things in black and white whenever he could, and simply decided not to think about why he was drawn to this woman who violated all his notions of female decorum.

There was one man among the Greeks, though, who was not content to spend the long, lazy days and nights feasting, swimming, and making love: the ill-natured Soloon. Morosely he watched his companions abandon themselves to the she-demons. Trying to convince them that they were wasting their precious seed on whores was useless. His protestations fell on either laughing or deaf ears, and Soloon's mood grew ever uglier.

The biggest disappointment was the behavior of his revered idol Heracles. On the long sea voyage, Soloon had not fantasized over full breasts and the sweet path between a woman's thighs, as the others had. Instead, his gaze had surreptitiously followed Heracles as the huge man strode vigorously about the galley, balancing easily against the ocean's movements on his powerful, sun-browned legs.

Heracles did not notice the younger man's adoring scrutiny any more than he noticed how Soloon contrived to be perpetually near him. But all of Soloon's thoughts, waking and sleeping, were of the expedition's noble leader. Lying on the rough wooden deck, he had dreamily concocted elaborate fantasies wherein he would save Heracles from some horrible danger, and afterward the hero would turn to him with gratitude and . . . dawning love.

Now it seemed that his dreams had actually become reality. However, the horrible danger was not some hideous monster from the depths of the sea. It was a woman, mysterious, incomprehensible, and therefore threatening, as all women were. And what made it worse was that Heracles did not recognize his peril.

Watching him put his brawny arm around Hippolyte's slender waist and kiss her rosy, smiling mouth made Soloon physically ill. The lewdly exposed flesh of these pseudo-women was only a cloak. They were demons who wished to steal men's souls.

He had tried. By Apollo, he had tried to make Heracles aware of the threat. But his cherished idol had only let out a familiar bellow of laughter. "Take one of these women and put your manroot to work, lad," he had said good-naturedly. "When you're well mounted between her legs thrusting away, you won't have time to think about such drivel." And clapping Soloon on the shoulder, he had walked away to rejoin Hippolyte.

So the unhappy Soloon had been left alone once more to brood. And this he did—chewing on his resentment and jealousy the way a dog will gnaw an injured paw until it becomes raw and festered. From the canyons of his inflamed mind, an idea slowly took shape, an idea that made increasing sense the more he thought about it. . . .

The day had been an exceptionally warm one, and thunderstorms had rumbled during the black of the night. When the first hint of dawn came, it carried the pink and blue scented freshness following rain on summer days.

Very early, when hardly anyone was stirring, a shadowy figure slipped toward the heap of weapons piled on the beach, well covered to protect them from the damp. Over the passing days the rigorously enforced guarding had lessened as both peoples relaxed with each other. The Greeks had ceased posting a guard entirely; and while the Amazons had not gone that far, they were nevertheless more easygoing than they had originally been. Only two of them maintained the unexciting vigil, and as the end of their shift approached, they waited with sleepy impatience to be relieved by the next set of guards.

Moving from rock to rock, Soloon worked his way nearer the pile of arms. He had imagined himself to be moving noiselessly, but the heads of both sentries jerked up. In consternation he realized they had somehow sensed his presence. He stood up quickly, his mind racing, and called, "Peace be with you. It is only I."

The two warriors regarded him with suspicion in the murky half-light. "Why are you skulking about seeking to come upon us in secret?" one of them demanded.

"I did not intend to! It is just—" *Think, you fool, think!* "My wits deserted me," he finished lamely. They stared at him, and he stumbled on. "You see, I have never been with a woman before. These past days I have watched my fellows and tried to get up the courage to approach one of you. But you are unlike any women I have ever seen and—and I feared that when you learned of my inexperience . . . you would laugh at me." There, he thought. They had to believe him. They had to!

It appeared they did. The Amazon who had spoken started to chuckle, and the second one nudged her. "Inexperience is nothing to be ashamed of," she said, not unkindly. "But creeping about and spying on people can get you killed. Didn't your elders teach you so? If you want to ask us something, ask it. That's always the best way."

"Then . . . will one of you lie with me?" It was not his original plan, but he had underestimated their vigilance, and anyway, if the gods were with him, this new scheme would work even better.

The women consulted briefly with each other in low voices, then turned back to Soloon. "Our guard duty will soon be over," the second one said, a tall brown-haired girl only a year or two older than Soloon himself. "My sister prefers sleeping to mating just now, but I will lie with you. Inexperienced though you may be, your seed should still be able to get daughters."

"I . . . uh, thank you," he mumbled, not quite sure what else to say.

"But first—" the Amazon continued practically, "we will look about to satisfy ourselves that this is not some sort of trick."

"Of course," Soloon said hastily. As he spoke, the carefully concealed knife meant for the cutting of meat—the only weapon each man had been allowed to keep—pressed its cold point into his side.

He fidgeted as nervous anticipation flowed through him, stiffening his shaft so that it reared up against his belly. But it was not the thought of the brown-haired woman that brought on his erection. It was the sharp feel of the knife—that and the look of proud devotion he was sure would fill Heracles's eyes when he realized how Soloon had rescued them all from these she-devils.

"Treachery! Treachery!"

The high voice rang out, freezing in their tracks the two Amazon warriors coming to relieve the present set of guards. A figure ran past, shielded by trees. In the uncertain light the guards could not tell who it was, but there was no mistaking the chilling message that floated on the still dawn air.

"The Greeks have betrayed us!" the voice called. "One of our people lies dead with a dagger in her throat—a Greek dagger! Murdered! Murdered!"

The cry pierced the ears of the listeners as the obscure harbinger of this terrible doom ran on. "Stop!" one of the warriors shouted. "What has happened? Who among us lies dead?"

There was no answer. Both warriors had turned to follow the runner, when footsteps suddenly came pounding toward them from the direction of the weapons pile. The remaining guard ran up, her eyes wild and staring.

"Philippis has been killed by a Greek dog!" she screamed. "Even now, her blood stains the ground, crying out for us to avenge the spilling of it!"

A red haze swirled up around the three Amazons. In the savage bloodlust roaring through their veins, none of them stopped to wonder about who had dashed by a few moments earlier. As one person, they whirled and flung themselves toward Themiscrya, their thoughts solely on revenge.

Even as they disappeared, new footfalls sounded from another direction. Soloon—having dropped his deception the moment he was beyond earshot of the Amazons—made straight for a group of five Greeks returning from a swim in the river.

"It is as I feared," he gasped out, waving a bloody arm in their astonished faces. "These female demons have meant treachery all along. As I was in the bushes skewering one, I heard others talking about how they mean to kill us. My bitch realized I'd heard and tried to gut me with my own knife, but I slit her throat instead. See how she marked me!"

The wound was little more than a scratch. Soloon had no liking for pain, and he'd had to force himself to inflict even so slight a cut. But in the weak light it bled convincingly, thus having the desired effect on Soloon's listeners.

Nestor, the highest ranking of the group, took over immediately. "Quickly! We must get to the weapons and arm ourselves. Soloon—go you to the others and warn them as you have warned us."

They raced off into the shadows, and Soloon looked after them with satisfaction. His blood still tingled with the excitement of his deed—piercing that creature's woman-flesh with both his body and the cold blade of his knife had been pleasurable, far more pleasurable than he had anticipated. Things were going well. Very well indeed.

He began to run again, an uncontrollable giggle of exhilaration bubbling out of his throat. It was all in motion now, and like a cart rolling downhill, it could no longer be stopped. And it had been easy, so very, very easy.

The clang of fighting outside the palace awoke Heracles. Rolling up in Hippolyte's bed, he found himself alone, and for an instant he hesitated, hoping this was a dream.

Then the chilling sound of the Amazon war cry split the air. It galvanized Heracles into action. With a single leap, he was out of bed, buckling on his swords, pulling on his lionskin, and racing from the chamber.

As he ran down the now familiar corridor that led outside, the clamor grew louder. Anger and dread filled his mind. What terrible thing had happened? Could Soloon have been right all along about Amazon treachery? And where was Hippolyte?

He emerged into the open space before the palace and was just opening his mouth to bellow an order, when the Amazon closest to the entryway saw him. "Untrustworthy lying dog!" she yelled above the din, and swung her battle-ax in a vicious sweeping arc at the hero's head. There was no time to argue or explain, only time to protect himself.

The Amazon was a tall, powerfully built woman, and the blade of her ax was already stained with bloody proof of her prowess. But never had she encountered the armor of Heracles's lionskin. The shining ax thudded against the white-fanged head enclosing Heracles's, then glanced off harmlessly. In the same instant, the hero gave an angry roar and drew his long sword. He struck off his attacker's head with one mighty blow.

The headless body fell twitching into the crimsoned dust, and four other Amazons swung away from the tumult to confront this new threat. Heracles had a confused impression of a main battle raging on the distant beach, bordered by smaller pockets of conflict such as this one. Then his foes were upon him, and there was no more time for questions, apologies, or attempts at conciliation.

The warriors charged the bristling figure singly, each eager to claim the glory of destroying the leader of these treacherous erstwhile guests. The first of them flew across the flat ground like a whirlwind—and was cut down just as suddenly, when her ax failed to slice through the hero's furred protection. In rapid succession, one after the other hurled herself at Heracles, only to be slain as the impenetrable hide blunted her weapons.

By now, the struggle had drawn the attention of the remaining Amazons. They had handily disposed of their

Greek opponents who, having neither lionskin armor nor the skill to protect themselves against the fierce Amazons, had died quickly.

The sight of his men's sprawled bodies and the stench of their spilled blood and entrails filled Heracles with an uncontrollable fury. All his animosity toward the rule of women, which had been temporarily quelled by Hippolyte's beauty, surged through him with redoubled strength.

The origins of this tragedy no longer mattered. The only thing that mattered was teaching these deceitful, murdering she-wolves a lesson they would never forget.

With his most ferocious war bellow, the hero lunged forward. A half-dozen spears, flung with deadly accuracy, met his charge, but they clattered harmlessly off the shaggy lionskin. Brandishing his sword, Heracles plunged into his opponents' midst. Valiantly the women fought back with sword and ax, circling and slashing as if they truly were wolves. But it was futile.

The magical properties that had once shielded the living beast from its enemies now shielded the man who wore its pelt. And for all his bulk, Heracles was amazingly light and quick on his feet. He had to be. The one real danger to him lay in being completely encircled, then attacked on his unprotected arms and legs.

To counter such a maneuver, he swung his arm with all its legendary might, disposing of his adversaries with obscene swipes of the long, blood-covered sword. One by one, the brave women met their deaths, and when the last of them had fallen, Heracles glanced about him, seeking to mark the progress of the main battle.

The outlying skirmishes had ceased as the savagely proficient Amazons overcame their Greek foes. Now the general mass of warriors had combined to drive the main body of men back to their ships. The Greeks were fighting desperately, but they were outnumbered and outmatched by these women who had studied warfare since the time they could walk. Roaring like the very lion whose skin he wore, Heracles ran to join his beleaguered comrades.

Seeing his furious approach gave new heart to the beset Greeks, and also aroused new ire in the breasts of the Amazons. Sending out their war cry, a contingent deployed itself to surround him with practiced ease. Dispensing with foolish battle pride, these warriors did not make the mistake of seeking to engage Heracles in single combat. Instead, they adopted the strategy of encirclement with more effectiveness than their fallen sisters.

Lightning swift and deadly as leopards, some leaped in and out in a slashing frontal attack, seeking to rivet the hero's attention. At the same time, others slipped behind him and, with the fluidity of eels, endeavored to capture the swinging ropelike tail or loosely dangling hind legs of the pelt, and yank it from Heracles's sweat-drenched body.

Like a bear defending itself in the midst of a wolf pack, Heracles whirled and spun on his massive legs, determinedly parrying every thrust and fending off with powerful blows of his sword each attempt to snatch at his armor. But he was beginning to tire. The breath tore out of him in hoarse grunts, and his face turned brick-red with the effort of his exertions.

His faltering did not go unnoticed. With reckless speed, Theseus, Peirthoos, and Telamon hacked themselves a path through the fray, and ran to protect their leader's sides and back. Heracles snatched at the precious opportunity for a respite. Bending forward, he placed his hands on his thighs and dragged great gulps of air into his lungs, then straightened and tucked the hind legs and tail of the lionskin into his belt.

As he regained his wind, the three bold Greek captains were being challenged. Theseus, Peirthoos, and Telamon found themselves fighting for their very lives, and it was with panting relief that they saw two more comrades— Tiamides and Cadmus—coming to their aid.

But as these last two joined the battle that swirled around Heracles, a young spear-woman named Pantariste marked their path. She had just seen her birth-mother collapse onto the sand—killed by Tiamides. And now, every fiber of Pantariste's being was on fire, thirsting with the hot desire for revenge. She worked away from the main combat, circling wide to come up on Tiamides from his left side.

Cadmus looked up and saw her, then sprang forward to meet her. With ferocious skill, Pantariste seized the shorter man by the hair and jerked him off his feet. Before Cadmus could twist free, her spear had ripped open his breast and his lifeblood flowed out to stain the trampled ground.

But another muscular Greek had already sprinted up out of nowhere, his sword raised and ready. Unable to free her spear, Pantariste leaped erect to face him. It would have gone hard with her had not a new battle yell shrilled through the deafening clamor.

Antiope, clad in a blue-starred tunic and without shield, her hair roughly tied back with a leather thong, hurtled through the press, her face a rigid mask of fury. The glittering curve of her battle-ax whined viciously, and Pantariste's attacker shrieked horribly as he fell, his body cut almost in half.

Pantariste raised her arm in a quick salute, retrieved her spear, and made for Tiamides. Above the shouts and screams, Tiamides somehow heard that single cry meant for him alone. Sensing his danger, he turned, but it was too late.

Even as he instinctively raised his shield, Pantariste tensed and her powerful arm became a blur of motion. Her enemy moved to cover himself too slowly; the mightily flung spear struck the edge of his shield, knocking it aside and thrusting onward to bury its lethal point deep in Tiamides's body. The death of her mother avenged, Pantariste swept up a discarded battle-ax and sped off to join the fighting by the ships.

Antiope, however, remained behind, slashing at one Greek foe after another. Seeing her thus, Theseus felt a crazy pain in his chest that had nothing to do with any external wound. It also gave him an impossibly daring idea. Somehow he managed to get close enough to shout into Heracles's ear. Nodding his great, dripping head in agreement, the hero roared out new orders to whatever men were within earshot.

Suddenly Antiope found herself at the center of an especially savage skirmish that resolved itself with her being surrounded by Greeks, one of whom she noted distantly was Theseus.

Eyes bright with rage, she launched herself at him, only to feel a burly arm roughly encircle her waist. She twisted with supple strength, almost succeeding in delivering a backward slice at her assailant, but other hands brutally wrested the battle-ax away and took her prisoner. Above her head, a bull-like roar erupted as Heracles bellowed at the top of his lungs.

"Get back, or your queen dies!"

Struggling against the cruel grasp of her antagonists, Antiope shrieked, "Don't listen! Kill them! Even if it means my death! Kill—"

Heracles's massive fist impacted solidly against her temple, and under Theseus's worried eyes, Antiope crumpled into silence. Screams of rage exploded around the group of beleaguered Greeks, and a throng of Amazons surged toward them in a lethal wave of ferocity. Heracles whipped up his bloody sword and pressed the tip against the unconscious Antiope's throat.

"Stop, or I'll slit her from ear to ear!" he thundered.

The warriors slowed and hesitated. Word of what had happened was spreading rapidly throughout their ranks, and the main body of women near the ships was turning its attention to this new drama. And not a moment too soon.

The harried Greeks were on the verge of a complete rout, and every man who still lived had resigned himself to joining his fallen comrades in the halls of the dead. Theseus's idea of taking Antiope hostage was nothing short of brilliant. It not only served his own purposes, but was very clearly the one possible way for the Greeks to leave Amazonia alive.

A path grudgingly opened through the muttering crowd of adversaries as Heracles and his train backed cautiously toward the ships, bearing the insensible Antiope with them. A number of Amazons had leaped aboard the galleys during the fighting, and a fierce battle had been raging between them and whatever Greeks had sought safety there.

Seeing the rows of enraged female faces along the railings of his fleet, the hero shouted, "You on the ships! Give up your weapons, if you want your queen to live!"

The warriors glanced uneasily at one another, but made no move to do as ordered. A bright drop of blood welled forth from Antiope's slender neck as Heracles pressed the sword-tip in harder.

"By my noble father, the mighty Zeus," he roared, "she'll die before we do!"

Still the warriors hesitated. To an Amazon, few things were more dishonorable than being forced to surrender her weapons. Then a new voice rang clearly and coldly through the gathering.

"Lay down your swords and battle-axes, my sisters on the ships. At least for now."

CHAPTER 13

～～ Just as Dorian had predicted, Thalassa healed rapidly, although the swiftness of her recovery was due as much to a fervent desire to escape the humiliation of lying helplessly in bed as it was to her natural strength. The savage defiance that had characterized her every action was gone, replaced by an air of morose pondering.

Silence sat on her, a silence of brooding and despair. Within that silence, the memories of her life paraded before her as though she were a ghost looking back from the land of the dead. She no longer flung herself about with the madness of an animal seeking escape from its cage, but her thoughts continued to hurl themselves against the unyielding walls of the evil fate enclosing her.

It was useless to go on attempting escape or death by her own hand. If sacred Artemis had willed this destiny upon her and that divine wish were disobeyed, Thalassa could expect the most dire of punishments to be visited on her in the afterlife. Yet it made no sense.

Artemis was the guardian of women, not men; a fierce

deity who had little use for males. Any man unlucky enough to stumble upon Her bathing in Her secret pool deep in the woods would be instantly transformed into a bear, hunted down, and killed.

Therefore, Great Mother, Thalassa prayed, *why have You decreed that I must dwell here, in this place of magic and dread, among strangers—to give up my precious freedom and honor to live with a member of the race of men; they who are ever seeking to destroy our kind, and—if the prophecy of his Elders is true—may be doing so even now while I stay here helpless? Why have You laid such a heavy lot upon the shoulders of one of Your faithful daughters? Why?*

Again and again, Thalassa's tormented mind howled these questions in anguish and confusion. But from the Goddess, there was no reply.

Physically well again, Thalassa wished only to find a dark corner and grieve over her lost life, as an injured beast in the woods crawls away to die. But this Dorian would not allow. He did not yet know her as well as he intended; nevertheless, there was something he already understood.

His golden lioness was a creature of movement, and her wounds could only be healed under the balm of constant action. Inured to hard exercise from birth, her body demanded it. Even though her mind wanted nothing more than to huddle in a ball of misery, she found herself given little opportunity to do so.

With determined cheerfulness, Dorian dragged her through every chamber of the exotic abode. Much of it Thalassa had seen before, but frantic with rage, she had paid little heed. Now she looked in awe at statues, murals, and furnishings more beautiful, she was sure, than any contained in the opulent palaces of either the Hittites or the Minoans. Most incredible were a dozen large rooms lined with alabaster shelves, each one of which held innumerable scrolls covered with writing and pictures.

Amazons did not read or write. Their history was passed from generation to generation solely through story-telling. Thalassa knew that writing existed. The Phoenicians, Greeks, Hittites, and Egyptians, who came to trade for Amazonian copper and gold, made various symbols on clay tablets or papyrus sheets. But she had never viewed anything like these elaborate scrolls, encompassing, Dorian explained, the entire history of the merfolk, in addition to every civilization that had thus far arisen on land.

The depth and power of these people was incontrovertible, and faced with example after example of it, Thalassa began to feel as insignificant as a fly seeking to light on the mane of a galloping horse. She looked on the things Dorian showed her with hostile, wondering eyes, saying very little, her reactions kept carefully to herself.

Yet, ever keenly intuitive, Dorian perceived in his chosen one the beginnings of a reluctant curiosity. Sensing she would make no further escape attempts, he eased his close guardianship. For short periods Thalassa found herself able to wander about as freely as any merman or woman.

It was a false freedom, of course, for she could not leave the abode. Nor did she wish to. The very mention of the interlocking chamber was enough to make her eyes glaze and set her limbs to trembling. Dorian's palace, cage though it was, had in some strange way become a sort of haven, a welcome barrier between herself and the terror of the *midnight sea*.

Still Thalassa distrusted her limited freedom, although Dorian had carefully explained the reasons for it. During her illness he had neglected his duties as king; now there were disputes awaiting his judgment, harvests of food and other riches from the sea to be supervised, and agreements to negotiate with the denizens who shared his watery kingdom.

While such tasks were normal for a ruler upon the land, imagining how they might be done *here* made Thalassa's head ache. And Dorian's reference to other seafolk sent shivers down her spine. If these others he spoke of were like the creatures she had already seen, she was overwhelmingly relieved that he did not demand she be at his side when he met with them.

So with caution, as though she expected Aricia or some other guard appointed by Dorian to prevent her, Thalassa began to explore the abode on her own. With Dorian busy at settling merfolk affairs, she could have acceded to her still strong desire to huddle in a corner and grieve. But vying with that need was one emotion she would not have expected—boredom. She was astonished that this should be so, and yet it was. The complete absence of all of her accustomed physical pursuits was fast becoming a torment. Not only did her body and mind cry out for stimulation, but sitting dully by herself gave her time to think—far too much time.

She often found herself drawn back to the marketplace Dorian had taken her to on that first day, so long ago it seemed when she thought of it now. It was one of the least threatening areas in the abode; one where she could satisfy the budding curiosity she felt toward her captor's people and yet remain unobtrusive.

The Barterers' Hall, as Dorian called it, was a busy and noisy place, full of color and commotion, shouts and laughter, heated arguments and the slap of palms as deals were struck. In this large, open chamber the abode's primary commerce occurred. All manner of things were traded: iridescent fish arranged on beds of wet seaweed; great stone tubs of seawater packed with crabs, lobsters, shrimp, clams, and oysters; alabaster tables laden with intricately crafted jewelry; sculptures, mosaics, paintings, statues, and colorfully illustrated scrolls crowded into stalls carved from red or black coral.

Despite the merfolk's penchant for nudity, Thalassa even saw clothing offered—beautifully draped tunics and robes that fluttered gaily in the rushing spray from the chamber's several fountains. There were numerous other items whose functions totally mystified her, and they continued to do so, for Thalassa was unwilling to ask questions or even to speak.

Yet it was evident that Dorian's kindred greatly desired to be hospitable. Men and women alike smiled, waved, made little bows of greeting, and in a dozen different ways showed their friendliness. Still Thalassa turned a wary face to all these signs of welcome. In silence she would appear in the great marketplace, and in silence she would remain, seated upon a bench near one of the fountains until Dorian came to fetch her.

The people were alien, their tongue utterly foreign, yet she took an odd comfort in the atmosphere of the Barterers'

Hall. It reminded her of when traders would visit Amazonia, spreading their wares on the sand to hawk them in the wheedling tone of merchants everywhere, even here, so far below the sea.

It was also in the marketplace that Thalassa saw her first merfolk children. Darting past the crowded stalls and tables, playing in the fountains, and begging samples from the food vendors, were boys and girls alike, healthy and active.

They were few in number, though, and that made Thalassa uneasy. Although Dorian had never broached the subject of children with her, she was well aware of a ruler's need for heirs. Even the Amazons, despite mating only once a year, required their queens to produce daughters in order to carry on the royal blood. Was that why Dorian needed a woman from the land so badly, because his own kinswomen could not breed sufficient offspring?

During her third visit to the Barterers' Hall, when she was brooding upon that very question, one of the children approached her. She was a tall, coltish girl of perhaps eleven or twelve summers, though with the incomprehensible age of these people it was hard to tell. She was naked, as all the children were, with disheveled light-brown hair that hung almost to her waist and bright green eyes. Around her sun-browned neck hung a magnificent necklace of emeralds set in heavy gold, an ornament that contrasted oddly with her urchinlike appearance.

"Lady?" The girl tentatively held something out to Thalassa. "Would you like one of my *lobash* tails?"

When Thalassa hesitated, the child added in a coaxing voice, "It is already cracked, so all you need do is pick out the meat. See?"

She held the bright orange appendage of what appeared to be a shellfish closer. Her eyes glowed with such an eager and hopeful friendliness, Thalassa could not bring herself to refuse. She took the unfamiliar object and said gruffly, "Thank you."

The girl did not move. "Are you not going to try it?"

Thalassa reached into the vividly colored shell and plucked out some of the white flesh. Slowly she ate it. It was delicious, as tender and sweet as anything she had ever tasted. She sampled some more.

The girl was watching her anxiously. "Does it please you?"

Thalassa smiled slightly. "It is very good."

A delighted grin broke out on the girl's face, and she thrust a big handful of *lobash* meat from the other tail she held into her mouth. "*Lobash* is one of my favorite foods," she confided, chewing busily. "Is this the first time you have eaten it?"

"I have no idea." Thalassa picked absently at the brittle shell. She truly didn't know. Since being brought there she had given up trying to identify all the strange foods Dorian had courteously but firmly forced upon her.

"My mother says that even though your birth-people live beside Mother Ocean they eat almost none of Her bounty. I think that is very strange. What sort of foods could they find to eat that are better than what the sea provides?"

Thalassa gave the girl a sharp look. "And did your mother also teach you to ask disrespectful questions of those who are supposed to be guests here?"

The child looked stricken. "Indeed not, Lady. I . . . I did not mean to offend. Please do not be angry, I am truly sorry—"

"Never mind." Thalassa took another bite of *lobash* and sighed. "What is your name, girl?"

The eager friendliness back on her face, the child said quickly, "I am called Lisala, my lady."

"Well, Lisala"—Thalassa stumbled a little over the pronunciation of the unfamiliar name—"you speak the Amazon tongue well for one so young. How came you to learn it?"

Lisala seemed puzzled by the question. "I wanted to talk with you, that is all. And Mother said I must do so in the Amazon tongue, for you do not yet know our language. Are the folk of land not able to speak with each other even if their languages are different?"

"Not easily," Thalassa said, studying her suspiciously. "At least not as easily as your kind seem to. I have never heard of being able to speak a strange tongue simply because one *wanted* to."

"Truly? I heard an Elder say once that landfolk possess as many different languages as there are spines on a sea urchin. If you cannot understand each other it must be very confusing. Of course . . ." Lisala munched reflectively on her *lobash*. "Even among us some are better at languages than others." She giggled. "Valya speaks your birth-tongue poorly. I heard him when the lord Dorian brought you here to the Barterers' Hall for the first time. I laughed until my stomach hurt!"

"Daughter!"

Thalassa jumped. A tall robust woman was striding toward them, an older version of Lisala, even to the heavy emerald necklace around her throat. But unlike the mer-child's merry eyes, this woman's green gaze was stern.

"What kind of manners are these?" she demanded in flawless Amazonian. "To entertain yourself at another's expense because his ability in a certain area is not the equal of yours? You shame me, child." She turned to Thalassa. "I apologize for the behavior of my daughter, Lady. You must excuse her, for she is yet a babe, having barely seen the passage of her first hundred seasons."

Seasons? thought Thalassa. Could the woman mean *years*? She swallowed and said nothing. Misunderstanding her silence, the woman gestured to the furiously blushing Lisala. "Come, child. She wishes to be by herself and we are intruding. Let us leave."

"No, wait." The words popped out before Thalassa realized it, surprising her as much as them. She did not want these unexpected visitors to leave. Lisala's friendliness had knocked a chink in the protective armor with which she had surrounded herself, easing not only Thalassa's boredom, but something she found even more difficult to acknowledge—her loneliness. "Your daughter does not offend me," she said with difficulty, and was rewarded with brilliant smiles from both Lisala and her mother.

"In that case"—the woman plopped herself down on the stone bench—"a short rest would be welcome indeed. This has been one of my busier trading days." She turned to her daughter. "Lisala, run over to Rodan's stall and fetch me one of those *lobash* tails—a nice fat one—and a goblet of *vishnak*. And make sure the *lobash* he gives you is from the bottom of the tub, not the top." A disgusted look passed over the woman's strongly featured face. In a confidential tone she explained to Thalassa, "Sometimes he'll take the tails from the day before and put them on the top layer to pass off as fresh."

Lisala grimaced. "I'll go, Mother, but he will ask me again when the armbands and earrings are to be ready. He asked me when I went to get these." She waved her half-eaten *lobash* tail in the air.

The woman snorted. "Let him ask. You tell him the order he contracted for will be ready on the evetide of the next full moon as agreed upon, and not a moment before. Go now, child. I missed my mid-meal and am perishing of hunger."

When Lisala had darted off through the milling throng, the woman shifted to a more comfortable position on the bench. "She has a good heart, my daughter, but she is young and the words leave her mouth before the thoughts behind them have reached her brain."

Thalassa nodded. It surprised her how comfortable she felt with these two foreigners, though perhaps there was reason for it. It would have taken a harder heart than Thalassa possessed to rebuff Lisala's disarming warmth, and the bluff, open manner of the girl's mother was a poignant reminder of the many older warriors she had grown up around. "How will she pay for the food you have sent for her?" she asked curiously.

"Pay? Ah yes, pay. Well, Lady, we have no purpose for money. What would we do with coins of gold and silver, unless we used them to make jewelry or other ornaments? In our world we trade for what we need or desire, just as landfolk often do. Of course, our customs are different. For example, the members of my clan arrange what we call contracts—long-term arrangements during which we receive goods or services from our customers until we deliver the items they have requested."

The woman grimaced. "It is such an arrangement that I have with Rodan the Gatherer. Although that one is a pushy sort, always seeking to get more out of a contract than was originally agreed upon. Still, he is very fond of decking himself out, so I suppose I mustn't complain."

This last part made little sense to Thalassa. She puzzled over it as the woman said, "By the way, I am called MoAt." There was a polite pause. The woman was apparently waiting for Thalassa to give her own name in return, but Thalassa remained silent. MoAt finally shrugged and said, "I am of the Artisan *Stratum*."

Thalassa looked even more confused, and the merwoman frowned. "Has the lord Dorian told you nothing of the Eight *Strata*?"

"He may have mentioned it," Thalassa said reluctantly. She was sure, in fact, that he had. Overwhelmed as she was by all that had happened to her, though, she had paid little attention.

"Well," MoAt said heartily, "one in your place can hardly be expected to pay heed to such things, at least at first. In any case, all merfolk belong to one or more of the Eight *Strata,* which are"—she ticked them off on her fingers—"Barterers, Historians, Gatherers, Teachers, Healers, Elders, Artisans, and the Ruling House. Both my mother and father—may their spirits find favorable currents in the Sea Beyond—were Artisans, and I have been content to follow their calling, though to do so is not required of us. Lisala, for instance probably will not take up my *stratum*. She has shown little interest in it thus far."

Thalassa gave the woman a bewildered glance. Among the Amazons there were individuals who showed a particular aptitude for, say, the breeding of horses or the growing of especially fine grain. But while such pursuits were acknowledged as critical to the survival of the tribe, they were secondary to the all-important occupation of becoming a warrior. Amazon girls had no say in this matter. It was simply expected, in the same way the sun was expected to rise in the morning and set in the evening.

To be given a choice as to whether or not one wished to learn the arts of her elders was . . . well, it was unnatural, Thalassa decided. "But should she not do as you bid her?" she asked. "You are her mother after all, and a mother knows better than her daughter what is best."

MoAt smiled. "Is it best for a parent to force a son or daughter into doing something the child dislikes and has no talent for? That is not our way, Lady. Our lifetimes last a great deal longer than those of the people of the land. There is time for us to master more than one *stratum* during the span of our years if we desire it. Lisala is not interested in working with fine metals now, but who knows? In a few centuries she may decide to learn her mother's craft."

"You are a metalsmith?" Thalassa looked at the woman with increased respect. "Do you make weapons?"

"I can, yes, but I do so only rarely. Here there is little need for such things, except as novelty items. Ah, the child returns at last with my meal."

Thalassa looked up to see Lisala threading her way through the crowded marketplace, a heavily laden tray wavering precariously in both hands. Reaching them she said excitedly, "When Rodan heard with whom we were talking, he sent along extra. He is delighted that you enjoyed the *lobash*, Lady, and urges you to try his *vishnak*. He says you will taste none better were you to visit every abode in every sea."

"He would say that," MoAt muttered, selecting one of three alabaster goblets, all of them brimming with a frothy liquid that foamed pale red over the polished rims. The merwoman drank deeply, smacked her lips as she placed the goblet on the bench, then began to pull apart her *lobash* tail. "He does make a fine *vishnak*, though," she said through a full mouth. "You should try it, Lady."

Thalassa ignored the tray and its contents, staring instead at MoAt with amazement. "Do you mean that there are more dwellings—more places beneath the sea—more than just this one?" she asked in consternation.

Mother and daughter looked at each other in surprise. "Why, of course there are," MoAt exclaimed. "Surely you did not think the merfolk were so few in number?"

By the expression on Thalassa's face it was evident that she had, and the merwoman shook her head. "Has the lord Dorian told you nothing? Mother Ocean is composed of many different seas, and within each sea there are a multitude of abodes, some of them small and others much larger. This one is, of course, the largest and most ornate, for it is the Royal Abode, the ancestral home of Dorian's clan, they who form the *stratum* of the Ruling House."

Thalassa was speechless. It shouldn't matter, she told

herself. The Goddess had decided her fate, regardless of how great or how few in number her captor's people were. Yet for some reason it did matter. Just as she was beginning to take the first tiny steps in adjusting to this bizarre existence, it was daunting to discover that the vast ocean was virtually filled with these godlike beings and their strange habitations. It made the mysteries of Dorian's world all the more frightening.

MoAt touched her arm with a sympathetic hand. "I have upset you, which was certainly not my intention. Perhaps—"

"It does not matter." Thalassa pulled her arm away and grabbed one of the goblets off the tray. The frothy drink was refreshing, ice-cold, and had a pleasant tang that indicated it must contain fruit of some sort. She gulped it down, then asked, "If you do not use your skills to make weapons, then what do you make?"

"She makes jewelry." Lisala's young voice vibrated with pride. "Some of the finest in all the seas. Look."

The girl leaned forward so Thalassa could better see her necklace. It was indeed beautiful, but she was disappointed that MoAt's obvious skill in metalsmithing should be wasted on baubles. She was about to say this when something in the necklace's glittering design caught her eye.

The two largest stones at first glance were merely emeralds. Peering more closely, Thalassa saw they were the eyes of a creature, an animal depicted so perfectly within the necklace's gold background that she recognized it as an otter, like the ones that inhabited the river Thermodon at home. She would not have expected these people of the sea to be familiar with animals that stayed within the boundaries of land. Putting out a hesitant finger, she touched the gleaming surface.

"Do your people know all the beasts of water, then?" she asked. "Whether they live in the sea, or the rivers and streams of land?"

"No—" MoAt started to say, when Lisala broke in.

"But this is a creature of the sea, Lady. It is a giant sea otter—"

"Child," MoAt admonished gently. She smiled at

Thalassa. "I know that otters live within the waters of land, but there is also a different and larger type that make their homes in the cold salt seas far to the north. Those waters are the wander grounds of my clan. Otters are lovely beings. I use them quite a bit in my art."

"Look closer," Lisala invited. "My mother creates more than just otters."

Thalassa studied the necklace. She saw that the otter was indeed only the centerpiece of a vastly detailed pattern that spiraled through every facet of the heavy necklace. Fish, long, streaming plants, birds, and a myriad of smaller otters writhed and danced in the glowing metal. And that was not all. Within each creature or plant twisted a smaller design and within that another, and then another, until they became so small it seemed impossible that human hands could have crafted such incredible detail.

Even the emeralds told stories, their jeweled depths reflecting tiny secretive beings that smiled at Thalassa from the green fire of an otter's eyes. She stared until her own eyes watered, and still she could not look away.

"Is it not beautiful?" Lisala asked in a pleased voice.

"It is extraordinary." And Thalassa meant it. "Never have I seen anything like it."

"You honor me." MoAt's tone was modest, the voice of a master who knows her work is superior and therefore has no need to boast. "I began it on the day of my daughter's birth, just as my mother began one for me."

"Requests are made far and wide for her creations, Lisala boasted. "Why even the lord Dorian himself has commissioned her to make your—"

She stopped abruptly, and glancing up, Thalassa saw that MoAt's cold stare had silenced the girl. "Make my what?" she asked pointedly.

MoAt sighed. "My daughter's tongue runs away with her thoughts once again. The lord Dorian has asked me to design the Jewels of Matebonding for you and him. When the time is right, of course."

Thalassa looked at her, knowing she should ask what the woman was talking about. Yet, did she truly want to know? Learning of the Sea Spell from Valya and his companions had been bad enough. And by their very title she could well imagine what the purpose of these jewels might be.

Shifting on the hard stone bench, she hastily changed the subject. "Are there a great many of you living within the sea?"

"Enough," said MoAt.

Thalassa frowned at her. "But if your people live forever as gods do, then how is it your numbers do not increase until even the sea is no longer large enough to contain you?"

"Merfolk do not live forever, Lady." MoAt gazed at the new queen with puzzlement. Her lack of knowledge about her new home, as well as her persistent refusal to identify herself as one of the merfolk, was unexpected. The king's chosen mate did not behave like one who had had the Sea Spell placed upon her. Indeed, the ties that bound her to land seemed largely unaffected, and MoAt found that very curious.

These were the lord Dorian's matters, though, the Artisan reminded herself with a mental shrug, and surely he must know what he was doing. "We only conceive children when there is a need to increase our numbers," she explained. "Thus we remain in harmony with the world of Mother Ocean."

Reassured, Thalassa nodded. At last something about these people made a small measure of sense. Like the Amazons, they lay together infrequently, and only then in accordance with ritual. If that were so, she might be spared—at least for a time—the indignity of Dorian's physical attentions. She smiled in her relief and said, "My people, too, mate but once a year."

Lisala and MoAt looked at her strangely. Lisala was opening her mouth to speak when MoAt said smoothly, "Well, the end of this trading day beckons and there is business to be taken care of before it does. Lisala, child, take this tray back to Rodan. Make sure you thank him for his generosity, and then come and help me."

Lisala's mouth turned down. "Could I not stay here instead?" she begged.

"No, child. The hour grows late and we have monopolized enough of the new queen's time as it is."

The relief Thalassa had been feeling evaporated. To hear herself referred to as a queen! She could pretend not to hear when Dorian's royal sister, or even Dorian himself, called her that. But to realize that MoAt—so much like an Amazon herself—thought of her in such a way sharpened the reality of Thalassa's position with terrifying clarity. Brooding and apprehensive once more, she responded absently to Lisala and MoAt's farewells, barely hearing Lisala's hopeful promise to visit with her again.

The Barterers' Hall was emptying, those who had come there to transact business packing up their goods and departing to wherever it was they disappeared to at the end of the trading day. Among the last to leave were the purveyors of shellfish, shouldering their stone tubs as though the heavy vats were made of air, and calling cheerfully to one another as they headed for the many arching doorways that led from the hall. A few of them stopped to speak with someone who had just appeared, a tall figure Thalassa recognized instantly. Dorian.

He walked toward her, pausing occasionally to exchange a word with this person or that. His powerful body was mantled in the glittering cape of kingly office, its long folds sweeping about his ankles as he walked. But his sleek black head was bare of its crown, which relieved Thalassa. Dorian made her nervous enough as it was, and with that wide gleaming band of gold and black stones set upon his head, he was almost unbearably imposing.

"Greetings, my sweet," he said upon reaching her. "Have you had a pleasant day?"

Still seated on the bench, Thalassa looked up at him. Her awakening curiosity struggled against her desire to remain insulated by whatever small measure of ignorance was left to her. The curiosity won. "And what might these Jewels of Matebonding be?" she asked bluntly.

CHAPTER 14

〜 Dorian hesitated for a moment before answering Thalassa. "I had heard," he said finally, "that you passed a pleasant visit with the Artisan MoAt and her daughter. MoAt would not be intemperate enough to mention such a subject, so her youngling must have broached it. What did Lisala say before her mother stopped her tongue?"

His assessment of what had happened was so accurate, Thalassa was nonplussed. "Just that you had commissioned the woman her mother to make them," she managed to say, and glanced away from his piercing eyes.

She regretted having brought this up at all. Her first instinct in not questioning MoAt or Lisala regarding the jewels had been correct. To ask about such things, particularly of Dorian of all people, was a mistake. She saw that clearly now. Far from being disturbed, as he had been when learning she knew of the Sea Spell, Dorian seemed unconcerned, even pleased by her inquiry. And this in itself was worrisome, as was the speculative way in which the man was looking at her.

"It is a bit premature to be discussing the Jewels of Matebonding," he said. "There are other events which must take place first."

The silky undercurrent in his voice sent a shiver down her spine. She gazed steadfastly about the room, fixing her attention on the last remaining folk, three traders in statuary who stood gossiping near the smallest fountain. Lisala and her mother had been among the first to depart the Barterers' Hall. Thalassa wished now that she had gone with them.

She shivered again as Dorian asked, "Have you no interest in knowing what those other events are?"

"No," she snapped. "I have not!"

Dorian smiled slightly. He had not intended discussing the Jewels of Matebonding with his chosen one for some time yet. The exchange of them was the very last step in the lengthy process of making Thalassa his own, and it would most certainly be years before MoAt had crafted pieces worthy of being worn by the royal king and queen. But though her awareness of the jewels was not his doing, Dorian found himself glad—no, delighted—that the matter had arisen.

He lowered himself onto the bench, pretending not to notice how Thalassa stiffened and edged away from him. "I can tell you this much," he said. "The Jewels of Matebonding are a gift, an exchange of love from one person to the other. And an important part in the development of such feelings is, of course, making love."

Thalassa stared at the three traders who still stood by the fountain. Misreading the intensity of her expression they flashed uncertain smiles at her, exchanged glances, and walked hurriedly from the hall, leaving her alone with Dorian.

In the absence of the traders' voices, the music of the fountains suddenly became louder, echoing through the deserted chamber so that Thalassa could almost believe she had not heard Dorian correctly.

"You are so quiet, Lady," he murmured. "Have you nothing to say?" Silence answered him. "Do you understand what lovemaking is, Thalassa?"

"I do indeed!" Her tone was sharp, disguising, she hoped, the fact that she spoke from bravado more than actual knowledge. Only once had she heard the mating act referred to as "making love," and then it had been Oreithyia using the term, the war queen's voice harsh with derision as she mocked the absurd notion of love being in any way connected with the physical business of getting daughters. As if he understood this, Dorian cocked a black eyebrow.

"You surprise me, then," he said, "for I would not think your birth-people would consider it as such."

"They do not—I mean *we* do not . . ." Thalassa's thoughts were fragmenting under Dorian's steady blue gaze. She jumped to her feet. "I must go."

"Why?" The folds of his robe whispering about him, Dorian rose also. "Does speaking of this cause you unease?"

You know it does! she thought. "Of course not. I merely tire of sitting on this bench, that is all. Indeed, I grow tired of a great many things, not the least of which is lazing about with nothing to do! By the Goddess, my body is coming to disgust me. It grows soft and white as new milk from being shut up in this place. If I am not able to feel the sun and get some exercise soon, I vow I shall go mad!"

The words had burst unbidden from her lips. With a defiance tinged by embarrassment, she scowled at Dorian before turning on her heel to stomp toward the nearest doorway.

A considering expression on his face, Dorian watched the sword-straight figure stalk away from him. He was neither deceived nor upset by her outburst. He well understood the reasons behind it. But his own needs, which despite the demands of the Elders he had been determined to hold in check while Thalassa adjusted, were fighting their way to the surface, growing harder and harder to ignore. . . .

He caught up to her just outside the wide doorway. "I quite understand your frustration," he said. "I wanted you to grow healthy and strong again, you see. I did not realize your convalescence had become such a burden."

"I am perfectly well," she said in a surly voice. "You need not treat me as if I were some weak-footed sop of an invalid."

He smiled. "Then I shall strive not to do so."

Thalassa glanced down the corridor. A man and woman were strolling toward them. As they drew closer, she saw with surprise that the man was carrying a baby, strapped into a holder of some kind upon his back. Smiling at her, they stopped to speak with Dorian for a moment.

Snug in its cradle, the baby waved tiny fists in the air. Thalassa studied the infant nervously. It was impossible to tell if the child was male or female, but the small creature looked as normal as any other baby she had ever seen. The sight of this particular infant, however, was an uncomfortable reminder of the mating act. The mating act that Dorian apparently wished to engage in with her. *Making love*.

She shifted her weight from one foot to the other, relieved when the little family had continued on down the hall but more nervous than ever at the speculative look on Dorian's face. "Is there always such perfect peace among your people?" she demanded testily. "Are there no battles here? Do none of you fight or struggle against *anything*? Surely there must be dangers to face, enemies of *some* kind that need killing. If I am to live here I will doubtless wither away from the dullness of this kingdom you rule over!"

Somewhat startled, Dorian gazed down at her. "Merfolk have developed differently from folk of the land, Thalassa. To us, being one with Mother Ocean is all-important. Conquest or violence toward one another is frowned upon and rarely, if ever, seen." His mouth twisted contemptuously. "Conquering lands, developing superior weapons, increasing territories, amassing wealth, and acquiring power—all those are Terran desires, not merfolk ones. We have no interest in such nonsense."

But Thalassa was unconvinced. "Have your people always lived in this fashion?" she asked skeptically. "Without wars or even the mildest of strife?"

"For the most part, yes."

"Then perhaps you should find some ways to make the passing of life in this world of yours more interesting!"

Dorian eyed her sternly. "Merfolk are not the only advanced people within the sea, Lady," he said, and there was a quiet, cold absoluteness in his voice. "The whalefolk, the grayfolk, and the Selkies have also lived in the same manner for millennia. They have never seen a need to change, and neither do we. Their ways and ours are timeless, blending harmoniously with the ancient rhythms of the sea. To live within the Mother and to follow the endless patterns of the tides, as every creature of the sea, from the simplest to the most complex, does, is all we require.

"The merfolk will not change, Thalassa, any more than the Mother will alter the times at which she sends forth her tides. We are not like the people of land. Remember that."

The ocean, with all its vast and chilling weight, seemed embodied in his imperious words. Suddenly Thalassa felt foolish and uncertain, not only of this enigmatic man-being, but of herself as well. She stared down the winding corridor. "I am not likely to forget it," she whispered.

"Well, then." Dorian's tone lightened. "There are pursuits enough to occupy you if you are so inclined. Our Historians, who spend their days chronicling what goes on in both sea and land, would be more than delighted to teach you how to read and write. Then you could understand the fascinating things contained in the scrolls they create. Or if you wish to see how we prepare food or learn about the harvestings, there are those among the Gatherers who would be happy to speak with you. Perhaps there are skills among the Artisans that you would like to learn—"

"Only one," she interrupted. "The making of weapons."

"And for the physical testing of our bodies," he continued as if he had not heard, "we have chambers set aside where we wrestle and engage in other forms of strong exercise." His gaze lingered on her. "Although to me, your body does not look flabby and soft as you fear it does, my sweet."

Thalassa swallowed hard, at a loss for words as she always was when his voice took on that disconcerting murmur that was so much like a caress. Desperately afraid of what his next words might be and determined to forestall them, she said in as unpleasant a tone as she could call up, "Leave me alone. I have no desire to look upon your face a moment longer."

She turned her back, only to feel strong hands descend upon her shoulders as Dorian pulled her around to face him.

"But, sweet Lady," he said, and though his voice remained soft, there was a glint of anger—or even hurt—in his eyes. "What of my desires?"

Every muscle in Thalassa's body tensed. "Satisfy them with someone else."

Now it was most definitely anger that glittered in his eyes. "I intend to satisfy them with you, Thalassa. To-night."

At the expression on her face, Dorian could have struck himself. He had not meant to use his power with such callous disregard, had not planned that this night would be the one on which he brought Thalassa to his bed. He had only intended to discover how much, if anything, she knew about lovemaking, and to begin getting her used to the idea. Yet, the words had been spoken and he would not—*could not*—take them back. He was too selfish, his drive to join body and mind with hers too strong.

For so long now, he had been filled with the wanting of this woman. Made more sensitive by that wanting, he'd been caught off guard by her harsh refusal. You're a fine one, he reproached himself. A callow youth could have handled this better.

But however poor his methods, he had a compelling reason beyond his own need for joining with Thalassa. Healed from her illness, the physical adaptation to his world complete, she was ready to enter the sea again. Only the barrier of her fear prevented it. Making love to her—mentally as well as physically—would provide him with the means to remove the fear, or at least control it so she could be reintroduced to the ocean safely.

"I have restrained myself with you, sweeting," he said gently. "Perhaps more than is wise, considering the circumstances. Now, though, it is time for us to get on with the business of learning about each other. And lovemaking is part of it. An important part, Thalassa."

He waited, hoping for a response. Even a show of further anger or defiance would have been welcome. But Thalassa stared dumbly at him, her expression one which he unhappily likened to horror. At length, he sighed. "Perhaps some time alone might be good for you, after all. I have some matters to attend to. You could have something to eat—"

"I am not hungry."

Her voice was almost inaudible, and he sighed again. "Very well, then. Wander where you please. I will join you in a little while."

Before she could draw back he bent and touched his lips lightly to her forehead, then strode off down the hall. Heart pounding, palms slick with sweat, Thalassa watched him go. The relief she had felt over the infrequent mating habits of the merfolk had been short-lived indeed. It was upsetting, though inevitable, that this man whom the Goddess had ordained should carry her off would in time take her to his bed. But that it should be tonight!

Yet it was not the idea of physical coupling that disturbed Thalassa. The love aspect—or lack of it—aside, there was no secrecy about such matters among the Amazons. All her life Thalassa had seen animals mate, had listened when older sisters spoke matter-of-factly about their spring meetings with the Gargarians. No, it was not the act that disturbed her. It was the implications behind it.

Going off to the mountains to couple randomly in the dark with strangers was one thing. That was how it should be between Amazons and men: reproduction for the sake of strengthening the tribe through the begetting of daughters, and nothing more.

Dorian had made it quite clear that he desired something entirely different. He wanted a mate, and who knew what that meant among these people? Surely a great deal more than she wished to give, Thalassa thought savagely. And yet, if the Goddess intended for her to stay there, She must also intend for her to lie with Dorian.

The glimmering stone wall was cool against Thalassa's back, and she reluctantly pushed herself away. With the exception of the couple and their baby, the corridor had remained deserted while she and Dorian talked. Almost as if, she mused, his people knew the subject of their discussion and had wished to give them privacy. Now, a few people appeared in the hall, but though they looked at Thalassa as they passed, they did not speak. To her their glances seemed filled with sympathy, and she shivered, her trepidation increasing.

The minutes bore down upon her, crushing her spirit. What would she do, where could she go, while awaiting the moment when Dorian summoned her? There was no place in the abode where she could hide that he would not find her. For a desperate instant she considered the interlocking chamber, but quickly thrust that thought aside. In all truth, her dread of Dorian and what he might do to her was exceeded only by her panic at facing the ghastly blackness outside the abode.

Aimlessly she walked down the corridor. There seemed to be no alternative to what lay ahead. That very night the godlike man would make her sleep with him, and she dare not refuse lest she incur the Mother's displeasure.

As she walked, an insidious idea coiled through Thalassa's thoughts. What if lovemaking possessed a different meaning under the sea than it did upon the land? Perhaps Dorian had not been speaking about the act of mating at all, but of something far more ominous.

What if he burnt her to a cinder the moment his body pierced hers, the way she had heard Zeus the Greek man-god had incinerated Semele, a mortal woman who had insisted he show himself to her in his true form?

Could it be one of the Moon-Goddess's mysteries that Her daughter was to be delivered up as some sort of offering to this unearthly race of beings?

The more Thalassa thought on this, the more it seemed the only possible explanation. Now, the sympathetic glances of the passersby made chilling sense, as did MoAt's reaction when Lisala had mentioned the mysterious Jewels of Matebonding. Obviously the jewels formed part of some ritual, the end result of which would be her sacrifice.

Clumsy with nerves, Thalassa stumbled, trying to decide which would be worse. To die as a sacrifice, or to live on as a slave? At least death would bring an end to this nightmare. It was not an honorable end, the way dying in battle would be, but it was better than slavery.

She lost track of how long she wandered the corridors in silent contemplation of her fate. When Dorian came to take her hand and lead her to his bedchamber, her fatalism was complete. And in some way, it was a relief. In other circumstances, she would have fought him tooth and nail, but she was a daughter of sacred Artemis, and bonds lay upon her.

If it be the Goddess's desire that she sacrifice her body, and perhaps her life in the service of some mystery beyond mortal comprehension, then there was nothing more to be said, she told herself, and entered Dorian's chamber with back straight and head held high.

CHAPTER 15

～～ Observing Thalassa's rigid stance, Dorian could not keep from chuckling. Since leaving her earlier his mood had greatly improved, the chagrin he felt over his harsh ultimatum giving way to an ever-increasing excitement at what this night would bring.

"Storm and waves, Lady," he teased. "You look as if I'm about to devour you. Surely, you don't still believe I mean you harm, do you?"

Thalassa stared at the brilliantly colored sea fresco adorning the wall in front of her and said nothing. With an audible sigh, Dorian took her hand again. "Come and sit down," he suggested. "I promise I will endeavor not to offend you."

Stiff and silent, she let herself be guided to a small couch, carved in ebony and piled with soft cushions. A round enameled table, whose four legs were crafted in the shape of sea horses, sat next to it, bearing a delicate, jeweled carafe and two matching goblets. Thalassa watched as Dorian filled both chalices and offered her one.

"Take it," he urged, a smile lurking about the corners of

his mouth. "I will drink from mine first if you like, so that you may satisfy yourself it's not poisoned."

Nearly trembling with apprehension and the desperate need just to get this over with, she glanced from the sparkling goblets to his warm eyes. "There is no need to ply me with drink," she said. "Do whatever it is you wish to do and be done with it."

"And what is it that you think I wish to do?" he asked in some surprise.

"There is also no need to treat me as a fool. It is obvious even to a child that you intend sacrificing me to your gods in a mating ritual—"

"A *what*?"

"Therefore, cease toying with me and get on with it. I am prepared. But believe me, no matter what you do, I will at least deny you the satisfaction of hearing me cry out."

Thunderstruck, Dorian stared at Thalassa's pale, set face. Then he was torn between laughter and the impulse to gather her into his arms and provide lavish reassurances. Realizing that neither would be advisable, he held onto his composure and forced himself to speak calmly.

"Lady, I do not recall doing or saying anything that would place such a thought in your mind. In any case, such evil practices are unknown among my people. Why, I would no more hurt you than I would myself!"

She merely looked at him in disbelieving silence, and he tried another tack. "Where in the name of all the gods did you get the idea that I wished to *sacrifice* you? I've told you repeatedly how I brought you here to live in health and happiness as my mate—certainly not as an offering to some bloodthirsty deity!"

Thalassa heard him out in more than a little consternation. The shock on his face and in his voice convinced her he was telling the truth. She was overwhelmed with ambivalence.

If he wasn't going to offer her to his gods, then that meant he would indeed lie with her as a man lies with a woman. She would not be burned to a cinder when he penetrated her with his man's part, but neither would she be freed from this captivity by the finality of death. Instead she would be forced to sleep with him again and again, like a helpless prisoner of the spear or a slave, sold in the marketplace to the highest bidder.

Yet for some unfathomable reason, the Goddess had willed this to be so, and Thalassa glumly reminded herself of the penalties that could befall her for disobeying divine will.

Dorian's gaze was roving across her face, as if to search out and capture her thoughts. "Indulge my curiosity," he said abruptly. "If you believed such a terrible fate lay in store, why did you intend to submit so tamely to it? You, who are so determined a fighter and competent a warrior?"

She looked away without answering. It was bad enough that this was happening. She certainly did not need to add to her humiliation by allowing the man to see her inner torment. Astonishingly lifelike dolphins and seals cavorted through the wide mural ornamenting the arched ceiling, and she gazed at them with wistful envy, wishing herself anywhere else.

"Is it because you still think me a god?" he asked.

Silence.

Dorian thought of her life and the belief systems of her people, searching for some clue that would explain this baffling turn of events. "I know your people sometimes sacrifice male captives to Artemis," he said. "Is it because of this custom that you felt I had such a fate in mind for you?"

Still no answer. Dorian shook his head. He went back over all the conversations he and Thalassa had held since her abduction, and a hunch suddenly occurred to him. "Your very name means 'sea,'" he said slowly. "That in itself is highly uncommon among your tribe. How did you come by it?"

She continued to stare fixedly at the mural, but he saw the way her body tensed.

"Did your Goddess bestow it upon you?" he asked. "Has She somehow ordered you to submit to being a sacrifice because of your name?"

His probing questions had unerringly placed him within reach of the truth, and Thalassa felt the last shreds of her privacy ripped away like bandages torn roughly from an open wound.

"What possible difference does any of this make?" she burst out. "Am I not here as you wish? Take my body then, and be done with it!"

The air between them quivered with the intensity of her pain, and Dorian shook his head again. "Taking you is the furthest thing from my mind, dear one," he said quietly. "And I want far more from you than just your body. Now come. Drink with me."

He proffered the goblet once more, and this time, Thalassa took it. She stared suspiciously at the luminescent liquid for a moment, then gulped the entire contents in one swallow. It was an appalling breach of courtesy to drink before one's host did, but could this man really be considered a host?

Unlike the fruity *vishnak,* this unfamiliar liquid burned all the way down to her toes. Thalassa tried to decide what it reminded her of. It tasted like neither wine nor mead, but something totally unknown—sweet and strong, with subtle hints and flavors that teased the palate and made her mouth tingle. Seemingly oblivious to her lack of manners, Dorian reached over and politely refilled her cup. It occurred to Thalassa that he was seeking to make her drunk. She downed the second goblet the way she had the first, and smiled cynically as he filled it a third time.

"I see there is at least one thing about us that you approve of," he said in amusement. "But take care, Lady. Our drink is heady stuff and it creeps up on one unawares."

"You'd like that, wouldn't you?" She glowered down at the sparkling drink. "Well, it won't happen. We are taught from childhood to handle strong drink."

It was true. Oreithyia and every war queen before her had a standing policy that all young girls develop good heads for alcohol, to protect them from men who might seek to take advantage of them in just such a way. Schooled on a potent mead made from mare's milk, the average Amazon could drink the average man into a stupor with little or no difficulty.

Unconcerned, Thalassa tossed off the third goblet, eyeing Dorian in morose challenge as she did so. He did not fill her chalice right away, but gazed at her meditatively as he sipped his own drink.

"Is the prospect of entering my bed so terrible a thing?" he asked after a moment. "Amazons do sleep with the men of neighboring tribes in order to get daughters, just as you would have done had I not found you."

Smiling, he added lightly, "And despite whatever fears you may have to the contrary, I am physically no different from landmen when it comes to lovemaking. So tell me, little one, why do I frighten you?"

Thalassa turned her head away from his beguiling gaze, focusing her attention once more on the ceiling mural. The dolphins and seals, to her surprise, were wavering and moving as if they were really swimming. She blinked fiercely to make them stop, and wondered for the dozenth time how it was that this creature knew so much about Amazons. "You don't frighten me," she said curtly.

"Ah, but I do, my tawny lioness. I frighten you dreadfully. But because you are a warrior, you hide it, and because for some strange reason, you have decided you must submit yourself to my desires, you will lie sullenly beneath me like a clump of dead seaweed. Is that not so?"

"Just-get-on-with-it," she bit out through clenched teeth.

"It does not have to be that way, you know." His voice became a low, husky murmur, and she fidgeted as those warm tones seemed to enfold her. "And nor will it be," he continued seductively, "if you can bring yourself to trust me even the tiniest bit."

With infinite care—as tentatively as if he were approaching a shy animal for the first time—he stretched out a hand and laid it lightly on the back of Thalassa's neck.

She went absolutely still. Her heart raced as though she were battling three opponents at once, but hopelessness reigned as strongly as her apprehension and resentment. She had known this would happen, and perhaps if he slept with her once, or even a few times, he would tire of her and let her go.

His long fingers slipped under her heavy hair and gently kneaded the tight muscles of her neck and shoulders. "Softly, my golden one," he whispered. "I promise I will not hurt or upset you in any way."

Alarmed and dismayed, Thalassa realized his hand

actually felt good. His dexterous fingers seemed to know exactly where all the tension in her lay. Seeking each spot out, they worked leisurely until the knot melted away. But even while her body was responding to his skill, her nerves were quivering with panic.

This was not what she had expected—this unhurried and subtly arousing campaign to lull her fears. If he had possessed her quickly, with no regard for any pleasure but his own, she would not have been disturbed nearly as much. To assert power over a woman's body was not the way to possess any part of her intrinsic self. Dorian could have taken Thalassa a hundred times under such circumstances, and her soul would still have remained inviolate and remote from him. But like all intelligent men, Dorian understood that, and because he understood it, he represented an even greater threat than Thalassa had first comprehended.

His fingers trailed delicately along the ridge of her collarbone, leaving a path of fire in their wake. She pulled away abruptly, unable to bear his disquieting touch another instant. The sudden movement caused the room to spin. Thalassa was horrified to discover she felt very much the way she had as a child when first introduced to strong mead. She glared down at the empty goblet still in her hand. "You must have put some manner of bewitchment on this potion you've given me."

"Not at all." Dorian laughed easily. "On the contrary, I warned you of its potency. But you are not bewitched, my sweet, only drunk. Whereas"—he gently uncurled her taut fingers from around the goblet and placed it on the table—"I am sober. No bad thing in our present situation."

He turned her to face him, and she had no choice but to meet his eyes. Immediately she was impaled upon that gaze, as if he had thrust a spear through her. All possibility of independent action or even thought vanished. She stared fixedly into those jeweled eyes, wanting to look away but unable to. Filled with curious concentration, his dark, expressive face seemed to flow toward her. For a second, part of her spirit sought to rebel. Then Dorian lifted her chin and bent his head to hers.

He kissed her at first with a tenderness that was almost comforting. But as Thalassa's lips softened ever so slightly, the texture of his kiss changed. His mouth became insistent, coaxing the stiffness from hers with an erotic sensitivity that left the inexperienced Thalassa devastated. He probed and teased at her lips until they parted of their own accord, permitting him to enter the unexplored cavity of her mouth with his skillful tongue.

The kiss went on for a very long time, and when Dorian finally lifted his head, her eyes were filled with shock and a startled, reluctant pleasure.

"I see you are beginning to enjoy kissing," he murmured. "An excellent start, indeed."

Struggling to regain her breath, Thalassa did not reply, and he bent to her again. This time he slid his arms around her and drew her firmly against him. His warmth enveloped her like a woolen cloak, and the strong, regular thud of his heart sent its rhythm directly into hers.

Her head was swimming, and she had no idea whether it was because of this extraordinary intimacy or the unexpectedly lethal alcohol. All she knew was that the world had shrunk to nothing more than this man's mouth on hers and the embrace of his powerful, cradling arms.

He continued kissing her until she discovered that to kiss was to kindle a strange, melting fire deep within one's belly—a fire that was not content to stay in a single spot, but spread its burning tentacles throughout every part of her body.

When he was sure those flames had been lit, Dorian went on to show her what it felt like to have breasts swell in response to stroking fingers and caressing lips. He had loved countless women in his long life, but he had never lost his ability to marvel at the beauty and complexity of the human form.

And this uninitiated young woman was magnificent. Not only in her physical perfection, but in the uniqueness of her proud and strong spirit, which had unknowingly reached out to him all the way across the seas. That spirit was bruised and bewildered by the ordeal of her abduction, but bonding with her would begin to heal the pain of these last months in a way that nothing else could.

He rose from the couch, drawing her up with him, and slowly led her to his broad bed. The queer drink, the hypnotic power of his eyes, and the sensual artistry of his kisses had all combined to work their magic on his chosen one's unwilling psyche.

It seemed to Thalassa that she floated across the wide chamber, her feet hovering a few inches above the luxuriant white carpet. Her mind had disassociated itself from her body and stood aside, watching critically as Dorian disrobed first himself and then her. When they were both naked, he took her in his arms, pressing their bodies together from chest to thigh.

Feeling the bizarre thrust of his jutting manhood, she instinctively tried to recoil, but he was holding her too tightly. As she stood against him, he ran warm hands down her back and gently squeezed her firm buttocks.

The cool texture of soft coverlets warned her that he had laid her on the bed, and her benumbed wits strove to return. Now it would happen, the thing she had tried so hard to resign herself to because it was the will of the Mother. She closed her eyes and waited for it to be over. To allow a man to use her body violated all honor, but unfortunately, one did not die of such things. She could only hope he would sate himself quickly, then leave her alone.

But rather than pulling her thighs apart and roughly plunging into her as she anticipated, Dorian simply lowered his body onto hers, careful not to burden her with his full weight.

"Look at me, Thalassa," he ordered in a low voice.

When she did not, he cradled her face in his hands and dusted her eyelids, cheeks, and throat with light, teasing kisses. "Open your eyes and look at me, my love," he murmured. "I won't stop until you do."

Her angry cat's eyes glinted at him through thick lashes, like a trapped lioness glaring out from behind the bars of her cage. He smiled. "I promised I would not hurt you," he reminded her. "Look well, and you will see that I spoke the truth."

She had little say in the matter, with his large hands imprisoning her head and his face looming directly over hers. Fresh panic seized her as she felt herself once more becoming entangled in the depths of his uncanny gaze. But as she stared up at him, an eerie calm descended over her, blanketing her trepidation, wrapping it up and bearing it softly away to some far-off place that no longer had anything to do with her.

In its stead remained only a feeling of tranquility, so profound it almost seemed she could fall asleep, despite the vulnerability of her position. Dorian's eyes continued to delve into hers. She felt her mind detaching itself from her body again as her will gave itself over to another, stronger will. A will that she somehow understood meant her no harm.

"All I wish is to give you pleasure," he said, and his words vibrated against her breasts from his broad chest.

It would have been too much to say that Thalassa truly believed him, but mesmerized and entrapped by the spell he had so masterfully woven about her, it no longer mattered. The sense of peace he instilled in her was temporary. In effect, he had drugged her using both the power of his mind and the potent drink she had gulped so defiantly. He would have vastly preferred her wholehearted participation, but that would come later.

In her present state, he could teach her body about love, and at the same time, bond with her mind in ways that would leave his chosen mate remembering sensual bliss rather than fear and resentment. For, above all else, Dorian wanted to give Thalassa joy, to plant the beginnings of trust within her hostile soul and to show her the beauty that could exist between a man and a woman.

Keeping his gaze locked with hers, he lightly swirled his palms over her round breasts. The dusky nipples sprang erect in response to the tantalizing motion, and she stared at him in paralyzed wonder. But he had barely started. As his hands and lips began a leisurely yet thorough journey over her supple body, her look of wonder intensified.

Thalassa was as unprepared for the concept of receiving sexual pleasure from a man as Dorian was experienced in giving it, and the reaction of her body was shattering. Waves of an unfamiliar tingling followed in the wake of his explorations, and she was overwhelmed to find herself quivering and straining toward some elusive goal.

Inexorably Dorian's black head traveled downward, and as if it were a dream, she felt his hands first caressing, then gently spreading her thighs. Dazed and bewildered, she opened to him, and jerked in surprise as the tip of his tongue sent torrents of sensation raging through her. The ecstasy was double-edged like the sharpest of knives—filling her with the keenest of pleasure, yet tormenting her with the need for more and still more.

Gasping cries rang throughout the room, and she foggily realized they came from her. She wanted to pull away—to withdraw in body and mind—to flee wildly from these unbearable feelings and the one making her feel them. But the alien desire that Dorian had aroused so skillfully was fully unleashed now, and it would not be stopped or controlled.

It surged forward relentlessly, sweeping Thalassa along in its wake. Her entire being dissolved into one enormous throb of sensation, and unaware of what she was doing, she arched her hips up to meet Dorian's mouth. His lips and tongue claimed her, seeking out her untried body's innermost secrets, until with shuddering spasms, a first shattering release swept through her, followed swiftly by another, and yet another.

Even as the intense ecstasy was still washing over her, Dorian pulled himself up and slowly thrust the length of his manhood into her moist flesh. Well prepared by his devoted ministrations and her resultant orgasms, her body welcomed him. Nevertheless, he took great care.

Knowing she'd spent a rigorous life mostly on horseback made him almost certain she no longer possessed her maidenhead. Still this was not the time to rush, for he was huge with need, and she was newly opened. He lay still, savoring the exquisite tightness of her and giving her a chance to adjust to his pulsating invasion.

And invasion it was. Thalassa felt him everywhere, not just in his foreign flesh intruding into hers, but throughout every corner of her mind. There was no escape, no place to hide from the powerful presence flowing into her, and terror began eroding her haze of passion.

Her elders had never described the act of mating as being so all-consuming and devouring. It could be enjoyable, but essentially it was nothing more than a pleasant physical exercise between two healthy animals. That was how it was supposed to be. Not this sense of being engulfed in another's mind; of being joined to his very heartbeat and pulse, caught up totally in the rhythm of that other life. Fear clogged her throat. Flinging her hands up to cover her eyes, she sought desperately to break free from this man and the unwanted spell of intimacy he had wrapped her in.

"Ah no, my dearest," he whispered. "Don't fight me." He stroked the damp hair back from her forehead, then pressed her hands down and recaptured her distracted gaze with his own.

Held once more in the grip of those steady sapphire eyes, Thalassa felt her momentary resistance fade. Bemusedly, she found herself relaxing under his whispered reassurances and gentle touch.

She comprehended that he had placed some type of enchantment upon her, but there seemed to be no way of battling it. And oddly enough, she no longer wanted to. It was so hard to go on fighting. And despite the strangeness of his body within hers, she felt no pain. In fact, she was becoming aware of astonishingly pleasurable sensations from his penetration.

"Let go, beloved." His voice was a breathy murmur in her ear. "Trust me, and we will share such delight together, you and I. Such delight, my golden one."

He kissed her, and under the persuasion of his warm, caressing mouth, her eyelids fluttered shut and her thoughts drifted lazily away.

It was a relief to give in at last, to allow the bewildering feelings to take over and carry her wherever they would. The presence of his consciousness in her mind was as comforting now as it had originally been terrifying.

He lapped her body in ripples of a desire so tender, it was almost restful. She was rocked by smooth, even thrusts that lulled her as gently as the sunlit ocean had the morning of her abduction. A deep sense of peace and security eased the last vestiges of anxiety from her taut muscles, and unconsciously she fell into Dorian's rhythm.

Intertwined on every level, bound together, they moved as one being, their separate selves temporarily merged. It was a joining more profound than anything Thalassa could have imagined, and had she been in control of herself, its power would have appalled her.

"Thalassa." The sound of her name carried an implicit command, and she once more met Dorian's gaze. She glimpsed tenderness in the depths of his eyes, and a solemn determination.

As her glassy, wandering stare fastened onto his, the cadence of his body changed. The tempo of his thrusts grew swifter and more forceful. A tide of unbelievable pleasure swamped Thalassa, and with an involuntary moan she surrendered to his deep, compelling rhythm. Endless moments passed, and she was consumed by those eyes and the driving power of his body.

Her muscled thighs clenched around his lean hips in an effort to draw him farther inside her, and the sensations that accompanied that movement toppled Thalassa into a realm where nothing existed save this irresistible and maddening rapture.

She heaved and lunged beneath him, every inch of flesh—inside and out—trembling in turbulent response to his thrusts. Through it all Dorian's gaze remained fused to hers. He had set out to inflame her with passion, and now that passion burst over her like whitecapped breakers. She cried out wildly as her body spasmed and convulsed in an excess of erotic frenzy. And yet her eyes were still chained to his.

He spoke to her in his own incomprehensible tongue, and the grave, mysterious words resonated on the deepest level of her soul, penetrating and marking her in some unexplainable manner, even though she had no idea what he said. An icy tendril of fear slithered through the fiery tumult surrounding her, but before she could react to it, Dorian gave way at last to his own burning urgency.

Sliding his hands underneath her, he cupped Thalassa's buttocks and pulled her to him. The vitality of his long-held release was so forceful, it swept her up again, and together they exploded, then fragmented in timeless shudders of rapture.

Hours seemed to pass before Thalassa managed to reassemble the splintered shards of her being and come back to herself. She was still on her back, but Dorian's weight no longer pressed down upon her. Instead, he lay close beside her, breathing softly as though he were asleep, his arms locked possessively about her limp form.

A host of conflicting emotions roiled through her brain, mingling with one bewildering physical image after another. The texture and heat of Dorian's male flesh, the feel of his seed flooding her, and, most incredibly, the total abandonment of her response. The memory of it made her cringe, and she became aware of a damp tenderness between her legs that increased her shame.

Dorian stirred lazily and rolled onto one elbow so he could study Thalassa's face. What he saw there convinced him that the bonding had been successful. She would need a great deal of reassurance in the days ahead, but the newly established link quivered between them with tenuous delicacy, allowing him a window into her reeling consciousness.

A tremendous love surged through him. She was his now. They were truly united on all levels, and blissful exultation pervaded Dorian's entire being. He yearned to share his feelings of closeness with Thalassa, to hug her to him and make love all over again. But, sighing inwardly, he held back, knowing it was too soon. He traced the line of her jaw with a gentle finger, and murmured teasingly, "Well, my love, was that as terrible as you had imagined it would be?"

She did not answer and, humor lurking in his voice, he went on. "At least my fears about you behaving like a clump of dead seaweed were not realized, so I can only assume you enjoyed it as much as I did."

Uneasily, Thalassa turned her head away, still stricken by this foreign emotion she belatedly recognized as embarrassment. "I enjoyed it too much," she muttered more to herself than to him.

He chuckled. "Such a thing is not possible," he told her. "And you will find, my lovely one, that your enjoyment is just beginning. The next time we make love, you will experience even greater pleasure."

His words extinguished her small hope that perhaps he would now be satisfied and leave her alone, and Thalassa flinched as she tried to envision how much more unrestrained he was capable of making her.

"My freedom would give me greater pleasure," she said, seeking in vain to ignore the sensations racing through her.

She felt raw and exposed, the privacy of both soul and body laid bare and open to this man. And she had done it willingly. It was the potion she'd so foolishly drunk, she reminded herself, that and the spell he had put upon her with those eyes of his. But the explanation brought her no comfort. If she had been truly strong, no amount of magical drinks or sapphire-eyed enchantments could have broken through her defenses. She was weak . . . weak. . . .

"It is not a matter of strength or weakness, you know," he said quietly. She stared at him numbly, too miserable to question how he had known her thoughts. "I have told you that we were fated to be together, and now we are. But I am yours as much as you are mine, Thalassa. I took nothing from you that I did not give back equally. In time, you will come to see that for yourself."

For some reason that she could not even begin to understand, the softly spoken words touched a chord in Thalassa's heart—a new chord, one that had never been there before. She wondered where it came from, this dawning sense of intimacy toward a *man* of all creatures!

She searched inside herself for harsh retorts to stem the curious thoughts and feelings coming to life within her, but without success. His nearness no longer brought on the disquieting unease it once had. Instead, it gave her a bewildering sort of solace. She suddenly became aware of how tired she was as Dorian fitted his warm, hard body against hers.

"Sleep well, my beloved," he murmured, and kissed her ear.

So he intended that she stay there in his bed in case he wanted her again! The thought should have made her angry, but it did not. Musing on the strangeness of it all, with Dorian's unfamiliar and yet familiar body pressed close against her, Thalassa fell asleep.

As she slept, Dorian lay staring into the shadows, the conversation he had had with the Elders earlier that evening

FREE-LIGHTED MAKEUP CASE!
FREE-6 LOVESWEPT NOVELS!

- ● NO OBLIGATION
- ● NO PURCHASE NECESSARY

(DETACH AND MAIL CARD TODAY.)

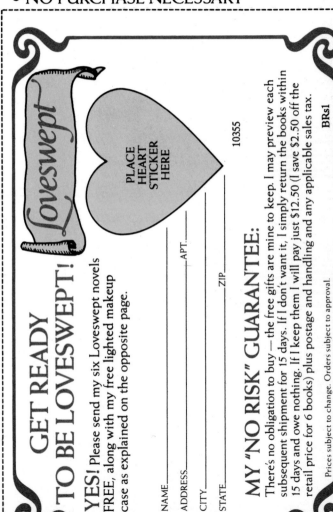

GET READY TO BE LOVESWEPT!

YES! Please send my six Loveswept novels FREE, along with my free lighted makeup case as explained on the opposite page.

Loveswept

PLACE HEART STICKER HERE

10355

NAME _____

ADDRESS_____ APT._____

CITY_____

STATE_____ ZIP_____

MY "NO RISK" GUARANTEE:

There's no obligation to buy — the free gifts are mine to keep. I may preview each subsequent shipment for 15 days. If I don't want it, I simply return the books within 15 days and owe nothing. If I keep them I will pay just $12.50 (I save $2.50 off the retail price for 6 books) plus postage and handling and any applicable sales tax.

BR5s1

Prices subject to change. Orders subject to approval.

REMEMBER!

- The free books and gift are mine to keep!
- There is no obligation!
- I may preview each shipment for 15 days!
- I can cancel anytime!

ringing in his ears. "Have you done it?" they had questioned in the echoing chamber of the heated pool. "Is the Sea Spell finally upon her?"

With the mind-shielding skills that Nomar himself had taught him, Dorian had done the unimaginable. "Yes," he had lied. "Yes, it is."

CHAPTER 16

≈ Hippolyte strode forth from the opposite end of the field, her once snowy tunic splashed and stained with Greek blood. Her eyes were as hard as the ice that covered the river Thermodon in winter.

"I see that Greeks are as other men, after all," she said bitingly. "Dogs without honor, who feel no shame in violating the ancient customs of hospitality."

"*We* did not—" Heracles began indignantly, then stopped. There was no point in arguing with these creatures. Too much blood had been shed on both sides to put things back the way they had been, and the sight of some of that blood on Hippolyte's tunic filled him with anger. "If we are dogs, then you are soulless bitches," he snapped. "But unnatural as you are, I will still spare this one"—he gave Antiope a cruel shake—"in exchange for our leaving this accursed land in safety."

There was a long tense moment of absolute silence, broken only by labored breathing and the groans of those who lay wounded. At last, Hippolyte nodded. "You are dung on the shores of our fair land," she said in that same icy tone. "But my beloved sister is too young to die at the hands of a Greek cur. Release Antiope, and then take your ships and go."

Under hundreds of hate-filled Amazon eyes, the remaining Greeks, exhausted and wounded, stumbled onto the galleys in their leader's wake. The men already on board had wasted no time in seizing the reluctantly discarded weapons of their foes and taking the women on the ships prisoner. They made way eagerly for their fellows, believing for the first time that they might actually see home again.

Gaining the deck of the lead galley, Heracles carelessly slung Antiope's body into Theseus's arms and began issuing terse orders for casting off. But even as he snapped out his commands, the hero's gaze remained on the tall, regal Hippolyte, his former lover who had bewitched and ensnared him with her unparalleled beauty. It seemed such a waste to leave behind a woman so obviously created for a man's pleasure! Her only fault lay in her stubborn refusal to acknowledge the natural superiority of men as the gods had ordained it.

Hippolyte's only thoughts were for her younger sister's safety. It seemed that hours had crawled by since Heracles's fist had sent Antiope into a deathlike sleep, though in reality not more than five minutes had passed. Impatiently she stepped forward.

"We are waiting for you to keep your word," she called. "Free my sister and those others who gave up their arms to ensure her safety, Greek!"

The peremptory note of command in her voice provided the final goad to the idea slowly taking shape in Heracles's mind. Planting his balled fists on his hips, he shouted back arrogantly, "When we have passed the headland and are safely beyond range of your spears and arrows, then will we release them . . . on one condition."

New mutterings, fraught with outraged menace, eddied and swirled throughout the Amazon host. Hippolyte's dark eyes blazed with fury.

"And what condition is that, son of a dog?" she asked in a dangerously controlled voice.

"That you board this galley without your weapons and

accompany us. With both you and your sister as hostages, we need not fear further treachery from the rest of your pack of she-wolves."

Cries of "Do not do it, Lady. It is yet another trick!" rose all about the Amazon queen, and in the clamor, Theseus touched Heracles's sweat-drenched shoulder.

"We have one royal hostage, Lord," he said in a low voice. "Why do we need another?"

"Because I intend to take her back with me as a slave—following behind me like a bitch at the heels of her master!"

As he spoke, Heracles did not notice Soloon hovering nearby, listening to every word. After having set the two peoples at each other's throats, Soloon had made directly for the dubious safety of the lead galley, where he had also succeeded in avoiding the worst of the fighting. From the moment his idol set foot on the ship, he had striven to be near him, and thus he heard Heracles's words in a paroxysm of rage.

Despite all his clever planning, this noble son of Zeus still wished to continue debasing himself with that lowbred whore! Crazed—in a frenzy of jealous longing—he muttered, "I must save him from himself."

At that moment, Hippolyte held up her arms. The commotion of her worried kinswomen subsided into restless murmurs that blended with the ceaseless wash of the waves lapping the beach. Contemptuously she dropped her crescent-shaped shield and short sword to the bloody, trampled sand, then placed her hands on her hips in the same arrogant posture as Heracles.

"And what guarantees will you give," she demanded in a voice that carried to the ears of every Amazon and Greek present, "that this is not simply another deceit from you honorless dogs?"

Glowering, Heracles opened his mouth to reply, but the words never left his lips. An insane Soloon lifted his spear and, with the strength and accuracy of the truly demented, flung it straight at the Amazon queen.

Hippolyte's eyes had been fixed on Heracles. Nevertheless, a sixth sense warned her and she tried to dodge that terrible cast. Had she not put down her shield, she might have succeeded in at least blunting the spear's aim. But Hippolyte's shield lay on the sand at her feet. . . .

Pandemonium broke out as the spear found its deadly mark. Some Amazons rushed to aid their fallen queen while others ran to storm the ships. A hail of arrows pierced the air, but Heracles had already screamed the order to cast off. In the strong winds of morning the galleys rapidly gusted beyond reach of the deadly missiles.

The unfortunate warriors who had been taken prisoner struggled against their bonds with the ferocity of wild animals, shrieking out their war cry and vowing terrible revenge for Hippolyte's blood. Their cries carried across the harbor to mingle with those of the Amazon host. The sound of their captive kin maddened the women on shore. In helpless fury, they could only watch as sisters, comrades, and their young queen were borne away. But the sense of futility did not last long.

Hooves pounded through the uproar as horses raced down the curving beach, carrying several squadrons of heavily armed bowwomen. On their way out to open sea, the Greek ships would have to sail along the borders of Amazonia, and there were places where they might come within range of Amazon arrows.

Heracles was well aware of such a threat, and his men were frantically responding to his shouted orders. Those who were not engaged in rowing lashed shields together on the landward side of each ship, forming a bulwark against the pursuing archers. Only when this was done did Heracles allow some of his weary men to tend the wounded.

He himself did not rest, but stood in the prow of the lead galley, anxiously scanning the shoreline. The hero's heart was sore within him. His rage toward Hippolyte had evaporated with the sight of her lying in a pool of blood, the spear protruding grotesquely from her sun-gilded breast. Now, all he felt was a deep sense of irrevocable loss, and reluctantly he turned at the sound of Theseus's voice.

"Everything is secured, Lord. Here, I've brought you some wine."

Heracles took the proffered cup. The dark red wine reminded him jarringly of his lover's blood, and he held the goblet without drinking.

"The prisoners are still fighting their bonds like madwomen," Theseus went on, "and Antiope is awake now. We had to bind her as well, for she struck down two men and very nearly succeeded in getting hold of a sword."

The young king's tired voice held puzzled resentment. He had tried to explain that he was doing what was best for her, but she had refused to understand. Instead, she had sought with all her strength to kill him, and he had been forced to order her tied like the other captives. Why could she not see he was taking her to a civilized life, one far better than the savage existence to which she had been born?

"Keep her bound then," Heracles said gruffly. "She and the others will quiet down soon enough when we're out to open sea and well beyond reach of their she-demon sisters." With an abrupt gesture, he lifted the cup of wine and tossed down the contents in one swallow. "I suppose you want to claim her as your slave." When Theseus nodded, he grunted. "Very well then, she's yours. By Zeus's balls, you certainly earned her."

The Athenian ruler smiled with relief. Heracles's temper was legendary, and Theseus had truly feared for Antiope's life. Equally great had been his fear that with Hippolyte dead, Heracles might exercise a leader's prerogative and keep their royal captive for himself. "Thank you, Lord," he said happily. "I'll be a good master to her, and I'm sorry about the older queen. She was a magnificent-looking woman."

"She was, indeed." Heracles's voice held real regret. "Treacherous and evil her tribe of misbegotten creatures may have been, but I never saw a better woman to breed sons on. With her, I could have replaced my poor, luckless children, whom I destroyed when the gods sent that terrible madness upon me."

In sympathy, Theseus remained silent. It was the first time he could remember Heracles ever mentioning the ghastly incident that had led to his accepting service in Eurystheus's court.

Suddenly Heracles flung the cup far into the sparkling waters and turned to glare at his crew. "Where is Soloon?" he bellowed. "Bring him to me at once!"

"There is no need, Lord. I have been awaiting your call." The young man's voice was eager, filled with barely concealed triumph as he hurried to the foredeck.

At last the moment for his reward had arrived! He could hardly wait to see the look of love and pride that must surely be filling his idol's eyes. But the look greeting him when he faced Heracles was neither loving nor proud, and Soloon faltered in confusion before the rage in the black gaze.

"The Amazon queen had laid down her weapons," the hero said slowly. "It was not necessary to kill her. With her and her sister as hostages, we could have left these shores safely, without any more of our men dying. Now we are being pursued. There are places where we must pass close to land, which means we will be vulnerable to those she-devils' arrows. Your action was ill-considered and foolish, and has endangered us all. What have you got to say for yourself?"

Soloon's reply was barely audible. "I did it for you," he mumbled.

"I can't hear you, lad! Stop whispering to yourself and speak up like a proper man!"

"I did it for you, Lord! I had to save you from the wickedness of those creatures. Especially from *that* one, who had entrapped you in her witch's spell. If you had brought her with us, the evil would have continued! That's why I planned everything out so carefully, and it was all working until that bitch acted as if she wanted to join us. I had to kill her! I had to!"

Heracles and Theseus stared, taken aback by the venomous intensity of Soloon's outburst. It was the sharp-minded Athenian king who asked, "What is this plan you speak of, Soloon? In the name of all the gods, what have you done?"

Soloon did not answer, and Heracles's massive fist shot out to seize the front of his tunic. Jerking the smaller man forward, the hero roared, "Answer him, boy, before I break your spindly neck! What have you done?"

In a welter of bewildered grief, Soloon shouted desperately, "I thought up a way to bring all of you back to your senses! I pretended that I wanted to lie with one of those whores, and when I had her under me, I stuck my knife in her throat. Then I ran and told our men I had overheard the Amazons plotting to kill each and every Greek. Nothing more had to be done. And now we are all free from the clutches of those creatures! Can you not see I have saved us all?"

Heracles's face turned a dark mottled red, and his hand closed spasmodically on Soloon's tunic. The fury gusting through his mighty frame was so violent that for several moments he was incapable of speech. When at last he found his voice, it was almost unrecognizable, so twisted with rage was it.

"Hippolyte was right, then. The laws of hospitality *were* violated—and not by them. You have heaped shame and disgrace upon my name. The brightness of my honor is stained and defiled with the offal of your treachery. Even though they were only women, they were still our hosts. You have made all of us appear as lowbred curs who have no respect for agreements made under the ancient traditions. You will be punished."

His other hand came up to close inexorably around Soloon's neck. The latter struggled, crying frantically in a high shrieking whine, "Please, Lord, please! It was for you! For you! Please, Lord! I love—"

There was a hideous popping and grating sound, and Soloon's pleas became a rasping gurgle as blood burst forth from his lips. Slowly he went limp as the life faded from his eyes, and when the swollen tongue bulged out of the slack mouth, Heracles lifted the corpse and pitched it over the side like refuse.

Soloon sank heavily beneath the waves, then bobbed to the surface, as if to bid his living comrades farewell.

Still in the grip of his wrath, Heracles stood with foam-flecked lips, his fists clenching and unclenching as though he was yet throttling Soloon. No one, including Theseus, dared speak to him. Finally sanity returned in enough measure for the hero to sigh heavily and speak.

"Well, it is done, and cannot be undone. Were we to go back and try to explain, those women would be too busy firing arrows at us to listen. Therefore, we have no choice but to continue on. And after all, we did succeed in obtaining what we came here for: the golden girdle. With that, we must be content."

"And the Amazons we hold prisoner?" Theseus asked. "What of them?"

"I've already said Antiope belongs to you. As for the others, I want none of them. The men can toss dice for which ones they want and divide them up however they like when we reach home. But as soon as we're beyond pursuit, I want all the women confined on one ship. It'll be easier to guard them that way."

Heracles paused, then added generously, "Except for your captive. You may keep her with you to serve your needs. Not only because your idea of taking her hostage saved all our lives, but her presence among the other captives will only cause more trouble—"

Shouts of warning rang out from the carefully posted watchers. Looking down the beach both men saw a cloud of dust that clearly heralded the approach of Amazon riders.

But Poseidon, who ruled the sea, continued to answer Theseus's prayers by sending forth favorable winds to aid his son. As fast as the Amazons' horses ran, the galleys outdistanced them—speeding before the wind and veering far enough away from land so that the arrows shot at them fell short.

From the decks of each ship, where the captive Amazons lay bound, new cries and curses rose as the women sensed the pursuit of their kindred. In the stern of the lead galley, Antiope squirmed and twisted against the ropes that held her. Six other warriors lay alongside their young queen, struggling with equal ferocity. But the ropes were knotted tightly, with the skill of sailors, and try as they might the women could not break free.

Antiope's head ached fiercely from the blow she had suffered from Heracles. The pain in her head, however, was nothing compared to the pain in her heart. Mercifully she had been spared the sight of her beloved sister's death, but that was all she had been spared.

The return to her senses had taken place amidst a tumult of shouts and screams. Dazed by the blow, Antiope had at first not been able to make sense out of what was happening around her. Then she had become aware of several things, none of them reassuring. The world was rocking crazily about her; the raised voices were both male and female; and the women were shrieking the name of Hippolyte over and over again in anguished rage.

Struggling to her feet, Antiope had beheld a scene sent by the raven-headed woman of nightmares. She was on board a ship. The shores of her home were rapidly receding, and that was not the worst of it. Other Amazons lay on the wooden deck, bound hand and foot. When they saw Antiope, they screamed, "Untie us, Lady! These dogs have murdered your sister!"

The impulse to free her comrades was instantaneous, outweighing even the horror of the words shouted at her. But as Antiope rushed to free her bound sisters, strong hands brutally seized her arms and a harsh male voice snarled, "You are no longer a queen, *Lady*, but a captive of the spear. Your new master will soon teach you womanly obedience!"

Antiope spun about and struck the man down with a savage kick to the groin. But directly behind him were others, their hands digging roughly into her flesh as they sought to subdue her. The cries of her kinswomen ringing in her ears, Antiope fought as one possessed by demons. She succeeded in injuring another man, and had actually gotten her desperate hands upon his sword before the Greeks' sheer numbers had overwhelmed her.

Through the mists of her rage, she heard the voice of Theseus, pleading with her to accept her fate, promising that he would treat her well. She paid no more heed to his words than she would the buzzing of insects, and so he reluctantly ordered her bound like the others.

Now Antiope lay on the heaving deck, the coarse ropes chafing cruelly at her wrists and ankles as she struggled against them. Amazonia had become nothing more than a faint blur on the horizon, and the iodine smell of the sea was overpowering, adding to the nausea she felt from the blow to her head and the unaccustomed movement of the galley beneath her.

The huge cloth sail creaked and billowed above her head. On either side of her, those Greeks who were able to sat at the rowing benches, manning the long oars with rhythmic slaps against the sparkling blue water. Bitterly, Antiope saw that her attempts—and those of her comrades—to free themselves were being ignored. Clearly their captors were confident that the securely tied women could not escape, and that only increased Antiope's rage.

A number of wounded men lay groaning a short distance away from the captives. Tecmessa, who lay closest to Antiope, wailed through bloody, bitten lips, "May their wounds blacken and shrivel until they die shrieking in agony, and may their shades find no peace in the land of the dead!"

Antiope's tormented eyes went to the ship's bow where Heracles stood with Theseus. "The Goddess will visit tenfold that fate on that black-bearded pig in the shape of a man, and the noble shade of my beloved sister will pursue him even into the halls of the dead. And as for Theseus, I will kill him with my own hands. On my sister's blood, I vow this!"

Tears rolled down her dirt- and blood-streaked face as she spoke. Tecmessa had told her what had transpired after Heracles knocked her senseless, and Antiope was frantic with fury and grief. That she had been taken into slavery barely touched her beside the enormity of Hippolyte's murder. Being a captive was only temporary. In her heart, Antiope knew the Goddess would send merciful death to release her from such a fate. But first, her sister's sacred blood must be avenged.

She twisted her aching neck to see Tecmessa's face. "How many of our people are captured?" she rasped in a voice that was so cracked and raw, she scarcely recognized it as her own.

"I am not sure. But all of their accursed ships escaped from Amazonia's shores and the wrath of our sisters, and I hear the cries of other warriors carried on the wind."

Antiope listened. "I hear them too." Her mind worked furiously. Surely Amazon horses were swifter than the boats of men, and could overtake them before they got too far out to sea! "They have not yet escaped the wrath of our sisters, Tecmessa, or the wrath of the Mother. These fools think us helpless, but we will show them how wrong they are before we kill them. Can you see if we are passing near land once more?"

"The shores of our home grow ever more distant, Lady." Tecmessa's hoarse voice cracked with desperation. "While you lay deathlike, the boats veered toward the land, and mounted squadrons pursued us along the beach. But Holy Artemis did not heed our prayers. The wooden creatures of these evil men ran faster than our beautiful horses and faster than the arrows of our kinswomen. Now our people are left far behind, and these boats show no sign of going near land again."

"Then we must formulate a plan," Antiope said firmly. "We will wait for darkness and then gnaw each other loose from our bonds. When that is done, we will seize weapons and kill as many Greeks as we can before we ourselves are killed. As for our sisters on the other ships, we will pray that the Goddess aids them to do the same."

Fresh tears filled her eyes as she thought of Hippolyte. *I will join you soon, my beloved sister, when your death has been avenged!* "But no matter what else happens," she said aloud, "Heracles and Theseus must die. When their blood stains these decks, then will I give up my life and go happily to the Goddess."

Tecmessa nodded. "So be it, Lady. I will tell the others when I am sure that the eyes of these dogs are not upon us."

The rocking movement of the galley suddenly intensified, and Antiope had to fight back her increasing nausea. Neither she nor her companions had ever been on a boat before. She would not have guessed that the sensation could be so sickening. Tecmessa apparently felt it too, for she moaned, "By Artemis's sacred doe, I feel sick. In another moment, I fear I may spew up my guts and disgrace myself. Do you think these curs have poisoned us?"

"I don't see how. It must be the motion of these ships that makes us so ill. Look you, Tecmessa. The Greeks have stopped rowing."

And so they had. The twenty oars on each side of the galley were pointing up at the cloudless sky in two dripping rows, and Antiope heard male shouts ringing out from what must be other ships. Desperately she craned her neck to see what was happening. It looked as if the galleys were being drawn up alongside each other. Groups of men were securing them while their fellows lifted writhing shapes into the air, to the accompaniment of lewd comments and much laughter.

Helpless fury hit Antiope like a kick to the stomach. Beside her Tecmessa snarled in wordless rage, and beyond her, the five other Amazons made similar sounds. Antiope fought to bring herself under control.

"Courage, my sisters," she called, sure that the men's commotion would cover her words. "It seems that they wish to put us all on one galley. What fools they be! This will only make it easier for us to loose each other's bonds when the Moon-Goddess covers us with night. Do not lose heart, my sis—"

She bit off her words as a group of men came laughing toward them, balancing easily on the swaying deck. Antiope recognized most of them from the feasting held during their stay in Amazonia. But these erstwhile guests looked upon her with no more respect or acknowledgment than if she had been the commonest slave girl. Now their true natures stood revealed, she thought fiercely. How right Oreithyia was. All men were utterly evil!

A burly Greek, his bare chest streaked with blood and sweat, bent over Tecmessa. "Offal!" she screamed as he slung her over his shoulder with no more care than if she had been a sack of grain.

The big man only laughed and ran his hand familiarly over her buttocks, poking a brutal finger in between her cheeks until Tecmessa shrieked that she would kill him with her bare hands. The man ignored her. "I like this one," he confided to his fellows. "She's nice and tight. Never been ridden there before, I'll wager. If Apollo favors me, I'll win her when Heracles lets us dice for them."

He bore the struggling, cursing Tecmessa away. Antiope could scarcely believe that she might be seeing her friend and age-mate for the last time. "Tecmessa!" Her cry rang out in anguish, but another Greek, this one sporting a fresh sword cut down the side of his face, blocked her vision.

Leaning down, the man squeezed Antiope's bared

breast. "This is the woman I want. I kept watching her with Theseus, but as far as I could tell, he was the only one mounting her."

Antiope twisted around and sank her teeth into the Greek's dirty hand. He let out a yell, and had swung back his uninjured hand to strike her when the oldest of the men intervened.

"Hold, Chlemias. She is Theseus's property still, and he'll continue to be the only one in the saddle until he says different. Heracles gave her to him in reward for getting us out of that demon-riddled land. You'd better choose another."

"Well"—Chlemias looked down sullenly into Antiope's face, and she glared back at him with all the hatred she felt in her heart—"she's not a virgin, Nestor, and what Theseus doesn't know won't hurt him. I'm to be in the first group set to guard these slaves tonight, and if I spread her legs and take a few gallops on her, who's to care?"

Nestor shrugged. "Not I, but that doesn't matter. She's not going on the galley with the other captives. Heracles gave orders that she's to be kept here to serve all of Theseus's wants. Another boon for his quick thinking in saving all of our hides, no doubt. Theseus has already ordered a tent to be set up. I suppose he wants to do his riding in private."

Horror engulfed Antiope at the man's words. She despised the king of Athens all the more sharply for her weakness in coming to care for him during the gentle days of peace between her people and his. But to be named his slave was not the cause of her stomach-churning dismay. It was the separation from her kinswomen that drove Antiope to twist against the unyielding ropes in wild futility. To be left on this ship alone with naught but enemies surrounding her!

The men took no notice of her struggles. Roughly they reached for the other warriors, taking every opportunity to fondle the women's breasts and thrust casually possessive hands between their squirming thighs. As she watched helplessly, an ancient and terrible power swept through Antiope.

"The curse of our foremother, Lysippe, be upon the

manhood of each and every one of you!" she screamed in a strangely old voice. "No joy will you draw from our suffering. Instead will you see your manroots attacked by a wasting disease that causes them to shrivel and bleed until they rot off, leaving you gelded, bleating eunuchs! Thus does the Great Mother punish the murderers of Her queen and the violators of Her daughters. This destiny I swear upon you in the name of Hippolyte!"

There was an uneasy silence. The Greeks gave one another nervous, sidelong glances, and several of them surreptitiously made the sign for the evil eye and backed away.

"Ho, Nestor!" a deep voice suddenly shouted from the other side of the galley. "You and your men—get those women over here. Heracles is growing impatient!"

Nestor shook himself. "Let's get out of here," he said in a voice that quavered ever so slightly with superstitious fear. "Her words are naught but the ravings of a woman who has been newly carried off. They all whine like that in the beginning. Theseus will have her tamed soon enough."

He and the others reached for the Amazons again. Despite the fresh curses and imprecations rained upon their heads, they bore them to the galley designated to hold the prisoners. Cries of "Remember us, Lady! We will never surrender!" tormented Antiope's ears, but she could only watch in agony as her sisters disappeared on board the other ship.

She lay back on the gently tossing deck—bound hand and foot—powerless and utterly alone. "Oh, Hippolyte," she whispered, "give me your strength, dear sister. I beg you."

CHAPTER 17

≋ *You can't hold your breath forever, love. Breathe*
in. You'll be pleasantly surprised, believe me.

The words came from directly inside Thalassa's head,
the melodic voice ringing throughout every facet of her
mind. The astonishing intimacy of it caused her to gasp, and
in that instant she took her first breath of seawater.

When she realized what she had done, she was terrified.
The salt water went down easily, though, feeling
no different than if she had taken a gulp of air. There was no
burning or choking at all. Bemused, she took another
tentative breath. The second went down as easily as the
first.

Now she became aware of a completely alien sensation—
that of water rushing in and out of the newly opened gills on
either side of her neck. Just as Dorian had promised, the
feeling was no longer painful, not the way it had been that
other time. Yet it was so totally foreign that Thalassa hung
suspended in the water, momentarily oblivious to everything but what was going on inside her.

Dorian floated by her side, one arm laid supportively

across her back. Smiling, he watched his mate, giving her the time she needed to adjust before he took her any farther. The sea beckoned to him, though, and at last—unable to wait any longer—he urged her out of the interlocking chamber's vast opened doors and into the midnight sea.

Thalassa went unresistingly, overwhelmed by these events so far beyond her comprehension. In Dorian's abode, the very thought of reentering the sea had continued to arouse sheer terror within her. How he had managed to calm her fears and bring her to this point, Thalassa understood no better than she understood anything else about this waking dream.

The sea was not the cold and suffocating black tomb she had remembered. Her eyes pierced the shadowy gloom with extraordinary ease, and she puzzled over this until Dorian spoke again into her head, explaining their people's ability to see in the darkness. She stiffened at the shock of his being able to send his thoughts into her very mind. Truly, this was magic of the most awesome sort.

Dorian had told her the merfolk communicated with each other in this way when in the sea. No magic was involved, he had insisted, only physical ability passed on from generation to generation. Yet with the sound of his deep voice resonating throughout her, Thalassa felt differently. Still, her belief that this was further proof Dorian was a god competed against her fascination with the underwater world he was revealing to her.

Behind them, the coral abode rose, curving into the dim shadows. Seen from the outside, Thalassa thought it resembled a huge reef more than a palace, where people moved through magnificently furnished chambers, filled with light, air, and warmth. Dorian's strong arm tightened around her, and she felt herself being drawn into movement as he slowly guided her upward.

As they swam, he loosened his supportive hold little by little. He did it with such subtlety, Thalassa was surprised when she realized she was swimming unaided. Though she was alarmed, her body of its own accord emulated Dorian's smooth, rippling movements.

The uncoordinated sluggishness—the feeling of struggling to move through mud that she had experienced during her ill-fated escape attempt—had completely vanished. She felt weightless and powerful at the same time, her entire being caught up in a freedom beyond anything she had ever known.

Marveling at this effortless strength, she stared about her as Dorian led her through what he referred to as the "rocky plains." Schools of fish, their colors brilliant in the softly filtered gloom, darted around and past them, and Dorian told her the names his people had for some of them. The gold cardinal fish with its glowing purple eyes; silver-sides, their sleek, little bodies shining in the blue shadows; and the brilliant damselfish, its tiny, graceful form the same luminous sapphire hue as Dorian's eyes.

Abruptly, sediment swirled in a powdery explosion. When it had settled once more, Thalassa made out the form of a long, light gray creature lying motionless on the ocean floor. It regarded her with round, incurious eyes, so completely lacking in expression that she shivered.

Dorian's hand touched her back, and his voice spoke reassuringly in her mind. *That is what we call a nurse shark. Do not be afraid; it will not hurt you. There are many different types of sharks in these waters, and in time you will grow accustomed to seeing them. They never attack our people because we use our powers to warn them off. Sharks can be deadly, but they are stupid creatures. Watch.*

For several moments, he stared hard at the motionless shark. Thalassa felt an almost physical sensation of menace building, as if some terrible threat was bearing down on them with awful speed. She started, but Dorian held her fast and nodded toward the shark. It was whipping its tail back and forth in an inexplicable frenzy, its cold eyes glancing wildly about. An instant later, it shot away, swimming as if its very life depended on it.

Thalassa stared after the fleeing creature in amazement, and Dorian grinned. *I sent it the message that great danger was approaching. It works not only with sharks, but with any other creature that could harm us, such as sea snakes or scorpion fish. Our highly developed mental strength is an effective defense against danger. But truly, Thalassa, sea creatures prefer to lead a peaceful existence and attack only when they feel threatened.*

Thalassa listened to this explanation without really hearing it. In truth, she was in the hands of a god, a god with powers the extent of which she was just beginning to learn. Dorian guided her forward again, and she was mesmerized once more by the multitude of life around them.

She saw fiery orange sea cucumbers inching along the ocean floor, tirelessly sifting the sediment for food with their mass of writhing tentacles. Bright purple sea urchins lined rocky outcroppings, sharing their homes with heart urchins, sand dollars, and tiny starfish of all shades and hues. Flexible sea fans—the color of burnt umber—grew out of the ocean bottom itself, looking like small trees as they bent gracefully in the surges of prevailing currents.

Sea anemones were everywhere, as numerous as brightly colored flowers in a field, and they reminded Thalassa jarringly of the wildflowers that bloomed on the plains of Amazonia. Then the pain of her remembering was forgotten as she gazed in wonder at a big, soft coral, its rubbery, treelike body an iridescent white and glowing eerily out of the shadows. Scarlet growths studded the coral's body, gleaming like startling red blossoms against the paleness. Thalassa stared until Dorian tugged her on.

Leisurely he took her higher. The deep monochromatic blue lightened as they moved upward, and the water gradually warmed in response to the distant sun. More creatures lived at this depth. Dorian identified many of them as they hurried past, although their names made little sense to Thalassa, overwhelmed as she was. An undulating, large brown eel slithered ominously by, almost touching her as it passed. She stiffened, but Dorian completely ignored it. Reassured by his lack of concern, she turned her head to watch as the eel disappeared harmlessly into the depths.

The sun lit the water—brighter and then brighter still. Abruptly their heads broke through the shimmering surface, and sunlight poured hotly down on Thalassa's face, as sweet and strong as warmed honey. The feel of it was beyond words. Tipping her head back, she closed her eyes and forgot everything.

The wet, heavy odor that was uniquely the sea's flowed into her nostrils, the sun kissed her cheeks, and for a moment, Thalassa was home. Once again, she floated lazily in the gentle waters off the coast of Amazonia. The nightmarish abduction by a god of the sea had not happened after all, and in another moment she would begin the swim back to her familiar beach.

"Are you rested now, my love?"

The deep voice jolted through her, and in consternation she jerked her eyes open to meet Dorian's gaze. Treading water with unwitting ease, she glared at him.

Her captor's eyes sparkled back at her—as ever-changingly blue as the ocean around them. His hair gleamed black as the sea's midnight depths, and his skin was as smooth and brown as burnished copper. He grinned at her, and his teeth flashed like pearls. The torque and arm-rings of heavy gold that he wore shone wetly in the sun. Truly, he looked like a king, Thalassa thought, and an odd sensation gripped her heart.

Dorian laughed joyfully. "But I am a king, dearling; and you are my queen," he said, reading the thought in her mind, as well as something else he was far too wise to tease her with.

Thalassa was relieved his voice no longer sounded inside her head, but she frowned angrily nonetheless. "I do not want to be a queen," she said hotly. "Yours, or any other male creature's. And I do not like your seeing the thoughts in my head and speaking them aloud. I wish you would stop."

It was hardly wise to talk to a god in that way, she thought belatedly. She had heard that the deities of men were notorious for their uncertain tempers, and she wondered, somewhat apprehensively, if Dorian's response to her insolence might not be to blast her into a bloody spot upon the waves.

He seemed disconcertingly unoffended by her sharp words, though. "It bothers you because you are not used to it," he said, "which I can well understand. But you will find, my sweet, that you possess the ability to look into my thoughts as well. It is simply a matter of learning how to use your newfound abilities."

Dumbfounded, she stared at him. A dozen questions sprang into her mind, but in the end she asked none of them.

It was too much to deal with—this notion that the one who had abducted her would actually gift her with powers like his. He could not mean it, she decided, and looked away from him, hoping to glimpse some sign of land.

All she beheld was the sea, a limitless expanse of jewel-bright water, rolling under a blazing sun in whatever direction she gazed. Far below, the ocean world Dorian had shown her teemed with life, but here on the surface he was the only living thing to be seen. This far from land, not even the cries of birds arose to disturb the immensity of sea and sky. The sea moved as it had for millennia—ceaseless, eternal, with a primeval, rushing murmur that had no beginning and no end. Somewhere to the east—lost in that infinite universe of waves and sky—lay Amazonia.

Thalassa's sense of isolation heightened until it was a knife blade in her vitals. She had lain with Dorian several more times since he had first taken her to his bed, and just as he had said, her pleasure had increased. It appalled her, the way she responded to his body's embrace. Was she to become like one of the Greeks' timid, housebred women after all—craving nothing but the touch of her lord—a bitch in heat, waiting to be mounted?

Even if the Goddess were to remove this destiny and allow her to return home, how could she face her kinswomen with the knowledge of her willing submission lying heavy on her breast? A wave splashed saltily into her mouth, and Dorian's hand closed lightly on her arm.

"Come," he said. "It's a long swim for one's first time out, and we've been treading water a good while. You grow tired—as well you should. Let us return to my abode now. Tomorrow, we will come out again."

His voice was courtesy itself, but Thalassa had learned to recognize the note of command in those gentle tones. She knew it would be useless to argue. In any case, there was nowhere to escape to in this vast, wave-tossed land of his, and even if there were, she could hardly hope to outswim the obvious ruler of these waters.

"It matters little to me where we go," she said dispiritedly. "For I am still your captive, am I not?"

Dorian sighed. The uneasy progress of Thalassa's thoughts was as clear to him as his own, and he wished he could bethink himself of some way to spare her this distress. The bonding between them had helped, but Thalassa had yet to give her heart—to either him or this life.

She could not lay aside his abduction of her, but clung instead to her Amazon teachings, though her grip grew more slippery each day. He would loosen her hold eventually, he thought as he studied her unhappy face. But it would not be today.

"You are no longer my captive," he said at last, then abruptly changed the subject. "You are greatly troubled about what the Elders may have foreseen, aren't you?"

Thalassa looked at him. To her, the Elders were shadowy figures, made even more mysterious by the custom that forbade her to have any contact with them until after the Ceremony of Matebonding—the ritual that would formally make her Dorian's queen and a member of his people once and for all.

Dorian had apologized about this. Far from being offended, though, Thalassa had felt only relief. She had no desire to confront these Elders, who were far more awesome to her than Dorian, who was at least familiar now. No, she was not in the least interested in meeting the Elders.

But their prophecy—that was another matter. Neither Dorian's lovemaking nor even this incredible entrance into the sea had been able to drive the lowering heaviness of doom from her thoughts. The idea that some terrible fate might be descending upon the Amazons was an ever-present torment, preying upon her constantly.

Despite her preoccupation, she had noticed that her status among the merfolk had changed since Dorian had taken her to his bed. In that way they were no different from the man-ruled tribes, she had reflected bitterly. They still treated her with great friendliness, but there was a respect in the sea-people's geniality now that had not been present before. Even the irrepressible Lisala seemed a bit intimidated, as though Thalassa's entering the king's bed had placed her beyond the pale of ordinary friendship. In any case, Dorian's guardianship, light as it had become, had ceased completely. Thalassa was permitted, even encouraged, to wander the abode for as long as she wished, with neither Dorian nor anyone else to gainsay where she went or what she did.

She would have been surprised to know that Dorian's relaxed attitude stemmed not from any notion of male possession, but from the telepathic union that now existed between them. With that invisible thread in place, he could keep track of her far more closely than if she was under the guard of a hundred men. But for all the link's unseen power, he was extremely delicate about its use. He took great care not to intrude upon her thoughts, and for that reason, he did not know what she had done. . . .

"Thalassa." Dorian's deep voice sounded gruff and, to Thalassa's surprise, almost ill at ease. "Would you like to return to the waters of Amazonia?"

Thunderstruck she stared at him, her mouth opening in astonishment so that a particularly large wave washed salt water down her throat. The resultant fit of coughing was a mercy. It saved her from having to reply, at least for a moment, to his incredible question. Stalling for time, she gasped, "Y-you would let me go home—after all that has happened?"

"I should never have told you about this accursed prophecy. It was a stupid thing to do. I am not given to doing stupid things, though it seems I have done little else since bringing you into my life." He slapped the water with an open palm. "Yet I have told you and there is no help for it. We may as well go to Amazonia to see how your birth-people fare. I wish you to be happy in your new life, Thalassa, and as long as you brood upon the fate of the Amazons, that cannot happen."

Of all the things she might have guessed he would do, she could never have suspected this! Did he know of her most recent talk with Valya, and was he toying with her? No, such did not appear to be his way. Despite the impediment of his maleness he seemed quite honest, and after all, he *had* told her things that he could have kept to himself.

If he knew that Valya and his cohorts were not bound for the southern reaches to swim with the whalefolk, as they had told everyone, but were instead heading east, toward the Sea of Amazonia, he would surely have stopped them.

But what would be their punishment *and* hers, if Dorian discovered the duplicity, which he surely would if he took her back to Amazonia? Yet, refusing to go would arouse his vigilance. She could already see suspicion spreading across his features in the blazing sunlight.

"I thought this would please you," he said with a puzzled frown. "Your reaction seems very strange."

"I . . . I was thinking," she replied, then improvised hastily. "What if something terrible has already befallen my sisters in my absence?"

His face cleared. "Ah, so that's what troubles you. Well, my soul, if that is the case, then at least you will know and no longer have to wonder. But Thalassa, the matter of prophecies is a tricky business. The Elders themselves admit it. Perhaps nothing has happened to the Amazons. If so, you can embark on your new life with a peaceful heart."

He was looking at her with a pleased expression, obviously expecting her to be as delighted with him as he was with himself. And if it weren't for her having already taken matters into her own hands, she would have been. Dorian's offer was stunning in its generosity. Certainly there was no need for him to be so kind, so concerned with her happiness. It was a side of him she was unprepared for—in him or any other man.

"There is something you can agree to, in return, of course," he added.

Her newfound feelings of tenderness promptly evaporated. "I should have known," she said sarcastically. "You would not grant me such a kindness without demanding a price."

"Not such a great price, but one that requires your cooperation nonetheless."

Reaching out an arm, he drew her against him so she could rest from the downward pull of the sea. The gesture, along with the sensation of his warm and wet body against hers, reminded her all too sharply of the morning he had risen out of the waves to capture her. But she was too tired to pull away, and he seemed unaware of her tension.

"The Ceremony of Matebonding remains to be done." Above the rush of the waters, his soft voice was strangely penetrating, filtering through her entire body. "It's a private ritual, so I . . . we can hold it wherever we choose."

Thalassa found this odd. Among the Amazons, the naming of a queen was an event that lasted for days, marked by prayer, fasting, countless sacrifices to the Goddess, and a formal ritual before the entire tribe. "Don't your people expect to see this happen?" she asked in genuine curiosity. "How else do they know that I am"—She could not bring herself to say the words, *your queen*. "That it is done?"

Although her back was to him she could almost see him smile. "As I've told you, merfolk are not like the people of the land. They will know."

Later, when the lights in the abode had been dimmed for night, Thalassa drifted into wakefulness within the darkened chamber of the king. She lay alone in Dorian's big bed, wondering what had awoken her from the deep sleep brought on by the long and exhausting day, and confused as to where he had gone. Then she heard voices.

They were coming from the opposite end of the room. Though the two spoke softly, she recognized Dorian's voice and that of his sister, Aricia. She even understood them. Since the joining of her body to Dorian's, she had discovered an instant comprehension of the merfolk's murmurous tongue, if not an ability to speak it.

". . . are sure she will not awaken?" It was Aricia, her vibrant voice low and hushed.

"She won't. The sea tired her greatly and she should sleep through the night undisturbed."

"You could check her thoughts to make certain."

Thalassa puzzled over Aricia's comment as Dorian said, "No, I don't think that's necessary. Anyway, I haven't been probing her thoughts at all as yet, and I don't want to until she's become more used to all these changes."

"Brother, do you think that's wise?"

"It's wiser than what I've already done." There was a pause, and Thalassa struggled to maintain the deep regular breaths of sleep, so as not to alert them to the fact she was awake. "Aricia," he went on, "I must confide in someone and there is no one closer to me than you. I told the Elders I placed the Sea Spell upon her."

"What of it? You did, didn't you?"

There was another pause, longer this time, then Dorian said, "No, sister, I didn't."

"By all the tides . . ." Aricia's soft voice shook with disbelief. "You *deceived* the Elders—lied to them! Dorian, why? And how? Did they not see the lie in your mind?"

Dorian's own voice was heavy and sad. "I used the skills Nomar himself taught me—skills I never expected to put to such a purpose."

"But why, brother? The Sea Spell would not have hurt her—"

"Who are we to say that, Aricia? We, who have never experienced it? It would have robbed her of her will and made her forget much about her past. Oh, she would have become tractable and surely more pleasant to deal with . . . and far less interesting. I want a woman as my mate, Aricia, not some docile milk-fed creature, which is what she has so often accused me of desiring."

"Is that how you think of our mother?" Though Thalassa's eyes were closed, she conjured up a picture of Aricia, the merwoman's back stiff and her eyes blazing with righteous indignation. "*She* was no dull-witted and tame sea cow, Dorian, and well you know it!"

"Neither was she an Amazon." There was a deep exhalation of breath that Thalassa assumed came from Dorian. "Sister, our mother was a slave owned by a cruel master. Any life was better than the one she had, so to her the Sea Spell was a blessing. She had no desire and certainly no need to remember all the abuses she suffered before Father took her. But Thalassa is different. I don't wish to take away her memories, Aricia. I want her to stay with me because she chooses it, not because she doesn't remember any other life."

"Dorian, have you forgotten what you're risking? No ruler has ever done such a thing. I don't know which is worse: your not using the Sea Spell or that you deceived the Elders about it. They themselves can't declare you unfit to rule, but when they find out what you've done, they will surely bring it before all the people for a judgment. Dorian, your kingship could be stripped from you—our entire line dishonored!"

"They won't find out, Aricia, at least—"

"Of course they will! The Ceremony of Matebonding must be performed, and afterward she is to be formally welcomed by the Elders. They will know at once the spell was never laid! And even before, someone in the abode will surely see she's not acting properly and the Elders will know!"

"Let me finish. No one will notice anything because at dawn tomorrow I am taking her away. The Ceremony of Matebonding will be done far from here and by the time we return, she should be content. The Sea Spell becomes irrelevant then, and while the Elders may be angered by my unorthodox methods, they will hardly be able to argue with the outcome."

"You mean she'll be with child."

"And happy about it, and this life as well, if I have my way."

"You had better," Aricia said somberly. "Your kingship could be at stake here, my brother. I don't agree with any of this, but . . ." A long silence followed, and when Aricia spoke again, Thalassa had to strain to hear the softly uttered words. "I love you and I've never seen you act unwisely before. Therefore, I will say nothing of your plan, mad as I think it is."

"Thank you, beloved sister. Now let us go to the state chamber. There are matters we need to discuss if you are to rule in my stead while I am gone."

Footsteps padded across the tiled floor, then the door softly closed. Thalassa's eyes flew open in the darkness. Bolting upright in the huge bed, she sat there, struggling to comprehend what she had heard.

The ominous and terrifying Sea Spell had hovered over her from the first moment she had learned of it. Other than the conversation they had had after her escape attempt, Dorian had not spoken of it, and fearful of what the result might be if *she* did, Thalassa had not dared to. Now the mystery was explained, though the explaining of it confused things far more than it clarified them.

Why should Dorian care so much that she stay with him

of her own choice? It made him more difficult to understand than ever . . . and it lent new strength to the strange emotions she was feeling for the man-creature she had once hated with all her heart.

Thalassa forced herself to lie back down in the rumpled bed. Dorian might return at any moment, and he must not find her sitting there, wide-eyed and stunned. Falling back to sleep with her thoughts awhirl seemed an impossible task, but she had to attempt it. She turned on her side and lay tensely in the darkness, fruitlessly trying to relax so the furious beating of her heart would not give her away to Dorian when he came back.

But long moments passed and he did not return. Her pounding heart gradually slowed, her eyelids grew heavy, and soon feigning sleep was no longer necessary. She never knew when Dorian slipped silently back into bed and fitted his body against the curve of hers.

CHAPTER 18

∼ Days had passed, and Oreithyia, war queen of the
Amazons, still stalked about Themiscrya as one
possessed. Victorious from her foray against the Cappadocians, she had returned with her force of warriors, to find
chaos and grief raging unchecked through the bright plains
of Amazonia.

On being told of the death of one sister and the
abduction of the other, Oreithyia had not wailed or torn her
hair, or shown any outward signs of anguish. All she had
done was whisper, "So this is what the Goddess sought to
warn me of in the dreams She sent me. A black-bearded
man from the Greek lands . . . a man who would bring us
great harm. If only I had heeded those dreams."

After, she said nothing more. As the solemn preparations for Hippolyte's burial went forward, Oreithyia paced
the broad banks of the Thermodon for hours, a silent and
ominous figure upon whose thoughts no one dared intrude.

Cloaked in the mists rising off the river each dawn, she
eerily resembled her murdered sister, as if Hippolyte's spirit
still walked these familiar lands, unable to find peace in the

glowing afterworld of the Goddess while her earthly blood lay unavenged. Oreithyia neither ate nor slept, and in her taut, ravaged face, her eyes burned like live coals—deep with reddish-black flames that lit her whole body with an aura of malevolent hate.

Four days after the fleet of Heracles had fled, the Amazons gathered to give their queen back to the breast of Earth Mother. The burial was at dusk, for it was at night that the powers of the Goddess were strongest.

The dirt and blood of Hippolyte's brutal death had been cleansed tenderly from her, and the once beautiful body dressed in a tunic of the softest Egyptian linen. A heavy breastplate of purest gold hid the gaping wound that had ended her life. Greaves of the same rich metal gripped the long, lovely legs that had so bewitched Heracles; and fillets of gold and silver bound the long black hair, lusterless now in death.

To replace the one taken by Heracles, a shining new golden sword belt studded with jewels encircled her slender waist. It had been designed in tears, and made with all the skill the master craftswomen possessed. Carefully placed by the dead queen were her crescent-shaped shield and a wave-patterned quiver filled with arrows tipped in that rare black metal called iron. In her hand reposed the final mark of royalty, a ceremonial *bipennis*, the ax's great double blades fashioned from the finest gold.

Amidst the funeral songs and the prayers supplicating Artemis to give her queenly daughter a warrior's welcome in the Bright Land, Hippolyte was borne to her final resting place. As the garland-decorated litter was carried to the waiting grave, people crowded around it, sobbing and reaching out to touch their queen one last time. The plain of Themiscrya was filled with Amazons—from the most ancient grandmother to the youngest suckling babe. Each and every Amazon who lived was there to bid Hippolyte farewell.

Snorting and tugging at their gilded lead ropes, two horses pranced nervously along on either side of the queen's litter. One—a milk-white stallion—was intended as a gift to the Mother, so that Hippolyte's entrance into the afterworld would be assured. The other was a striking bay mare with mane and tail of midnight and a hide the color of burnished copper. Raised by Hippolyte from a foal, she had been the queen's beloved comrade. Now the mare would join her human companion in the Land of the Dead.

Oreithyia watched stonily as her sister was laid reverently in the soft, deep bed dug for her at the first light of dawn. With gentle skill the mare was guided into the pit. Her hooves flailed as if she sensed her coming death, then a razor-sharp knife sliced swiftly across her jugular vein. White-eyed and rearing with terror at the heavy smell of blood, the big stallion was led forward and dispatched just as quickly.

The bodies of the two horses, still quivering and kicking with the last echoes of life, were carefully arranged around the dead queen. Blood streamed from their severed throats, flowing into the dark, loamy soil, creeping along the edges of Hippolyte's white linen tunic, and soaking the feet of the women in the grave. Oreithyia's lips drew back in a silent snarl as the smell of death rose hot and thick on the evening air.

The sun trailed crimson streamers as it sank into the ocean. Oreithyia's eyes blazed as she stared at the waters stained bloody by the dying sun. The ocean. That alien element her people had never learned to navigate. It had brought them nothing but evil in the form of men in their vermilion galleys—galleys painted as red as the blood of these two dead horses, as red as the blood of her sister. . . .

The sun was almost gone, night was coming, and all the world looked and smelled of blood and death. Oreithyia raised her arms.

"My sisters!" Her voice was deep and it croaked hoarsely, sounding to her more like the raven-headed woman of nightmares' voice than her own. "Look well on this sight. Burn it deep into your very bones, so that you may carry it with you always. Our queen and my beloved birth-sister lying in the bloody grip of death—and all because of the treachery of men!

"How many times have I said it? *Men cannot be trusted!* Now do you see what comes of welcoming men into our midst. Look well, sisters. Carve the vision of our slain queen into your eyeballs, for you will have to carry it a long way. All the way to Greece—where we will avenge Hippolyte and free Antiope from the humiliation of slavery!"

Oreithyia's voice had risen to a shriek. It truly seemed as if the spirit of the raven-headed woman had entered into her, and Oreithyia welcomed it—welcomed the cleansing, murderous lust for blood that would make her a better war queen and perhaps ease the terrible pain in her breast. The air shuddered as her kindred shouted crazed battle cries in response to her words, and the red coals that had become Oreithyia's eyes glowed with joy. The blood-price would be paid. Men would swim in a sea of blood before she deemed payment was sufficient.

So, as the tragic summer faded into a crimson-hued autumn, and an unseasonably early first snow whitened the ground that held Hippolyte within its embrace, the Amazons—like a great beast stretching its muscles before the hunt—prepared for war.

The expedition Queen Oreithyia planned was no inconsequential border raid, but a full-fledged campaign against the entire world of men.

But such an expedition required prodigious organization, endurance, and discipline. Fully realizing the magnitude of the revenge she intended, Oreithyia sought out allies to augment the Amazon host. A war treaty was concluded with the Gargarians, and special envoys sent to the far-off Scythians. Through her messenger, Oreithyia reminded King Sagillus that Amazons and Scythians were of common stock. They both were menaced by these ambitious Greeks, who had already sent a war fleet to Themiscrya, and if left unchecked would challenge Scythia as surely as the rising sun.

Sagillus, keenly aware of any threat to the sovereignty of Scythia, promised to send his son Panasagoras with a large number of mounted troops. Within days, they arrived, a shouting and boisterous multitude of wild, unkempt horsemen, riding horses as shaggy as themselves and eating everything in sight.

With their arrival and that of the Gargarians, there was no more need to wait. But before taking the far-going road to Athens, Queen Oreithyia performed one final act. On the day the sprawling army was set to leave, the war queen roused herself several hours before dawn, gathered up her weapons, and left the royal house she had shared with her two sisters. Her tall, ominous figure flowed past the snoring clusters of Gargarians and Scythians like a wraith of the night.

A small retinue of warriors awaited her at the beach. In silence they followed Oreithyia into a coracle held steady for them by two elderly priestesses. As the two grandmothers poled the round, little boat into the lapping waves, Oreithyia settled herself uncomfortably, her dark gaze brooding on the star-silvered sea. There was only one exception to the Amazon's lack of affinity with the sea—the secret trip to the Isle of Otrere, that flat, bird-haunted island named for one of her people's greatest queens.

Queen Otrere had built a temple there when the Amazons first settled along the coast, and the war queen still offered sacrifice at the temple on the eve of any great battle. Oreithyia rubbed her sleep-crusted eyes and bit back a yawn. For the last two days she and every other woman of fighting age—seasoned warrior or unblooded fledgling—had been lashing herself into a frenzy at the shrine to Holy Artemis.

Dozens of sheep and cattle had been sacrificed. After each offering, the women had performed a wild shield dance, followed by an even wilder circle dance. During the latter, the dancers shook arrow-filled quivers and stomped the ground in unison to the accompaniment of pipes. Their full-throated howls of ecstasy chilled the blood of the listening Gargarians and Scythians, and penetrated to the heights of the very mountains themselves.

Now, only one last group of sacrifices remained. The coracle's wooden hull scraped against the Isle of Otrere's rocky shore, and Oreithyia's sharp eyes made out the dark roofless shape of the temple of Artemis looming blackly against the purple predawn sky. Pulling her short mantle tighter about her shoulders, she disembarked from the boat and led the way up the rocky path.

Her feet in their short boots of untanned leather embroidered with stars found the route by themselves. She had been there before, but never with such a terrible pain in her heart, a pain that only the spilling of blood would ease. Ahead of her the temple waited, deliberately built without a roof so that the daughters of the Goddess could always feel the closeness of Her presence.

The nervous whicker of horses came to Oreithyia's ears, mingled with the heavy breathing of men. The priestesses who lived on this sacred island had already assembled the sacrifices to Artemis, and everything was in readiness for the ceremonial ax of the war queen. By the crude altar constructed of pebbles, they stood in the flickering yellow torchlight: four unblemished two-year-old stallions, taken from the Goddess-consecrated herd that roamed unfettered throughout the island, and four male slaves bound hand and foot. An even number, as was pleasing to the Goddess.

Oreithyia's gaze rested coldly on the four trembling men. Slaves, she thought contemptuously. But they would have to do.

Oreithyia turned to the eldest priestess and said in a ringing voice, "When we return, Grandmother, I will bring Greek men without number to Holy Artemis. Here on Her altar, they will offer up the gift of their lives. And one of them will be Theseus of Athens—he who thinks he can enslave our youngest queen with impunity. Soon he will find out what the rule of women truly means!"

The tall, ancient priestess inclined her gray head. "Well spoken, my queen," she said in a deep voice. "Now let us begin. The hour for sacrifice draws near."

The first of the slaves, a stocky, dark-haired man whose knees had locked with dread, was jerked forward and stretched out upon the black stone set in the middle of the altar. Artemis had bequeathed this massive stone to Queen Otrere in a dream, and it had since become the Amazons' most sacred object. To burn offerings of sheep or oxen on the black altar was forbidden. Only the blood of horses and men was considered rich enough to give the Goddess, here in Her most hallowed and secret place.

The priestesses began the invocation, drowning out the doomed man as he babbled frantically in his own language. The young stallions, whose turn would soon come, shifted their hooves and tossed their heads at the smell of fear-sweat. The women, long experienced at this sort of thing, soothed the uneasy animals and held them still.

The chant to Artemis crescendoed, and with a flourish, the chief priestess handed Oreithyia the sacrificial *bipennis*. As the great double blades whined in a glittering arc above the war queen's head, the slave's babblings became a wordless shriek of utter terror—a high, shrilling sound that was abruptly and horribly cut off as the ax smote his skull.

The quivering corpse was quickly removed and laid beside the altar. Oreithyia's mouth curved grimly. The thin, weak blood of slaves was poor compensation for the life of Hippolyte. But soon the hot, thick life-fluid of Greek warriors would cover her hands, and then . . . *then* the blood-price would be paid!

The stars had dissolved in the gray blanket of a cloudy dawn, when Valya's head broke through the surface of the sea. With bright and worried eyes, he took his first look at the coast of Amazonia. To his amazement the beach and the rolling fields that lay beyond were black with men—small, shaggy-looking men who lay sprawled in sleep among herds of tethered four-legged animals.

Horses! Valya was more fascinated by his first glimpse of these legendary creatures than by their human masters. A second head popped up beside his own, and brushing long strands of blond hair from her mouth, a young woman called Latora frowned at him.

"Valya! Why do you dawdle about on the surface while we wait below for your report? All of us are as eager to see this land as you— Oh . . ." Her green eyes widened as she saw the crowded beach. "But there are so many of them—all jammed together like barnacles on a rock! Is *this* how they live?"

"I don't think so. For look you, Latora, they are all men, and the lady Thalassa said men do not dwell among the Amazons." A new and terrible thought suddenly struck him. "You don't think we could have traveled to the wrong land, do you?"

The girl shot him a disgusted look. "Of course not. The Elders may have forbidden us the abodes of landfolk, but not the knowledge of how to reach them if we choose. At least, *I* know how to find my way about!"

Stung, Valya retorted, "Then if you be so wise, explain why the shores of this woman-ruled place are filled with men!"

Latora squinted at the distant beach. "Sea and sky, Valya, I don't know. The ways of the landfolk are a mystery to me as much as they are to you. One thing I do know: we had better go back and tell the others about this so we can decide what to do."

"Do?" Valya glanced at her in surprise. "We know what we must do, Latora." He thought of the lady Thalassa, of the desperation in her face when she had come to him. "I am resigned to staying with your lord," she had said, "so I will not ask you to risk exile by helping me to escape. But there is something you can do for me if you still wish to see the land. . . ."

"We must deliver the message as was agreed," he went on firmly, "for the lady Thalassa is relying on us to do so. And anyway, if we don't go ahead with our plan, then what was the use in our coming here? I certainly didn't risk the anger of the lord Dorian and the Elders simply to turn around and go home."

Latora shook her head doubtfully, but as it turned out she was the only one of the small group who had any hesitations about going ashore. Ferne and Ellice—the two other women—as well as the two men—Badru and Matteo—all were as eager as Valya to set their feet upon one of the great lands of the Terrans. And so, with Latora reluctantly bringing up the rear, they swam close in to shore, searching for a place where they could unobtrusively leave the sea.

This proved more difficult than any of them—even the dubious Latora—had anticipated, for the rows of unkempt snoring men stretched for miles along the sandy beach. Finally, at a spot where the sands ended and the waves blew white foam around jagged boulders that glistened black under a weak, cloud-filtered sun, the six young people slipped ashore. Climbing over the slick rocks with native-born ease, they quickly traversed the pebble-strewn beach and regrouped under the huge, spreading trees of the first true forest any of them had ever seen.

Valya could scarcely contain himself. From the sea he had been able to glimpse the majestic mountains of Amazonia, their flanks clothed in green and their heads capped with the silvery stuff he had once heard called *snow*.

Trees, just like the gigantic one under which he stood, marched all the way up to those very peaks. It was an intoxicating sight, and it filled Valya with a yearning to follow the strangely orderly progression of this towering forest over the mountains' steep sides and witness for himself what lay on the other side.

He jumped as an impatient hand shook his arm. "Valya!" It was Badru, his thick auburn hair plastered wetly against his forehead. "What ails you? I've asked you twice who it was the lady Thalassa instructed us to seek out. Didn't you hear me?"

"He heard you," Latora said in a tone of weary exasperation. "He has been this way ever since we struck these waters and he surfaced to look at the land."

Valya glared at her. "Or-ei-thy-ia." He pronounced each syllable of the difficult Amazon name with the utmost care. He had been practicing it endlessly during the several days of their journey and was determined to say it correctly when the all-important moment arrived. "They call her their war queen, and she is responsible for defending them in times of danger. Lady Thalassa said there are two other queens as well, but this Oreithyia is the one we must speak to about the prophecy."

"Well, let us go find her then." Petite, black-haired Ferne stared off through the trees, her dark eyes alight with nervous excitement. "Their city is at the mouth of that river we saw, which means we have a goodly distance to walk."

The little party set off toward the river Thermodon and Themiscrya, following the beach but staying within the screening protection of the trees to avoid the strange men, some of whom, with grunts and muttered curses, were now beginning to waken. Fitful sunlight rippled through the forest's dense living roof, and as the young people walked, their feet pressed deep into an earth that was cool and damp with mold and generations of fallen leaves.

It was like nothing any of them had ever felt. Oh, they had occasionally visited small islands inhabited only by animals and set in the vastness of tropical oceans. But the sea dominated those tiny pieces of land, surrounding and dwarfing such islands with its indifferent immensity. Here the sea receded. Even its very smell grew faint before the odors of ancient woods, mountains, and plains.

Snow rarely fell this close to the beach, and the traces of its first early coming had already melted away, except for a stray patch here and there. The visitors came upon these infrequent spots with delight, joying in the alien feel of the cold stuff upon their toes. Though they had begun their walk quietly enough, the snow, along with each new incredible sight, gradually caused them to wax more exuberant. Now they were noisy.

Startled by their approach, a pair of deer burst from a heavily wooded copse, bounding up a nearby slope as though on wings. All six merfolk froze in their tracks. In bemused wonder they stared at these unknown animals until the graceful creatures had vanished among the trees. Then they turned to continue on their way, only to find four tall women dressed in leggings and leather tunics that left one breast bared, standing in front of them, feathered arrows nocked to bowstrings, eyes fixed in cold menace.

"Who skulks about the shores of Amazonia?" a grizzled-looking female with heavily muscled arms demanded. "You had better give an answer that satisfies me, or we'll kill you here and now!"

CHAPTER 19

≈ Oreithyia sat glumly in the queen's house, her eyelids heavy with fatigue and her morning meal of fermented mare's milk, barley bread, and dried fruit untouched. The exhilaration of the blood sacrifices to Artemis had passed along with the lives of the four unfortunate slaves. She wished she could seek her couch and lose herself in sleep, rather than having to sit there brooding upon the omens portended by the baffling arrival of six strangers, unarmed and unclothed in the cool weather of autumn.

Panasagoras, leader of the Scythian host, sat with her, partaking heartily from the dishes set before him. Sloshing a crust of bread in the bowl of mare's milk, he drained the bowl, popped the bread into his mouth, and belched lustily. "I'll say one thing," he said, his bearded jaws working busily over the bread crust. "You women certainly know how to feed a man."

Oreithyia slanted him a look from the corners of her black eyes, and the Scythian amended hastily, "I mean— you have shown us great hospitality." He quickly poured

himself a goblet of wine from the flagon at his elbow and
drank half of it off at once.

Oreithyia returned to her brooding, for which Panasagoras was grateful. He would have gladly let one thousand of
his shaggy Scythian ponies trample over him before admitting it, but these Amazons—Oreithyia, in particular—made
him nervous. Yet the strong wine, combined with the bite of
fermented milk, sent a warm glow of contentment through
him. Feeling cheerful, he pushed himself back against the
piled cushions.

"So, War Queen, what do you intend to do with these
strangers who have delayed our departure? Are you going to
sacrifice them to your Goddess?"

Absently Oreithyia cracked a nut in her strong brown
fingers. She scarcely heard him. From the buzz of the
voices outside she could tell the sentries were approaching
with the booty they had caught. She sat straighter in the
carved wooden chair, her gaze fixed grimly on the open
doorway. Within a few moments, the sound of many
footsteps rang in the hall and the sentries entered with the
prisoners in tow.

"By my balls!" Panasagoras rose on the cushions. "You
did not say there were women, Lady. And such women! I
hope you're not going to waste *them* in sacrifice. Give the
females to us instead. We'll make good use of them, I
promise you."

The war queen ignored him. Flanked by the scowling
sentries the six captives stood before her. Despite her
determination to remain impassive, she found herself
staring at them incredulously. Just as the runner had
reported, they were astonishingly tall, easily overreaching
the Amazons who guarded them. Their tanned limbs bulged
with powerful rippling muscles, and even the shortest of
them—a dark black-haired female—would have towered
over Panasagoras had the bow-legged Scythian stood up. A
fact that, judging by the frown on his bearded face, was
obviously not lost upon him.

Oreithyia shifted in her chair, disturbed to realize that
these strangers must have come willingly to the queen's
house. Though they carried no weapons, any one of them
looked capable of overpowering even Chylldia, the tough

sentry commander. Quickly the war queen pushed this disloyal thought aside and gazed at the foreigners' one adornment, necklaces of heavy gold worked with such magnificence, simply looking upon them was enough to hurt the eye.

The wearers of the necklaces returned her scrutiny with wide, friendly smiles. Considering the gravity of their situation, these trespassers were strangely unafraid. Oreithyia watched in irritation as they gazed about the chamber with birdlike curiosity, studying it, the Scythian, and her as though everything had been arranged solely for their entertainment.

"We would have slain the men right off and brought just the women to you," Chylldia said sourly, "but they speak our tongue, and they said some things that are . . . uh, disturbing."

Oreithyia glanced at her sharply. "What things?"

"We bring you a message, Lady," one of the young women said in a low, clear voice. Her cool green eyes met Oreithyia's with a directness worthy of any Amazon. "It is from one of your kinswomen who fears you probably think her dead."

"And who is that?" A cold breath of wind ran along Oreithyia's spine, despite the braziers set about the chamber to warm it against the morning chill. With her own eyes she had seen Hippolyte laid in the earth, but was her murdered sister sending her some word on this, the most important campaign the Amazons had ever faced? Or was it Antiope who was trying to reach her? Hope and fear racing through her veins, she demanded, "Answer me! Who sent you here?"

The green-eyed girl whispered something to the tall, handsome youth next to her, then nudged him. Casting a nervous glance at his companions he stepped forward.

"Oreithyia, war queen of the Amazons," he began formally, "your kinswoman Thalassa sends you her greetings—"

"Thalassa!" The mouths of Oreithyia and the four sentries dropped open.

"Who's Thalassa?" Panasagoras asked impatiently.

"One of our sisters who disappeared at the start of the

summer. We thought her captured by slavers"—Oreithyia's black eyes hardened—"or dead."

"She is not dead, Lady," the blond youth answered, "but very much alive. And she has not forgotten her people. Her heart aches for the sight of them, yet she cannot come here herself, so she bid us come instead, to say that she loves you, and to warn—"

"Why can she not come herself?" interrupted one of the sentries. "Who holds her captive?"

"And who are *you* that you know so much about her, and us?" another put in. "Thalassa would not give her name to those who took her by force—"

Oreithyia motioned brusquely for silence. "Let him finish. Go on, boy."

The youth drew a deep breath. "She told us her name so that you would know this message indeed comes from her. Lady, the wise ones of my people have the gift of seeing, and they foretell that harm may come to your tribe"—he cast an uneasy glance at Panasagoras—"from men who visit your shores."

The five Amazons stared at him in profound silence, and Panasagoras muttered an incantation to protect against evil. "This is ill-omened," he growled to Oreithyia.

His words unbound the war queen from the spell the youth's words had put upon her, and she let out a horrible, croaking laugh that was almost demented in its mirth. "Ill-omened, eh? You're certainly right about *that*, Scythian. This warning of theirs comes too late!" Turning dark, wild eyes on the disconcerted strangers, she snarled, "The harm your wise ones foresaw has already swooped down upon us! One of my sisters lies dead, and the other, along with some of our bravest warriors, is even now being carried off to the worst of all fates—enslavement to men!"

Aghast, the young merfolk looked at each other. Of all the possible scenarios as to how they might be received, this one had never occurred to any of them. But Valya was especially horrified, for he had come to know Thalassa better than the others. It was he whom she had chosen to confide in, he whom she had entrusted with the delivery of this vitally urgent message! Her plight, and that of her people, was all the more real to him because of it, and though Valya well knew that nothing could ever come of such a misplaced attraction, he was a bit infatuated with this landwoman who was the lord Dorian's chosen one. Saving the Amazons from an evil fate was the one thing he could have done to earn her undying gratitude, and now he had failed, failed miserably.

"L-Lady," he stammered, "we came as soon as we could. Indeed, we thought the men who are here"—he carefully averted his gaze from the glowering Panasagoras—"might be the ones . . ."

"That your so-called warning spoke of?" Again Oreithyia cackled that dreadful laugh. "These men are here as allies, to march with us against the Greeks. *They* are the men of this ill-timed prophecy—treacherous dogs who dishonored the ancient laws of hospitality and shed the blood of my sister and my kinswomen. It is they whom we go to destroy—every last one of them!"

Valya heard a quick intake of breath from Matteo, then the tall merman asked excitedly, "Do you mean that you intend to go to war, Lady?"

War. It was something they had all heard of. Why, their own people had engaged in it with the Selkie folk at one time, though that had been long, long ago, and not even within the living memory of the Elders had such a thing happened since.

Panasagoras gulped noisily from his wine goblet. "Yes, she means war, you fool of a boy," he said irritably. "Don't they train men in warrior pursuits where you come from? War Queen, are you going to sacrifice them or not? We've already been delayed a day as it is, and my men chafe to be on their way, as do the Gargarians. If you want my opinion—"

"I don't." Oreithyia had recovered herself, and a chilling calm had taken the place of her mad humor. "Tell me of Thalassa," she said to Valya.

Obediently he launched into a carefully rehearsed explanation. This question he was at least prepared for, and whether or not they would believe him, the words came easily enough. He concluded with the sentence Thalassa herself had drilled into him. "She has received signs that the Goddess placed this destiny upon her, and though it be like a spear in her breast, she cannot set herself against that sacred will."

Gazing at the hard faces of Oreithyia and the four sentries, he added earnestly, "Our lord Dorian is a good man. He loves her already and will treat her well. Of this I am sure."

"And you expect us to make you welcome after bringing news that your lord carried off one of our sisters?" Chyl-ldia's tone was outraged. "This whole tale smells of trickery. People do not live under the sea like—like fish!"

Ferne steadily met Oreithyia's black gaze. "The lady Thalassa told us the Amazons are a tribe that lives by its honor," the small merwoman said with quiet dignity. "We have spoken the truth here, and though it came too late to save your sisters, it is no less the truth. Your kinswoman thought you would be grateful, both for the warning and the news that she is well. She said in return you would allow us to stay among you for a while, to see something of this wondrous land which we have heard of but never seen."

"Bah." Draining off his third cup of wine, Panasagoras slammed the empty goblet down upon the table. The appearance of these foreigners and their incredible story on the eve of a battle campaign could not be construed as anything other than the harbinger of a terrible doom. The Scythian leader was worried.

If it were up to him, he would pack the whole lot of his troops up and head for home. But it was not up to him. Sagillus had committed his men and his son to this enterprise, and Panasagoras shuddered at what the reaction of his doughty sire would be if they returned home, their high-wheeled wagons empty of booty and slaves.

It was irksome that the Amazons did not seem frightened by the implications of the situation, but then, that was what happened when women took on roles they were unsuited for. They lost all common sense. The Scythian shook his head. Since his female allies obviously did not possess much in the way of wisdom, he would have to take matters in hand.

"You should stop conversing with these creatures and consecrate them to your Goddess." His gaze lingered regretfully on the firm silken curves of Latora, Ferne, and Ellice. "Even the women. The gift of six unblemished, beautiful sacrifices will please Her, and in return She will protect us from any powers their undersea kin might throw at us in retaliation for their deaths. Do this now, Lady, so that we can leave with tomorrow's dawn."

The four sentries muttered angrily at the Scythian's peremptory tone, and Oreithyia favored him with a look as black and cold as winter ice. "These are Amazon matters, Panasagoras," she said in a voice as frigid as her eyes. "We do not need or desire your advice. Still . . ."

She sighed, and her voice became less icy. "You are right about one thing. We must not delay our departure another day. We will leave tomorrow." She studied the assembled merfolk, assessing their powerfully muscled frames with a warrior's eye. "Do any of you know how to handle weapons?"

Six eager smiles greeted this question. "We are all well able to take care of ourselves, Lady," Valya explained. "And you will find"—he gave Panasagoras a contemptuous glance—"that we are much stronger than the men of land. Including *this* one, who is so eager to see us die."

"He is not the only one!" The words burst from the youngest of the sentries, a warrior with dark disheveled hair and burning eyes. "Oreithyia, Thalassa and I are age-mates, and friends! We must avenge her abduction, not welcome the kin of he who carried her off!"

"We have no choice!" The war queen leaped from her chair, black hair whirling about her flushed and tired face. "If this story of theirs is true, then Thalassa herself has bound us by promising them safety, Hippothoe. Kin of an evil lord they may be, but we cannot kill them else we dishonor Thalassa's word as a warrior, and ours in the bargain! Unless . . ." Her voice lowered dangerously. "Unless they are lying."

"They are! They must be!" Hippothoe, Chylldia, and the two other sentries burst out in a chorus of angry denial.

Oreithyia sank back into her chair and regarded the silent merfolk. "Well," she said in a soft, sinister tone, "it seems that none of us believe your claim of living in the sea." She jerked her head toward the scowling Panasagoras. "He wants to see your blood spilled in Artemis's honor, and perhaps he is right. Yet if the Goddess did indeed have a hand in this, that would not be wise. So, because of the love we bear Thalassa, I will ask you this: Can you prove what you say?"

"I suppose we can," Valya answered slowly. He glanced hopefully at Latora, who was the most cautious of all of them, and also the most quick-witted. Of course, neither he nor any of the others took the threat of being killed by the Amazons seriously. Their confidence in the special gifts of their kind ran deep. Compared to folk of the land, they were virtually invincible—and in any case, the safety of the sea was very close.

Latora calmly gazed back at the Amazon war queen. "If it is proof you want," she said, "come down to the ocean with us. There we will give you all the proof you require."

As the late morning sun struggled to shred the thin gray blanket of clouds, they did just that. Oreithyia, Panasagoras, the sentries, and a crowd of Amazons, Scythians, and Gargarians stood clustered along the beach, watching as the six strangers waded unconcernedly into the chill waters of the autumn sea.

"This is nonsense," Panasagoras kept grumbling to whoever would listen. "No one can stay underwater for as long as it takes a horse to gallop five leagues. Utter foolishness. We should sacrifice them and be done with it!"

The foreigners were swimming now, cutting through the waves with smooth, powerful strokes. When their heads were specks on the heaving ocean skin, they turned and waved back to those on shore.

Oreithyia nodded. "Now, we'll see what's what." She raised an arm and looked behind her, to where Hippothoe sat, mounted upon a glistening chestnut mare. She watched the young Amazon rein in the impatiently prancing animal, and when the horse was still, slashed her arm downward.

The mare shot off down the beach in a chestnut streak. At precisely the same instant the heads of the six foreigners vanished beneath the sea. Moments passed, and a strange quiet descended upon the beach. Gradually, the rhythmic thunder of the mare's hooves faded away, until only the roll of the breakers and the cry of an occasional bird was left behind. Even Panasagoras's outraged muttering ceased, and he stood like all the rest, his eyes glued to the spot where those six heads had disappeared.

When Oreithyia's voice broke the eerie silence, those nearest her jumped. "I never realized it could take so long to gallop five leagues. Think you they swam down the beach and quickly surfaced to take a breath of air?"

All around her heads shook in negation. "No, Lady," Chylldia said. "There are watchers posted up and down the sand for as many leagues as you commanded. If they tried to deceive us in that way, someone would surely see."

Silence fell once more, and within it, Oreithyia stood pondering. She was no less sensitive to omens than Panasagoras, but unlike the squat Scythian, she was not convinced that the strangers' appearance portended doom. If they truly came from Thalassa, their presence was a sign of good rather than evil forces. Thalassa had been stolen, and yet—Oreithyia's thoughts flew—she had also sent word that Artemis had ordained the abduction, which meant the Goddess must have some purpose in sending these odd creatures to her.

"Hoofbeats!" The cry rang excitedly down the beach. "Hippothoe is returning!"

The steady thud of a horse's hooves drifted faintly to the war queen's ears. It rapidly became louder, then the chestnut mare came into view, galloping along the flattened sand at the water's edge with the effortless gait common to all the wonderful horses bred by Amazons. Mane and tail streaming in the wind, her hooves throwing up clods of wet sand, she pounded toward Oreithyia, with Hippothoe perched low along her outstretched neck. As they neared the war queen they slowed to a canter, a trot, and then a walk.

"Well, she is back," Chylldia said. "But where are they?"

"Drowned probably," Panasagoras said sourly. "And anyway, how could they know your warrior is finished galloping the five leagues, if they are truly beneath the sea?"

Oreithyia pinned her gaze upon the undulating waves. "They said the vibrations of the mare's hooves would tell them."

"That far out in the water? Hah! They are dead. Now let's put an end to this foolish—"

"There they are, Lady, there they are!"

Oreithyia did not need to be told. Transfixed, she watched six heads break through the dark blue surface with synchronized precision. As sleek and graceful as the otters her people sometimes glimpsed in the river Thermodon, the strangers swam toward land. All who stood there—including Panasagoras—watched them in utter silence. They rode the rolling waves with an ease that made Oreithyia think of the chestnut mare's effortless gallop, the mare whose loud snorting was now the only sound to be heard on this beach full of stunned observers.

As the strangers waded the last few feet in to shore, Hippothoe slid from her horse's back and said in a wondering voice, "By Artemis's holy bow, they told the truth."

"So it would seem." Oreithyia squared her shoulders and stepped forward.

The dripping wet merfolk stood by themselves, encircled by an invisible barrier beyond which none of the staring men and women dared to go. Silently the crowd of people opened a path for the war queen. Straight backed and grim, Oreithyia strode through it.

"Now hear me," she said, her voice low and hard. "I see that you are truly from the sea, but for that watery world of yours I bear no love. Never has the sea brought us anything more than grief. And your Elders are not the only ones who have visions.

"The Goddess, too, sent me dreams warning of evil in the shape of men, yet I was foolish and paid no heed to Her warning. For that I have paid a terrible price. Not again will I make such a mistake. I think Artemis has sent you here for a purpose, and I will use *any* weapon against the Greeks, even if it means allowing men to dwell among us for a time.

"So these are my terms. If you wish to stay here, then you must accompany us to Greece. If you fight well, *and* if you live . . . then we will see. If that does not please you, go back to the sea. Now."

She ignored the mutterings all around her and stared piercingly at the foreigners' tanned, youthful faces. They were the only ones who did not seem disconcerted by what she had said. In fact, they did not consult among themselves for even a moment. The one called Valya stepped forward, a wide smile on his attractive face.

"Lady," he said happily, "pleased indeed we will be to come with you."

CHAPTER 20

≈ Thalassa swam passively at Dorian's side as the sun heralded the first day of their journey to Amazonia. Since they had started she had been like this, following Dorian's lead and accepting his guidance with a meekness he would have found amazing, had he not himself been so preoccupied.

The previous night, after he and Aricia had concluded their meeting and she had sought her bedchamber, Dorian had been on the way to his own bed when a hearty voice had called out his name. It was Myrwyn, his younger brother, fresh from the southern reaches, still wet from having come through the interlocking chamber, and eager to hear of his brother's mate.

Dorian had greeted him with mingled joy and trepidation. Despite his silvery-white hair—a physical characteristic that often cropped up among the merfolk—Myrwyn was the youngest of the three of them, older than the troublesome Valya, but not by much. There was a deep bond between the two brothers, though since taking on the mantle of kingship, Dorian had not confided in Myrwyn to the extent he did the level-headed Aricia.

Myrwyn was generous to a fault, openhearted and completely devoted to his brother and sister, but given to an impulsive tongue. To trust him with the knowledge he had deceived the Elders would be a mistake. Such devastating information might slip all too easily from the ebullient Myrwyn's lips, before the friendly soul realized it.

So, squelching his feelings of guilt at adding his brother to the list of those he could not be truthful with, Dorian had spoken of Thalassa in the most general of terms. But as he guided his chosen one in the direction of her birthland, Dorian's thoughts kept returning to the final exchange he and Myrwyn had had before parting for the night.

Casually asking about the six meryouths who had left for the southern reaches, Dorian had been taken aback by Myrwyn's blank expression. "I have seen no one from these waters," the cheerful young man had said, "nor sensed their vibrations as I came here."

"But that is very odd." Frowning, Dorian had stopped in front of the chamber Myrwyn occupied whenever he stayed in his brother's abode. "Valya said they were going south to visit the whalefolk, and they departed only days ago. You should have met up with them."

Myrwyn had vigorously shaken his silvery head. "Well, I haven't. And neither have the whalefolk. A pod of them accompanied me here most of the way, and their senses are far keener than mine. If Valya and his friends were taking the southern pathways we surely would have known."

The brief conversation had troubled Dorian. Why would the six youngsters lie about their destination? True, they were all at an annoying and defiant age, but he would not have considered them capable of practicing deceit. Yet neither had he thought himself capable of it, and look what he had done. Deceit breeds deceit, his father had once said. How ironic and deeply disturbing to think that in some eerie way his actions might have given rise to theirs!

A fine king he was turning out to be, he thought bitterly, for how could he accuse them of deceit with the example he himself had set? Yet, like a school of feeding fish his thoughts kept darting around the mystery of the young ones' departure. He was unable to rid himself of the premonition that it was somehow connected to Thalassa.

In truth, he was growing tired of this whole coil. Aricia was right after all, and he was mad. He should put the Sea Spell upon Thalassa that night, perform the Ceremony of Matebonding, and return to his abode on the morrow, with her contented and acquiescent at his side. If Thalassa and the meryouths were indeed involved in some sort of duplicity, then she would tell him of it herself.

The brightening sun painted the water above their heads with gay fingers, and Dorian grew ever more convinced that he had been in the grip of a temporary madness. The risks were simply too great. How could he have placed an idea drawn from the philosophies of the discredited and long-dead Jabari above the kingship and traditions of his people—traditions that rested more heavily on the king's shoulders than anyone else's?

He had been selfish. The honor of his family must not be violated, as it surely would be if he persisted in holding to this dangerous course. The Sea Spell would not hurt Thalassa. Aricia was right about that, as well. Yes, Dorian told himself with a pang of regret, he would lay it upon her at sunset, then bid good-bye to this madness.

Belatedly he became aware that Thalassa had stopped moving, and indeed would have begun to sink into the depths had he not placed a firm arm across her back. Quickly he sent his thoughts into her mind. *What is it?*

Thalassa hesitated. Using this inexplicable method of communicating was a profound indication of the changes that had overtaken her, and she had avoided it despite his urging.

Just think of what it is you wish to say, and I will hear it, he encouraged.

I . . . I feel something. The thoughts were as halting as the spoken words would have been, and uncertainly she stumbled on. *As if there are people nearby. Many people.*

By the Great Mother Ocean . . . Dorian angrily sent his senses winging upward. Here she was, totally new to the sea and picking up the presence of galleys, while he mooned idly along, ignoring everything about him. *Your burgeoning powers grow keen, my love,* he told her ruefully. *Landfolk are indeed traveling above our heads.*

Can we look upon them?

It was Dorian's turn to hesitate. The sea-people often sensed the presence of galleys. Uniformly uninterested in Terran doings, they usually swam off without approaching them and that was the end of it. Dorian's initial reaction was to do the same. Yet hers was a simple request, one that seemed easy enough to grant, particularly in light of the prickling guilt he was feeling over what he intended to do at day's end.

Well, there seems little to be gained from gazing at the galleys of some merchant or group of pirates, he telegraphed reluctantly. *But if it will please you, we can take a quick look.*

Thalassa had grown accustomed to emerging from the depths into the vast, rushing stillness of a deserted ocean. This time it was different, of course. Distant shouts greeted her ears, and, stunned, she beheld a fleet of nine crimson-painted galleys bobbing in the sun-flamed waters of early dawn. Eight of the vessels were clustered together in an ordered formation, but the ninth drifted apart, and it was from this one that the shouts were being carried.

"Galleys, such as the ones Greek traders use," she muttered incredulously. "Only bigger. They are much bigger."

After so much time in her captor's enchanted world, she had almost come to believe the world of land that she sprang from no longer existed. This evidence that it did was a confusing and dizzying reality, and Thalassa wondered if she were dreaming this vision of distant men-filled galleys. Dorian's words convinced her she was not.

"Yes, they are Greek galleys," he said with disgust in his fine voice. "But they are built for war, not trade. And it sounds as though a battle is occurring on one of them."

He scowled as a shift in wind brought the shouts and cries closer to his and Thalassa's ears. "The landfolk never seem to weary of searching each other out in order to commit acts of violence. Bad enough that they must kill one another on the earth, but when they carry their love of killing onto the breast of the Great Mother Sea, I lose all patience. Come, Thalassa, we will leave them to their foolish violence. It has naught to do with us."

But Thalassa resisted the gentle pressure of his hand.

The wind now brought more than the shouts of men. There were women on that galley—Amazons! "I hear the war cries of my kindred," she whispered hoarsely.

Dorian paused. "Surely not," he said firmly. "You must be mistaken."

"By the Goddess, I hear the war cries of my sisters! They are in danger, and I must go to them!"

"No." Dorian's hand tightened implacably on her wrist. "The women are probably captives, taken in some battle with another man-ruled people. It's unfortunate, and I grieve for their fate, but it is a common enough thing. If I were to go about my kingdom rescuing every landwoman taken in such a way, I would never have a moment's rest or peace. Now come, my love. We have seen enough."

Desperation roiled through every fiber of Thalassa's being. In another moment, he would pull her below the sea. She could sense it, just as she could sense that she was not strong enough to prevent him. "Please . . ." she said raggedly. "In the name of the Mother . . . I beg you. Let me go to them."

He was silent, and she ventured a glance at his face. He was regarding her solemnly, his long fingers still encircling her wrist. "Is it so important you would swallow your fierce Amazon pride to beg me?" he asked slowly.

"Yes." She met his probing eyes without hesitation. The certainty that Amazon warriors were battling for their lives on the lone galley was so strong, she would do anything—including beg—to reach them.

He sighed. "Very well, then. Let us go closer to see if there are indeed Amazons aboard that galley. But if there are not," he added warningly, "then we will leave, and I will not permit you to argue. I will not have you harmed, or seeking to escape me by climbing onto a vessel of the landfolk."

He freed her, and she instantly dove beneath the waves. For the first time since Dorian had brought her into the sea, she was truly glad of the metamorphosis forced upon her. It seemed that she could not swim fast enough toward the distant ship. But fast as she swam, Dorian paced her, his big, naked body pressing lightly but watchfully against her side. As they neared the galley, the waters ahead of them exploded.

Thalassa saw the body of a man tumble into the sea, arms and legs spread wide as if to embrace it. His throat had been slashed from ear to ear, and blood fountained out in graceful spirals, forming a red cloud about the corpse. Three more explosions rapidly followed as additional bodies—all of them male—were pitched overboard to join the first.

It would not be wise to stay here overlong, Dorian said into Thalassa's mind. *The blood from these dead men will draw sharks, and it will take considerable power to persuade them that we are not part of their meal.*

Determinedly he took control of their course, steering her to a point just beyond the galley's bow. *We will surface here, so that you may see whether your kinswomen are aboard. Look well, sweetheart, and then we will depart this place.*

Thalassa thrust her head through the sea's glittering roof. Shouts of savage triumph, mingled with agony-filled screams, immediately battered at her ears. As her gaze raced over the ship, every muscle in her body went rigid. The combatants rushing back and forth upon the galley's wooden decks were too absorbed in slicing at one another to take notice of the watchers in the sea, but that mattered little to Thalassa.

On the very edge of the galley's heaving bow, two figures were engaged in a furious struggle. The one closest to Thalassa swung its sword in a sweeping arc and viciously decapitated the other. The headless body toppled into the bloody sea, and with an ululating cry, the victor dashed away in search of a new opponent.

Unaware that she did so, Thalassa clutched Dorian's arm. "That is my age-mate, Tecmessa," she cried, heedless of who might hear her. "She has been captured—along with the Goddess knows how many others of my people! I must help them!"

"It does not appear they need much in the way of help." Treading water beside her, Dorian narrowed his eyes thoughtfully as he watched the raging fray. "They seem to be disposing of the Greeks most handily," he added, and swiftly grabbed Thalassa's arm as she plunged forward.

Splashing wildly, Thalassa fought to be free of him. But it was useless. He simply captured her other arm, and with that impossible and maddening strength, pinioned her easily against him. Spitting water, she twisted around so she could see his face. "You say you care for me, yet you would force me to stand idly by while Amazons fight and die for their freedom! I am a warrior, and if you deny me the right to aid my people, I will hate you forever! This I swear on every drop of their spilled blood!"

Her frantic eyes blazed into his, and Dorian read the determination and anguish burning in those golden depths. He frowned and looked away, taking care that his grip on her did not slacken. The other galleys in the flotilla were trying to maneuver back to their battle-stricken sister ship. So far the winds had not favored them in their attempt, but as the morning breezes freshened, Dorian knew that could quickly change.

"I do care for you, Thalassa," he said, his quiet voice oddly penetrating above the rushing waves and distant shouts. "But I have told you over and over that you belong to my people now, and not the Amazons."

"Then hear me!"

The fever of confusion, of wild anticipation at seeing Amazonia once more, and of dread that Thalassa had been struggling with suddenly became unbearable. For hours she had been swimming next to Dorian, the conversation of the night before repeating itself endlessly in her brain. At any moment, she expected him to use his awesome powers and discover she had not been asleep, after all. And when he did? The things she had heard gave her power over him—a power he would have to neutralize, either by the terrifying Sea Spell or something even more dreadful.

True, he had told Aricia he would not, but Thalassa could not quite believe he had meant it. His apparent distaste for the magic that would take away her will would surely vanish if he found she had any sort of weapon to hold over his head. Above all, she had told herself, he must not discover what she knew. But now, with the cries of her sisters ringing in her ears, she had no choice but to wield the one pitiful weapon she possessed.

"Hear me," she repeated hoarsely. "If you take me from here, then I will go to your Elders and tell them of the deceit practiced by their king. I'm sure they will be very interested to know how he has lied to them."

She had not realized how utterly glacial his eyes could become—like shards of the blue glass Egyptian traders sold. Around them the ocean swells splashed and foamed, and the groans and shouts of battle continued. But Dorian held Thalassa motionless, staring into her face with those terrible eyes.

"And just what," he asked slowly, "will you say to them?"

"I'll say . . ." Her voice quavered shamefully, yet she forced herself on. "I'll say that you did not fulfill your duties as you told them, and that I am not under the power of any accursed spell!"

"Ah." The lightness of his tone turned the simple word into something chilling. "Then I should place you under a spell to remedy that, shouldn't I?"

She swallowed. All her fears were coming true, yet mixed with her dread and her desperate concern for the galley-bound Amazons was a crazy sense of relief. If this long-feared thing was to happen at last, then she had nothing more to lose.

"Do as you may," she cried despairingly, "I know that I cannot prevent you. But you have already lied to your Elders, and were you to place me under ten thousand spells, your deceit would still remain unchanged!"

The ice in Dorian's eyes turned to blue flames. His long fingers tightened upon her until she feared that in another moment, she would shame herself by wincing. "To hear such truth from the lips of one who understands so little," he muttered so softly, she wasn't sure she had heard him correctly.

The king of the merfolk was furious, as coldly angry as he had ever been in his entire life. Aricia had urged him to probe Thalassa's thoughts, but he had been too confident, too sure of himself, and her. *This* was what his arrogance had brought him.

She had a hold over him now—this untried innocent from the primitive folk of the land; this child-warrior whose abilities he and the rest of his long-lived people had viewed with such indulgence. He could put the Sea Spell upon her this very instant and it would make no difference. In her frantic ravings she had unwittingly stumbled on the truth.

The spell would affect her memories and her will, but it could not stop her tongue. And it might not be able to overcome the intensity of this experience, or her subsequent desire for revenge. His mouth twisted. Of course there were other spells he could lay, but at what point did one cry enough? When his mate's power for independent thought was completely gone?

Yet he could not allow her to go to the Elders. Despite his bravado with Aricia, Dorian had never intended to divulge his secret, even after he had brought Thalassa back content and pregnant with his heir. In the Elders' view the seriousness of what he had done might not be mitigated by a satisfactory conclusion. They could still bring the matter of his deceiving them before the people, with all its attendant embarrassment and potential for dishonor. No, his break with tradition was never to have become known, especially not by Thalassa, not *yet*. . . .

Thalassa had watched his face breathlessly during the few seconds it took for these thoughts to spin through his mind. In that beautiful frozen visage with its twisted mouth lay the failure of her sorry attempt to aid her captive sisters. Bitterness overwhelmed her fear, and she said savagely, "If you are so against my going to my kindred, *why* then were you taking me to Amazonia?"

He looked at her in surprise. "Why, to see how your people fared, of course. But at a distance! It was never my intention to let you approach them, Thalassa, nor is it now, although"—the anger in his deep voice matched the savagery in hers—"you leave me little choice."

She stopped breathing.

"It seems you have won a victory, my love."

Dorian's grip had never eased, and now it tightened again upon her shoulders until she did wince, expecting at any moment to hear her bones snapping beneath his hands. Then those terrible fingers loosened.

"But a small victory," he said deliberately, "and one that is only temporary. Believe me, Thalassa."

"I do," she whispered when she had recovered her voice.

Her face burned as if he had held a flame to it, and rage pounded through her with such fury, her body throbbed. Yet she controlled herself. Only a few minutes had passed since they had surfaced and seen the galleys, but who knew how many Amazons could have died or been wounded in that time? Since he was capitulating, she dared not lose her hard-won advantage by giving way to a foolish show of anger.

"You will let me go to them, then?"

He nodded curtly. "*We* will go, and by the eternal tides, woman, if you seek to use this as a means of escaping me, you will regret it. Now, if you wish to help your Amazons, we had better hurry. The rest of the fleet is seeking to turn about and come to the aid of their fellows, and if they succeed it will make things terribly difficult."

Thalassa's rage was forgotten. Not only would he not stop her, but he actually meant to help her as well? she thought in wonder. Her eyes glowed into Dorian's—not with anger or suspicion, but with a warmth and openness he had never seen before. She bared her white teeth in a feral grin. "Let us hurry, then. And I thank you for your aid to my people."

It was the first truly genuine response she had ever given him, and Dorian ruefully reflected that it was not his compelling persona but his willingness to shed blood in defense of her birth-people that had brought it about. Were Amazons not aboard that ship, things would likely be very different. He shrugged off these thoughts as they dove under the surface and swam cautiously toward the galley. As they neared its side, he drew close to her.

Listen well, Thalassa. He sent the words forcefully into her mind. *When we surface and go aboard this galley, you will find that you possess the strength of my people now. Your physical power will far exceed that of any man born to the land. But I caution you to take care. You are not invulnerable, and a well-placed sword can still wound or kill you. I cannot and will not allow you to be harmed. For that reason, I will remain close by your side . . . so do not behave foolishly.*

Foolishly? Thalassa was totally unaware of the ease with which she hurled her reply back into Dorian's mind, so insulted was she. *I am a blooded warrior and I do not behave foolishly in battle. Nor do I need your protection, man of the sea!*

Dorian smiled grimly. *Nevertheless, you shall have it. Now, are you ready?*

Thalassa glared in answer. So he thought he had to protect her, did he? Her newly born gratitude toward Dorian threatened to vanish at his condescending words, and only with the fiercest of efforts did she control herself. The heated blood of battle was already pounding through her veins, driven by a frantic and heartfelt desire to see the faces of her beloved kinswomen. Clearing her mind of all but the coming strife, she nodded curtly.

They swam forward again. The galley's untended oars were trailing aimlessly through the water, and Thalassa and Dorian slipped agilely in between the long flailing shafts to the low railing that lined the deck. The sun-warmed wood was wet with sea spray beneath Thalassa's hands, though she scarcely noticed the slipperiness of it in her eagerness to heave herself aboard. She landed on the swaying deck with the grace of a cat, and the first sight her eyes beheld was a bleeding, unarmed Amazon valiantly defending herself against a burly sword-wielding Greek.

Unbidden, the war cry of her people erupted from Thalassa's throat. In a single leap she was beside the unevenly matched pair, her hands closing on the man's arm as he raised the sword, aiming at his wounded opponent's head.

Dorian's assurances about her extraordinary strength had not really touched her—until now. In truth, she needed to use only one hand to stop the muscular Greek. Not knowing this, Thalassa used two, and thus not only broke his arm, but wrenched it out of its socket and sent him flying into the sea. Hideous shrieks promptly issued from the water as sharks—drawn by the bloody corpses—converged swiftly on this thrashing, live prey.

The entire encounter lasted no more than a few seconds.

Thalassa saw that the warrior she had rescued was staring at her as if she were a shade, come back from the land of the dead, and she smiled joyfully.

"Thalassa . . . ?" the other woman whispered.

CHAPTER 21

≈ "I urge you to exchange your greetings later."
Dorian scooped up the unfortunate Greek's
sword and handed it to the Amazon, who gaped at this
towering, naked man who spoke her tongue so perfectly.
Before Thalassa could intervene, he went on. "We have
been noticed, and since you are wounded, you have the
most need of a weapon. Thalassa and I will manage."

"Do not fear him," Thalassa said quickly. "He is a
frien—"

She had no time for more. Even in the midst of combat,
it was impossible for a naked man and woman to appear out
of nowhere on that crowded deck and not draw attention
from Amazon and Greek alike. To the latter, it rapidly
became apparent that these magical beings were not there in
their defense. Terror began to overcome the men's battle
fever, and soon their screams for help were carrying to their
companions on the other galleys as loudly as their battle
yells had minutes earlier.

Drunk with the power of her unimaginable strength,
Thalassa was a virtual hurricane of lethal force. She was

vaguely aware of Dorian's presence beside her, but he did not interfere, leaving her free to fight as she chose. She alternated between destroying her foes bare-handed and with a sword swept up from one of her fallen opponents.

The tide of battle had been turning in favor of the ferocious and skilled Amazons, outnumbered though they were. Dorian and Thalassa's arrival left the victory assured. As Dorian casually lifted two men off their feet, one in either hand, strangled them, and hurled the lifeless bodies overboard, Heracles stood in the bow of the lead galley, staring with uncharacteristic awe.

When at first light, the lookouts had called to him that the captives on the prisoner ship had freed themselves during the night, Heracles had been filled with exasperated anger. "Zeus blast these cursed women!" he had roared to no one in particular. But despite his ire, he had not taken the Amazons' revolt seriously. They were unarmed and outnumbered and female. Surely it would not take long before they were secured and under the control of their new masters once more.

This had not happened. Instead, he and the Greeks on the other eight galleys had watched in growing consternation as the determined Amazons fought with superior skill and courage. In an appallingly short time it began to look as if these defiant slaves might actually succeed with their rebellion, and a truly furious Heracles ordered the fleet to come about.

As the galleys struggled to obey his commands in the teeth of a capricious wind, Heracles growled to Theseus, "We will put an end to this nonsense. And when we do, each and every one of those women who still live will receive a good ten lashes for her insolence. Not enough to kill them, mind you. Just enough to break their spirits. That should finally teach them respect for their lords!"

Theseus did not answer. Behind them, Antiope lay in the small tent of oiled linen cloth that he had ordered erected for their privacy. During the twelve days at sea, the only influence over her hatred and fury had been seasickness. Even then he had still found it necessary to keep her bound for his own safety, and that of everyone else on board. The young king groaned inwardly. He was certain Antiope could hear the sounds of conflict on the prisoner galley, and he sighed at how much more intractable his new bed slave would be if her kinswomen were flogged.

The appearance of the two mysterious figures—seeming to have come from the heart of the very sea itself—had paralyzed Theseus with wonder. "Truly, it is my father, the lord Poseidon," he muttered to Heracles. "And the woman at his side must be the nymph Caenis—she who asked him to transform her into an invulnerable fighter as a love gift."

Heracles snorted. "Poseidon rules over the sea, and the sea is the province of men. Therefore, he is a god of men. He would not come out of his palace under the waters to help unnatural women such as these. And it is obvious that he is helping them, as is that naked creature with him." He hesitated, then said uneasily, "Perhaps Soloon was right, after all, and these Amazons are demons and have called upon other evil spirits to aid them."

"I do not think so. Even if they could summon such aid," Theseus said reasonably, "the demons they called would resemble females because of the Amazons' hatred of men. And he is too manly and proud in form to be summoned up by mere women."

Theseus's gaze was fixed on the black-haired man on the besieged galley. The stranger looked taller and more formidable than the mighty Heracles himself, truly a noble sire for the king of Athens to have! Pride rushed through Theseus at the thought that he might be descended from the loins of this magnificent being.

"No, my lord, I believe that we look upon Poseidon himself. We have offended him in some terrible way, and that is why he has turned away from his proper sons."

Heracles regarded his second-in-command worriedly. The gods were easily displeased. He, who had suffered the effects of their disfavor so horribly in the past, knew better than anyone.

Futilely the hero wracked his brain, trying to think of some sacrifice they had failed to offer the deity of the sea, some propitiation they had erred in making, but nothing came to mind. And Heracles, ever a man of action, grew impatient with standing in useless thought while his fleet dithered in the contrary winds, and his men were put to death with ruthless efficiency.

"What ails you?" he bellowed so loudly that he was heard on each of the other seven galleys. "Fumble-fingered, mewling, milksop virgins masquerading as warriors of Greece! Bring these ships alongside that galley, or by Zeus's mighty cock, I'll throw some of you overboard to feed the sharks!"

"My lord!" It was Peleus who turned from the task of directing the rowers on the lead galley. He struggled to remain respectful as he addressed his commander, but frustration was clearly evident in the slight tremor of his voice. "The gods bear me witness that we are trying," he said. "But the winds ill favor us. It's as if an evil spell has been cast to keep us from obeying your orders." He did not mention that he and the other men were completely terrified by the two obviously supernatural figures aiding the Amazon captives.

Heracles, however, divined this. "Fear is making all of you clumsy," he said, fixing Peleus with a cold eye. He raised his voice so that it carried again to all the galleys.

"I have vanquished the lion of Nemea and the many-headed Lernaean hydra. It was I who captured the Ceryneian hind—sacred beast to Artemis herself, the very Goddess those misbegotten Amazons worship. I took the savage Erymanthian boar alive and tamed the man-eating horses of Diomedes. And if that be not enough, it was I who drove away the bronze-beaked, bronze-clawed Stymphalian birds that feed upon the flesh of men. All these things I have done, and I say now that my might will conquer those two demons called up by mere women, as surely as I have defeated all my other foes. But first, I must get close enough to fight!"

"That's all very well for him," Peirthoos whispered to Theseus. The king of the Lapiths looked about him, then continued, "But how many of us will die in the meantime? Our numbers are already reduced by battling the Amazons. We cannot afford to lose more men, Theseus. We barely have enough to man the oars as it is."

"I know," the king of Athens whispered back. "But

what of our comrades on the prisoner's galley, Peirthoos? Do we leave them to die?"

Peirthoos shrugged. "Such is obviously their fate. It appears that they have been ordained as sacrifices to the powers of the sea, and it is not for mortal men to intervene, Theseus. To do so could bring disaster upon us all."

"You two gossip like women at the water well," Heracles's voice boomed out. "What do you natter about?"

Peirthoos looked at Theseus. The latter squared his shoulders and drew a deep breath. "We are thinking, Lord," he began carefully, "that Poseidon desires those on that galley—Greek and Amazon alike—as offerings. And we are thinking that it would not be wise to thwart the god of the sea in his desire."

A murmur of assent rose from the men within hearing distance, and Heracles scowled blackly. But before he could respond, the winds that had been merely uncooperative turned hostile. Billowing the wide sails out with their strength, they spun the eight galleys off the course Heracles had ordered set, as easily as though the forty-oared vessels were toys in the hand of a giant.

"You see?" Peleus cried as the rowers struggled with the oars. "Theseus has spoken truly. The god himself has sent this wind as an omen, and we must heed it!"

"Nonsense!" In a towering rage, Heracles stomped up and down the deck. But even his awesome strength was helpless against the powers of wind and sea, and in an astonishingly short time the entire fleet was pushed away from the lone galley.

On the bloodstained decks of that galley, a cheer went up as the vessels fled before the wind. Every one of the Greeks who had manned the prisoner ship lay floating in the crimson-dyed waters around it, his lifeless body surrounded by hordes of voracious sharks.

Standing beside Thalassa, Dorian blew his breath out in a gusty sigh of relief. "One would almost think the Mother herself had sent that wind," he murmured. "And it is well, for had they reached us, we would have been vastly outnumbered." He did not add that had this occurred, he would have seized Thalassa and borne her away forcibly, rather than staying to fight a battle there was no hope of winning.

Thalassa smiled at him, exhilarated and astonished by the fact that she was scarcely out of breath after all her exertions. "You are modest," she admonished him happily, "for it is clear as the river Thermodon that you called up the wind to save the lives and freedom of my kinswomen. And this, after fighting so bravely at our sides. We are all of us in your debt."

"Indeed," a woman said. "But what manner of man comes to the aid of Amazons, and speaks our tongue as if it were his own? And Thalassa . . . have you returned from the halls of the dead to fight with your sisters in their time of need . . . and brought this one with you?"

It was Tecmessa who spoke. Turning, Thalassa saw that her age-mate and the other surviving Amazons were clustered together at the deck's far end, regarding herself and Dorian with more than a little apprehension.

"But I am not dead," she cried joyfully. "And this one—even though he be a man and once my sworn enemy—has righted some of the wrongs he committed against me by what he did today." Not all of them, she thought, suddenly conscious of Dorian's pensive gaze upon her. For would he release her now, to go with her kindred, wherever they were bound?

"Thalassa . . . then the Goddess in Her great kindness has sent you back to us!" A dark-haired, stocky woman broke from the grouped Amazons and ran toward her.

It was Evandre, one of Thalassa's closest friends. With a sob, Thalassa flung herself forward, and the two women fell into each other's arms. Evandre's move shattered the holding spell that had lain upon the group. In an instant, Thalassa was surrounded by laughing, crying, and hugging warriors, all of them talking and shouting questions at once, while Dorian stood and watched, his mouth drawn forbiddingly tight.

Thalassa finally motioned for silence. From the corner of her eye, she could see Dorian, his face an inscrutable mask. Was he waiting to see what she told her people about her disappearance? She cleared her throat and took Tecmessa's hands in hers.

"Sisters, I will tell you of how I came to be here, but first, I must know what doom fell upon you that those maggot-ridden men took you captive. Did they come on you unawares as you were swimming, or hunting, as when those Cretan pirate dogs sought to take us? Remember, Tecmessa?"

"Of course, I remember." Tecmessa's voice was grim. "And by the sacred pool of Artemis, I wish it had been something so insignificant as Cretan pirates." As the other Amazons remained silent, she described the tragic events that had so recently taken place.

Thalassa's face grew white as she listened, and against that blanched skin her golden eyes blazed like a fire in a field of snow. "And Antiope?" she asked at last, vaguely surprised at how calm her voice was. "Why is she not here with you? Did they murder her as well after their galleys left the shores of Amazonia?"

"No, although I am certain that would have been her wish rather than what befell her. When these curs moved us all to one galley—so as to guard us more easily, they said—Heracles gave orders that Antiope was to stay where she was."

"Why?"

Tecmessa's gaze fell at last, and she stared miserably out to sea. "Because Heracles—may the Goddess rip the living eyeballs from his head—gave her to Theseus as a slave. With my own ears, I heard his men say this, as I also heard them say"—her voice became almost inaudible with rage—"that she was to be kept on Theseus's galley for him to use at his pleasure. In reward for his enabling them to escape our wrath, they said."

A vengeful murmur rose from the women, but it was drowned out by Thalassa's shocking, sudden scream. Throwing her head back, she let out another ear-shattering cry and clutched her head, spinning about in a wild, demented circle.

"In *reward?*" she shrieked. "Our brave sister queen *given* to the man whose idea it was to take her hostage—as though she were nothing more than a breeding heifer traded for a measure of grain? And this, when the blood of noble Hippolyte weeps upon the ground crying out to be avenged! They think to escape our wrath, do they? Well, there is nowhere they can flee to escape our revenge! Nowhere! *Nowhere!*"

She whirled about as a fresh wave of frenzied pain descended, and throwing her head back once more, Thalassa let it sweep through her. "Antiope, Antiope! My queen, my age-mate, my sister!" She heard her howls rising to the sky like those of a wounded beast, but she could not stop herself.

She yanked at her thick chestnut hair until handfuls of it came loose in her clenched fingers. And still, it was not enough. "Hippolyte," she wailed. "Beloved older sister, I shall not forget you. Oh, they shall indeed pay a terrible blood-price for their treachery—a terrible price!"

She screamed again, wordlessly this time. She continued to scream until her voice gave out, and she felt a large, warm hand laid gently on her shoulder. "Are you finished now?" Dorian asked. Before she could answer, he respectfully addressed Tecmessa. "If you will permit me a question, Lady—how did you manage to free yourselves in order to attack your captors? In truth, you fight so well that you really had no need of Thalassa or me."

"No need of you, or any other man, perhaps. Although we thank you for your aid." Tecmessa warily studied this godly male creature. "We waited until the sea no longer made our stomachs heave, and until the Greeks thought us meek and tamed to their wills. Then, under the blessing of the Moon-Goddess, we gnawed through each other's bonds, and right before the stars began to dull in the sky we attacked! They misjudged us—these stupid Greeks—and they are indeed poor fighters compared to us."

Her teeth and those of the other warriors flashed wolfishly as the women recalled those first glorious moments of revenge and freedom. Then Tecmessa looked at Thalassa, and her smile faded. "It was Antiope's idea," she added sadly. "Almost the last thing she said to me before we were . . . separated."

No one spoke, then Dorian broke the silence again. "Well," he said briskly. "Have any of you given thought to what you will do now? You float aimlessly upon the great ocean—lacking either helmsman or navigator—in a galley with forty oars, when there are but fifteen of you."

CHAPTER 22

≈ A spacious body of land lay within a day's travel of the galley, Dorian explained. Roving man-ruled tribes inhabited it, but it was a fertile place.

For the rest of that day and all through the night, the fifteen women rowed the galley toward the haven Dorian had described, a task which, if not as dangerous as their original taking of the vessel had been, was no less difficult. Without Dorian, in fact, it would have been impossible. It was he who set the course and kept them to it, he who assigned the small party to the oars in such a way to compensate for the lack of a full crew. Yet even with his careful division of labor, the mighty galley would still have been unmanageable had it not been for the prodigious strength of him and Thalassa.

Devoured with worry that at any moment capricious winds might allow Heracles's remaining fleet to give pursuit, Thalassa had said anxiously to Dorian, "We are moving so slowly. Can you not summon some of your people to aid in the rowing?"

He had given her a cool, appraising look. "If I did, they

would have many questions, not the least of which would be why I am allowing this at all. If you were truly under the Sea Spell, we would not be here. They would wonder about me, and they would wonder about you. Is that what you want?"

Thalassa did not raise the subject again.

The journey continued throughout the dark of the night, Thalassa and Dorian rowing with the same effortless strength. The one square sail snapped and sang over their heads, and the galley moved majestically toward its destination.

As dawn paled the waters about them, Thalassa gave in to Dorian's urging and took a much-needed break on the galley's foredeck. In the weak light she could see the first glimpse of land, a distant strip of beach wrapped in sea fog and gleaming faintly on the horizon.

Glumly she stared at it, feeling the embrace of a bitterness as pervasive as the mists enshrouding that unknown land. The land where soon her beloved sister-kindred would be left to fend for themselves—alone in an unfamiliar and, no doubt, hostile country. She yearned to join them there, to face whatever dangers awaited them.

When she had approached Dorian about it—tentative and defiant all at once—he had gazed at her as if her wits had flown. "Do you desire me to pilot this galley to land?" he had asked harshly. "Then take care not to push me too far. There is a price for what I do here, and threatening me with the Elders will not change it. Not this time."

It was an impasse, and with the lives of her people at stake, Thalassa knew better than to challenge it. But remembering those long hours spent in heartfelt talk with her sisters as they rowed the galley was almost more than Thalassa could bear, now that the time for parting rushed inexorably upon them. She turned her back on the slowly approaching land and saw Tecmessa and Evandre walking toward her.

"So that is the land he spoke of," Tecmessa said when they reached the foredeck.

"Yes." Thalassa stared at her hands, clenched on the deck's wooden railing. "I wish the journey could have taken weeks rather than a single day. For then, I could have been in the company of my beloved sisters much longer."

"Oh, Thalassa," Evandre burst out. "We cannot leave you with this man, god though he may be. You belong to us and not him. It would be a crime against the Mother Herself to leave one of our own to a fate not of her choosing!"

"Evandre's right," Tecmessa said, covering Thalassa's calloused hand with her own. "We simply cannot abandon you, sister. It would dishonor us, and how could we find happiness knowing we had left you behind?"

Thalassa smiled tremulously at the two women. What good and loyal friends they were! "Thank you." She heard the tremble in her voice and went on more steadily. "But none of us has any choice in the matter." She scowled as bitterness welled up in her anew. "Dorian has seen to that. You have seen his power."

"And yours," Tecmessa noted soberly.

Thalassa sighed. "And mine. But it was he who gifted me with strength, and who knows whether he could not take it away just as easily if I sought to use it against him? No, sisters, he is too strong. He will not let me go, and there is nothing any of us can do about it. And I cannot forget that if it had not been for him, your fates would have been very different. Even if those evil, treacherous Greeks had not retaken you, without knowledge of how to steer this galley, you surely would have perished in the sea."

Evandre nodded. "That is so, and we are grateful. But at what a cost, Thalassa! Our freedom in exchange for yours? There must be something else that will satisfy him."

"There is not." Thalassa set her jaw, recalling the unyielding sternness in Dorian's blue gaze as she had argued and pleaded. In vain.

"He agreed to conduct you to land on condition that I not accompany you. In that he is as immovable as one of the mountains of our home."

"The home none of us might ever see again," Tecmessa said, echoing Thalassa's thoughts so exactly that Thalassa looked up, drowning in a sudden wave of longing for Amazonia's familiar wooded peaks.

Anger sparkled in Tecmessa's eyes. "Such a bargain is

no better than the Greeks vowing to release Antiope if we allowed them to leave our shores unharmed."

But Evandre was intently studying her friend's troubled face. "Thalassa," she asked uncertainly, "is it perhaps your wish to stay with this man and his people?" The small, muscular woman rushed on when she saw Thalassa's shocked expression. "I would not fault you if you did, for we all face an uncertain future. And we've seen for ourselves how changed you are . . ." Her voice trailed off, and she and Tecmessa exchanged glances.

Thalassa crossed her arms over her chest. Last night, she had described to her sisters the merfolk and their existence beneath the sea. When they had not believed her, she had shown them the tiny gills on her neck. Though still incredulous, they had believed her then. But not even to Tecmessa and Evandre—the close friends of her heart— could she bring herself to describe the Sea Spell or Dorian's refusal to use it, and now she understood why.

Dorian might not have wrapped a spell about her, but the sea had. Without her realizing it, the rhythm of the tides had begun to beat through her. The call of the sea was terrifying in its power over her. Evandre's observation was only too accurate. A strangeness had indeed been born in her—a strangeness that she could hide from herself, but not from the eyes of these women who had known her since birth.

"Dorian," she said hesitantly, "is not the way men are supposed to be." Her voice hardened. "The way the Greeks are."

"Of course not!" Tecmessa snorted disgustedly. "He is obviously a god of some sort." What she and the others had seen of Dorian, as well as the incredible things Thalassa had described, had convinced all of them that their sister was, beyond a doubt, in the hands of an immortal being. It would be wise to treat him with respect.

"But you've said they seem to worship the Mother in some fashion," Evandre insisted. "If that is so, then She would not be pleased at his keeping one of Her daughters in this way."

"She would if it was Her will . . . and I believe it is," Thalassa said quietly, her thoughts on old Marpe's words of prophecy that a destiny had been laid on her by the Goddess.

She had never told Dorian of the reason behind her sullen and sudden acquiescence to her fate, though she suspected he had guessed. The shattering appearance of her people had given her the wild hope that the Goddess had relented. But even if She had, Dorian had not, and Thalassa knew she would not be able to bear it if Tecmessa, Evandre, or any of her other kinswomen were killed or injured because of her.

The galley was drawing nearer to the land. The rhythmic slapping of the oars sounded unnaturally loud in the quiet dawn sea, and the three women stood without speaking as their destination came closer. Below them, the other Amazons looked up from their rowing, their gazes intently fixed on the strip of beach that grew ever more visible as the galley steadily plowed its way through the mist.

The sun was brightening the violet-gray sky, its sparkling fingers reaching through the white fog to illuminate the land more clearly. Behind the flat sand beach lay wooded hills and gently rolling pastures, so eerily similar to Amazonia's shores that Evandre muttered to Thalassa, "I could almost believe this god of yours has brought us home, sister."

Thalassa nodded. It did indeed seem as if an early morning hunting party of mounted women would canter down the deserted beach at any moment. She had to forcibly remind herself that this was a land ruled by men, not women.

"The morning's greetings to you," Dorian said behind them, and the three women turned to face him as he came to stand next to Thalassa.

As if it were his rightful place! she thought resentfully.

"And greetings to you," Tecmessa returned carefully. "I see that we draw nearer the land you told us of."

"We do, indeed," he said cheerfully. "In fact, I intend to bring this vessel of men onto the beach itself and leave it there. We'll have no need of it, once you're safely ashore."

Tecmessa regarded this imposing giant of a man in frowning silence. "Thalassa has said you are not like other men," she said after a moment. "And this is obviously so.

You possess great powers, and you used them in our defense rather than aiding the men whom you resemble. So why must you now behave like all men do toward women—cruel and unreasonable, according them no will of their own?"

"I suppose it must seem that way to you." His expression softened, and he looked sympathetically at Thalassa. She deliberately refused to meet his eyes.

"But," he went on, "I am not as cruel and unreasonable as you think me. Your kinswoman has changed, and she would not be happy on the land. The tides of the Great Mother Ocean beat through her blood, calling her to the breast of the sea, as all of my people are called. There is no other home for her now."

Thalassa shivered as though the waves of that sea had already engulfed her—cold and clutching as only winter waters could be. Although Dorian had addressed Tecmessa, his gaze had rested upon her as he spoke, and it was only too clear for whom his words were meant. She shivered again. It was as though he had looked into her soul and deciphered every uneasy thought and feeling hidden there.

As the galley's low keel ground through the sandy shallows, Thalassa's stomach churned and knotted itself with an apprehension greater than any she'd ever felt. Only moments remained before she would be parted from her sisters forever. Tecmessa and Evandre gripped her hands, watching as Dorian vaulted easily over the galley's side. With the twin aids of the incoming tide and his enormous strength, he hauled the vessel up onto the shore, his muscles bunched and straining with the effort.

Land. The once captive Amazons were no less excited by the feel of it under their feet than was Thalassa herself. Followed by Tecmessa and Evandre, she eagerly leaped onto the beach. The sand was cool and silky between her toes, and with giddy delight she danced up and down in the gritty dampness.

"By the Goddess!" For just a moment, she gave herself up to the joy of being reunited with the Earth Mother. "My legs feel as wobbly as a newborn foal's!"

Evandre laughed delightedly. "Mine too. And after all those days on that accursed vessel of men, it is no wonder!"

Dorian remained beside the galley, his gaze sweeping gravely over the small group of celebrating Amazons. Then, with casual grace, he strode past them, heading for the sloping dunes that led up from the beach. Within a short time he came back. Neither his departure nor his subsequent return had gone unnoticed. Sharp gazes fixed on him, and Tecmessa called, "What news do you bring, man of the sea?"

Silence instantly fell upon the other warriors. Tensely they awaited his answer, and Thalassa's joy died away as the dreaded moment of separation rushed down upon her. Now the pleasure of walking on solid land was torture. All too soon she would be forced to return to the weightless, alien world of her captor, and this welcoming beach, along with the beloved faces of her sisters, would only be memories. Lost in her misery, she started at the sound of Dorian's compelling voice.

"Just beyond the largest of these dunes lies a rich pasture, and in it grazes a herd of horses, fat and glossy, and apparently waiting for you."

"Sent by Holy Artemis to aid Her daughters!" one of the women shouted exultantly, and the small group of Amazons hugged one another in joyous agreement.

The steadily rising sun was stronger now. Thalassa heard a horse's distant nicker carried on the first winds of morning, and she thought longingly of Alcippe as the breeze rustled on through the waves.

"Well," Dorian said, "I am eager to return to the sea. Take what you need from the ship's stores, for Thalassa and I certainly have no need of them.

"I wish I could tell you the land beyond this strand is filled with peaceful tribes who will offer you courteous welcome, but I fear that is not the case. The people here are called Samauratians, and rather than live in one place, they prefer to wander throughout the land, driving their herds before them and making war as it pleases them."

"Are all of these Samauratians ruled by men, or are there any that follow the ways of the Mother?" asked a tall warrior, an older woman whose black hair was shot with streaks of silver. She had been a close friend to Thalassa's birth-mother.

Dorian shrugged his broad shoulders. "Can any man born to the land truly follow the ways of the Mother? No matter what gods or goddesses they worship, the Samauratians will probably see women alone as fair game. Unless you persuade them otherwise, they will seek to take your freedom from you—forcing you to live in the giant-wheeled wagons they make their own women travel in, shut off from the wind and sun and being made to do what they call 'women's work.'"

"Spoken like an Amazon," the old warrior muttered to her companions.

She had not meant for Dorian to hear her, but he did, and he grinned. "Samauratians are good fighters and skilled horsemen," he went on, his grin widening. "But I doubt they are any match for Artemis's daughters. If you are wise about choosing when and where to fight, I believe that despite your small numbers you will be able to carve out a place for yourselves in this land."

He looked at the other women, and his expression sobered. "You will never be able to avenge the wrongs done you by the Greeks," he said softly, "but this is certainly better than slavery, is it not?"

"There is no question about it," Evandre said stoutly. She strode forward and faced Dorian, her hands fisted belligerently on her hips. "But I ask you to release Thalassa from whatever bonds you hold her in. We cannot be happy in our freedom if she is still a slave."

"Then I fear you will be doomed to unhappiness. And I will tell you what I have told her—she is not a slave." Dorian's voice was still soft, but there was a coldness in it that raised the fine hairs on the back of Thalassa's neck. His eyes were focused on Evandre's face, and while the stocky warrior paled a little at his wintry stare, she refused to drop her gaze.

Worriedly Thalassa glanced about the sunny beach. Her kinswomen were giving her concerned looks and murmuring angrily—both to her and to each other. Evandre's challenging words had given voice to their own growing reluctance to abandon her. Thalassa's breast ached, as though an arrow dipped in the poison the grandmothers made in times of great danger were embedded there. She made herself walk through the cluster of glowering warriors until she stood beside Evandre, who, glad of the excuse to look away from Dorian's chilling gaze, turned to her.

"Hold a moment," Thalassa said before the other could speak. Dorian was watching her, and she looked him straight in the eye. *You may be able to make me stay with you,* she told him silently, *but you will not see me simper and smile meekly about it!* She drew a deep breath.

"I gave my word as an Amazon warrior that I would not seek to accompany you, my sisters. I did this so you would have a chance to live again in freedom and strength, as the Mother intended Amazons to live. I do not want to bide with this man and his people. But if I break my bond, I will bring dishonor upon myself, and honor is all that is left to me. Too many of our brave kindred have died. I could not endure being the cause of any more suffering."

"Thalassa—" Tecmessa's voice was deeply troubled, but Thalassa put up a hand.

"No, sister, I will not argue this with you. It is my choice to make, and I make it freely. Go now, while my resolve is strong and I am able to do what is right. And may the Mother watch over all of you." She stopped before her voice broke. This was horrible enough without adding to it the shame of weeping before Dorian.

Only the waves made any sound, as they washed up onto the sand with a laughing, sibilant music that seemed to mock the tragedy of Thalassa's pending loss. She could feel the eyes of Tecmessa and Evandre upon her, but dared not look at them or any of her people. To do so would surely end in her calling out desperately for rescue from this cruel and lonely fate—a call her sisters would not refuse. Then all would have been for naught.

"Sister . . ." Evandre's voice was thick, as if she had swallowed something painful. "Are you sure?"

Thalassa nodded. "Yes, Evandre, I am sure. Even if I were not, it would make no difference. Can't you see that he will not allow me to leave? If I try, there would be a fight. Some of us would be hurt or killed—and in the end, he would still have me, as he does now. Truly, this is the only way."

Forcing herself to speak through a hurtful lump in her

throat, she raised her voice. "Sisters, I beg you: Go and find those horses he spoke of before their owners come back to claim them. You cannot afford to be abroad in this strange and hostile land without horses. You know that as well as I."

The assembled Amazons looked at one another unhappily, but the wisdom in Thalassa's words was inescapable. "Very well," said the old warrior with black and silver hair. "But to leave the child of my friend like this causes a great sadness in my heart, little daughter. It is a noble sacrifice you make for the good of your people, and we will honor you always for your bravery." She cast a sharp, angry glance at Dorian. "I hope *this* one—whether he be god or mortal—does the same."

"I honor her already," Dorian said quietly, his gaze resting on Thalassa's agonized face.

She ignored him. The struggle against tears was abruptly lost as Tecmessa and Evandre caught her up in a bruisingly hard embrace. "He is right about one thing," Tecmessa whispered. "We will never be able to avenge Hippolyte's murder and the taking of Antiope. Make a new life for yourself, my sister, as we must. Here in this land, we will erect an altar to Artemis in your name, so that you will always be remembered. This I promise you."

Thalassa drew back and looked at her. But before she could reply, the rest of her kindred were engulfing her. She and Evandre exchanged a last tearful hug, and then—with many backward glances—the fifteen warriors started toward the dune behind which the herd of horses grazed.

Evandre was the last to go. Staring at Thalassa for a long moment, as though seeking to fix her friend's face in her mind forever, she finally called out, "I will never forget you, sister!"

Thalassa swallowed hard. "Nor I you," she got out. She watched in anguish as Evandre turned to follow her companions. As the small group headed farther down the beach, it finally became too much to see this last link with home and family disappearing. Involuntarily she took a step forward, the cry for them to come back trembling in her throat.

Dorian grasped her arm with gentle firmness. "Let them go," he murmured. "They'll be fine. As will you."

"Will I?"

She tried to jerk free of his hold, but could not. Defeated, she stood motionless, straining for one last glimpse of her kinswomen as they climbed the sloping dune, slipping and sliding in the ankle-high sand. Long after Evandre, who brought up the rear, had disappeared over the rise, she remained, locked in a grief more terrible than anything she had ever known. It would have been better never to see her people again, she thought, than to have this brief time together, only to be separated with such finality. It was cruel . . . so cruel.

She did not think she had spoken aloud, but Dorian answered as if she had. "It seems so now, and I grieve for your pain," he said. "But one day, you will see that what you did was not only brave, it was the right and proper thing."

Savagely she yanked again to free herself, and this time he let her go. She stumbled away, staring blindly at the now deserted beach.

Dorian watched her, and for one of the few times in his life he wished he could cry. Native-born merfolk could not. Thalassa—because of her land birth—would always retain the ability to shed tears. What else would she retain without the softening aura of the Sea Spell? he wondered. There was no telling, for all of his predecessors had placed the spell upon their chosen ones without delay. Only he swam through unfamiliar waters, in the teeth of a dilemma that he had been foolish enough to impose upon himself. And it was indeed a dilemma.

He could not resume the interrupted journey to Amazonia, a country that would surely be in turmoil now. His only purpose in taking Thalassa there in the first place had been to reassure her that her people were well, thus winning her gratitude and her trust—elements he strongly felt were essential to her complete acceptance of her new life. But the landfolk's eternal love of bloodshed had brought that carefully laid scheme to ruination, and he scowled as his mind raced along the pathways of other plans.

Where could he take Thalassa? Certainly not back to his

abode, for he could not trust her there, not now, not with what she knew. Even unwittingly, she could betray him, jeopardizing his kingship so easily, it chilled his blood. Thalassa had wandered farther down the beach, and as he stared at her, Dorian's frown deepened.

He was well aware of his power to intimidate. He had used it often enough in the past, against far more formidable opponents than one uprooted landwoman. And Thalassa, despite her bravado, was still sufficiently daunted by him to be susceptible. Yet she had more power than she realized. It would not do for her to find out how concerned he was by this turn of events. He would have to act swiftly to bond her to him, so that she would protect rather than reveal his secret.

The Amazon war cry suddenly rang through the air, followed by a long equine neigh. Eagerly Thalassa swung around, her eyes searching the horizon with a wild yearning. Silhouetted against the morning sky, fifteen mounted figures had appeared along the rise of the highest dune. Frozen in space, they remained there, as if to give Thalassa time enough to carve their memory into her very heart. And then—with a last call—they were gone.

Thalassa stared at the empty dune for a very long time. Her eyes burned and stung with unshed tears when she finally turned her gaze back to Dorian, who stood behind her, lost in thoughts of his own. "Well, they are gone," she said, pleased by the steadiness of her voice, "and you have had your way. Now may we go on to Amazonia, to see how the rest of my people fare?"

He studied her without answering. Disquieted by the enigmatic expression on his face, she snapped, "Or is it your will that we stand upon this beach until we grow roots and become trees?"

At that he smiled. "We can leave, Thalassa. But before we resume any journey, there is something we must do tonight."

CHAPTER 23

≈ Thalassa could not ever remember being so tired. The battle with the Greeks, the long day and night of rowing the galley, and the emotional anguish of bidding good-bye to her sisters had all taken their toll. More than anything she wanted to sleep, even if it meant floating atop the waves, as Dorian had told her his people often spent their nights.

But with an uncharacteristic—almost cruel—disregard for her comfort, Dorian refused to let her rest. It was a side of him she had never seen before, and while at first it had baffled and frightened her, she was now so weary it no longer mattered. Her initial questions about where she was being taken had gone largely unanswered. They must reach a certain place by nightfall, Dorian had explained brusquely, and to do so they would have to travel hard throughout the day. Beyond that he would say nothing, other than advising her to save her breath for swimming.

He meant it. To Thalassa, it seemed as if he was deliberately trying to drain her of every ounce of strength by forcing this punishing pace upon her. And it was working.

They had been swimming steadily for hours, and she was so exhausted she scarcely knew that Dorian was virtually pulling her along.

She had long since ceased either to question or worry about the reasons behind this brutal trip. In fact, she was no longer thinking about anything other than sleep. Even the grief of the past day and night had dulled under the relentless travel. The meeting with Tecmessa, Evandre, and the others became distant and unreal, like a waking dream.

"Thalassa."

She heard an impatience in Dorian's voice, as though he had repeated her name more than once. His arms encircled her, and she groggily realized they had stopped moving at last. The knowledge had little impact on her. The spot where they had halted looked no different from any other spot in this vast, tossing wilderness of water and sound.

"Are we here?" she mumbled.

"Yes."

"Good." Her words were so heavily slurred, she could barely understand them herself. "Then I can sleep."

"For a time. At least until moonrise."

She did not hear him.

Darkness fell over the rippling sea, and stars blinked waveringly through the broken masses of clouds that drifted in from the east. Dorian smelled rain in the air, probably within the next several hours. It didn't matter. The moon would be up soon, and when the storm hit they would be far below the ocean surface. Thoughtfully he looked down at Thalassa. She lay in his arms like one dead, in a sleep so profound he knew she would provide little resistance to what was to come.

"I think," he murmured into her unheeding ear, "that seeing the past of the merfolk will do you a great deal of good."

Closing his eyes, he tried to relax himself into a light doze, but it was useless. Though he was tired, anticipation ran heatedly through his veins, until finally he gave up. With Thalassa resting heavily upon his breast, he rode the rocking swells and stared up at the threatening sky. The moon rose hesitantly, a thin crescent blade slicing weakly through fitful clouds.

With a gentleness that was quite different from the pitiless manner in which he had driven her there, Dorian woke Thalassa. "Come, love," he said, stroking the wet, tangled hair off her forehead. "The moon is nearly up, and we must go."

"No," she mumbled fretfully. "Leave me alone. I want to sleep."

"You will in a little while," he promised her. "A very deep sleep which we call the *dream walk*. Except that when you awake, the knowledge contained in this dream will not vanish in the way of most dreams, but will remain with you. Now come. The ceremony can only take place at moon-rise."

He gave her no further chance to protest but, tightening his arms, rolled off his back and plunged them both beneath the waves.

Thalassa drifted slowly out of the soft, heavy fog. Her feet felt oddly weightless, as if she were floating rather than walking. The sensation should have frightened her, but did not. She was no longer in the sea with Dorian, but alone under a blazing sun. Ahead of her lay a huge city.

Breathtakingly beautiful, it sat proudly on a ridge of land that jutted far out into a wide, marshy lake. The harsh noonday light of the unfamiliar sun glittered off palatial buildings of white marble inlaid with gold and precious gems, creating a glare so dazzling she had to look away.

Her gaze fell on the lowlands surrounding the marsh. At the western end, a broad river emptied into the swampy lake, and there fruit trees grew in such abundance that she thought with a pang of Themiscrya's fertile orchards. There were other familiar sights. Tall, sturdy women in orderly ranks were drilling at military exercises out on the level plains, and vast herds of sheep and goats grazed nearby, tended by sullen-looking youths.

Warm grass tickled Thalassa's bare feet. She was walking toward the magnificent city as casually as if she had lived there all her life. She passed the drilling women and the young men with their flocks, and none seemed aware of her. Now she was within the arching gates paneled in gold and studded with rubies. The paved streets of Cherronesus—how had she known its name?—teemed with life and sound.

Soldierly women rattled by in horse-drawn chariots, shouting at those on foot to make way. Sheep and goats bleated under the curses of herders, who struggled to keep their charges from dispersing along the teeming streets. Vendors cried out their wares, and bands of shrieking girl-children ran unfettered through the maze, nimbly dodging chariots, merchants, and animals. Thalassa saw that those on foot were, without exception, male.

Men guided the bleating herds through the narrow streets, or carried large woven baskets filled with succulent fruits to the rows of crowded but comfortable-looking dwellings. Indeed, any type of menial work seemed to be exclusively the province of men. In front of many of the houses, Thalassa saw swaddled infants and crawling toddlers tended by men, who were also engaged in preparing meals, milking goats, mending clothing, and performing all sorts of tasks normally delegated to slaves, or wives.

Just as on the lowlands outside the city, no one seemed aware of Thalassa's presence, and she studied the men of this strange yet familiar land with curiosity. Most of them were plump and soft looking, as if they never did anything more strenuous than house minding and eating. The boy-children did not appear to have the freedom to run about as their sisters did, but instead helped their fathers in the household work with meek and quiet expressions on their small faces. Only the young men seemed to have any freedom, and it was strictly limited to the tasks of herding animals or picking fruit.

Two powerfully built women shouldered past Thalassa, calling out greetings as they approached a dwelling with what appeared to be a forge next to it. A sweating, heavily muscled woman wearing an apron of tanned leather came out in response to their call. "Good day, good day!" she shouted cheerily, then poked her head in the house's doorway. "I have guests," she called. "Bring out refreshments and be quick about it."

A boy of about fourteen stood to one side, eyeing the guests with open interest, and the muscular woman gave

him a fierce box on the ear. "How dare you raise your eyes
to women without my permission!" she roared. "Act like a
properly brought up young man and fetch cushions for us."

"But I was about to bring in the goats," the boy
protested, nursing his bruised head. This time he received a
clout that knocked him down. "Insolent whelp," the woman
bellowed. "I'll teach you to backtalk! It's not up to men to
decide what their tasks are, or even to speak unless a
woman orders them to. Now get those cushions!"

The youth clambered to his feet and scuttled into the
house, past a plumpish man who hurried out bearing a tray
loaded with wine and plates of flat cakes. Eyes lowered, he
served each of the guests in turn as the mistress of the house
apologized for the boy's unseemly behavior. "Three sons,
and not a single daughter to pass my craft of weapon
making to," she grumbled. "All I can do is teach them
proper manners and marry them off. Ah, it's a curse, all
right."

The youth had come back out with cushions, and after
he had arranged them, the weapon maker curtly told him to
fetch in the goats. Turning to her husband, who still stood
with his gaze on the ground, she delivered a hard smack to
his buttocks. "You've done a poor job of raising that one.
What woman's going to want a husband who tries to act as
if he can think for himself? Get back into the house now. I'll
deal with you later."

"Yes, my lord mistress," the man murmured, and
disappeared through the dark doorway.

Thalassa had been a fascinated witness to this entire
incident, although the women, the submissive husband, the
youth who ran past her on his goat-fetching errand seemed
unaware she was there. This was how she had always heard
life described for any woman unfortunate enough to be born
or kidnapped into a man-ruled society. Indeed, it was
exactly how she had expected her life to be as Dorian's
captive.

In appearance and demeanor, these women were astonishingly similar to Amazons. The only major difference lay
in their keeping husbands the way men kept wives. Other
than having a few male slaves about, Thalassa's people
would never dream of cohabitation with men. Yet these

women did it with no danger to their freedom or self-sufficiency. Obviously the secret was in keeping these husbands and sons of theirs cowed and subservient.

But as Thalassa gazed at the three women helping themselves to more cakes and wine, she decided she still preferred her own people's way of life. These fleshy, servile males seemed more a burden than a pleasure to have around.

True, they freed their mistresses for warrior pursuits by taking care of all the onerous work, but at the same time they imposed a weighty responsibility on the women who kept them. Soft and dependent, they did not seem at all capable of caring for themselves. That meant some woman would always have to be saddled with the obligation of directing their lives, even their very thoughts.

It all seemed like a great bother, Thalassa thought. And with their pudgy bodies and flabby limbs, these men were not even comely! At least Dorian—despite the animosity she felt toward him—was undeniably fair to look upon. For a man, anyway. And she had to admit that he made things interesting. These docile creatures did not appear to be very entertaining—in bed or out. Yet, in all other places in the world this was how men wanted women to be. She certainly could not see why. Such passivity seemed equally boring whether it was in a male or a female.

Without warning, the scene in front of her blurred. She blinked to bring the three women back into focus, but the surroundings blurred still more. A new scene was forming, and Thalassa vaguely wondered why she was not frightened by these magical happenings. She found herself standing on the broad meadowlands outside the white marble city, but now the flat, green plains were black with warriors.

Thousands upon thousands of them, they darkened the ground as far as the eye could see. Thirty thousand foot soldiers, Thalassa's experienced gaze noted, and three thousand cavalry, at least. All of them were heavily armed with spear, bow, and sword, all of their limbs swelled with strength and agility, and without a single exception—all were women.

What was even more impressive than their sheer numbers was the armor they wore. Thick and scaly, it resembled the skins of gigantic reptiles.

A roar went up, as from the gates of the city two chariots rolled forth. One of them raced forward to position itself at the head of the cavalry, but the other, drawn by a team of glistening white mares, thundered on until it reached a small hillock. There the chariot's lone occupant pulled in her rearing horses and paused to survey the host.

She was a tall, stately woman with strong muscles and a mane of unruly black hair. By her dress and appearance, Thalassa marked her as the queen of these people, and the woman's first words confirmed it.

A stern smile curving her lips, she shouted, "Well met! None can hope to prevail against us. I, the swift-bounding Myrina, queen of the Amazons, declare it! Glory and riches beyond imagining shall be ours when we conquer the treasure-laden lands of the Atlantians, those unnatural people who were spawned from the sea, and who dare to say men and women are equal to one another! Blasphemy! Outrage!"

Battle shrieks erupted on the word "outrage," drowning out the queen's voice. Myrina waited until the clamor had died away, then she looked westward and raised her hand. The signal given, the army surged forward like the wind preceding a thunderstorm. Thalassa gazed on in wonder. Amazons . . . These stalwart women were Amazons! And the Atlantians Myrina had referred to so contemptuously . . . Could they be kindred of Dorian's?

No sooner had she thought this than the scene changed again. She stood before another city now, one that was larger and even more magnificent than Cherronesus. Sunlight glittered off graceful spires of pure gold and lit up massive buildings that boasted domed roofs encrusted in rubies, garnets, and other precious gems Thalassa could not identify. Never had she seen such wealth, or even dreamed that it could exist. In the white-hot reflection of the sun, the city blazed with a thousand sparkling lights, as though a rainbow had fallen to earth and caught on fire.

Before the towering walls that enclosed this dazzling metropolis, the Amazon army was drawn up in battle formation. Thalassa could see the helmeted heads of men peering over the ramparts at the awesome force come to menace them. As she watched, Queen Myrina lashed her whip and sent her war-chariot thundering up to the city's gates.

"People of the Atlantian city of Cerne," she cried in her ringing voice. "I am Myrina, queen of the Amazons. Acknowledge me as your conqueror and surrender your wealth, else I lay waste to your city and take by force what you could give peacefully and without bloodshed!"

The horses pranced nervously, and the chariot's spiked wheels rolled back and forth, their viciously sharpened points glittering in the heat of day. Moments edged by, and still no response came from the inhabitants of Cerne.

Scornfully Myrina shouted, "It is as I've heard, then. All Atlantians are sniveling cowards. Spineless and timid like men everywhere—cowering behind your fine walls hoping they will protect you and that we will go away. And you weak fools dare to call yourselves the equal of women! Pah!"

"Take care with your words, queen of the Amazons," a man calmly called down from the ramparts. "We do not meekly surrender our freedom to every braggart who comes swaggering to our gates. If you have come here to test our bravery, then so be it."

No sooner had the man finished speaking than the portals swung ponderously open, and Cerne's inhabitants poured out to do battle with the invaders. As with everything else she had seen in this strange country, Thalassa did not exist for these people who proceeded to fight and die in front of her. But for her, the ensuing combat was only too real.

The Atlantians withstood the opening flight of arrows that greeted their entrance upon the field. Again and again the sky thickened and the very air rattled with shafts sent from such a distance. It was beyond the strength of the Atlantian bowmen to respond, yet the valiant defenders refused to yield, and the Amazons were compelled to close.

Thalassa winced at the dreadful impact of battle shock. Weapons rang against each other, and the screams of dying men and wounded horses blended with the savage Amazon war cries in a horrible cacophony of death. These Amazons did not utilize the battle-ax as Thalassa's people did, but their spears and swords created the same lethal effect as the most skillfully wielded *bipennis*.

Tirelessly they drove at their opponents until the Atlantians began darting this way and that, seeking to organize an orderly retreat to the safety of their walled city. Their obvious distress at the Amazons' ferocity only incited the warrior-women. Maddened with bloodlust, screaming as though their wits had left them, they surged to fresh slaughter. Outnumbered and outmatched, the Atlantians fell in droves.

Like wolves on the track of a wounded deer, the Amazons pursued their prey over the quagmire of the slain and wounded. The remaining inhabitants of Cerne had opened the gates in a desperate attempt to rescue whoever still lived on the blood-drenched battleground. But before those hastily opened gates could be closed, the Amazons swarmed through and took possession of the city.

When Cerne was secured, Myrina issued her standard command: all males from youth upwards to be put to the sword. For all her warrior training, Thalassa had never witnessed the sacking of a city. Now she saw that the reality of it was brutal beyond belief.

Blood-spattered patrols immediately set to work, ranging the broad, smoothly paved streets and ransacking the beautiful jewel-encrusted buildings and the smaller but no less magnificent dwellings. Whenever a man was found, he was seized by wrists and ankles and dragged off to the squadrons appointed to carry out the executions.

Some were hauled to their fate screeching and pleading for mercy; but Thalassa saw many others go proudly, somehow maintaining their dignity despite the humiliation of being pulled along like a calf to the butcher. They were tall, handsome men, those doomed ones, but they obviously did not possess the godlike strength of Dorian's folk. If they had, even the Amazons with all their terrible prowess could not have defeated them.

Night fell, a dusty, red-tinged night, and still the bloodbath went on. All through the endless hours of torch-lit darkness punctuated by screams, Thalassa wandered the streets of the raped city and saw the same scene repeated over and over. When a murky dawn finally illuminated the vanquished Atlantian metropolis, the carnage seemed spent at last.

But Thalassa stared in horror as Queen Myrina's next orders were carried out. Cerne was to be razed, and all the precious metals and gems loaded into a multitude of wagons drawn by sturdy oxen and mules. This in itself was not surprising, for with its vast wealth, little else could be expected for the conquered city. But the command that all the women and children were to be taken into slavery shocked Thalassa to her very bones.

Warlike and bent on conquest the Amazons of Themiscrya might be, but the taking of women as slaves was something they would never do. Women were sacred to the Goddess. Was it possible that these Amazons did not worship the Goddess? Weary of being a ghostlike spirit, unseen and ignored, Thalassa yearned to put this question to her newfound sisters. But suddenly the rubble of the destroyed buildings of Cerne wavered.

A bright, towering city stood once again, and in astonishment Thalassa saw that Amazons walked through the wide streets, mingling with Atlantian men and women in the most perfect peace imaginable.

And to her further amazement, she saw tall Amazons strolling with equally tall Atlantian men, their arms wrapped affectionately about each other. What had happened to bring about this incredible change?

CHAPTER 24

"Queen Myrina raised a new city bearing her name on the same spot where Cerne once stood. Then she freed all the women she had enslaved and gave the city to them as their new home, also allowing any Atlantian man who wished to, to live there."

The deep, musical voice ringing through her mind was unmistakably Dorian's. Thalassa, reeling in confusion, found herself back in the sea, securely wrapped in his arms. The transition had been so swift that for a moment she instinctively strained to free herself, lashing about in unthinking panic.

"Gently, gently," Dorian soothed. *"You have left the* dream walk *and are back with me now. There is nothing to fear."*

Thalassa's struggles slowly ceased. The still unsettling intimacy of feeling his thoughts within hers paled before the enormity of this experience, and her first question came of its own volition. *"Where have I been?"*

"Your body has been here with me, but your mind has just returned from a journey that led it far into my people's past."

"*Your people! But I saw Amazons—or women who called themselves so. They lived in a great city with men to serve them, and in a mighty army they went out to conquer a people called Atlantians who were supposed to have come from the sea—*"

"*I know.*"

He sounded amused, and she twisted around to see his face. He was smiling at her, his features eerily illuminated in the uncanny light of this flooded cave so far beneath the waves. A trick of the Mother had dazzled this tiny part of the *midnight sea*, filling it with mysterious lights that glowed like a magical underwater rainbow. Wildly patterned, the colors danced in the ocean currents, flickering and darting over the rocky walls and ceiling of the cave, so that if Thalassa looked at them too long they made her dizzy. She looked instead at Dorian, though in the twinkling light his eyes were ghostly hollows and his smile jewel-lit and strange.

"*Where are we?*" she asked.

"*In a sacred place, one that is filled with power and known only to merfolk. When they are deemed ready, each young man and woman among us visits this place alone, to embark on the* dream walk. *And it is here that the kings of my people have always brought their mates—the chosen ones—who enter this holy spot as landwomen, and leave it as queens.*"

Thalassa shivered. She could almost feel the presence of those other women—women like her—torn from the familiar world of their birth. "*Has . . . has Valya come here?*" Thalassa asked.

"*No.*" The frost of the single word was like the bite of an icy wind. "*Neither he nor those he swims with are ready yet.*" He added grimly, "*They may not be for some time.*"

She trembled with apprehension. "*Do all who come here see what I did?*" she asked quickly.

"*No. It is different for those born to the sea. For us, the* dream walk *is in many ways a passage into adulthood, not unlike killing an enemy in battle is among the Amazons. The merfolk's greatest strength rests in the mind, and our minds blend with the power in this place to create openings into the past, dream journeys that help us to learn and gain in wisdom.*

"When a young person goes to sleep here, the deep part of his or her thoughts—those secret threads that lie buried during one's waking moments—come to life, in different ways for each. Whatever aspect of our history will do a dreamer the most good is shown to that person, with his or her own mind determining what that will be. But not being born to the sea, you could not make such a choice, so I had to make it for you, as all my ancestors have done for their queens. I hope I chose wisely."

He had, Thalassa thought, filled with a sudden resentment at how keenly he understood her.

"With all you could have shown me, why did you choose what you did?" she asked.

He did not answer immediately. *"I wanted to bring you back to me,"* he said at length. *"Before we came upon the Greek galleys, it seemed as though you were finally growing accustomed both to me and to this life I had brought you to. Then I became your captor and your enemy again. Yet, Thalassa, Amazons have lived harmoniously with men of my blood in the past and not lost their freedom in doing so. I thought it was time to reveal the common ancestry that lies between us."*

Thalassa wondered why his words did not arouse the desperate fury in her they once would have. Had she changed so much?

One of his hands was caressing her breast, and now the other trailed through the water to trace the line of her hip and belly. *"The ceremony is not yet finished."* The whisper of his thoughts floated across her consciousness. She could almost imagine that he had spoken aloud, his warm breath stirring the wet hair about her cheek.

His hand moved lower. *"There is one more thing left to do in this place so that we are truly bound together, with you as my queen. You know what that is, I think."*

As his fingers teased between her legs, she closed her eyes and did not reply.

"Would it please you?" he persisted, his sensitive fingers continuing to toy with her.

She drew in a deep breath, feeling a familiar tremor

deep in the pit of her stomach. *"Yes,"* she whispered in her mind at last. *"May the Goddess and all the grandmothers forgive me, it would."*

Dorian brought her back to the surface of the sea. It was deep night. A storm had come and gone, washing the iodine-scented air clean with the sweetness of rain. After the cold of the *midnight ocean*, the waves beneath them were as warm and inviting as the softest of couches. They rocked Thalassa. Cradled in his arms she lay against him, tired, strangely at peace, and sad.

"Were those . . . Atlantians truly your kindred?" she asked drowsily.

"Distantly, yes."

"Then why did they not have the powers you possess? They were defeated, their city crushed, the men all killed, and the women and children enslaved. And what were they doing living on the land anyway? If they were from the sea, why did they not stay there?"

He chuckled. "So many questions. You see, my love, many, many centuries ago, a branch of my people tired of living in the sea and decided to try life upon the land. Why they should have wished this is beyond me, for I cannot imagine leaving the beauty and freedom of the sea for the dubious pleasures of the land."

Thalassa grunted. "I can," she muttered, more awake now.

There was a silence. "Can you?" Dorian asked in a troubled and almost angry voice. "Well, to me such reasoning is a mystery. In any case, that is what they did. They chose a vast, fertile land on the shores of the Mother Ocean, sun-kissed and more enormous than any country that exists today. There they settled and built proud, beautiful cities like the one you saw. But there was a price to be paid for leaving the Great Mother Sea.

"Over time, the gifts bestowed by the Mother upon Her children faded for those sons and daughters who had chosen to desert Her. The powers they were born with— extraordinary strength, longevity, breathing underwater, special vision, navigating the depths—all these abilities, even the gills on their necks, waned, until at last they disappeared."

"So that is why they could be defeated in battle," Thalassa murmured more to herself than to him.

"Exactly. Had they retained their abilities, not even the Amazons, as terrible foes as they were, could have prevailed against them."

"But if Queen Myrina went to all that trouble to destroy them, why did she rebuild their cities?"

"Cerne was the only city she needed to rebuild. Myrina was a wise commander. She destroyed Cerne as an example. The rest of Atlantia surrendered to her without another spear-cast or casualty on either side.

"And once the Atlantians accepted her as their queen, she strove hard to conciliate her new subjects with acts of kindness and magnanimity. Eventually the two peoples came to live in harmony."

"That simply could not be." Thalassa spoke dutifully, almost reflexively. The teachings she had grown up with had been so seriously shaken, she could never again espouse them with the single-mindedness she once had. Yet, like the echo of a dying soul that cannot accept its death, they prompted her to argue. "In their own city, I saw the Amazons behaving toward men the way the man-ruled tribes treat women."

"Ah, but as often happens when one people subjugates another and then comes to dwell among them, the line between conqueror and conquered blurs. The Amazons learned a great deal from the Atlantians. They were unlike any people the warrior tribe had ever come across. Atlantian women were independent and proud, much like Amazons in many ways. And the men, well, eventually there were marriages between Amazon and Atlantian, and the unions were happy ones, without either being forced into subservience to the other."

Thalassa listened intently. "The grandmothers never spoke of these things," she said hesitantly. It was both an admission of defeat and an acknowledgment, and Dorian drew her a little closer.

"That is because they did not know of them. All this happened long before your people ever began the tradition of keeping their history in songs and chants, and it took place in a land that is no more."

She was startled by the sadness in his voice. "No more? What happened to it?"

"It's difficult to say. The Elders believe that in a strange way the Great Mother Sea Herself rose up and obliterated the civilization of those who had left Her depths. Since all nature is ruled by the forces of the Mother, this is no doubt true. At any rate, a huge underwater volcano that had been sleeping peacefully beneath the land for uncounted ages came to life. There was a terrible eruption, followed by an equally devastating earthquake, and the country that had sheltered Amazon and Atlantian alike broke apart and sank into the sea."

"All of them perished?" Thalassa was horrified, thinking of the bold, robust warrior-women and the noble kingdom they had carved out for themselves. They were her ancestors, those stalwart women, yet they and their empire had vanished without a trace. "Did no one escape?"

"Not as far as we know. It's always possible, of course, but not very likely. Still, my people find it curious that aeons later the Amazons came to life once again in your own birth-people, so perhaps some of them did reach safety. As for the Atlantians . . . that was the end of any merfolk venturing onto the land with the idea of staying there."

Thalassa listened to the steady thud of Dorian's heart and wondered how much—if anything—he knew of Valya and his comrades' whereabouts. Caught up in the events of the last day and night, she had given little thought to the desperate plot contrived with her young allies, but as Dorian appeared to doze, she found herself able to think of nothing else.

The small group would have reached Amazonia after the Greeks' treachery, coming upon a land ravaged by the murder of one queen and the abduction of another. What sort of welcome would they receive, these innocents who had been so eager to help her? When she had made her bargain with them she had not really cared.

But so much had happened since then. Worry at what may have befallen those friendly, good-hearted youths gnawed at her. As incredible as it seemed, they were kin to her, as much as the fierce long-dead women in their lizard-skin armor were her ancestors. Had she sent Valya and the others to meet death at the hands of women who were also their distant kin? The thought made her sick.

Off in the distance a series of splashes signaled the presence of a group of sea creatures. Thalassa lifted her head from Dorian's broad chest. In the east, a pale swath of gray presaged the dawn, and she could barely discern several round heads poking out of the dark waters. A family of white-bellied brown seals, perhaps. Dorian had told her they were quite common in these waters. As she contemplated the distant shapes, she realized Dorian was awake. He carefully brought them both upright in the water.

"Thalassa, do you feel able to tread the waves for a few moments by yourself?"

"Yes, but—"

"Good. Wait here, then. I will return quickly."

Before she could say anything else, he was gone, leaving her alone in the sea for the first time. Nervously, she stared about her. Even with Dorian's reassuring presence, the immensity of the sea was intimidating. Without him, it was appalling.

How she had once longed for this moment—for the one chance to escape him finally! Now, unbelievably, it had come, and to her mingled confusion and dismay, the driving urge to flee had lost much of its strength. Truly, she was no more free of Dorian than if he had chained her to his side, as he had once threatened to do. Bound more securely by the compelling mysteries of the past night than by any manacles made of the strongest metal, she flailed in the warm, heaving sea, railing against her impotence. When Dorian glided back to her, she was almost relieved to see him.

"Your kinswomen," he said without preamble, "have raised a great force to march against the Greeks. They follow the coastline and will soon be within reach of Athens."

Thalassa gasped, fired with excitement and filled with a potent yearning. The Amazons were going to war! Ah, to feel a horse's warmth between her legs once more. To ride into battle with her people, a war cry swelling her throat and her *bipennis* singing its deadly song over her head!

She saw that Dorian was frowning at her, and breathlessly demanded, "How do you know this?"

"Do you remember the Selkies who came to my abode? Well, those seals are also Selkie folk, but in their animal form. They told me."

"Oh." She absorbed his simple explanation in wonder. She remembered the Selkies, of course. How could one forget those astounding creatures with the bodies of men and the eyes of animals? Yet she had never dreamed the seals bobbing a short distance away were anything other than seals, even though both Dorian and Aricia had told her of the Selkies' ability to shape-change.

Then the Selkies were forgotten. The Amazons were going to war! It was hardly unexpected. Indeed, how could it be otherwise? Yet the news sent the blood pounding through her veins. The call of that grave retribution roared within her breast, and she was a blooded warrior once more. Heart and soul, she belonged to the Amazons—the gills on her neck, the strange spell of Dorian's eyes, all the wondrous and terrifying changes that had befallen her were swept aside in the obsession to see Hippolyte avenged and Antiope freed. So filled with the desire for revenge, she could scarcely concentrate on Dorian's next words.

"The Selkies say that Amazonia has emptied herself. Every woman of fighting age who can sit a horse and carry a weapon seems to have joined this campaign." He paused and asked grimly, "Do you not think it unwise for them to leave their capital city and all their lands so ill-attended? Your birth-country is a rich and fertile place. What if other tribes seek to take it over in their absence?"

She bristled at the unmistakable note of criticism in his grave voice. "What would you know about warfare—you who spend all your time in the sea? Amazons are the best fighters in the world!"

"My life may be in the sea, little one." His melodic voice sounded heavy and sad—almost distressed. "But not all of my time has been spent there. When you have lived as long as I have, you learn a great deal about the world, whether on land or sea.

"I understand your loyalty," he went on earnestly, "and I honor you for it. But, Thalassa, I have seen many land people rise to power, then watched their tragic fall to destruction. It grieves me to say it, but I fear this may be the prophecy the Elders spoke of. The same doom that has struck down so many others awaits your noble kindred."

A chill wracked Thalassa's body, and she whirled around with outrage and a wild need to refute him. "You know *nothing!*" she spat out, but he cut her off impatiently.

"I know that no tribe, no matter how powerful, can afford to go off to war leaving its borders and capital city unattended. I certainly need no prophecy to tell me *that!* And judging by the size of their force, that is exactly what your people have done."

She could not deny the logic in what he said. But Oreithyia was a wise and sharp-minded war queen, one of the best the Amazons had ever had. Surely she would not make such a tragic error in judgment. Even if she did, the grandmothers would gainsay it, wouldn't they? Thalassa's hands clenched. Unless rage over the murder and abduction of two of their queens had swept away all reason, for Oreithyia and everyone else.

"Thalassa," Dorian asked softly, "have you thought of what will happen if the Amazons lose this battle against Athens?"

"That will not happen, for they—we—fight in the name of the Goddess."

Dorian grunted. "And the Greeks fight in the name of their gods as well. Landfolk always fight in the name of whatever deity they venerate. Yet in a war there can be only one victor. And if the Amazons do not succeed to that exalted position, the survivors may not have a home to return to."

It was a thought beyond comprehension, and Thalassa took refuge from it in anger. "You don't understand. The blood oaths of our people demand that we seek payment for the wrong done us. It's a matter of honor!"

"It is also a matter of survival," he said steadily. "This campaign could be the ruin of your people, Thalassa."

"Nonsense! You speak as though you possess great wisdom, but you know nothing—nothing!"

She tried to pull out of his encircling arms, but succeeded only in swallowing seawater. Almost absentmindedly Dorian continued to hold her, his thoughts whirling in dark circles. The plans he had concocted with such painstaking care were all falling apart, and the subsequent lack of control was as unpleasant to him as it was unaccustomed.

Even before the Selkies' arrival he had known the Ceremony of Matebonding, which he had counted on to bring her to him without reservations, had failed. She had come to him, yes. But with her she had dragged the heavy weight of Amazonia, a mammoth burden that, unless he could sever her from it, would forever keep her from swimming free and unencumbered at his side. Looming and ugly it stood between them still, and he hated it—this vast rival composed of memories and people both alive and dead, this stubborn mountain that kept his chosen one imprisoned on its rocky peaks, rather than in the welcoming sea where she belonged.

For all its power, the Ceremony of Matebonding had not released Thalassa from the bonds of land. Without that one all-important transformation, Dorian knew he had accomplished nothing. He scowled savagely. If he had performed the ceremony a few days earlier, or if the blood-mad landfolk had managed to contain themselves only a few days longer, none of this might have happened. Like so many deeds, he concluded glumly, it was all a matter of timing.

Twisting in his arms Thalassa saw the anger in his face and instantly assumed the worst. She had finally driven him too far. Now he would retaliate and gain control over her once and for all. She cursed the tender new feelings that had prevented her from fleeing him when she had had the chance.

"What magic do you intend putting upon me now?" she asked bravely.

He stared at her. "I wish it were that simple. But since it is not . . . I intend to take you to Athens."

"You—you do?" She must have looked as foolish as she felt, for a mocking smile whispered across his mouth. "Why? Why would you do this?"

The smile turned grim. "Do not question me too much, dearling, lest I think better of my decision."

Wisely Thalassa held her tongue. But she was incredulous. Athens—where she would see her people in their full might, perhaps even participate in the freeing of Antiope and the avenging of Hippolyte! From the moment Dorian had imparted the Selkies' news she had thought of nothing else. And here he was, granting her this great boon without her even asking it of him! An emotion strangely akin to the deep love she felt for her closest heart-friends swept over her, and in the grip of this powerful new sensation she very nearly kissed him.

At the last moment she remembered herself and drew back, confused and embarrassed. The frightening pleasure of their lovemaking had, in her mind, always been an intimacy she'd had no choice but to share in. Never had she shown Dorian any sign of physical affection that he had not wrung from her with his own passion. The thought of doing so had not even occurred to her. Until now.

"Thank you," she said awkwardly. "I do not know how . . . Thank you."

It seemed as though she had angered him yet again, for his face became thunderous. "Why must you always pull away?" he asked harshly. "Have we not grown as close as two people can? *When* will you finally come to me?"

Yanking her to him, he kissed her, his lips hard and almost punishing upon hers. Yet within that brutal kiss, which lacked his usual erotic control, there was pain, an aching vulnerability that touched Thalassa's soul in a way nothing else ever had. She put her arms around him and kissed him back, and for an instant it was she who offered comfort and he who accepted. Then his mouth slowly left hers.

"Do not be too free with your thanks, my love." His eyes, in the brightening dawn, were sad. "You may yet have cause to regret our going to Athens."

She smiled at him. "I do not think so, man of the sea," she said, turning what had once been a term of anger into an expression of endearment.

Her eyes were aglitter with excitement, and this time it was Dorian who held his tongue. Perhaps this last reckless measure might bear fruit after all. If witnessing what he suspected was the Elders' prophecy come to pass succeeded in bringing her to him of her own free will, then the risks would be well worth it. But there was no point in telling her what he had decided to do if it did not.

CHAPTER 25

≈ The city of Athens stood four miles from the sea. From the bastion of the temple of Athena—that beautiful Goddess who had defeated blue-haired Poseidon for possession of the city—one could look out over the wine-dark expanse of the Aegean. It was on this lonely spot that Antiope—queen, Amazon, and slave—stood as the eastern horizon slowly pinkened with the deep rose of dawn.

Here, King Aegeus, mortal father of Theseus, had waited for his heir's return from the island of Crete. He had been taken there with six other youths and seven maidens in his sixteenth year. Minos, king of the mighty Minoan civilization, had demanded this human tribute every spring. The unfortunates were taken to his magnificent frescoed palace at Cnossus, and then sacrificed to the Minotaur, a horrible half-human, half-bull monstrosity.

Confidently the young Theseus had vowed to his tearful father that he would kill the monster and return in triumph. "Watch for my sails," he told Aegeus. "If they are white, then I was successful. If they are black, then I am dead."

But in the excitement of his victory and his return home after his long absence, Theseus forgot to change the sails. Aegeus, watching the sea each day, finally saw his son's galley returning, its black sails a stark contrast to the bright waters of midday. Overcome with grief, the old king had thrown himself off the rampart of Athena's temple, to land a battered, lifeless hulk on the jagged rocks below.

Theseus himself had told Antiope of the tragedy, moved as much by guilt as by the desire to impress her with his bravery in killing the Minotaur. But Antiope had not been impressed. To her it seemed the height of irresponsibility to forget something as important as a prearranged signal, especially one so grave as this. Also, she had been new to Athens when Theseus had related the story, and so was not much interested in anything he had to say. Then.

Antiope sighed and wrapped the long mantle of fine Greek wool tighter about her shoulders. She had grown soft in this man-ruled land. Once the dawn chill would have barely aroused her notice, and now she was bundling herself up like an old woman. There had been a time when she'd battled everyone and everything there, when the longing to shed Greek blood had outweighed all else. Then that murderous urge had faded, replaced by an equally fierce desire to end her own life. Now that was gone as well.

The sea was taking on a golden shimmer under the lightening sky, and Antiope gazed on the quiet waters with sullen antipathy. Almost a year had passed since Theseus had carried her off to Athens. She had changed in so many ways during that year, but her hatred for the sea had remained constant.

It was the sea that had brought death to Hippolyte and so many others, and it was the sea that had provided the means by which she'd been abducted from home and kin. Yes, the sea was at the root of all her troubles, and she hated it.

Repeatedly Theseus had sought to make her understand what had happened that terrible day in Amazonia; how Soloon had betrayed Amazon and Greek alike with his treachery. Eventually Antiope had come to believe him, but it made little difference. The truth would not bring Hippolyte back, and for all his eagerness to please her, Theseus refused to grant the one request she had made—that he free her and allow her to return home.

Oh, he was sly about it. For all his youth, the king of Athens was an extremely clever man. That was another thing Antiope had learned about him. The journey was lengthy and fraught with dangers, he explained. He had been absent too long from his responsibilities as king, and could spare neither the time nor the expense of mounting a large enough fleet to deliver Antiope safely. And what if on reaching Amazonia he and his men were slain by enraged warriors before Antiope could prevent it?

To make matters worse, Antiope found herself with child. She sought to hide it, but Theseus's sharp eyes detected it. Triumphantly he seized on the fact of her pregnancy, adamantly declaring that he would not even consider allowing the mother of his unborn son to undertake such a journey.

Antiope's lip curled. His son. He had been so certain the child growing within her would be a boy. And so it had been. But perhaps it was better that way. How could she endure seeing a girl-child grow up in this man-ruled place?

Yet Theseus had offered Antiope her freedom. It was just that she did not consider it as such. When she gave birth to a squalling, lusty boy, the overjoyed king of Athens had informed his slave that he wished to free her and make her his wife. "You will be queen over all of Athens," he had declared happily.

But Antiope had snorted in contempt. "I am a queen already," she'd said. "And as far as I can see, being a man's wife is no different from being his slave. So I may as well remain a slave."

To give him his due, Theseus had not punished her for such insolence, as well he could have. The young king genuinely loved his intransigent captive, and now that she had given him such a fine son, he loved her even more. But there was no longer any hope of his releasing her. He wanted to make more sons with her. As if she were his prize brood mare, Antiope thought resentfully.

Yet even she had to admit Theseus had tried hard to make her content. He had ordered that she be given every courtesy. Indeed, he took pains to see that she was treated more like his queen than his slave. Antiope knew that many in the palace disapproved of the exalted position Theseus had given his spear-won captive. She had heard the whispers and mutterings that he should break the Amazon slave to his will and train her to follow at his heel like the cur bitch she was. But Theseus seemed oblivious to such criticisms, or perhaps truly did not know of them.

Antiope left the temple and walked down the stony path that led to Piraeus, the port of Athens. High walls rose in the distance, forming a corridor that ensured the city could not be cut off from its wooden fortifications on the sea. Rocky crags towered above Antiope's head, all of them crowned with limestone buildings that sparkled boldly in the hard, clear light of the Greek morning. The most magnificent of them by far was the Acropolis, the largest structure Antiope had ever beheld.

Theseus had once admitted, rather reluctantly, that, compared to the mighty kingdom of Mycenae, or the powerful walled city of Tiryns, his city-state was not a major power. But to Antiope's eyes, accustomed only to Themiscrya with its stone hall, thatched huts, and rambling queen's house, Athens was quite the most impressive metropolis she had ever seen.

She would have never thought so many people could live comfortably in one place. The *Agora*—Athens's marketplace—swarmed with farmers, merchants, fishermen, nobles, and slaves . . . always the slaves. Cephalus, the wealthy and well-known weapons merchant, owned one hundred and twenty of them alone. They labored in his factory making swords and spears for the aristocracy. Even the smaller businesses, of which there were many crowded along every street in Athens, kept no less than six slaves apiece to make life easier for their masters.

The *Agora* had its own particular aroma, compounded of rare perfumes and spices, fish and freshly slaughtered meat, human sweat and animal dung. Even at this early hour the odors teased Antiope's nostrils long before she reached the open square. People were already about, and as was usual for this Greek city, they were almost all male. It was considered poor manners for highborn women to go out in public. Thus it was rare to see a female other than a slave or the wife of a farmer or poor merchant walking the streets of Athens.

Antiope drew more than one disapproving stare as she strode along, her manly gait awkward in the long tunic worn by women. Despite her lowly status as a slave, Theseus had gifted her with *chitons* of the softest wool, accompanied by magnificent brooches of gold to hold the garments in place upon her shoulders. In these fine clothes she had the appearance of a noblewoman, not a servant. Therefore, she was eyed with censure by those who knew a highborn lady had no business striding about the streets as though she were a man.

Antiope stumbled over an uneven paving stone and cursed. She hated the *chiton*, hated the way the material flapped annoyingly about her ankles, hampering her every move. It was no wonder women there were so helpless. How could they ride or fight or do anything worthwhile with these ridiculous skirts constantly tripping them up?

At first she had adamantly refused to put on the humiliating women's dress, but when her belly had swelled with child, her one tunic had threatened to split from the strain. She had reluctantly donned the *chiton*, only to find that after she had birthed the babe, her precious Amazon tunic—the last link with home and family—had mysteriously disappeared and could not be found. With her tunic gone, her servitude seemed assured.

On the street of the slave dealers, she tensed as she approached the wooden auction block, set in a large open area at the end of the street. It was here that the slave merchants brought their human merchandise, to be sold to the highest bidder at midmorning every day. The auction would not be for some hours yet, but the slaves to be sold that day—most of them women and children—were already chained together behind the block, on display for whatever prospective buyers might wish to inspect them.

Antiope's dark gaze swept over the dejected group. She had been there many times before and had always left in disappointment. Yet she continued to return, obsessed by the hope that one day she might find Thalassa, or one of her sister warriors taken prisoner by Heracles, chained among the other women fated to be put up on the block and sold.

A slave herself, Antiope had no means of purchasing a captive Amazon, even should she find her. However, Theseus did, and Antiope had decided she would do anything to convince him to buy a kinswoman if that possibility ever arose.

But today was not to be the day. With a heavy sigh, she left the street of the slave dealers and climbed the hilly path that led to the palace of Theseus, perched high on one of the rocky crags.

Clustered around the great palace complex were the small, flat-roofed limestone houses of the Athenian populace, terraced one on top of the other in the hilly Greek terrain. Antiope found her way through the stepped streets that connected one level to another, and as she neared her destination, she glanced at the imposing buildings that rose on either side of her.

Here were the royal workshops and the houses of the great merchants, those who were among the wealthiest citizens of Athens. Just beyond these stately edifices lay the gates to the palace itself which Antiope passed through with no more than an uninterested glance from the guards.

Entering the courtyard, Antiope carefully picked her way through the untidiness, which she had found was typical for the outside of a lord's house. Geese waddled back and forth picking wheat out of long wooden troughs, and dung from horses, mules, and cattle lay in odorous heaps everywhere. In front of the vestibule a chariot was being unharnessed by two stable slaves, and she stopped to watch as the three lathered horses were unyoked and led to the watering trough.

They were fine horses and had been driven hard, she noted critically, by someone who had little care for their well-being. She would never be able to get used to the way men treated horses here, making them wear massive, wickedly curved bits that cut their tender mouths, and mercilessly using whips on their shining coats. But she could no more do anything for mistreated horses than she could for herself.

Shaking her head, Antiope went through the wide doorway with its woodworked threshold sheathed in the finest of bronze. The rumble of male voices signaled that guests were in the Great Hall, but that mattered little to her. She had learned that a woman was not welcome in the hall or any other place where men gathered, unless she was summoned there to provide service of some kind. Shrugging, she walked toward the passage that led to the women's quarters. The less she had to do with men in this Goddess-less place, the better it suited her.

"*Potnia.*" The respectful term of address for a highborn lady was uttered with ill-concealed resentment. Antiope turned to see a slave woman of middle age approaching her. The woman's black eyes glittered with hostility as she took in the appearance of her royal lord's favorite concubine.

Though showered with gifts by her noble master, the woman thought resentfully, the stupid chit would accept almost none of them. Not the ornate ivory combs for her hair, the long ropes of beads made from carnelian, gold, and the highly sought-after amber, or the beautifully crafted ivory hand mirrors and jewelry boxes. And as if that were not bad enough, the girl did nothing to make herself attractive for her lord.

She absolutely refused to darken her eyes with kohl, and at the suggestion that she apply white lead to her disgracefully tanned face and shoulders so that they would take on the snowiness of a dove's breast, she had actually laughed most scornfully. She would not even use a bit of alkanet juice to heighten the rosiness of her cheeks!

Her behavior was an insult to the royal son of the great Poseidon, and it rankled the older woman to be forced to address this unfeminine creature as though she were nobly born. Yet to disobey the order of Theseus, or any other man, was unthinkable. Would that this ill-mannered, uncivilized savage followed her example!

"What is it?" Antiope finally asked, tiring of the woman's unfriendly stare.

"The king, *your noble lord and master,* has done you the great honor of summoning you to his presence in the Great Hall. Now come. We have been searching the palace for you, and there is not much time. You must prepare yourself so that you are pleasing in the eyes of your master. Hurry now! Your lord must not be kept waiting!"

The woman's bony fingers tightened on Antiope's arm, and she gave her a hard yank in the direction of the women's quarters. Antiope set her bare feet on the white-plastered floor. She easily pried off the woman's fingers with one hand, then with the other, gave her a shove that sent the slave woman tumbling to the floor.

"I am not a slow-witted ox to be tugged here and there," she said coldly. "It would be well if you remembered that. And no woman in this man-ruled land looks like a proper woman. Only Amazons can make that claim. I will go to see what Theseus wants the way I am, and if he is not pleased with my appearance, then so be it."

Turning her back on the glowering slave, Antiope strolled off toward the hall, moving with deliberate and unhurried nonchalance. Rubbing her bruised buttocks, the other woman got awkwardly to her feet and glared after her. "Bitch of a cur," she spat. "I hope she does displease the king, and then may he flay all the flesh from her living bones for her insolence! Ill-mannered slut!"

The hall of Theseus was crowded with men when Antiope entered. Talking in low voices, they stood around the central feature of the room, a gigantic hearth flanked by four enormously tall columns of hard blue limestone.

The fire lit in the great hearth every night regardless of the weather still burned, but the air in the hall was amazingly pleasant to breathe. A massive terra-cotta chimney, the first Antiope had ever seen, filtered out the smoke. Remembering the buildings of the Amazons with their crude holes cut into the roofs, Antiope had to admit the Greek system was far superior.

Female slaves were scurrying back and forth with platters of food. As she walked toward the men, Antiope's stomach grumbled. The rich smell of pork sprinkled with white barley, and mutton stewed with leeks and peas smote her nostrils. There were also dishes of vegetables fried in olive oil, and loaves of freshly baked bread.

Theseus's guests had to be important to warrant such a feast, she thought, as several slave girls rushed past bearing gray pottery jugs filled with goat's milk or the watered wine she still found so unappealing.

"Ah, she comes at last," a voice boomed. The red-bearded king of Athens stepped out of the cluster of men, smiling at the sight of her.

Antiope regarded him unenthusiastically. "I was told that you asked to speak with me."

"I see you still have not succeeded in teaching the wench manners," a second male voice said gruffly, and the lion-draped figure of the mighty Heracles stepped out to stand beside Theseus.

Antiope stiffened at the sight of that familiar face, with its square beard and the long black hair tied in three pigtails. How had she managed to miss him when he towered above all other men like an oak tree in a forest of saplings? She truly was becoming soft and dull-minded in this accursed land!

Heracles was looking at her with frowning disapproval. "Your lord did not ask to speak with you, girl. He ordered it, as is his right. I should have thought you'd have developed womanly respect by now." Before Antiope could snarl out a reply, he turned to Theseus. "Oh, well. She's obviously a good breeder of sons, so I suppose that's why you're not riding her with a tighter rein."

Antiope reached for her dignity and drew it around her. "If the purpose of your summons was to impress upon me my servitude," she said quietly to Theseus, "then you have done so. I will leave you now, since I am sure you *men* wish to be alone."

Theseus caught her arm as she turned. "No, dearest, that is not why I called for you. And well do you know that I wish to free you from servitude and make you my queen. No, there is another reason you are here."

He looked haggard and drew a deep breath. "Messengers brought word to the lord Heracles three days ago that your kinswomen have raised a vast host and are marching toward Athens at this very moment."

Thunderstruck, she stared at him. A fierce and terrible joy surged through every thread of her being. Her people were coming to rescue her . . . and now these arrogant men were terrified, as well they should be! Throwing her head back, she let out a wild peal of laughter that caused several of the men to make furtive signs against the evil eye.

"So their coming affrights you, does it?" she exulted. "That is most wise of you, for every man among you has good reason to fear the wrath of my kin! Over and over have I prayed to the Goddess these long months. At last She has heard me—and Her answer to the prayers of Her daughter is your destruction!"

A swell of angry, frightened voices rose about the echoing hall, but they were drowned out by Heracles's deep growl. "You see, Theseus? It is as I said. You can cage a she-wolf, but just when you think you have her tamed she turns on you. This one's like all the rest of her kind. You were a fool to think she would help us."

"Help you!" Antiope repeated shrilly. "In the name of the Mother, what makes you think I would help those who slew my sister and carried me into slavery? Fear has addled your wits and made all of you mad!" She laughed again, looking around a room that had gone suddenly quiet.

The men watched her intently. She seemed to them the very embodiment of the Goddess her barbaric people worshiped: a cruel and bloodthirsty female deity. A Goddess who would only be satisfied by a river of male blood.

But the king of Athens still stood beside her, neither apprehension nor loathing in his eyes as he studied her. "Lady," he said gently, "will you do nothing? If there is fighting and it reaches the palace, your child could die. Then you will have lost both a sister and a son. I know he is not the daughter you hoped for, yet I have watched you with him at your breast. I know you care for the boy."

Antiope bit her lip, unable to meet Theseus's steady gaze. His words were deeply disturbing, for she did love the bright, robust boy-child she had birthed. And there were times when, to her horror, she felt strange and shameful emotions toward the father as well.

When her son had been born—after a labor that the midwives said was indecently easy—she had given him the name Hippolytos in memory of her sister. Fully expecting Theseus to reject her naming and choose one of his own, she had been astonished that he did not. Suspiciously she had waited for him to grow weary of such indulgence and give the child a Greek name. He hadn't. She had never let Theseus know how much that pleased her.

Her gaze fell on the serving girls. In each corner of the Great Hall they stood huddled together, their hands clutching unemptied wine jugs and platters full of cooling food. Their round eyes were fixed on her in fascinated dread, and she felt a stab of pity. These girls had not asked to be slaves. They had either been born into it or abducted, as she herself had been, Yet if the Amazons took Athens, they would most likely die.

"Very well," she said, "here are my terms. My freedom, horses and weapons of my own choosing, and practical clothing to replace this"—she tugged disdainfully at the *chiton*—"absurd woman's garment.

"You, Theseus, along with eight of your most trusted officers, will escort me to my Amazon sisters. In return, I pledge that I will persuade Oreithyia, the war queen of my people, to leave these lands without further violence." She paused, then added, "The boy may stay with his father, of course. For no Amazon may raise a son."

She was surprised at how painful it was to say that she would leave Hippolytos behind, but she hid this and smiled sardonically as the men exchanged relieved glances and nods of approval. All except the king of Athens. Yet his glowering expression did not really matter. Theseus would agree to her terms. His nervous men would not let him do otherwise.

"It is a good trade, my lord," an older noble with a grizzled beard said when Theseus remained silent. "The freedom of one female in return for the safety of your entire kingdom. Women are like fruits on a vine. Pick one, sample it, and then pick another. You've already enjoyed this girl and can easily replace her with ten or twenty slaves just as comely. The son she bore you is the only important thing about her."

"Lykaon speaks wisely." Heracles gave Antiope a contemptuous stare, which she coldly returned. "Let this she-wolf go back to her pack, and good riddance to all of them. But I don't mean to overstep myself. This is your city, Theseus, and the woman is also yours, to do with as you wish. So, will you release her?"

Theseus spoke at last. "No," he said. Antiope's tormentingly brief taste of freedom died before the hardness in his voice and in his light-blue eyes.

"This woman is the mother of my son, and intractable as she is, I love her. She belongs to me. Not for anything in this world will I let her go. And if the Amazons desire a contest, they are welcome to test our mettle. The brave men of Athens will defeat them!"

CHAPTER 26

≈   "Oreithyia! A rider approaches!"
        At the sentry's call the war queen looked up
from currying her mare. A lone warrior was thundering into
the army encampment that sprawled along one of the plains
on the Greek mainland. As the woman dismounted from her
lathered horse, Oreithyia strode forward, followed by
whomever else had been in earshot of the sentinel's cry.

"What news do you bring me?" the war queen demanded.

A tired smile creased the warrior's dust- and sweat-
streaked face. "Success, Lady. I bring you success. The
detachment you sent into the Peloponnesus has penetrated
as far as Laconia. Its mission of terror and conquest has
borne fruit. The Peloponnesians are thoroughly cowed. Any
ideas they once had of reinforcing their king by marching
across the isthmus have been abandoned."

"Hah!" Triumphantly Oreithyia slapped her thigh as the
listening Amazons cheered. "Where is our force now?"

"In the Pyrrhichan region of Laconia. Two shrines have
already been erected with wooden images, one to the

Mother and the other to Artemis." The messenger stroked her mare's damp neck and smiled fiercely. "In the isthmus we came upon a stone pillar put up by order of Theseus. On one side the letters *Athens* were cut, and on the other it said *The Peloponnese*. We tore the pillar down and trampled it beneath our horses' hooves."

"Well done!" Oreithyia clapped her exhausted herald on the shoulder. "You have ridden long and hard to bring me this fine news. Tend to yourself and your valiant mare. Both of you have earned a good rest. See that you get it, for tomorrow, we march!"

The warrior led her horse away to a chorus of eager questions directed at the war queen. Oreithyia held up a hand for silence. "Yes," she said. "The moment for the final advance has arrived at last. Now that the Peloponnesians are quelled, the last obstacle to the city of Theseus is removed. Soon Athens will be in the hands of women, and *then* let Theseus and all the curs of this man-ruled land look to their heads—as we strike them from their shoulders! Spread the word, my sisters. We march at dawn!"

As the assembled Amazons scattered to do her bidding, Oreithyia spread her arms and smiled up at the hard, blue skies of Greece. She was exultant. The last menace to this great campaign was gone, and now she could ride on Athens as a conqueror. The months-long and arduous march from Themiscrya was thundering to a close. Soon it would climax in the stronghold of Theseus.

"Thank you, O glorious Mother," Oreithyia whispered. "Be strong of heart, Antiope, for your days as Theseus's slave are coming to an end. We will ride home side by side, younger sister. And the proud king of Athens shall stumble along behind us in the dust, a future sacrifice to the Goddess of women!"

Her softly uttered words had been meant for Artemis alone, but though he stood at quite a distance from the war queen, Valya heard them. Shaking his head he strode heavily away. To those who glanced at him as he walked through the milling camp, the young merman looked immeasurably different from the bright-eyed youth who had risen out of Amazonia's waters only months ago. And no one was more aware of those changes than Valya himself.

His shining blond hair was pulled back from his face with a leather thong, and a tunic of finely tanned cowhide clothed his towering body. A broad leather belt encircled his lean waist and from it hung a bronze long sword—given to him by Oreithyia herself—and a short stabbing dagger, its glittering blade fashioned from silver. But it was in his face that the real changes could be seen.

The innocence that had so struck Thalassa—the untried childishness stamped across his attractive features—was gone. His face wore a new expression now, a hard look, born of cynicism and weariness and blood. Blood. It was something Valya had seen enough of to last him all the remaining eons of his life. He had done his share in the spilling of it, too, which was why Oreithyia had gifted him with the long sword.

After their first battle she had given swords to all of them, in a formal ceremony held before the entire assemblage of Amazons and their allies. At the time Valya's own blood had still been on fire from his first taste of combat, and the acceptance and approval of those fierce warriors had filled him with delight. But as battle upon battle had followed, the exultation had faded, and the sword at his side was a burden now, rather than a joy.

War involved far more than the simple business of two opposing forces striving toe to toe. Valya had learned this lesson in ways that he suspected would plague his sleep for centuries. The orange glow of whole villages put to the torch; the piles of the slain, their limbs sprawled in the graceless postures of death; the agonized faces of women who had just seen their men killed and were about to be raped; the shrieks of mothers and children as they were torn roughly apart and bound with the chains of slavery.

And the blood. Always the blood. Pools of it, rivers, so much that even the cleansing embrace of the Great Mother Sea might never lift the reek of it from his hands. The sights and sounds of this long campaign haunted Valya. More and more he yearned for the clean bite of salt air, the rolling rush of the blue swells—rather than the foul odor of spilled entrails and the groans of the dying. Yet he and his companions continued to fight as Oreithyia wished, acquitting themselves so well on the battlefields that all around them sang their praises.

It was easy to kill men of the land, Valya thought sadly, so easy, it shamed him. In the first battle of the campaign Oreithyia had forbidden the six meryouths to be given arms. When one of her officers had protested that such a decree was tantamount to murder, the war queen had smiled coldly. "They claim to possess special strength," she had said. "Let them show it." Valya fingered the sword at his waist. They had shown her, so well that they were accorded an honored place in the army's vanguard from then on.

In truth, Oreithyia could have continued to keep weapons from them and it would have made little difference. Valya was keenly aware that he, as well as his friends, lacked the power and skill of, say, Dorian. But what they did possess set them so far above these warriors of the land, it made killing them repugnant. Plucking a sea urchin off a rock was more painful than taking the sword from one of these men, many of whom barely reached his ribs. He had discovered that most had no knowledge of unarmed combat. Take away their weapons and they were helpless.

Their superior prowess had shocked the six of them at first. Then, pushed by the admiration of the Amazons, they had delighted in it. Now they felt only disgrace. The desperate men who came out to meet the advancing army were farmers and villagers, fighting not for lands or riches, but simply to protect homes and families against a ravaging host. Their deaths had begun to eat at Valya like a festering wound, and even Oreithyia's praise, her promises that they might stay among the Amazons as long as they wished, could not ease the acid bite of his guilt.

As he neared the spot—one of the choicest in camp— where Oreithyia had ordered tents erected for them, Valya saw his kindred gathered together. Their faces looked very grave, though perhaps no graver than his did, he reflected. "Have you heard?" he asked, walking up to them. "We march on Athens tomorrow."

Latora nodded somberly. "They are crying the news all over camp." Like Valya, she'd tied her golden hair back from her face, and she and the others were clothed as he was.

Valya heard the unenthusiastic note in her voice without surprise. Latora had grown disillusioned with the killing even before he had. But he was not prepared for her next words. Clasping burly Matteo by the arm, she said quietly, "Matteo has decided to leave us and return to the sea."

"What?"

Valya rounded on the heavily muscled youth in bewilderment. Of all of them, Matteo had been the most excited about making war with the landfolk. Further, though it made Valya profoundly uneasy to think about it, he alone still took pleasure from the killing.

"Matteo, you?" he blurted out before he could stop himself. "I thought you—"

"Enjoy bringing death to these puny Terrans?" Matteo broke in roughly. "Well, I do, Valya. That is why I must leave." He ran a hand over his square solid jaw, and for the first time Valya saw the deep hollows in which his friend's normally dancing eyes sat. Did they all look like that? he wondered. So haunted . . . and so weary? He brought his wandering mind back to attention as Matteo gripped his shoulder.

"Something evil has awakened in me, Valya, and I am afraid. Even sharks in a blood frenzy do not kill as these landfolk do, with such wantonness, such waste. And for what? At least sharks when they slay do so because they're hungry."

Matteo's voice held an urgency that Valya, who had known the brawny young merman since birth, had never heard. "But Matteo, we are together in this," he protested, "just as we have been in everything from the time we were small. You *can't* leave us!"

"I must! *I must!*" Matteo's anguished cry rose into the hot dusty air and quivered there. It made the Amazons, Gargarians, and Scythians who were hurrying by glance over at them curiously, but because the merfolk were speaking their own tongue, the glances were uncomprehending and the ones who looked went quickly on their way.

Matteo drew a deep, shaky breath. "I have to leave, Valya. My soul depends upon it. Don't you understand? I pleasure in the shedding of blood far too much. A black monster has entered me, and with each life I take, it draws its tentacles ever tighter. Only the sea can help me. I sense it. I must go to the Elders, have them heal me of this dark sickness that waxes stronger and stronger, before it is too late . . . before I am lost. Forever."

His bloodshot eyes met Valya's with a look of desperate pleading. "Please, old friend, do you not see?"

"He sees." Badru spoke heavily. "We all do, Matteo, for there is not a one of us who has not felt what you describe, though it seems we were able to protect ourselves against the blackness of this evil, when you could not."

"Exactly," Matteo muttered feverishly. "You sickened of the killing, but I haven't. May the Great Mother Sea forgive me, I haven't!"

The suffering in the voice of his childhood comrade cut Valya to the bone. "Oh, Matteo," he said sorrowfully, "why did you not speak of this sooner?"

"I thought it would leave me on its own. As it left the rest of you. When I realized it would not, we were yet too far from the sea, so I had to wait. Thank the tides we are finally here. Had this accursed journey been any longer, I might not have had the will to forsake this black delight that seeks to possess me."

Valya nodded. The torment on Matteo's face was painful to see. What had happened to him, to all of them, he wondered, on this journey that was supposed to have been filled with excitement and adventure and the learning of new things? Gladly would he give up the experiences of these last months to erase the look on his friend's face, and to cleanse his own soul of the burdens it carried. Not for the first time the wish that he had never left the sea seeped into his thoughts. "I understand," he said slowly. "How could I not?"

"Then come with me." Matteo gazed around at his companions. "We came to see the land, and we have seen it. Indeed, I have seen enough of it to make my gorge rise at the very mention of land for the rest of my days. The Elders were right, my beloved comrades. This is no place for people of the sea. Let us go home. All of us."

No one spoke. Looking about him, Valya could easily picture what was going through the others' minds. The original plan had called for them to live among landfolk indefinitely, to return after several centuries perhaps, older, wiser, and far more self-assured.

None of them had ever imagined going back, as suppliants meekly admitting their expedition had been a mistake and asking for forgiveness. But the Elders, in their depiction of the land tribes as vile and barbaric, had been right, and each of the six meryouths now knew it. Yet their pride still burned unabated. It was that pride which fought at the idea of being humbled before the Elders.

Black-haired Ferne spoke for all of them when she said, "We understand your need to go, Matteo, and I pray the Elders heal you of this illness quickly. But the thought of facing their wrath just yet is something I do not think any of us is ready for." She smiled crookedly. "After all, we did start out to see the land city called Athens. We may as well follow this journey to its end."

Matteo shook his head but did not argue. Had it not been for this dark evil within him, he too might have wanted to continue on to Athens, if for no other reason than to see the Greek city that was reputed to be far larger than the Amazon capital of Themiscrya.

Silently the six merfolk walked through the shouting, excited encampment. Everywhere preparations for the next day's march were being made, the warriors rushing about, making themselves and their horses ready for the dawn. No one paid much attention to the merfolk.

As they passed the huge herd of tethered animals, Matteo paused briefly. "I will miss the horses," he said to Valya.

Valya nodded in understanding. As part of their champion status, Oreithyia had given them horses from the Amazon herd and had assigned warriors to teach the merfolk how to ride the animals. They had learned quickly, but bestriding intelligent, feeling creatures such as these soon became distasteful—particularly when it meant riding them into battle.

The sight of wounded and dying horses was, in some ways, even worse to the merfolk than the sight of wounded and dying humans. After all, the horses had no choice in going to war. Why should they suffer because of their masters thirst for blood? Following one especially fierce engagement, Valya and the others had decided not to ride their horses into battle again. Oreithyia had been baffled and a little offended by their decision.

In the gently lapping waves of the Aegean, Matteo turned to his comrades and solemnly embraced each of them in turn. Valya was last. The two friends clasped each other tightly, then Matteo stepped back with a sigh. "Oreithyia will not be pleased when she finds I have gone. It means one less champion to fight for her against the Greeks."

Valya merely shrugged, another measure of how much he had changed from the youth so eager to win the war queen's approval.

"Take care, my friends," Matteo said. "And please, do not delay too long in coming back to your true world. My heart will be sore until we are all together . . . again." His voice broke. In silence he hugged each of them once more, then ran swiftly into the diamond-sparkled sea and was gone.

For long moments the five meryouths stood without speaking. Latora finally broke the quiet by muttering, "I hope the Elders are not too angry with him."

"The Elders?" Valya stared worriedly out to sea. "I wonder what the lord Dorian will say when Matteo tells him we lied about going to the southern reaches. And what of the lady Thalassa? She was resigned to her fate when we left, but what will she do when she finds her birth-people have gone to war?"

CHAPTER 27

≈ Dorian poked his head out of the waves. "There," he said to Thalassa, who had surfaced beside him. "Athens lies before you. What think you of it?"

Thalassa stared at the city beside the sea. The fierce Greek sun was dying slowly, and the white limestone of the city's buildings shifted from mauve to crimson-hued shadows in the bloody light. The beauty of Athens caught her unprepared. Somehow, she had not expected it to be so lovely. And it was much larger than she had imagined as well. Where was Antiope in that winding maze of streets and dwellings constructed by men? Was she even still alive?

She had eagerly followed Dorian through his unfathomed kingdom of waters in order to arrive there. Past the narrow strip of land the merfolk called "the Terrans' boot," with its swirling whirlpool so dreaded by Greek sailors, entering finally the wine-dark Aegean, dotted with myriad islands and tiny headlands.

The sailing season that would last until the first storms of autumn had begun. Twenty-oared traders' galleys rowed across the indigo waters, bound for distant eastern ports;

and the small, round coracles of peasant farmers hugged the coastline as they ferried their produce to market in the populous centers of Crete and Tiryns. The threat of Amazon invaders did not appear to have forestalled trade. Indeed, it seemed to have increased it, as if each man felt an urgency to make as much profit as possible before disaster struck.

"I have not been here in some time," Dorian said, squinting up at the large structures that crowned the rocky crags of Athens, "but the palace of old Aegeus rests atop one of those hills. I assume it is now the home of his heir. It is there that Theseus would have Antiope."

"If she still lives," Thalassa muttered, unable to keep from voicing her fears any longer.

Dorian gave her a somber look. "I do not know what kind of man Theseus is. But if your queen is as stubborn as you, my love, then I can only hope he is as patient as I."

"You are not like the men of land. You've told me that often enough yourself." She forced from her mind images of what a man in this land might do to a captive who displeased him, and thought instead of the Amazon host she and Dorian had seen on the plain that morning, breaking their camp in the darkness of false dawn. "Oreithyia probably paused to tidy up her lines and secure her rear," she said reflectively. "No doubt that is why she was camped on the plain."

"Most wise of her."

Thalassa chose to ignore the slight edge in Dorian's voice. "They have begun their final advance." As she spoke a fleeting desire stabbed through her. Oh, to be riding with them on the last leg of that glorious march! "How long will it take them to reach the city?" she asked, ashamed of the wistful note of longing that had crept into her voice.

"They must first cross the plains of Attica, but with a force of that size, I doubt they will meet with any opposition. With Theseus so vastly outnumbered, he will wish to protect Athens and not fragment his own forces by sending valuable fighting men out to what can only be certain death. So their way should be clear." Dorian thought a moment. "Tomorrow, or the day after perhaps."

"Time enough for me to find Antiope, then."

"And how do you propose to do that, my love? You,

who have never been in such a large city in your entire life, and do not know your way about."

"I'll manage." Her jaw jutted out pugnaciously. "I possess the strength of your people, along with the courage and warrior training of my own. If my queen and age-mate is alive to be found, then I will find her."

He sighed. "Indeed. But there is no need for you to go alone. When the night sets in, we will go ashore, and I will take you to the palace of Theseus myself."

She stared at him. "You would do that?"

"Of course. You hardly thought I would bring you all this way to let you blunder about the streets of Athens stark naked, do you?"

"I . . ." It was embarrassing to admit that she had thought he would do exactly that—or even worse. That he would not permit her to go at all. "I thank you," she muttered lamely.

"Do not thank me, Thalassa." His musical voice took on an unyielding note that instantly put her on her guard. "There is a price for my help."

She looked at him warily. "There always is. What is it this time?"

"I will help you to find your kinswoman, and if she lives, to free her. But I will ask something of you in return. To persuade her and her war-queen sister to put aside their revenge and go home."

"But what about the slaying of Hippolyte, and the humiliation of Antiope being held a slave all this time? Why should you care about the fate of Athens? Is it because you are a man and care only for the causes of men?"

"You know that is not the reason." Maintaining his control, Dorian ignored the fury he knew was sweeping through Thalassa. He reached out and took her balled fists in his large hands. "I care for the fate of your birth-people because I love you, and you sprang from them. War is wasteful and foolish. It will not restore Hippolyte to life, and it will not erase the months of Antiope's slavery. All it will do is cause more death, to as many women as men."

She drew her hands out of Dorian's. "I will speak to them," she muttered. "But I cannot swear that they will listen."

He lightly kissed her forehead. "I can't ask for more than that," he said. "And they would listen more to you than they would to me."

When Athens and the sea around it lay cloaked in darkness, Dorian did just as he had promised. Under the pallid light of a waning moon, he and Thalassa slipped into the sleeping city. It was not difficult. Knowing his foes approached by the land route, Theseus had wisely elected not to spare precious men by increasing the fortifications along his seawalls.

The night was warm, and the stones in Athens's streets still held a vestige of the day's heat. In her excitement, Thalassa barely felt them beneath her bare feet, just as she paid little heed to the night breezes brushing against her body. She was surprised when, after telling her to wait in the shadow of a large shop, Dorian disappeared inside, then returned with two men's tunics and a length of twine to bind up her thick hair.

"If someone looks closely," he said as they pulled the tunics on, "he will see that you are no man, but clothed we can at least move about more freely."

As she followed him up a hilly, winding path, Thalassa wondered how Dorian could find his way. Never could she have searched out the path to the palace by herself. It would have taken hours, perhaps the entire night. Even with Dorian, her progress was slow, for away from the safety of the sea, Athens was a city girded for war.

More than once they were challenged by gruff male voices that came out of the darkness, and only Dorian's deep, commanding voice and his faultless Greek enabled them to go on their way unmolested. Tension and fear sat heavy on the night air, and Thalassa could not help but take some pleasure: *Amazons* were causing it. The very thought of women warriors marching toward their city made these arrogant Greek men stiff with terror.

By the time the palace of Theseus rose blackly against the sky, Thalassa could barely contain her exhilaration. "These men quake like wheat before the wind," she whispered to Dorian. "I can smell the stench of it everywhere. I'll wager they now regret the treachery of their king and his comrades. But regret will save neither them nor Theseus from the wrath of my kin."

She had forgotten momentarily her promise to seek to dissuade her kin from that very wrath. But Dorian had not. He gazed gravely at her and whispered back, "Has the vision of what it looks like to see a city destroyed as Cerne was already left your mind?"

The memories of jewel-bright Cerne reduced to ashes and rubble, and the screams and sobs of the dying and bereaved filled Thalassa's mind. Chastened, she fell silent. When Dorian motioned for her to follow him, she did so with an unaccustomed meekness. Like two pieces of the night, they stole past the nodding guards and into the Athenian ruler's echoing palace.

Thalassa froze as the rumble of male voices floated toward them. Dorian touched her arm. "Whoever they are, they are not near. In that direction lies the king's Great Hall."

She wondered how he knew that, but only nodded. "Theseus must be holding a war council. If I were in his place, it's what I would do."

"And so would I. My guess is that noble Theseus will not sleep this night, which will make it easier to find your kinswoman alone."

They set off cautiously. As they glided through the deserted corridors, Thalassa gazed about her. Once she would have been awed by the splendor of this, the first Greek palace she had ever seen. But after the magic of Dorian's royal abode, Theseus's domain seemed plain, even a little rough.

She glanced at Dorian's profile in the golden light of oil lamps set in niches along the walls, brooding on how she would view the queen's house if she could see it again. Had living in the large buildings of the Greeks changed Antiope, as well? She sighed and nudged an elbow into Dorian's ribs. "Know you where the bedchambers are? We should look there first."

Before he could answer, their ears both caught the sounds of voices and approaching footsteps. By unspoken consent they swiftly ducked into the shadows. Three burly soldiers swaggered down the hallway, dragging behind them an equal number of girls whose coarsely woven *chitons* marked them as slaves. "But master," one of them was protesting halfheartedly, "I am to bring wine and cakes to the Great Hall."

"You'll spread those pretty legs while I sheath my sword in your belly first," the man to whom she had spoken growled. "After those Amazon she-beasts arrive, noble Zeus only knows if I'll live to mount another woman, so I intend to get in all the gallops I can while I'm still able to enjoy them. Now shut up. It's your body I'm interested in, not your flapping woman's mouth."

"Unless that flapping woman's mouth is being used to stiffen a man's rod so he can shove it between her legs again," one of the other soldiers observed with a coarse, whinnying laugh. Jerking his girl to a halt, he thrust a hand up her skirts and roughly fondled her until she cried out with pain. Ignoring her cry, he shouted, "Let the old, dried-up slaves whose bodies no longer please a man bring food and drink. The young ones are here to serve the pleasures of the brave men who will fight for Athens!"

The group went on down the corridor, and when their laughter had died away, Thalassa turned to Dorian. Disgust and rage blazed from her golden eyes. "If that is how the *men* of this land have used Queen Antiope, then I do not know if I can keep my vow to you," she said hoarsely.

"Let us hope Theseus has had better sense. Likely he kept her for his own use, at least at first. If she bore him a son during that time, then he would not hand her freely about, to be used by any man who desired her. Among the man-ruled tribes, the mother of a king's son—even though she be a slave—is usually deserving of a little better treatment."

Thalassa clenched her fists, fuming helplessly as she thought of her proud and royal age-mate. For a queen of the Amazons to have her worth judged by whether or not her belly swelled with some man's brat, after he had repeatedly raped her! "Now that those swine are through interrupting us," she said harshly, "let us find the bedchambers."

It did not occur to her to think in terms of women's quarters or men's, so it was fortunate Dorian was there to guide the way. Yet it was an awkward business. The area of the palace where women—highborn and slave alike—spent their lives spinning, weaving, and attending to other female tasks was unusually crowded.

Many of Theseus's officers and nobles had brought their families and most valued slaves to the great palace for safekeeping. The chambers overflowed with them: infants, children, young wives, and elderly grandmothers. All of them were highborn and they all lay snoring on the beds and couches, muttering and sighing in deep sleep. The female slaves lay wherever they could find space to throw down a blanket. Even the most beautiful concubines, who spent their days preening in the all-too-brief favor of doting masters, had to be content with a corner of the floor.

Added to the large number of regular palace women, the newcomers made the corridors and chambers a veritable mass of slumbering humanity, through which Thalassa and Dorian picked their way with the utmost care. Yet nowhere in this murmurous, heavily breathing throng could they find Antiope.

"It's no use." Dorian's whisper was so soft, it was almost as though he were speaking into Thalassa's mind. "The sun will be high in the sky before we finish looking through all of these women, and if one of them awakens and sees us . . ."

"I know." Desperately Thalassa stared about her. "There is a passage we have not tried, though. Please. Let us look there."

The passage led to a columned porch that looked out over a walled courtyard. Just beyond lay a megaron with a brightly painted hearth and two chambers separated by yet another corridor. In sharp contrast to the overcrowded women's quarters, this area was completely deserted. "How strange," Thalassa muttered. "Where are we?"

"I believe these are the queen's apartments, and since Theseus has no queen, he must have ordered them to remain unoccupied."

"Then why is the door to one of those chambers barred, as though someone were inside?" She gripped Dorian's arm. "I think we may have found her!"

The rough wood of the heavy beam cut into Thalassa's hands as she and Dorian lifted it from the door, but in her haste she barely noticed it. Inside, the chamber was dimly lit by a single oil lamp. A lone woman in a white sleeping robe, her long black hair unbound, stood tensely next to the corded bedstead. "Who comes here?" she challenged in a firm voice as they entered.

Dorian paused as Thalassa ran forward. "Antiope, it is I—Thalassa!"

"Thalassa . . . ?"

Incredulously the two women fell into each other's arms, talking and laughing at once. Their first rush of emotion finally exhausted, Antiope stepped back. "So many times have I gone to the slave markets searching for you. I had begun to think you were dead at the hands of men . . . as so many others are."

"And I feared the same fate may have befallen you. But there is time enough for that later. We must get you away from this evil place before anyone comes."

"We?" Antiope's gaze slid to Dorian, who still stood by the door. "So you, too," she mumbled, her voice dulled, "have been robbed of your freedom."

Thalassa felt the warmth of Dorian's gaze upon her, as if he was touching her with his hands. "Not exactly." The words stuck in her throat, but she said awkwardly, "You may trust him, Lady. He is not like the men of Greece. Now come, we must make haste."

Still Antiope held back. "To where?" she asked, eyeing Dorian with suspicion. "Two days have I been imprisoned here by Theseus, to prevent me from fleeing to join our sisters." She gripped Thalassa's hands. "They are already within the borders of this man-ruled land, Thalassa! Orei-thyia is riding to avenge Hippolyte and me. And now you will be free as well! Did you know this?"

Thalassa gently withdrew her hands. "Yes. I knew."

"Then have you news? How great a force has my sister raised? Are they outside Athens yet? Oh, Thalassa, tell me what is happening!"

In her excitement, Antiope had completely forgotten Dorian's presence, and she jumped at the sound of his deep voice. "Your sister has raised a great force, Lady. The greatest host that has ever been seen by the people of this land. They vastly outnumber the men of Theseus, which is probably why he dared not spare two, or even one soldier to guard your chamber. They could reach Athens as soon as tomorrow, and the city prepares itself desperately for war."

Antiope gaped at him. "Thalassa, how comes this man to speak our tongue? Did you teach it to him?"

"No, Lady." Thalassa sighed and threw Dorian an irritated glance. "I told you. He is . . . a friend."

"I have had bitter cause to learn what poor friends men make . . ." Antiope turned away as a sleepy whimper sounded from the rumpled bed, and she gathered a small form into her arms.

"Antiope." Thalassa could scarcely believe her eyes. "You have a babe?" She fell silent as images of what her friend must have suffered in this foreign land filled her mind.

"A son. Better that than a daughter in this man-ruled place. He is called Hippolytos in honor of she who died through men's falseness, and Theseus is the father."

"Has Theseus acknowledged him, as is the custom here?"

Dorian asked the question softly, and Antiope swung around to glare at him. "Yes, curse all men and their customs! That is why he would not release me. I offered him a good bargain: my freedom in return for the safety of Athens. His nobles pleaded with him to take it, but he would not. The fool wants to keep me so that I may bear more sons for him!"

"It could be that he loves you and cannot bring himself to part with you," Dorian suggested gently, his gaze resting on Thalassa's face as he spoke. She ignored him and concentrated her attention on the child in Antiope's arms.

In her whole life she had never seen a baby boy. Infant sons were separated from their Amazon mothers at birth and returned to the villages of their fathers. It was hard to believe this tiny being would grow up to be only another man, believing that women existed solely for his pleasure. Looking at the sturdy dark-haired child, Thalassa could see Antiope in the small, drowsing face. She felt a surge of warmth, as protective as anything she had ever felt toward the girl-children of her own tribe. And the boy was not even hers! What, then, must Antiope feel for this son of her body? She saw how tenderly her age-mate held the child and knew the answer to her question.

But there was nothing tender in the look Antiope gave Dorian. "Why are you here, and what is it that you want of Thalassa and me? What hold do you have on her?"

"I love her," he said evenly. "Just as Theseus probably loves you. She has asked for my help in freeing you, and I have agreed to give it, if you will speak to your war-queen sister about foregoing revenge against the Greeks and returning to your own lands."

"And if I do not?" Outrage was written all over Antiope's face. "Will you leave me here as Theseus's slave?"

"No!" Thalassa glared at Dorian. "*We* would never allow a queen of the Amazons to remain enslaved to these Greek swine!" She hesitated. "But I did promise to talk with you, and some of the things this man has said do bear listening to. Also, it is not the first time he has helped our people."

Antiope looked at her in puzzlement, and Dorian broke in. "While we stand here talking, the night is waning. If you are going to accompany us, Lady, then I suggest you do so. It would not be good for any of us if Thalassa and I were found here."

There was no denying the sense in his words. Antiope wrapped the baby more securely and nodded to Thalassa. "Let us go, then," she said in a brisk voice.

"But the babe . . ." Thalassa stared worriedly at her friend. Surely Antiope could not mean to take a *son* back to the Amazons! "A boy-child, Lady . . ." She could feel rather than see the corners of Dorian's mouth quirking in a wry smile and refused to look at him. "What will Queen Oreithyia say?"

"I care not what she will say." Antiope's chin rose stubbornly. "If Theseus had agreed to my terms, he could have kept the boy. But now, I will take him, and who knows? Perhaps I can raise him so that he will not be like all other men."

"A noble thought, Lady." Gallantly Dorian opened the door and stepped aside so that Antiope could pass.

Thalassa stalked after her. "I just hope Oreithyia also finds it noble," she growled to Dorian. "But somehow, I don't think she will. No Amazon has ever kept a son before."

Dorian grinned fondly at her. "There is a first time for everything."

Wraithlike, the three of them slipped back through the women's quarters and out of the palace. The night was indeed waning. The stars had faded and a faint ribbon of gray lightened the eastern sky. Dorian looked up at it with a worried frown. "We must move quickly," he told the two women. "It is even later than I thought."

Antiope thrust little Hippolytos into Thalassa's arms, then bent down to tear her sleeping robe off at the knees. "There." She retrieved the baby and smiled. "Now I can move as one should."

They made good time on their way down the hilly path, keeping to the shadows and taking turns carrying the baby in a sling fashioned from the extra cloth of Antiope's robe. Thalassa's arms still tingled from the brief moment she had held the baby. He was a good child, barely making a sound despite being bounced around on someone's back as they hurried along.

She found herself wondering what it would be like to hold a son of Dorian's and hers. Would such a child have his father's piercing blue eyes, or his mother's golden ones? Her thoughts shocked her. How could she even think about sons, she who had been brought up to want only daughters? Yet Antiope had been raised the same way, and here she was declaring her intention to bring a boy-child back to the Amazons.

Thalassa was relieved when they reached the outskirts of Athens, and she could turn her thoughts to something less confusing. Before them lay the plains of Attica, the wheat fields and olive groves that dotted them just beginning to take shape under a brightening sky. The first true hint of the approaching day—a breathy south wind—ruffled through her hair, and from the shelter of the stone wall she could look back into Athens and see the flicker of torches as soldiers moved through the streets.

"Do all Greek cities have such poor defenses as this one?" she asked scornfully. "Our people could gallop through here as easily as riding down the beaches of home."

Antiope took Hippolytos back from Dorian. "Theseus has said that there are mighty cities in this land—cities with massive, thick walls and giant gates in the shape of lions, and that Athens is not considered great compared to them."

Thalassa snorted in agreement. "We will need to steal some horses if we are to find our kindred."

"That will not be necessary," Dorian said, and both women glanced at him sharply. "Your kindred are about to find us." He paused, his black head cocked to one side. "Can you not hear them approaching?" he asked Thalassa.

Antiope took several steps forward, listening to the dawn with all her might. "I hear nothing!" she muttered in frustration and anger. "You are jesting with us. Thalassa, you don't hear anything, do you?"

But Thalassa did, for she heard with the ears of the merfolk now. That knowledge froze her. Suddenly she felt separate from Antiope, her native queen and childhood friend who could not read the warm south wind's message as she could. The Amazon host was coming upon Athens, the long-awaited moment of its revenge spreading murderous tentacles out toward Theseus's city.

CHAPTER 28

〰 Oreithyia entered Athens before the sun was three hours into the sky. As a horse twitches its hide to rid itself of annoying flies, so had the Amazons contemptuously shaken off the skirmishing parties Theseus sent out to delay their advance. Now the very ground vibrated with the hoofbeats of Oreithyia's cavalry, as it advanced on a city that was strangely deserted.

With the arrival of daylight, Thalassa had witnessed an amazing sight. Long lines of people snaked up a winding path to a plateau of rock that stood some two hundred feet high. Carts drawn by complaining oxen struggled over the stony ground, sharing the narrow trail with heavily burdened donkeys and herds of bleating sheep and goats.

Their destination was the Acropolis, a mighty stronghold that sat atop the rocky plateau. "Theseus told me the entire populace of Athens would take refuge there," Antiope said. "All his palace folk were to go at first light, including myself and Hippolytos. If you had come any later . . ." She gave a triumphant little laugh. "Theseus will be wild when he discovers that I've escaped him after all."

"I suspect Theseus has a good deal more to occupy his mind at the moment," Dorian said dryly. "I doubt his men have even told him of your disappearance yet."

The army of invaders was spreading across the plain in a mass of dust, yells, hoofbeats, and high-pitched whinnies. From the vantage point of the boulder-strewn ridge where they had taken cover, Thalassa watched this army of her people and whispered to Dorian, "It reminds me of the great force my ancestors raised in the visions you showed me."

He nodded soberly. "Yes. But whether the fate of Athens is to be the same as that of Cerne remains to be seen."

Thalassa glanced over at Antiope. The young queen was absorbed in this first sight of kindred whom she had thought never to see again. Lips parted and eyes shining, she was oblivious to her companions, and Thalassa returned her gaze to Dorian. "So you still intend to hold me to my vow?" she asked softly.

"I do, indeed."

"Even though it will likely do no good?"

"That also remains to be seen."

She sighed. "My thoughts are very confusing where you are concerned. It was much easier when I hated you with all my heart. Yet twice now have you aided my sisters, and so I must warn you that I fear for your safety. Even under the best of circumstances, Queen Oreithyia's dislike of men is well known. And after all that has happened . . . Well, she could easily order you slain, despite your freeing of her sister. Can even your powers protect you against so great a host?"

"Probably not." He ran a finger along Thalassa's bare arm. "Though your concern warms me, my sweet. But that is why I think it would be best that you and Antiope go alone to Oreithyia once her forces have settled in."

"Settled in?" Antiope caught Dorian's last few words and swung around. "Surely my sister will order an immediate attack!"

"I think not. Look again, Lady." He gestured toward the distant army. "It appears that she has already selected her base of operations."

A prominent mass of rock reared up directly opposite

the Acropolis. Atop it, the tall figure of the war queen astride her white mare stood etched against the sky. Below her, tents were being thrown up, wagons and pack animals unloaded with practiced speed. The side of the prominence that faced away from the Athenian stronghold formed a gentle slope, and along this easier route supplies were already being carried to erect the camp of the commander and her officers.

"Ares Hill," Antiope muttered. "That is what the Athenians call it."

"A good choice," Dorian said approvingly. "Oreithyia is wise to make it the center of her spearguard. See the steep side that faces the Acropolis? From there she can observe the Greeks' every move. And she can use the plains that border the hill to extend the right and left wings of her battlefront."

Thalassa was listening abstractedly. Dorian's statement that she and Antiope should go alone to the Amazons still rang in her ears. Did he not realize the import of what he had said? Once she was back with her own, no power was great enough to make her forsake them and return to him. Or was there?

Hippolytos awoke and set up a fretful wail that quieted as soon as Antiope gave him her breast. The baby nursed contentedly while the three adults sat in silence, watching the huge Amazonian army take over the peaceful plains of Attica. When her son's tiny mouth had ceased to pull at her nipple, Antiope smiled at Thalassa over the dark, fuzzy head. "Now that this one's hunger is satisfied, we can rejoin our sisters."

"You go ahead, Lady. I will follow shortly."

Antiope's smile faded, and she looked dubiously from Thalassa to Dorian. Thalassa put a reassuring hand on her arm. "Do not worry. He will stay here."

Antiope rose to her feet, her expression still uncertain. "Very well," she said doubtfully, and turned to face Dorian. "I am in your debt," she continued. "I still do not understand why you helped me, or what is between you and my kinswoman, but . . . thank you."

She set off toward the bustling tumult of her people, walking faster and faster as eagerness overtook her. "You should go with her," Dorian said casually, and Thalassa stared at him.

"Are you giving me my freedom, then?" she finally burst out, and added bitterly, "Or is this some cruel means of testing your power over me?"

"No, my heart. It is I who am being tested, and for both our sakes I pray I do not fail." At her uncomprehending expression, he smiled ironically. "And as for power, it is the Great Mother Sea who holds that over you. It is She who will call you back to Her depths, not I."

Thalassa pushed aside the troubling sensations his words evoked and stood up. "Perhaps," she said guardedly. "But I was an Amazon before you took me, and I am an Amazon still." She started to walk away, but his voice halted her.

"You will keep your word?"

She faced him. "Yes." The word came out brusquely, yet when she met Dorian's eyes, Thalassa heard an unbidden softness creep into her voice. "I will."

"There is one other thing I would ask of you," he said before she could turn away.

"And what is that?"

"There are five merfolk in Oreithyia's camp. One of them is Valya. Send them to me. But say nothing of why you and I are here. And tell them they would do well not to tarry."

Shamefaced and shuffling nervously in place, Valya, Badru, Latora, Ellice, and Ferne stood silently before Dorian. They had been standing that way for some minutes while their cynical self-assurance, gained at such cost over these long weary months, evaporated under the piercing, all-too-knowing gaze of their lord.

Finally, unable to bear the silent censure another instant, Valya mumbled, "How . . . how long have you known?"

"Since we first struck these waters. But I suspected before that." Dorian threw this revelation out deliberately, letting his young subjects stew for a few moments longer before inquiring, "And Matteo? Why is it that he alone possessed enough sense to return to the sea, when the rest of you did not?"

Five pairs of eyes focused instantly on his face. "You have spoken with Matteo, Lord?" they all cried out together.

Dorian fixed a severe look on them. He had no intention of revealing the shocked dismay he had felt when he'd sensed Matteo's presence in the Aegean, nor explaining why he had used his superior skills to conceal his and Thalassa's whereabouts from the young merman. "It is I who am asking the questions here," he said in a freezing tone. "Answer me."

There was another uneasy pause, then Latora told him everything, starting from their first meeting with Oreithyia, to the bloody campaign and Matteo's horrifying realization about himself. When she had finished, she asked anxiously, "Will the Elders help him, Lord?"

"I believe so. But he has a great deal to answer for." His gaze traveled over each of their faces. "As do you." Before that icy gaze, even the normally composed Latora lowered her eyes, and the miserable silence descended once more.

At length, Badru whispered, "Lord, what is our punishment to be?"

"What do you think would be fitting, in light of what you have done?"

Badru's eyes remained fixed on his feet. "I—I do not know."

"My lord." Valya squared his shoulders and met his king's fierce gaze with a resoluteness born of sheer desperation. "Whatever you decree, I beg you to show leniency toward the lady Thalassa. It was we who approached her to aid us in seeing the land. Had we not done so, she would never have sought to conspire with us."

Dorian's dark features remained expressionless. Given Thalassa's ingrained distrust of men, he could well believe she would not be the one to initiate a scheme involving her abductor's kin, three of whom were male. But he had no intention of sharing that thought and relieving, in any way, these disobedient youths' apprehension. "We are not speaking of she who is my queen," he said in a soft, menacing tone. "I will deal with her part in this later. The issue before me at the moment is what should be done with you."

He watched their young faces blanch, and felt a surge of anger both at them and at himself. "You came to the land before being deemed ready, and you lied to me and to the Elders in order to do so. You revealed the existence of our people to landfolk. By my father's sacred memory, you even lowered yourselves to take part in one of their senseless wars simply for the amusement of it!"

His voice whipped at them. "Now Matteo is afflicted with soul-sickness, and you stand before me in the garb of landfolk, your hands covered in blood, fouling the very air with the stench of your betrayal and your shameless interference in the union between myself and my queen! All this have you done for your own selfish, shortsighted ends." He drew a deep breath and thundered, "What have you to say for yourselves?"

Thoroughly cowed, the meryouths shrank from him. Facing Dorian was worse than any of them could have imagined. Never had they seen their lord so angry. Indeed, only Valya had ever seen him angry. It was an awesome and frightening thing, this rage of his, and for the first time the true seriousness of their predicament struck them.

"We meant no harm," Ellice said in a quavering voice. "Truly, Lord, we did not. Indeed, the lady Thalassa implored us to take her to Amazonia, but we refused." She ignored the glare Valya threw at her, and adamantly continued. "We explained instead, that by sacred decree she had been named your chosen one, and to interfere in her destiny as your queen would be unthinkable."

Dorian's eyebrows lifted. "Most wise of you," he said dryly, "though it be unfortunate that such wisdom did not extend to your own ill-fated deeds. And did it not occur to any of you that by delivering a message to her birth-people, you were, in fact, intruding upon matters that were not your concern?"

Ellice studied the rocky ground at his feet. "No, Lord. It did not."

"What did you think would happen when your deception was discovered, as it most certainly would be? That you would receive nothing more than a tongue-lashing from myself and the Elders, and then be allowed to go merrily on your way?"

They stared at him wordlessly. This was exactly what they had all thought, but none of them could find the courage to say so.

Dorian pondered the stricken faces before him and contemplated what he should do. The misdeeds of these young rebels were grave, yet they paled beside his own actions. In their consternation at his unexpected and wrathful appearance, the five had not thought to question why *he* was in Athens, with a mate who was obviously not under the power of the Sea Spell. Dorian's mouth twisted. He was indeed in a precarious position, far more precarious than that of these foolish young kindred, though they were too unnerved to see it. So far, the weight of his authority had given him the upper hand. He must keep that, at all costs.

"Well," he said, and sighed. "You have come to the land, and there is naught I can do to change it. But tell me this: Do you wish to return to the sea, or"—his deep voice grew harsh with contempt—"do the joys of living among these Terran creatures still appeal to you more than your own true world?"

"Lord." Their voices—even Valya's—all rose at once. "More than anything, we wish to go home. Please, Lord!"

Dorian held up a hand. "Good. Then here are my commands. Remove those barbaric trappings of land from yourselves, go into the sea that borders this land city, and wait until my queen and I join you. Perhaps by then, my anger will have cooled and I will look more favorably on going lightly with you when we return to my abode."

The relief that emanated from them was almost palpable. With one masterstroke, Dorian had given them the best of both worlds. The sparkling blue Aegean offered many vantage points from which to see the final scenes of this long drama unfold, and now they could watch it in safety, no longer a part of the violence they had all grown to abhor. Only Valya's expression did not reflect this overwhelming sense of reprieve.

"But, my lord," he began with unaccustomed timidity,

"there is to be a great battle, and the war queen of the Amazons expects us—"

The others drowned him out. "Our fealty is to the lord Dorian, not Oreithyia! We have done our fighting, Valya! No more! Do not listen to him, Lord. Happy are we to wait in the sea as you command!"

As their voices died away Dorian stepped forward until he stood toe-to-toe with Valya. His height overreached the blond merman's by several inches, and before him Valya appeared slight, completely subordinated by the older man's more powerful, heavily muscled build.

"Boy," he said dangerously, "I do not believe what my ears have just told me. Are you saying the foolish oath made to a queen of these—these savages binds you beyond loyalty to *me,* your blood king?"

"No, my lord! It is not Oreithyia who concerns me." A flush rose into Valya's tanned cheeks. "It—it is the lady Thalassa, she is yet in the Amazon camp, and when the fighting begins, what will become of her?"

Dorian stared down at him with such intensity, Valya seemed actually to shrink before the eyes of his comrades. "The lady Thalassa," Dorian said at last, "is my concern. Do you dare question my ability to protect she who is my queen?"

Valya's blond braid bounced against his cheeks. "Of course not, my lord," he said quickly.

"Then you had better consider your interference in matters between her and me at an end. Unless you would prefer me to banish you from the sea here and now, a decision that, given your transgressions, the Elders will surely approve of."

"That won't be necessary, Lord!" Latora and Badru each seized one of Valya's arms. "He will not interfere again. None of us will. We have had our fill of the land, and all we desire is to go home, truly!"

But the sapphire knives that were Dorian's eyes bore relentlessly into Valya's pale blue eyes. "Let him answer me. Is that what you wish?"

Caught between his hopeless infatuation for Thalassa and his own aching need for the sea, Valya gave the only reply he could. "I will obey you, Lord," he said tonelessly, "for I, too, want to go home."

"Leave?" Oreithyia smashed her wine goblet onto the rough trestle table. The wine splattered her arm, staining it as though she had been stabbed. "Have the gods of men robbed you of your common sense and sent madness upon you in its place?"

Thalassa sighed. The blazing eyes and twisted features of the war queen made her want to say, *No, but unreasoning hatred and the thirst for revenge have robbed you of yours*.

"Lady," she said instead, "we have Antiope back. And between the Greeks' treachery when they came to our lands and those who have fallen on this campaign, we have already lost too many of our sisters as it is. An ocean of men's blood will not put Queen Hippolyte back among the living. We are the best fighters in the world. All of these man-ruled tribes know that. Why not go home?"

Oreithyia eyed her coldly. "You speak strangely, Thalassa, as though you are no longer an Amazon warrior. In truth, I do not understand you or Antiope—she who is the only blood sister left to me. Has your captivity among men broken both your spirits so that you talk like mealymouthed housewomen protecting their masters? Well, get back your stomach, Thalassa, for I will hear no more of this nonsense!"

She turned and reached for the wine flask. Recognizing dismissal, Thalassa shook her head and slipped wordlessly from the tent. The fiery midday sun slashed at her as she stepped outside. On top of barren Ares Hill, the heat was worse than below, where one could at least find some shade.

Well, man of the sea, she thought, I have kept my word, for all the good it did any of us. She cringed as she recalled Oreithyia's scornful observations about her. Had she truly become a mealymouthed, man-ruled woman, which was exactly what she had feared would happen in those first days of an abduction that now seemed so long ago? She could never forgive Dorian for the way in which he had shattered her world, and yet . . .

She kicked a rock out of her way on the path and stopped to gaze at the sun-dappled Aegean. The sea appeared calm—untouched and far removed from the bloody doings of landfolk—and Thalassa trembled with longing for its cool depths. It was not the first time she had experienced such yearnings. During the four days that had passed since her reunion with the Amazons, the disturbing feelings had steadily grown more intense.

The last two nights had been the worst. Lying under the star-strewn sky, she felt as though another heart had joined with hers, sending its alien beat pulsing through her very blood and bones. The voice of the distant ocean had echoed thunderously in every thread of her being. When she finally slept, it had been a restless sleep, enfolded by the rhythm of the tides and the feel of Dorian's arms as he sheltered her on the long, rocking swells.

He had said the Mother Sea would call her back. Was this aching need for the cool murmur of endless blue horizons what he had meant? Four days, and not a sign of the man who had held her captive for so long. And they had not been an easy four days either.

When the first joyous excitement of being back with her kindred had dissipated, Thalassa had to face an unpleasant realization. She was not the same person who had gone down to the sea alone to practice her swordcraft on that early summer morning. Neither, for that matter, was Antiope.

In some ways, it was far worse for the youngest of the sister queens. As much as Oreithyia railed at Thalassa, she was infinitely harder on her sibling, whom she had gone to such lengths to find. It was bad enough that Antiope seemed lukewarm—even opposed—to her older sister's goal of destroying Athens and dragging Theseus home in chains as a sacrifice to the Goddess. But to show up with a *male* child and adamantly insist she would keep him!

Under any other circumstances, prompt exile would have been the punishment for such outlandish ideas, even for a queen of the tribe. But despite their horrified dismay at her actions, the Amazons had rallied to Antiope. Her behavior had to be the result of her long ordeal and the suffering she had experienced at the hands of Theseus, they told each other. Given time, and the help of the Goddess, she would surely return to her senses.

So they had said to Thalassa, and so they had said to Oreithyia, in an effort to calm her rage at her younger sister's heresy. Thalassa's position—at least outwardly— was easier. That she had been abducted by a god, even a loathsome man-god, was more acceptable than showing up with a son, as Antiope had.

As she left the footpath and began walking through the far-flung tents and long picket lines of the assembled host, the pervasive mood of the sprawling encampment enveloped Thalassa. It was an atmosphere of tension accentuated by boredom. Amazons, Scythians, and Gargarians had each set up their own separate areas, and within these enclaves, warriors sat in the shade idling away the hours.

The Amazons' male allies slept, or amused themselves with slave women taken during the campaign, or with boisterous games of knucklebone. In the camp of the Amazons, pursuits were more disciplined. Quietly, women mended their travel-stained tents and tunics, and cared for their precious horses. Arrows were feathered with new reeds and plumes, and bows and spears grimly oiled and reoiled in impatient preparation.

The expedition had assumed the character of a siege, with neither side appearing particularly eager to open hostilities. Oreithyia wanted to rest her forces after their long and arduous trek from the east, and the Athenians . . . Well, jeering speculations were being made in all three camps about the reluctance of Theseus and his men to engage in full-fledged battle. Yet the Greeks were not cowards, Thalassa thought, gazing up at the stone walls that encircled the Acropolis.

Two days earlier Oreithyia had tested the citadel's defenses by sending several squadrons of volunteers up the rocky, winding trail. They had assailed the walls and made camp in a place known as the Hill of Muses, before the Greeks drove them back. A truce had been called to allow the women to bury their dead. Many had fallen in the suicidal mission, and in the shadow of the lower walls, Thalassa could see the hurriedly erected monuments that marked their graves.

A familiar voice called out, and she saw Antiope beckoning to her from the shade of a gnarled fig tree. "Join me. You look as if you could use a cool drink."

Thalassa threw herself down beside her friend. "I could, indeed." Gratefully she accepted the water flask Antiope proffered and drank deeply.

Antiope studied her shrewdly. "You've just come from seeing Oreithyia, haven't you?"

"How did you know?" Thalassa leaned back against the rough bark and closed her eyes.

"I saw you climbing the path. But even more, you look as I must after one of her tongue-lashings."

"I tried to persuade her that we should go home, now that you've returned safely to us. She said she understood neither you nor me, that we've become mealymouthed—"

"—man-ruled women. Yes, I know. She's accused me of the same." Antiope gazed down at Hippolytos, who lay on a piece of tanned hide gurgling happily up at the sky. "Shall I tell you something?" Her voice was low. "Once I thought nothing would give me greater joy than to wield the *bipennis* that scattered Theseus's living brains over the sacred black stone. But now my thoughts give me no peace. The idea of spending the rest of my days here makes my gorge rise in disgust. My very bones ache for the sight of Themiscrya. And yet, I do not want to see Theseus die."

Thalassa opened her eyes and looked at Antiope. The young queen met her gaze anxiously. "You are the only one I can say that to, for you also have been with a man. No one else would understand. Thalassa . . . do you understand?"

"Yes." A deep empathy flowed through Thalassa. The memory of the last time she and Antiope had sat together came back with painful clarity. The night of the honor-feast celebrating her blooding as a warrior. She remembered Antiope's face as it had been then, bright in the firelit hall as she teased her about the spring meeting with the Gargarians. How young and untried they had both been, so blindly unaware of the fates the Goddess held in store for them!

She reached out to take her age-mate's hand. "Antiope, my sister—"

"Ho, there!" A tall warrior raced past, then stopped when she saw the two women under the tree. "Ho, there!" she called out again, and jogged toward them.

"What is it, Aella?" Thalassa and Antiope rose tensely to their feet, eyes fixed on the panting messenger.

So it has come at last, Thalassa thought. Even before her friend Aella opened her mouth, she knew what she would say. The waiting was about to end, and whatever destinies awaited all those gathered there would soon descend, whether for good or ill.

"The king of these gutless dogs has finally begun preparing for battle," Aella said. "Our watchers on top of the hill saw him making sacrifice—to his god of war, no doubt—because now all the men are scurrying about the stronghold like mice fleeing a brush fire."

"He must have received favorable advice from the oracle then," Antiope said. "On the day before Thalassa and the male stranger freed me, he visited my chamber and said that the oracle would instruct him on the best way to deal with my people." Her lip curled. "Apparently, he did not think it necessary to consult it about my possible escape."

Aella let out a loud and contemptuous laugh. "Little good would it have done him if he had, and little good will it do him now. As for me, I am glad his oracle gave him good sign. All this lazing about has made me so weary I can scarcely bear it. My weapons thirst for a hearty drink of Greek blood, and soon they shall have it! Now I must hasten, for there is much to be done." She started to turn away, then added to Antiope, "Your sister asked me to send you to her should I see you."

Clapping Thalassa on the shoulder, Aella took up her swift pace once more, her calls ringing out to all within earshot. Disturbed by the commotion, Hippolytos began to cry, and absentmindedly Antiope picked him up. Her face was tight with worry, and looking at her Thalassa wondered if that same strained expression was mirrored on her own features. "Lady, will you fight?" she asked quietly.

"How can I not?" Antiope gazed unseeing over the baby's head. "With my sisters going out to shed their blood in my name, how can I not?"

CHAPTER 29

~~ Theseus moved out the next morning as daybreak
gilded the craggy hills and limestone buildings
of the deserted city. Massed and ready, the Amazon host
watched in an eerie silence as the Greek troops marched
forth from the Acropolis's opened gates. Unwilling to risk
chariots on the treacherous path, and with cavalry unknown
in this part of the world, the forces of Theseus would fight
on foot. To the waiting Amazons, it was plain that the men
were unnerved by the stillness of their foes. Such deadly
quiet was infinitely more ominous than the shrill war cries
Theseus and Heracles must have told them to expect.

In Oreithyia's carefully positioned right flank, Thalassa
sat astride her restless black mare. During her absence
Alcippe had been adopted by the openhearted Aella, who
had immediately returned the mare upon Thalassa's astonishing reappearance. To be one with Alcippe once more, to
feel the mare's warmth between her legs and the weight of
weapons—borrowed but familiar, nonetheless—loading
down her arms, was a joy she had never thought to
experience again.

Yet questions ran continuously through Thalassa's mind. Where was Dorian? Was he watching all this from the protection of the sea? And where were Valya and his companions?

Since that first day when she had found them in camp and whispered Dorian's message, neither she nor anyone else had seen them. His face stiff with dread, Valya had nodded, whispered back that they had delivered her message as well, and then, along with the others, he had vanished.

Oreithyia, who had looked forward to using the meryouths' unnatural strength in the upcoming battle, had been infuriated by their mysterious disappearance. She repeatedly demanded that Thalassa call them back. It was a useless request. Thalassa was no more able to summon the missing youths than was the war queen herself. Perhaps her telepathic powers did not extend to the land, or perhaps she was simply too unskilled in their use. Or perhaps Dorian had commanded the young merfolk not to respond. Whatever the reason, Oreithyia had finally been forced to resign herself to the loss of her supernatural allies.

"Look you, Thalassa." Aella maneuvered her white mare closer and nudged Thalassa. "Yonder is the accursed one called Heracles. See how he towers above all the others? Him, I would like to kill with my own hands, for he took many of our sisters' lives. Take care if you find yourself facing him. Our blades and arrows are useless against the magical lionskin he wears. Go for his legs and arms, which are unprotected."

"I will remember." Thalassa studied the lion-draped figure standing arrogantly atop the Acropolis walls. She recognized him from among the men who had stood on the galleys, watching as the Amazon captives regained their freedom. Once she would have thought the burly Greek hero a giant, but after knowing Dorian, Heracles did not impress her. The king of the merfolk might even be taller, she decided, and there was certainly no doubt that he was the stronger.

A mutter rippled along the women's lines, as the Greeks suddenly loosed a clamor of battle yells and surged forward. Their numbers looked pitifully small compared to the rows and rows of warriors arrayed against them, but they raced forward bravely, roaring as if to give themselves courage, and fell upon the Amazons' left wing. With grim resolution they attacked, seeking to close with these silent foes. And then . . . Oreithyia gave the signal.

Thousands of lips curled back in response, and from countless throats the first blood-freezing war cries of the Amazons pulsated forth. Like the wind heralding a storm the chorus rose, billowing and rolling in wave upon wave of ghastly sound. It beat relentlessly at the ears of the terrified Greeks. Added to the unearthly horror were the soul-curdling shrieks and howls of the Gargarians and Scythians as they spurred their small, shaggy horses forward into battle.

The Athenians in the forefront struggled to brace their nerves against the shrilling, their fear as great an enemy as the warriors that came to meet them. They strove to press in close, and by grappling hand to hand evade the women's deadly arrows and use what must surely be superior male strength against these female foes. Up and down the lines, men and women locked toe-to-toe.

Out in the dark waters of the Aegean, five heads were bobbing nervously atop the waves.

"It has begun," Ellice said in a low, excited tone, then her voice rose sharply and was joined by the others in a frantic chorus. "Valya, where are you going? Come back, Valya! Come back! *Valya!*"

In the struggles that followed, hope seeped from each Greek in his turn. The Amazons fought like demented, wild-eyed dancers, shrieking above the din and whirling about their disconcerted opponents in a mad gyration of arms and legs. Their lightning-swift feet threw up the dust in thick swirls, and their battle-axes and swords clanged, slashed, and bludgeoned in a raw orgy of bloody prowess. In that terrible onslaught there was scarcely a breathing hole, and a sickening knowledge preceded every man's imminent death—that the Amazon gripping him was faster than he, stronger, and utterly bent on taking his life.

Over and over, this ugly truth was made violently real, until the uncommitted men in the rear lines shuddered with terror and revulsion. Throwing down their weapons, they stampeded in a herd of wild, panicked men. Queer, high-pitched croaks rattled from their throats as they ran, as if their tongues were strangling in their jaws. Bound in suffocating coils of fear, they fled to the nearest safety, a place ironically known as the Temple of the Furies.

Holding in her rearing mare, Aella shouted exultantly, "They run like frightened cattle! Why have we not yet been given the signal to charge?"

All up and down Oreithyia's right flank, similar emotions were being expressed. Battle fever ran like wildfire throughout the ranks, and only the women's lifelong warrior discipline kept them from spontaneously charging into the fray.

Thalassa was as affected by the flush of war as anyone. Excitement bubbled and frothed through her, imbuing her with one desire: a flaming eagerness to spill Greek blood. This flood of bloodlust washed away Dorian's dire predictions about this campaign. How could any man-ruled tribe hope to stand against the glory of the Amazons?

Alcippe danced wildly in a circle, and as Thalassa reined her in, she saw the gates of the Acropolis swinging open. "See you there!" she yelled above the tumult. "The Greeks are sending out reinforcements!" Now Oreithyia's wisdom in holding back part of her battlefront was clear. Obviously the war queen had suspected that wily Theseus would not commit his entire force at once, and she had been right.

Fresh troops poured down the rocky slope, and at their head were Heracles and a tall, helmeted figure, who Thalassa assumed was Theseus.

"Not a moment too soon," the warrior on Thalassa's other side shouted. "Another moment, and these craven weaklings would be routed without our even getting the opportunity to fight!"

No sooner had the words left her lips than it came: the signal to charge. Neither Thalassa nor her comrades needed a second urging. Like witches riding the winter storm winds that shrieked over Themiscrya's mountains, they rode screaming down the plain.

Knee to knee Thalassa galloped between her kindred, her head bent low over Alcippe's flying black mane. With the wind whipping her face, the thunder of countless hooves and the ringing Amazon war cry throbbing in her ears, it was the most supremely happy moment of her life, and Thalassa knew she would remember it the rest of her days.

Then the crash of impact came, and there was no more time for thought. On seeing help arriving in the shape of Heracles, Theseus, and additional troops, the panic-stricken Greeks already on the field had rallied and turned back to the fight. Now both wings of Oreithyia's battlefront were engaged, and the combat raged unchecked through the plains and hills outside of Athens.

In the midst of it, Thalassa hacked and swung in a mindless frenzy of killing. The men she encountered were no match for the almost instinctive skill and power with which she wielded her *bipennis* and fired her arrows. The greatest danger came from the Athenians' long javelins, which they stabbed savagely at their foes' horses in an effort to bring the gallant animals down through hamstringing or disembowelment.

It was an astute battle tactic, but one that enraged the Amazons as nothing else could. To attack them was one thing; but to attack their beloved horses was quite another. Numerous men paid a horrible price for the strategy of their leaders, as the infuriated women responded by slaying them in the most torturous ways possible. Yet more than one Amazon mare collapsed into the crimson-tinged dust, shrieking out in almost human pain as she fell.

With the uncanny clarity that a single sound can take on in the roaring confusion of battle, Thalassa heard an agonized scream. Peering through the swirling tempest with the keen eyes of the seafolk, she saw that one of the long javelins had found its mark in Aella's mare. Blood spread out in a scarlet flower on the animal's snowy belly as she reared up and fell over backward. Aella managed to leap off in time to avoid being crushed, but her action left her afoot in the midst of a half-dozen javelin-wielding Greeks.

Setting heels to Alcippe's sides, Thalassa charged through the melee to her friend's defense. Three of her arrows dropped an equal number of the Athenians stabbing at Aella, and with almost careless blows of her *bipennis* she swiped the heads from the men who sought to seize Alcippe's reins. Then she was directly upon Aella's adversaries. The unnatural strength that flowed through her enabled her to make short work of the remaining Greeks, and she hauled her unhorsed comrade up onto Alcippe's back.

But Aella was wounded. To her horror, Thalassa saw the thick glutinous blood that portended mortal injuries seeping from the other woman's stomach and chest. Her one bared breast was soaked with it, and Thalassa desperately tried to staunch the flow as she maneuvered Alcippe away before the tide of battle turned toward them. Aella opened her eyes. Already their brightness was dulling with the remoteness of approaching death.

"You have grown stronger, my sister." Her voice was a thready whisper that even Thalassa with her sharp ears could barely hear. "Use that strength to slay Heracles, as I would have, had I lived."

"Do not speak so!" Thalassa cradled Aella's suddenly heavy head against her. "I will get you behind the lines where your hurts can be tended. Aella! Aella!"

But the older sister-friend who had taught her how to hunt and fight, who had kept Alcippe for her, who had fought the Cretan pirates at her side, was gone.

A great sob tore out of Thalassa's throat, but there was no time even to carry Aella to a quiet resting place. The battle was sweeping forward to engulf her once more, and all she could do was tenderly lower her friend's limp body to the reddened ground beside her lifeless white mare.

"It's not really them any longer," she said into Alcippe's wet neck. "They are both galloping through the Bright World of the Goddess now."

As Thalassa's tear-filled eyes fought to regain their focus, she finally looked up to see a powerful figure looming over the Greeks who fought beside him.

Heracles.

Grimly Thalassa freed her bloodstained *bipennis* from

the leather sling that held it across her back. The battle-ax whined viciously as she whirled it through the air, and her eyes narrowed as she carefully marked the route she would have to take to reach her target. "Come, black one," she said to her mare. "Let us go kill this hulk of a man for Aella."

It almost seemed as if Alcippe understood, for with eager swiftness she carried her rider through the press, finding openings that even Thalassa's keen gaze had missed. A pool of battle swirled about the mighty hero of the Greeks.

Scores of Scythians and Gargarians had flung themselves at Heracles, each one whooping delightedly at the thought that he might be the man to down the Athenians' foremost champion. The Amazons had warned them of the infamous lionskin, but they had ignored the women's cautionary advice. Now they were paying for their inattention with their lives.

Laughing in mockery, Heracles smashed the Gargarian foot soldiers who sought to vanquish him. Contemptuously he seized the jaws of the Scythians' shaggy ponies—one in each huge hand—and broke the animals' necks, disposing of their riders almost as an afterthought. The Amazons attacked with more sense but little more success, and the pile of the dead and dying grew.

Screaming, Thalassa galloped through the quagmire of death, Alcippe's hooves thudding sickeningly on soft, still-twitching bodies. Aella's warning rang in her brain as she hewed right and left at the Greeks who fought next to Heracles. With surprising speed for one so massively built, the hero shot out his beefy hands to seize her leg and yank her from her horse. But Heracles had not reckoned with Thalassa's own speed. Arrow swift, she threw her leg over Alcippe's withers so that she was sitting sidesaddle, and in the same motion swung her ax as she raced by him.

Heracles bellowed with pain and rage, sounding more like an enraged bull than a man. Thalassa cursed under her breath as she pulled Alcippe around for another pass. The delicate balance of her position had not permitted her to swing the *bipennis* with her full strength. Rather than severing Heracles's arm, she had only sliced a deep gash into it. Still, it was the first serious wound the Greek champion had suffered, and a lesser man would have been stopped by it.

A cry went up from the Athenians at their hero's wounding, to be drowned out by the gleeful howls of the nearby Amazons, Scythians, and Gargarians. With new ferocity they renewed the attack, until the hard-pressed men around Heracles called out desperately for aid.

Unheeding, Thalassa charged again. Heracles aimed a terrible blow at her head with his long sword as she passed, but Thalassa hooked her legs around Alcippe's belly and dropped down so that the deadly blade slashed only air. She had returned the battle-ax to its sling in favor of her bow. Now with lethal precision she nocked and released four arrows in rapid succession, and when she swung around for a third pass, Heracles was roaring so dementedly, it seemed as if the god-inspired madness had infected him once more.

Two feathered shafts protruded from each of his tree-trunk legs, sending bright streams of blood pooling down around his feet. So great was Thalassa's strength that the arrows had pierced straight through flesh and bone. The Amazons' hard-won knowledge about the lionskin's vulnerabilities had borne fruit at last in an opponent strong enough and quick enough to exploit them to her advantage.

Triumphantly Thalassa jerked the battle-ax loose. Her prick-and-dash strategy was working. Heracles was weakened now, and if she could hack off an arm or leg, he would be finished. A victorious war cry swelling her throat, she gave Alcippe her head.

The black mare leaped forward . . . and stumbled with a high-pitched scream of anguish. At the same moment, an inexplicable instinct made Thalassa twist violently from side to side. Two javelins whined past her, so close she felt the wind of their passage along her arm and side. Alcippe let out another shriek that ended in an agonized grunting, and lurched to her knees.

Appalled, Thalassa saw three javelins jutting from the sleek black hide. "Oh, my dear one!" she cried out, leaping off the mare's back and running to her head. Alcippe's brown eyes stared uncomprehendingly into hers. She tried gallantly to regain her feet. Then the eyes filmed over and the animal's long, fine legs relaxed into the dust.

Seared with a pain as terrible as that which had ended Alcippe's life, Thalassa swung around. A squadron of Greeks were fighting their way toward her. And leading them was Heracles, limping and tripping because of the arrows in his legs, but his face a black mask of fury.

"She is mine!" he bellowed, flecks of foam spraying over his lips and beard. "None of you touch her. The right to slay her is mine! By Zeus, I'll twist the bitch's head from her neck like a chicken being plucked for the spit!"

He came on, hurling aside with brutal whacks of his sword the warriors who sought to stop him. Shouts of "To Thalassa!" rang out, and Amazons in the vicinity began racing to her aid. But equally quick, the men around Heracles—all of them seasoned fighters—ran to engage them, the battle raging with new ferocity, leaving Thalassa still alone and unaided.

She gripped the battle-ax in both hands. "Come ahead then, O tiny-brained fool of a mad boar!" she shouted. "If you think you can kill me, you are welcome to try!"

"I would prefer that he not," a quiet voice said in her ear. Whirling around, Thalassa saw Dorian standing beside her.

Her whole body jerked with disbelief—and an odd happiness—but there was little time to react, for Heracles and those of his cohorts not already engaged were upon them. The taunting challenge of this lowly female, who had actually managed to wound *him* of all men, had goaded Heracles beyond reason. He was no longer capable of speech. Incoherent bellows resounded from between his foaming lips, and he was not even aware of Dorian's sudden appearance out of the dust of battle.

His bloodshot eyes were fixed on Thalassa as he hurled himself forward, roaring like the boar to which she had compared him. She leaped to meet him—but somehow Dorian was in her way. Before she could yell at him to stand aside, he had reached out, seized Heracles by the arm, and wrenched the sword loose with such ease, the hero might have been a child.

Pandemonium broke out among those who had seen—

elation on the part of the Amazons and dismay on the part of the Athenians. Dorian was unarmed. He wore only the Greek tunic he had stolen on the way to Theseus's palace, yet he presented a more imposing sight than any man present. His head topped Heracles's by several inches, and next to the burly massiveness of the Greek champion, the merman's iron-muscled bronze body rippled with sleek grace and latent power.

But Heracles was not impressed. His rage turned from Thalassa to this traitorous stranger who had the disloyalty to fight against his own sex. Never had he suffered so much as a scratch in battle, and now, in the space of a few minutes, he had been repeatedly wounded by a *woman* and disarmed by one of her allies! With a guttural bellow he yanked the short sword he used for close combat out of its scabbard.

"Die with your unnatural whore!" he bawled at Dorian, and struck at the merman with all the might of his stalwart right arm.

The blow tore through the air toward Dorian's head, but Dorian was no longer there. Only Thalassa's eyes were sharp enough to follow the move that brought him behind Heracles, and he twisted this second weapon free with inexorable fingers. "There," he said calmly, his quiet voice somehow making itself heard above the din. "Will you yield now, or must I do more?"

Heracles's eyes bulged with the strength of his fury as two Greeks rushed past him at Thalassa. With terrible skill she struck them both down with her *bipennis,* but two more were hard on their heels, and it might have gone badly with her had not Dorian intervened.

Grasping the swords he had taken from Heracles, he flung them as if they were javelins. The Greeks let out gurgling screams and went down, the blood-covered bronze blades protruding gruesomely from their chests, their bodies pierced all the way through. At the same moment, Heracles let out an inarticulate sound and lunged for Dorian's throat.

Rather than slithering away, Dorian met the Greek champion's bearlike charge with one of his own. Almost casually, he knocked aside the hero's brawny arms. A powerful fist flashed out. There was an awesome crack as it

impacted solidly against the other man's jaw, and like a
felled ox the mighty Heracles collapsed into the dust.

But Dorian was not yet through. He effortlessly slung
Heracles over his head, holding him there as though he
weighed no more than a feather. He spoke again, but no
longer spoke quietly. "Greeks, will you call a truce?" he
roared in a voice that seemed to reverberate over the entire
battlefield. "Or shall I kill your champion for you?"

"Do not kill him."

A tall, helmeted figure stepped forth from the men that
had been fighting around Heracles. "Truce!" he shouted.
"Spread the word! I, Theseus, declare a truce!"

Echoing shouts rang throughout the field in response to
his command. Panting for breath, Thalassa thought, So that
was Theseus. As she watched Dorian lower the flaccid body
of Heracles to the ground, fury seethed through her. The
battle's sudden slackening had caught her off guard. Her
bloodlust still flowed; the desire to rend and destroy still
urged her on.

"You should have slain him," she hissed to Dorian
when he strode over to her. "Who are you to take it upon
yourself to conclude a truce here?"

He glanced from Alcippe's javelin-studded corpse to
Thalassa's face, heavily streaked with sweat and dirt. "Who
indeed?" he muttered, and firmly steered her away, into a
small, secluded grove of trees left relatively untouched by
the fighting. When they were well within the grove he none
too gently made her sit down. "Had you done as you
promised, my interference would not have been necessary."

"I kept my word! I pleaded with Oreithyia until my
tongue grew tired and my throat hoarse. But she only said
I was no true Amazon to speak so, and would not listen.
That is the truth of it!"

Dorian regarded her with a look of grim disapproval.
"Unfortunately, I believe you. It was useless to expect that
folk of the land could behave with any sort of wisdom." His
voice rose angrily. "Yet, despite all my experience to the
contrary, I hoped there might finally come a time when
these foolish people would avert the bloody catastrophes
that constantly follow them. . . ."

His words trailed away, and he stared rigidly into the

distance. "By the Great Mother Sea, no," he cried out in a voice so altered, Thalassa hardly recognized it. The next instant he was on his feet and running through the trees.

"What is it?" she shouted, though he was already too far away to heed her. Utterly baffled, she followed after him, pausing at the edge of the grove to catch her bearings.

Among the bloody debris of the battlefield his tall figure was nowhere to be seen, and then, as if her gaze were being drawn by an unseen hand, she saw him—walking back toward her, his step heavy and slow like that of an old man.

Thalassa's hand went to her mouth. In his arms, head lolling and bright hair stained an unnatural crimson, lay Valya.

CHAPTER 30

≈ Silently Dorian lay Valya down upon the grass as tenderly as though the young merman were yet alive. Thalassa stared down at him with horror. Valya's face was so slashed and torn that, were it not for his height and the unbloodied portions of his blond hair, she would not have known him. Jagged craters gaped over his chest and abdomen, and bloody stumps oozed where one arm and one leg had been. He had taken so many sword cuts to his throat that his head was nearly severed. Both his eyes had been put out.

She stared stricken at the man at her side. "Oh, Dorian," she said softly, using his name for the first time. "My heart is torn. I grieve for you, I grieve for him. May Holy Artemis welcome Valya into the Bright World, and feast him as She does the most honored of warriors."

"He has seen quite enough of the land's welcome," Dorian said hoarsely. "He has no need of its gods, and behold for yourself how its warriors have served him."

His voice was so savage, his eyes so filled with anguished rage, that Thalassa could not look him in the face. "How could this have happened? The strength of merfolk is so much greater than that of the people of land, how—"

"It happened because he was careless, and too filled with pride in the powers of our kind." Clenching his fists, Dorian stood stiff and hardfaced, staring down at the mutilated body of his kinsman. "He saw your horse slain, and you thrown afoot. He shouted to the women around him that you needed aid, and tried himself to reach you before Heracles did. But he was too far away. And in his eagerness he paid no attention to protecting himself."

Dorian made an inarticulate sound composed of either anger or sorrow, and stumbled on. "Those who saw it said that ten times ten Greeks, or perhaps even more, swarmed over him, stabbing and slashing with javelin and sword. The Amazons tried to help, but the Greeks were thick in that part of the field, and it was over too quickly, they said."

His magnetic eyes sought and found Thalassa's gaze. "Perhaps it was. I will never know. I was so caught up in seeing that no harm befell you, I did not even sense his presence until it was too late. The merfolk are not immortal, Thalassa. I have told you before. Now the proof of it lies before you."

She swallowed, guilt and shame rising with the taste of bile in her throat. Never would she have expected to grieve for a man as she would for Aella, or even Alcippe. Yet this ebullient young merman, so fascinated with the world beyond the sea, had sincerely tried to help her. For that kindness, he had paid with his life.

"It is my fault that he is dead," she choked out.

"No more than it is mine." Dorian drew a deep shuddering breath. "I commanded him and the others to wait for us in the sea outside Athens. But I should have made them leave here, put as much distance as possible between them and this evil place. Now it is too late, and this youth, who should have lived for century upon century, is no more. Ah, the experiences that waited for him, all the glory of the seas that he had yet to understand, it has all been taken from him. And to what purpose?"

Waves of trembling racked his powerful frame. Suddenly he swung about, driving his fist into the nearest tree with such awful force, the trunk splintered and cracked, and the hapless tree was all but uprooted from the ground. *"To what purpose?"* he roared in a voice filled with the thunder of his rage and grief.

The awesome display left Thalassa curiously unafraid. Instead her heart went out to him. Stepping forward she laid a gentle hand upon his taut arm. "You must not blame yourself," she said softly. "Blame the cruelty of the land, or blame me for sharing with him my desire to escape, but do not hold yourself responsible. Even if you had commanded Valya to leave, I do not think he would have obeyed you. His beguilement with this world was too great. You, who are so content with your life in the sea, never could have understood that."

Her touch seemed to calm him. Dorian turned his head and looked at her as though he were seeing her for the first time. He brushed a hand against her dusty cheek. "I was forty kinds of fool to have let you fight today. It could have been you lying here, instead of . . . Valya."

A film of tears obscured Thalassa's vision. "With you to protect me?" She scrubbed quickly at her eyes. "I think not. But how will you—I mean, what is the custom when . . ."

"When someone dies?" His gaze went back to Valya, and he said slowly, his voice heavy and sad, "His clan and close comrades will find him a permanent resting place within the sea. Among us, death is a private matter, something we can accept because of the length and richness of our days in the world. But Valya's death is different. To lose one of our own at so young an age . . . is almost unknown. It is a tragedy that will haunt us all for centuries to come."

Kneeling beside the body, he pulled off the tunic he had stolen and gently covered Valya's ruined face. "In a few minutes I will take him back to the Mother Sea, to where his friends still wait for him."

Thalassa nodded. When Dorian remained where he was, she sat down next to him. The physical and emotional intensity of this terrible morning was taking its toll. Exhaustion made her eyelids feel leaden, yet when she closed her eyes, the scenes of the battle repeated themselves over and over: Aella dying in her arms; Alcippe faltering and screaming as javelins pierced her flesh; the biting, acrid smell of blood and dust. And nightmarish visions of what Valya's death must have been like.

Her nostrils stung with the foul odors of war, her ears still rang with the shrieks of the wounded and dying, and wearily she asked, "Why did you not slay Heracles? He deserved to die, and your power made his might a weak and puny thing. It would have been a simple matter for you to take his life."

"Too simple." Dorian's face wore a strange mask of regret and loss and fury. "Though now I wish that I had. Still, in this case, it was better to let him live. He is the champion of the Greeks and an exceedingly arrogant man in his own right. To defeat him in battle without considering him a worthy enough foe to kill is a humiliation far greater than mere death to a man like Heracles. What happened here today will gnaw at him the rest of his days."

It was true. In her eagerness to carry out Aella's dying wish, Thalassa had thought only about the glory of killing the Athenians' champion. Now the subtleness of Dorian's strategy struck her, and she found herself in wholehearted agreement. It would have been better if Heracles had suffered his humiliation at the hands of an Amazon—yet this would do.

She looked out over the plains of Attica. The midday sun was a jagged ball of flame, and uncaringly it blazed down over the morning's carnage.

Already the bodies of fallen warriors and horses were bloating in the unrelenting heat. An unnatural stillness had replaced the clash of warfare—a stillness in which no birds sang, no cattle lowed in the distance. Only the groans of the wounded disturbed the eerie calm; that and the droning of the flies, as they settled to feast upon the dead in heavy black clouds.

The stench of death hung in a thick miasma over the once fertile fields, and though the very thinking of it shamed her, Thalassa realized she was glad Dorian had managed to halt the fighting, at least for now.

As if he had seen her thoughts, he said savagely, "Ugly, isn't it? Do you think the Amazons consider themselves sufficiently revenged yet?"

Thalassa sighed. From where they sat, she could make

out the distorted shape of Alcippe, her beloved mare, who was now food for the flies. But she could not see the body of Aella. She sighed again and pulled up a stray arrow embedded in the grass. "I fear that Oreithyia will not be content until every man in Athens is dead."

As she spoke she saw that groups of opposing warriors were moving through the battle site, seeking out the wounded and arranging the dead for burial. The truce would hold until that task was finished, and then . . .

Thalassa tensed. "Look there," she said to Dorian. "Climbing that low rise to the south. Oreithyia, and with her, Antiope."

Even from a distance they could see the two women were arguing. Their angrily gesticulating figures came closer, and Thalassa shivered as a terrible premonition clawed into her mind. Apprehensively she got to her feet. Dorian rose also, and she felt the warmth of his arm as he supported her against him.

But his gaze was not on the two Amazon queens, as Thalassa's was. "What is it?" he asked, eyeing her in concern. "What troubles you?"

She shook her head. "I'm not sure," she whispered. "Something dark."

She watched as the argument escalated, then seemed to culminate with the taller war queen flinging herself around and stalking down the sloping hill. Thalassa held her breath. Antiope stood very still on top of the rise, her gaze not on her departing sister but on the battlefield spread out below her. When the young queen's clear voice finally split the air, Thalassa wanted to close her eyes, knowing in her bones what Antiope would say. She could do nothing but wait helplessly for the evil words to fall.

"I call on Theseus of Athens!" Antiope's bold cry vibrated on the heavy, stifling air. "Theseus, step forth. Queen Antiope would speak with you!"

Slowly the king of Athens strode out from the cadre of officers that had gathered around to revive Heracles. He had removed his helmet, shaped in the head of a boar, and in the noon sun his red-gold hair formed a bright halo about his head. "Where is the giant warrior who bested mighty

Heracles and then showed him mercy? It is him I would speak with, not you, my former slave."

His voice was deliberately cruel, but there was a note in it that made Thalassa wonder if some deep pain was hiding behind his harsh words. "They must not have seen us go among these trees," she muttered, and Dorian nodded, his attention caught now as well.

Antiope drew herself up. "I know not where he is," she said coldly. "And I am indeed no longer your slave. But you will speak with me, Theseus, if you want your son back and the fighting between us to cease."

"No." Unaware that she did so, Thalassa clutched Dorian's arm. "By the Goddess, she must not do it. Antiope!" she called out.

It was too late. Whether Antiope heard but deliberately took no heed of her cry, Thalassa would never know. Enveloped in foreboding, she heard Antiope's precise, fluent Greek, the language of her bondage.

"Too many have died here today," the young queen said, her voice loud yet controlled. "That Greeks lie among the slain concerns me not. But to see the lifeless faces of my brave Amazon kindred and their noble allies lying in the dust makes my heart ache with sorrow and shame. I will allow no more of my beloved sisters to suffer wounds or meet death on my account. Hear me, Theseus. I have already told my people, and now I say it to you. I will get Hippolytos and come back to live as your wife—if you still want me."

The reaction among all who heard this was clamorous, but Theseus paid no more heed to it than did Antiope. "I still want you," he called gruffly. "But what of your kin? Will you bid them leave Athens and the lands of my kingdom in peace?"

Antiope closed her eyes, but her voice did not waver. "Yes. I will."

Thalassa moaned in anguish. The lament was taken up and echoed by every Amazon present, until a chorus of wails rose into the cloudless sky. Then a wild and utterly frenzied shriek slashed the air. Oreithyia's progress down the slope had been arrested by her sister's hailing of

Theseus. Her features twisted and frozen, she had listened in rigid silence as Antiope spoke. But no longer.

"Defiler of our sacred ways!" she screamed hoarsely. "You desert your people and spit on our laws, preferring instead to follow at the heels of some man, fawning on him like a whipped cur bitch! You were born a queen of the Amazons, yet you throw your birthright of freedom away with both hands, to live as a breeding heifer—a slave—a lowly creature of men with no will of her own! Aaaaaaahhhh . . . the shame and dishonor you have brought to us! By the Holy Goddess, I declare that you are queen no longer—Amazon no longer—*my sister no longer!*"

Rushing back up the slope, she drew the short stabbing sword from her belt and thrust it viciously through Antiope's breast. A wave of agonized sound washed over the battlefield, but Antiope herself made none. Utterly silent, she gazed at her older sister as her hands locked convulsively about Oreithyia's on the haft of the sword. For an awful moment, the two faces that so closely resembled each other met and exchanged souls.

Then Antiope's hands slowly dropped away and, still soundless, she crumpled to the ground at the war queen's feet.

"Nooooo!" The roar that burst from Theseus's throat was like that of a wounded beast, as though it was his breast the sword had pierced and not Antiope's. "You are the bitch . . . to murder your own blood sister!" he screamed. Seizing up the nearest javelin, he reared high and flung it with all his might.

Oreithyia did not move. Indeed, to Thalassa's tormented eyes, it seemed she welcomed the javelin that flew toward her—hurling itself forward with unerring aim to bury itself in her breast.

CHAPTER 31

≈ An armistice was arranged before nightfall.

The Amazons' heart had left them. Two of their queens were dead, the war queen lay mortally wounded, and the Scythians and Gargarians, sullen over this turn of events, were anxious to leave Greece and cross the frigid mountain passes with their booty before the storms of winter set in.

As dusk fell on that long and bloodstained day, Thalassa strode through the silent and grieving camp. She had adamantly resisted Dorian's attempts to make her rest, and had also refused to accompany him in returning poor Valya's body to the sea. It was cruel of her she knew, but Valya was dead, and Oreithyia, last of a once unbroken line of sister queens, still lived.

When it became apparent the war queen had not been killed outright by Theseus's javelin, Thalassa had turned to Dorian with desperate hope. "Will you go to her with me? After—after you have done with Valya? The magic healing herbs in the sea that you have spoken of could help her, could they not?"

With bitter sadness Dorian had looked down at her. "There is naught in the sea, or anywhere else, that will help Oreithyia, any more than Valya can be helped. Her life leaves her quickly, and I think she is glad of it. Go to her if you wish, but your war queen would not welcome the face of a man beside her deathbed. I am sure of that."

So Thalassa walked alone to the tent where Oreithyia lay. Hundreds of warriors ringed the small tent, holding a wailing, tearful vigil for their fallen leader and bemoaning the tragic loss of Antiope. It took a long time for Thalassa to work her way through the crowd, and when she finally pushed open the tent's doorskins, tears were running uncontrollably down her cheeks.

Inside the dimly lit interior, the last queen of the Amazons drifted ever deeper into the dark waters that led to the river of oblivion. Her tanned, finely boned face was gray now and pinched with approaching death; her eyes stared dully into space. Around the bed of furs on which she rested were gathered her closest friends and comrades, softly murmuring prayers to the Goddess for the safe journey of Her royal daughter.

Thalassa touched the sinewy arm of an older woman, whose iron-gray hair and many battle scars attested to her status as a veteran. "How does she, Una?"

The warrior shook her head. "Not good, child," she said in a voice raspy from the day's screaming. "The will to hold on to life has left her in the sorrow of having had to slay her own sister. The Mother will call her to the Bright World very soon, and just as well, for Oreithyia's heart is broken. Yet what she did was meet and proper."

"Do you really believe so, my aunt?" Thalassa asked, using the form of address given to a respected older warrior.

Una's chin jutted out. "I do. Antiope acquitted herself bravely during the fighting, but she dishonored us all by using concern for her people as an excuse to run panting back to the penis of her master. It was shameful. She deserved to die, and as war queen, it was Oreithyia's business to kill her."

"But, Aunt . . ." Thalassa swallowed painfully. What was there to say? From what she had seen outside the tent, everyone else felt as Una did. There were those who grieved for Antiope, but even her closest friends mourned the loss of a queen more than they did Antiope herself.

The death of all three of their queens in just one year was a catastrophe of such immense proportions, the Amazons had not truly grasped its implications. Yet one thing was clear to Thalassa. In all the camp of the Amazons, not one person understood the emotions that had torn at Antiope, or the terrible sacrifice she had made. Except herself.

Oreithyia weakly turned her head, her pain-filled eyes struggling to focus in the shadowy tent. "I heard the voice of Thalassa," she whispered. "Was I dreaming?"

Thalassa stepped forward and knelt beside the bed. "No, Lady," she said gently. "I am here."

"Good." The war queen's reply was the merest thread of sound. Remembering the last occasion she had been in this tent, when Oreithyia had railed in her powerful voice, Thalassa wanted to weep.

Oreithyia reached out a hand, which Thalassa quickly took in hers. The flesh felt dry and frail, more like that of an ancient grandmother than a vibrant warrior in the prime of her strength and health. "Why did she do it, Thalassa? You were her friend and you brought her out of that man-ruled place of slavery. Why did she do it?"

Oreithyia's hand tightened in a pathetic caricature of her old vitality. "She knew I could never allow a queen of the Amazons to betray our values in such a way. She knew this, and yet she still chose to forsake us . . . her own kindred . . . her only living blood sister . . ."

Her voice trailed off, and Thalassa squeezed the hand she held between both of hers. "I do not think she saw it as forsaking, my lady. She loved you, and she loved her people. But so much had happened to change her. She was not the same as when she was so cruelly taken from Amazonia."

"Who amongst us is?" Oreithyia sighed. "It does not matter, Thalassa. The Goddess is calling me, and I go to Her eagerly. Antiope is surely in the Bright World by now and has forgiven me for what I had to do. No, my heart aches for the living now. For our noble people who are bereft of everything: their queens, the victory this campaign should have brought, perhaps even our own lands; for in the redness of my hatred, I left them poorly attended.

"It is a long and hard journey home, and the Amazons who begin it are already lost. They will leave this accursed land in grief, confusion, and despair, and not in the glorious triumph I had promised them." The long speech exhausted her, and a thick bubble of blood burst from between Oreithyia's lips and trickled down her chin.

Tenderly Thalassa wiped it away. "Please, Lady, speak no more. Words will change nothing, and you must rest. Perhaps it is not yet your time to join the Mother."

Oreithyia's pain-racked features twisted into a grimace of a smile. "I am dying, girl, and you know it as well as I. But do one last thing for me, if you will."

"Anything." Thalassa's eyes were so blurred with tears, she could hardly see. "What do you wish of me, Lady?"

"Take the whelp that Antiope brought here and give it back to Theseus. I had thought to order it killed, but Theseus would conclude no peace without the return of his son, my officers said, and I know Antiope cared for the babe. It would be a bitter thing to face my sister in the next world with both her blood and that of her child's on my hands.

"You are the only one I can ask this of," the weak voice continued. "I fear that even my most trusted comrades might let their sorrow overwhelm them and wring the cub's neck rather than give it to Theseus. Will you do this for me?"

"Of course, Lady. It would honor me."

The war queen nodded and closed her eyes. "Go then." Her hand dropped limply from Thalassa's. "Farewell, my sister, and may the blessing of the Goddess be upon you. If there is still some happiness left for Amazons, I hope you find it. But I fear that no joy awaits any of us. The Goddess seems to have turned Her face from a world that grows ever more crowded with the gods of men. Their power waxes as Hers wanes, and darkness rolls toward our people. I am glad . . . glad that I will not be here to see it. . . ."

Thalassa rose, her throat tight and aching with the bitter weight of her grief. She had turned to leave when Oreithyia's weak whisper called her back. "Wait . . ." Death was gathering swiftly in the queen's dark eyes, and Thalassa was not sure the dying woman could really see her any longer.

"Yes, my queen?"

"The man who fought by your side and defeated Heracles," Oreithyia gasped. "Was he the one who stole you from us, and then helped you to free Antiope?"

"Yes, Lady. It was he."

Oreithyia sank back. "I do not understand," she muttered, and said no more.

Oreithyia died later that night. As the sounds of mourning rose into the dark sky to follow the war queen's departed spirit, Thalassa retrieved little Hippolytos from the Scythian slave woman who had been keeping him. Alone she took the sleeping baby and went to the hastily erected camp outside Athens, where Theseus waited impatiently for his son.

"She's dead, isn't she?" he asked.

At Thalassa's answering nod, the bright-haired king laughed savagely. In the firelight his youthful face looked old and ravaged with sorrow, but his hands as he took his son were gentle. "Would that she suffered longer—that cruel and unnatural she-devil who carried the stone face of a demon where a woman's heart should be!"

"She suffered," Thalassa said curtly. "More than you can ever know, you who think women are either toys for your amusement or mindless bellies that think of nothing but swelling obediently with your sons. She suffered, Theseus of Athens. You will never understand how much."

"And what of my suffering? I care nothing for hers! She took the woman I loved from me. I would have made Antiope queen over all of Athens!"

Thalassa gazed steadily at him. "She was already a queen."

Theseus's hands trembled, and he looked down at the child snuggled against him. "She said almost that very same thing to me when this one was born."

Thalassa made no reply. She had turned to leave when the burly form of Heracles loomed up beside Theseus. Peering at her, he demanded, "You're the one, aren't you?

The brazen wench who managed to nick me during the fighting!"

She stared at him coldly. "*Nick* you? Even now you stumble like a hobbled ox from the arrows I sent through both your legs, and your arm is white with linen from the bandages on the wound I laid open with my battle-ax. I am no *wench*, you hulking, loutish fool, but the warrior whose skill and prowess overcame even the protection of that lionskin you cower behind. If you would speak to me, then do so with respect or not at all."

Heracles's face went brick-red, but Theseus intervened. "We are at peace here," he said. "And I charge both of you to remember."

"I have not forgotten it." Thalassa's icy gaze enfolded the Athenian king. "But I came here to deliver the child, not bear the insults of your fellow Greeks. Now that I have done it, I will leave."

"Wait." Heracles took several limping steps forward, his mouth working as he sought to contain his anger and speak civilly. "What about the man who was with you? Why did he spare my life?"

Thalassa said nothing, and the Greek champion persisted. "Is he a warrior of either the Gargarian or Scythian tribes? Or was he a god summoned up by them to aid you women during the battle?"

Thalassa realized she was smiling. Obviously neither man recognized Dorian or herself as the two beings who had risen so mysteriously from the sea to free the Amazons from the Greek galley.

"Well?" Heracles's tone was impatient. "Why don't you answer? Is he a Scythian—a Gargarian—or one of their gods?"

"No," she said serenely. "To all three."

She turned and began walking back across the dark plain, to the campfires of the Amazons that flickered in the distance. Behind her she heard Heracles telling Theseus in his booming voice that the unknown warrior had to be a god, for only a being with supernatural powers could have bested the mighty Heracles so easily.

Over the next two days, the vast army made its preparations to leave Athens. Funerals were held for the slain, and for those who had survived the battle but not their wounds. Amidst the greatest pomp and ceremony, Queen Oreithyia was buried under a tomb formed in the crescent shape of an Amazon shield. Despite the prevailing feeling that Antiope had betrayed her people, she too was given a queen's burial and laid to rest beside her elder sister. Over her grave was set a tall earthen pillar.

Thalassa attended these solemn events in a state of the most profound confusion. She had discovered that the toll of birth-friends lost in the fighting was far higher than just Aella, Antiope, and Oreithyia. Among the slain were Asteria and Eriobea and fierce dark-haired Hippothoe. The pain of loss had woven itself into the fabric of her soul—yet grief was not the only emotion churning inside her.

The sea voice that had awoken in her before these tragic happenings had faded during the intensity of the battle and its aftermath. But the voice had only quieted. It had not stilled. Now it spoke once again to Thalassa, even more strongly than before, troubling all of her hours whether waking or sleeping.

Soon—perhaps even as soon as the next day—the Amazons would begin the long and dangerous trek home. Whatever destiny awaited them the Goddess alone knew, but looking at the disheartened faces about her, Thalassa felt only dread. Dorian had been right after all, and Oreithyia's dying words haunted her. That the war queen had left Amazonia so ill-attended greatly compounded the disaster of her and Antiope's deaths.

What would the leaderless Amazons who survived the long march back find when they finally entered Themiscrya's fertile plains? Exhausted from the rigors of their journey, would they have to fight once again to reclaim their lands? And could the Scythians and Gargarians, who had been promised and then denied the riches of Athens, be trusted not to turn against their allies as they neared their own territories?

These questions ate at Thalassa, and she agonized over them. What would become of her people? And what would become of her? As an Amazon her duty was clear. But could she truly consider herself an Amazon any longer?

Trapped between two worlds, she was tormented over

not really belonging to either. She wanted to ride into the barren Greek mountains with her sisters when the Amazon army departed; yet the thought of leaving the sea behind made her ache with an odd, yearning hunger. She burned as though consumed with fever, a fever that only the cool salt waves could assuage. Desperately resisting the strangeness of it, she purposely stayed away from the sea—away from those wine-dark waters that beckoned with murmurous constancy. But it did no good.

If Dorian had sought to push her back into the sea, she could have turned all the turmoil raging within her against him. But he had taken Valya and returned to the sea—for all she knew, for good. Certainly she had seen no sign of him since, and unlikely as it seemed, she wondered if the youth's tragic death had freed her from the mer-king at last.

Perhaps he blamed her, after all, and had gone back to his Elders to repudiate her as his mate. She had heard that among man-ruled tribes, men routinely discarded wives who displeased them for one reason or another. Perhaps a similar custom existed among the merfolk.

Strangely, the thought that Dorian might have released her brought her no joy. . . .

At dawn on the third day of the armistice, the Scythians and Gargarians moved out. On the way to Greece, they had been content to bring up the invasion force's rear, but now they eagerly took the lead with their heavily loaded wagons, and the small horses of the Scythians cantering out in front. Standing atop Ares Hill in the grayish light, Thalassa watched as the lumbering wagons and dancing ponies kicked up great clouds of dust that trailed behind them in rolling white streamers.

The tents of Oreithyia and her officers had been dismantled from the summit of Ares Hill, and the rocky plateau was empty now, as it had been when the Amazons first came. A lone figure strode up the path, and with a wild intermingling of happiness and trepidation, Thalassa saw that it was Dorian.

"So they have decided to leave," he said when he reached her side. "They are very hushed about it."

He was naked, his body beaded with droplets of water as if he had just emerged from the sea. The shadows that had marred his brilliant eyes were gone, though the sadness remained. In answer to her unspoken question he said quietly, "Valya has been laid to rest far from here. His comrades are with him yet, and when they have finished bidding him farewell, they will begin the journey back to my abode. I, too, must go, for my presence will be required when they face the Elders. Valya's family must also be told, a duty that as king falls to me."

"I understand."

He made no mention of her accompanying him, and the turmoil within Thalassa's mind mounted. Distracted and miserable, she gazed downward. Activity swirled about the bottom of the hill as the Amazons prepared to follow their allies, retreating back over the same route they had used in their proud advance. But despite the flurry and commotion, little noise floated up to the two on the hill. The women went about the business of packing and loading in subdued silence, their faces sad and their hearts heavy.

"The Amazons find no joy in the thought of going home," Thalassa said, her voice hoarse with bitterness. "They are ashamed to return to Themiscrya under the blight of such failure as has happened here."

Dorian nodded in sympathy. Unable to contain herself, she suddenly burst out, "O my sisters! What will become of them?"

If Dorian noticed that she had not included herself in their number, he gave no sign. "I suppose I could tell you pretty lies to ease your pain," he said. "But you would not believe me even if I did. What I think is this. Few, if any, Amazons who leave here will ever see Themiscrya again. Since they are too filled with shame to return, most will allow themselves to be drawn into Scythian or Gargarian settlements along the way. Those who do not may die fighting in some distant, lonely place."

Thalassa tried to swallow past the lump in her throat. If there had been tears left, she would have cried for her doomed people, but all her tears were gone. As all her friends and age-mates were gone. "What a hard fate it is," she whispered at last, "to relinquish what makes them Amazons, or to relinquish their lives in its stead."

"I know." He laid a gentle hand on her shoulder. "Yet

to live with a man does not necessarily mean being enslaved to him, my love. I should think you'd have learned that by now. Your kinswomen whom we freed from Heracles's fleet apparently have."

"What?" She whirled to face him, her whole face a question, and he smiled.

"Before I came to you, I spoke to some Scythians who—after I convinced them I was not a capricious and dangerous god—were quite talkative. They told me a strange story about a group of warrior women who arrived mysteriously on the far reaches of their kingdom some months ago."

"Tecmessa, Evandre . . . ." Thalassa murmured.

"I believe so. In any case, the young unmarried men of a village in the area became quite enamored of the newcomers, and from what these Scythians said, the women convinced the men to go off with them and start their own tribe."

"By the Mother, if only it could be true!" Joy surged through her at the thought that some of her kindred could pull happiness from this debacle and still preserve remnants of the Amazon way of life. And to know that at least some of her friends still lived!

"There is no reason to believe it is not true," Dorian said. "Amazons are resourceful and powerful women. They will have a strong influence on any men they meet." His voice softened. "The way you have had on me, my sweet."

Thalassa was suddenly very aware of his hand resting on her shoulder, and she fixed her gaze ever more intently on the activity below. The dismantling of the giant encampment was almost complete. The eldest and most experienced of her kinswomen had already mounted their horses and were facing east, ready to follow after their departed allies.

"Why have you not sought to go with them?" Dorian asked. "Do you not want to?"

She bit her lip. It was the question she had been waiting for, yet she could not explain—even to Dorian who seemed to understand so much—the pain of those last partings, or why she was up there on that lonely hill and not down below with her sisters.

Not looking at him, she asked, "Would you let me if I did?"

"They surely must be looking for you."

The cavalcade of disheartened and low-spirited warriors had finally started, moving slowly toward the east. How gloriously the Amazons had ridden into Athens! And how grimly and silently they were leaving it!

"A horse waits for me at the bottom of this hill," she said at last.

"I have seen it."

"They expect me to ride after them . . . if—if that is what I choose."

He said nothing. A long silence stretched between them while the last great army of the Amazons strung itself out upon the green plains of Attica. The sun had risen on yet another of those cloudless, bright days that seemed to bless this land. Even this early, its rays were strong on unshaded Ares Hill. But Dorian and Thalassa stood without moving until the long procession had faded into tiny black specks on the eastern horizon.

Then—still without speaking—they took the winding path down from the summit to where a bay mare stood lazily switching her tail in the shaded side of the hill. Remembering her own black mare, Thalassa laid a hand on the animal's warm neck. Though beautiful as all Amazon horses were, this mare was no replacement for Alcippe. Yet there was no replacing any of what she had lost. There was only the will to go forward.

In a fluid motion she swung onto the bay's back, then waited—expecting Dorian to drag her off or seize the animal's reins. He did nothing, and disappointed and exhilarated at once, she looked down at him. He was gazing at her, his dark face utterly without expression. Yet there was an air of coiled tension about him, and she felt her own muscles knot and twist as though in the grip of a mortal wound.

Beneath her the mare fidgeted and tossed her head, eager to gallop after her vanished herd-mates. Holding the prancing animal in, Thalassa stared at Dorian a moment longer. Then she abruptly loosed the reins. The mare surged forward, and soon she and her rider were lost to sight.

≈ ≈ ≈

The wine-dark Aegean lapped gently at the shore. Ankle deep in the warm waves Dorian stood alone, his back to the sea that was his home. When his ears first caught the distant thud of hoofbeats, he thought he was mistaken, that his own desperate yearning had conjured up the sound of a galloping horse. Then she came into view, the bay mare lathered and fighting the bit in protest at being forced to return.

Sliding from the horse's sweaty back, Thalassa slapped her haunch and cried, "Thank you for bringing me back. Go now, and join your comrades!"

As the mare raced off she walked slowly toward Dorian. When her feet touched the very edge of the sea, she stopped, hesitating as though an invisible barrier faced her. Then Dorian reached out and drew her into his arms, and as he did she resolutely turned her face from the land.

They swam until late in the night. Thalassa felt an aching need to put distance between herself and the land of the Greeks. It was not until they had paused to rest that she told him what she had suspected for days, that she was with child. Dorian's eyes glowed like jewels in the reflection of the moon, and his smile was so bright, it made the night seem like day.

"Then we are truly joined at last," he said.

She clasped his hand and lightly, briefly, kissed him. "Yes."

≈ ≈ ≈

AFTERWORD

The war with the Amazons was unique in the recorded history of the Athenians: It was their first successful repulsion of invaders. The event was memorialized in rituals honoring the bravery of the fierce Amazon foes for centuries. More importantly, it marked the end of Athens's status as a minor city-state and signaled the beginning of its unparalleled rise to the center of the civilized world.

The debacle at Athens was far more than a military disaster for the Amazons. Their ranks decimated, the survivors left without strong leadership, it was the end of their civilization. Most never made it back to their fertile country, either dying or being absorbed into various cultures along the way. Those remnants making it back to their homeland found it in the hands of man-ruled tribes. Eventually these few survivors recovered a portion of their territories, but never again did they rise to their former glory. And they were left with a lasting hatred of all things Greek.

Thus passed a way of life based on women's strength and independence. A darkness descended upon those created in the Goddess's image—a darkness that would last thousands of years, a darkness during which history would be written by men.

And in those male-inspired accounts, the vanished glory, and indeed the very existence of the magnificent warrior-women, would be ridiculed or ignored, until its brightness flickered and finally went out.

The time of men was come upon the land, and in the man-ruled world there could be no place for proud women on horseback who sent their war cries ringing boldly onto the wind.

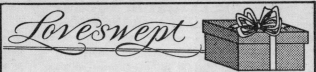

THE LATEST IN BOOKS
AND AUDIO CASSETTES